Magdalenes

To Victoria —
Enjoy the trip back in time
Channing Hayden

Magdalenes

Channing Hayden

Writers Club Press
San Jose New York Lincoln Shanghai

Magdalenes

Writers Club Press
an imprint of iUniverse.com, Inc.

For information address:
iUniverse.com, Inc.
5220 S 16th, Ste. 200
Lincoln, NE 68512
www.iuniverse.com

This novel is a work of fiction. Any reference to historical events, real people (living or dead) and actual events are used solely to lend the fiction its proper historical setting. All other names, characters and incidents are fictitious, and any resemblance to actual persons or events is purely coincidental.

ISBN: 0-595-17300-4

Printed in the United States of America

To Cheryl
An exceptional proof-reader, literary critic and my best friend,
who also happens to be my long-suffering wife.

PART I

FALL 1897

CHAPTER I

HER PAW WAS DRUNK AGAIN…happy drunk, but that would change. It always did.

Not quite thirteen years old and already life battered her, brutal cycles stretching as far into the past as she could remember and as far into the future as she could imagine. In her mind she began her week on Tuesday, sorry-day for paw. He apologized for everything he had done since Saturday, promised never to do it again and tried to make his family as happy as poor white trash with empty bellies could be. Wednesday was find-an-odd-job-day and, with luck, not-so-hungry-day. Thursday was work-or-hunt-day and usually full-pot-at-dinner-day. Friday was com-plain-day; never-had-a-man-worked-so-hard-for-a-family-so-ungrate-ful-day. Then came two-jug Saturday–anxious morning, agonizing afternoon, appalling night. Tomorrow the horror of Saturday would continue until her paw could only snore and drool, sleeping straight through until Monday, vomit-and-be-sick-day.

"Come here, ya vixen."

She heard her paw's liquor-slurred words and her momma's shrill, nervous laugh in reply, both firmly fixing their exact position in the demon's repertoire of brutality.

He always calls momma vixen 'fore he takes her the first time.

The child knew that had she been peeking through the cracks in the cabin's clapboards instead of hiding at the edge of the clearing where their shack stood, she would have seen her paw roughly undress her momma, then be quick about his business with her. All the while the woman praised the wonders of her husband, holding him close as he had his way with her and staring vacantly at the roof of the dilapidated hovel the four of them called home.

"Oh, you're a wonderful man," her momma always said as her paw, walking away unsteadily, pulled up his pants and went for his jug again.

Then the brief interlude in which the demon sometime actually bared his fangs and smiled would end; not all at once, but slowly, inevitably, like the Mississippi rising during spring flood. She had watched this ritual so many times through the chinks in the cabin wall she knew exactly what was happening inside. Today, huddled at the edge of the woods, she saw the minute details of each abomination in the archives of her memory, sounds from the cabin moving the images in her head toward their inevitable conclusion.

Her momma, dressed now, would be going about her chores as her paw sat in the family's only chair–a rickety, old ladder-back–pulling on his jug.

She waited. Without a breeze to stir them, the tall pines where she hid seemed carved from the cloudless blue background and painted in earth tones. In the grass at her feet, a spider ran the tightropes of its web, worried by the water collecting on the strands. *Where'd it come from?* she wondered, then realized she was crying.

After a while her paw's loud demand carried to the trees. "Where's m' woman!"

In her mind's eye the child saw her momma trudge to where he sat, putting on a forlorn smile as she came into his view, herding wisps of ornery, broom-straw blonde hair into place, uselessly smoothing the wrinkles in her apron. "Here I am, Herman. Can I get ya somethin'?" she always asked, anxious brown eyes flitting around the shack as if looking for some minor household god to make this Saturday different from all the rest.

"Got me an itch needs scratchin'. Takes a real woman. Think the likes o' you can do it?"

"Oh, I'll try, Herman, I surely will," her momma always said as she helped her husband out of his clothes, then undressed herself, frantically attempting to be erotic. But the poor woman never succeeded.

In all the years she watched her mother's inept, almost comic, efforts to be seductive, the child did not know liquor diminished a man's prowess, that the failure did not belong to her momma. She only knew her paw's manhood would not peak and he blamed his wife.

Waiting for Saturday's inevitable tragedy to play itself out, the child hunkered to insignificance in the scrub. Haunches to heels, she squatted, hugging her knees to her chest, barely breathing the pine-scented air. Cramped thighs, calves and arms ached; a muscle under her right shoulder blade knotted. She bit her lower lip until tiny drops of blood seeped through the skin. Tears fought against the pain in her body and the agonizing images in her mind. *Daren't cry out, daren't move, lest the demon catch me up in his nettle-cloth.*

"Damn you!" her paw yelled. "If I had me a real woman, I'd be all right. But I'm stuck with you. A real woman'd put me in fine fiddle, wouldn't she now? Not a cow, though. Not a floppy-titted bitch!"

"Oh, Herman, I'm trying. Don't you think…Well…M-Maybe if you didn't drink so–."

"Leave my drinkin' out o' this!"

The sound of an open-palm slap and her momma's scream reached the child, made her shrink further into the undergrowth.

Then the demon called for her. "Sarah Beth!"

This, the most recent vagary in the savage cycles of her life, had begun a few months ago. After her bout with yellow fever, Sarah Beth first noticed how strangely her paw stared at her, but dismissed it. *Just another puzzlement.*

"Oh, Herman, no. Please. *PLEASE!*"

Her mother's terror plain in the woman's voice, the child did not understand it.

"You don't need her," Sarah Beth's mother continued in a plaintive voice. "Ya got me. Let her be. She's so young. She's–."

"You surer-than-hell ain't no good f' me!" A slap and scream for punctuation. "That's just what-alls I need…A young 'un…*SARAH BETH*! Git yourself in here, gal! Ya old paw's got somethin' sweet f' ya…Somethin' real sweet!"

"No, Herman. Oh, God, Herman, no! Leave her be! You got me. You don't need–."

Her paw hit her momma again.

Sarah Beth wanted to run into the cabin and make him stop but could not, frozen by fear and promises.

"Listen t' me good, Sarah Beth," her momma had said time after time. "No matter what all happens t' me, promise you'll never get next to ya paw when he's drunk. Understand me?"

"Yes, 'um." But Sarah Beth only understood her momma took beatings meant for her.

"Swear it!"

"I swear, Momma."

The loathsome sounds of her mother being knocked into the cabin walls, the poor woman's screams and pleas drove Sarah Beth deeper into the woods. The scrub pulled at her, knotted in the thick mass of her scarlet-gold hair. Vines tripped her. Branches and brambles tore her clothes, ripped her skin. Captured in a hell gone green, she twisted; stumbled; fought the thicket; thrashed; punched her leafy, insubstantial captor; sobbed; saw her paw's face in the tree trunks; ran on legs that would not, could not move; gulped for air; lost her sight to tears; fell; split her knee; ripped her palms; pounded her forehead on the ground to banish the terrible sights trapped forever in her head. But nothing could release her from the scenes playing endlessly in the cabin and her mind. Eyes squeezed tight, every angle of her consciousness, like mirrors in a fun house, reflected her momma's plight to the far-off crannies of her brain. She had to find a way to stop the beatings meant for her. *But I promised!*

Lying in the undergrowth, bleeding, out of breath, the image of her paw's face, twisted and leering, came into view behind her closed eyelids. Bit-by-bit the bead of a gun sight assembled in her mind's eye and nestled between his thick eyebrows. She imagined the rifle's smooth, wooden stock against her cheek; the cool, metal trigger under her finger.

Fear and confusion suddenly gone, Sarah Beth knew how to keep her promise and still save her momma.

CHAPTER 2

ON TUESDAYS HER PAW DOTED on her momma. From the loft of their one-room cabin where she and her ten year-old brother slept, Sarah Beth would hear her parents do tenderly on Tuesday night what had been done so viciously just a few days before. And, surprisingly, her mother enjoyed it. Yet, Sarah Beth knew the cycle. As sure as harvest followed planting, the violence would come again the very next Saturday. She had never known her momma without a bruise blooming or fading on her face.

In the dark of the following Tuesday's midnight, Sarah Beth stole from the loft leaving her brother curled up on the old, moss-stuffed burlap sack they shared. She crept to the mantle and lifted her father's lever-action carbine from its wooden pegs. On many previous sorry-days he had showed her how to use it, taken her hunting now and again. He had even remarked in his thick Southern drawl, "You a tolerable good shot for a gal."

Now she would show him how good. In the quiet, one-room shanty, the clatter of metal on metal sounded like freight cars coupling as she chambered a bullet. Despite the noise, her paw continued sleeping in a death-like trance of satisfied exhaustion. She leveled the rifle at a spot on his forehead below his thinning, brick-red hair.

"What ya doin', Sarah Beth!" Her momma's demand came in an urgent whisper.

"He ain't never gonna hurt ya no more." Rage made the child almost luminescent in the gloom.

The specter shape of her momma floated from the bed and the tall, gaunt woman snatched the rifle from the child's hands. "That ain't the way," the older woman hissed, taking her first-born by the shoulder and hurrying her out of the cabin. On the porch, her momma asked, "How we gonna eat with him dead?"

"Don't eat much no how. 'Sides, I know how t' hunt."

Her momma bundled Sarah Beth into scrawny arms and hugged the child to her through a threadbare night dress, wincing as love tangled with the pain in her side.

"That spot still hurt, Momma? Been three whole weeks–."

"Killing him won't make it no better." Tears brimmed in her momma's brown eyes.

"How can ya say that, Momma? After all them lickin's he gived you. And little Jeremy, too. Now he wants t' beat me, too. And would, if ya let him. He's been callin' after me on a Saturday lately. I can't let ya take no more beatin's f' me, Momma. I got to do *somethin'*!" Though her voice did not waver, tears ran from Sarah Beth's green eyes and made diamond trails down her cheeks, rivulets that sparkled in moonlight bright enough to cast shadows.

Her mother began to cry, too–but softly, not to wake the sleeping monster just inside. "That still ain't the way, my Honey Girl. Soon ya'll have an age t' leave on out o' here. Ya nigh on old enough right now, if ya've the mind t'. Sure ya could. Get a job somewheres, maybe down t' Baton Rouge, and wouldn't never have t' worry 'bout him wantin'…Well, ya just wouldn't never have t' worry 'bout him no more."

"But what about you and Jeremy?" Sarah Beth argued, not understanding what she had almost been told. "I love ya both s' strong it aches me t' see what he does ya. I can't leave on out o' here with the two of ya–."

"Well," her momma said in her soft, slow drawl, "don't rightly know 'bout ya brother and me. 'Cept when ya get settled, maybe Jeremy can come meet up with ya."

"What about you, Momma?"

"Me? Well…Ma'be I can come meet up with the two of ya later on." Her momma's plain, care-worn face creased even more as the woman looked to see if the child believed her.

"Why we can't do that now?" Sarah Beth, excited by the prospect, bounced on the balls of her bare feet. "It'd be real easy. Sunday when he's drunk asleep, we'll–."

"He'd come after us, Honey Girl. And he'd be s' mad–."

"But he wouldn't never find us," Sarah Beth insisted. "Not if we done it right. We'd go somewheres he wouldn't never think of. New Orleans maybe. Take a packet boat on down. He couldn't never–."

"That all takes money, child. Money we ain't got."

"I'll get money, Momma. Just ya wait and see. I'll get money and a job and send for you and Jeremy. Then the three of us won't never have t' put up with him no more."

"That'll be fine, Honey Girl. Just fine," her momma said with a sad smile as she caressed the child's beautiful hair, a sleep-tossed mass that glittered silver-blue in the brilliant moonlight. "But there's one thing, Sarah Beth." The woman's smile fled as quickly as it came. "Don't hate ya paw too much. He's a good man down deep. Remember that. Maybe ya can't see it, but he is. I knowed him a long, long time and why he's like he is. He had dreams once, just like you. But his ain't come true and it ate up his innards. Remember, child, he was a good man once."

"Oh, Momma, I love you so much…And Jeremy, too," Sarah Beth said, truly adoring the woman. *Who else but momma could find good in a man like paw?*

"Oh, my Honey Girl, I love ya, too."

The woman hugged her daughter again and sent Sarah Beth back into the cabin with a gentle swat on her backside through the thin cotton of her hand-me-down night dress.

At the cabin door, Sarah Beth turned. "After I get me settled, how I send for you and Jeremy?"

Her mother knitted her brows, wrapped a wiry strand of broomstraw blonde hair around her finger and twisted it, then gave a wry smile. "Get somebody t' write a letter for ya and–."

Sarah Beth, slightly taller than average for her age, drew herself up to her full height. "I'll write it myself. I *am* gonna get me t' school, ya know."

The older woman's smile said she knew Sarah Beth would accomplish whatever the child put her mind to. "Just send that letter on down t' the general delivery in St. Francisville. I'll pass by from time t' time lookin' for it."

"But how ya gonna–."

"Addie Thompson...Ya know, the lady down to the General Mercantile. She and me go way back. She'll read me it."

The idea of running away had lurked in Sarah Beth's mind for a long time, buried between the crevices of other thoughts. She had taken it out and examined it several times, always putting it away because it meant deserting the people she loved. Now her momma coaxed it into consciousness again. *Must be the thing t' do. Momma wouldn't say so if not.*

Her momma's approval and her paw's incessant savagery gave her the courage to act. The rage that first led Sarah Beth to her paw's rifle became a fierce determination to face the unknown for the sake of her beloved mother and brother...and for her own sake, as well.

CHAPTER 3

SARAH BETH NEEDED MONEY TO make her plan work, but had no idea how much. She discussed the problem with her best friend, Lottie Mae Talbot, an eleven-year-old girl who lived with her family in a share-cropper shack about a mile from Sarah Beth.

"I axed my Maw, like you said, how much it take t' feeds all us'ns," Lottie Mae explained one day shortly after Sarah Beth had made her decision. "She say a good dinner f' all us'ns is 'bout fo' nickels. But ya know how she be, she gots t' tell me how it done. Wanna hear?"

"What she say?" Sarah Beth smiled, picturing the familiar sight of Elona Talbot hovering over Lottie Mae or one of her other two children. Sarah Beth spent as much time as she could at the Talbot's, drawn by the warm, bountiful love that made them wealthy despite the meager existence Josh, Lottie Mae's father, scraped from the delta mud.

"Ya gots t' be real careful at the store t' gets all yo' money can buy." Her hair in two kinky, black pig-tails that shook when she spoke, her only everyday dress red and black polka-dots, Lottie Mae looked like the nickname her mother had given her, Lady Bug. "Maw say ya go t' *both* Marse Bishop's store *and* Marse Ducros'. Take a dime and ax Marse Bishop f' a nickel o' red beans, two pounds, a nickel bag o' rice and an onion *lagniappe*. Then go see old Marse Ducros. Ax him f' a nickel-worth o' pickled pork, a *quartee* lard—ya know, a half nickel's worth—and a *quartee* bread. Then say, 'Gimme *lagniappe* salt 'n' pepper.'" Lottie Mae smoothed her dress. "Maw say ya don't never git groceries all t' the same store 'cause the more places ya goes, the more *lagniappe* ya gets."

"How much ya think it'll cost *me* t' eat while I get me some work," Sarah Beth asked, having already shared her plans with her friend.

"Now, that just depends." Lottie Mae studied the ground as if the answer to Sarah Beth's question lay in the dirt around them. "How long ya 'spect it gonna take t' find somethin'?"

"Don't know."

The two girls sat on an old tree trunk laying along the dusty road that led to the fields Lottie Mae's father tended. They twisted bare toes in the dusty delta mud while they thought, but there the similarity ended. A quick look and a stranger would have thought a white boy and a colored girl sat on the log. Closer examination would have shown that under the wide-brimmed, floppy hat, beneath the numerous patches on the baggy man's shirt, inside the over-sized coveralls, the white boy was, in fact, a strikingly beautiful girl on the threshold of womanhood.

Sarah Beth's boyish appearance vanished when she took off her hat to fan herself in the hot sun. The Conquistadors who explored the region would have found their El Dorado in the cascade of gold-on-fire that tumbled below her shoulders. Radiant, scarlet-gold hair framed a face with perfectly arched brows and long, fine lashes around eyes tinted the light green of an ocean wave about to break. Sarah Beth answered after ruminating a while. "A week, maybe."

Lottie Mae considered the estimate, scratching the end of her nose. "Sounds 'bout right."

"The five o' ya'll eat a good dinner on four nickels, how much ya think it'd cost me for a whole day?" Sarah Beth asked. "Two?"

"Yeah, that's 'bout right." After a thoughtful pause Lottie Mae asked, "How much that be all together?"

Both girls bumped hard against their greatest handicap, lack of education. Of the two, Providence had only given Sarah Beth the native wit to surmount the disadvantage. Not only did she possess great beauty, but great intelligence; both squandered on a tyrant's dirt farm in south Louisiana.

"Maybe we can figure it." When Sarah Beth found a twig and squatted, her loose-fitting clothes tightened around her and tattled the secret of her budding breasts and rounding hips. She began making lines in the dirt. "Say each o' these here is a day. Tuesday, Wednesday, Thurs–."

"How ya know you is leaving on a Tuesday, girl?" Lottie Mae asked.

"Don't make no difference. They just so many days. Wherever I start, it'll come out the same."

"You sure?" Lottie Mae knitted her brows.

"Yeah…So, each day's a dime," Sarah Beth continued. "And dimes got two nickels inside, so I put me two strikes under the days and them's the nickels I need. Now I put me five more strikes under each o' them nickel marks and them's the pennies I got t' have."

"What ya call all them many pennies?" Lottie Mae asked when Sarah Beth had drawn all her marks.

"Damned if I know," Sarah Beth said. "Paw ain't never let me go t' school…*DAMN HIS HIDE!* If he let me get t' school like I wanted, bet'cha I'd know whatcha call all them pennies. Bet'cha I could cipher 'em. But paw, he say school ain't nothin' but a waste o' time. Wants me home t' help momma with the chores." She sat quietly for a moment, mourning her lack of education. Her paw's decision in that regard was her second greatest curse. She wanted to attend school almost as much as she wanted him to stop beating her momma.

Lottie Mae shrugged. "So, now ya got it figured. How ya gonna 'member it? Ya can't take this here patch of dirt with ya, girl. And when it rain, it'll be gone all t' mud. So what's the good in all that figurin'?"

"I'll call t' mind the picture," Sarah Beth said.

Lottie Mae's brows drew down close to her dark brown eyes and her forehead wrinkled. "What picture?"

Sarah Beth waved her hand at the ground. "The picture o' this here in my head."

"Ya got *pictures* in ya head?" Lottie Mae touched hers as if something were missing.

"Sure. That's how I remember stuff." Sarah Beth's voice took on a note of concern. "Ain't it the same with you?"

"Ya mean like calling t' mind what Maw looks like when I can't see her? Yeah, I do that."

"Can you remember what dress she had on when she fixed that ham f' ya ten-year-old birfday?" Sarah Beth asked.

"Sure," Lottie Mae said in a off-hand manner. "She only got but the one."

"And remember the grease splattered on her when she was fixing lunch. Where was the stains?" Sarah Beth asked.

"On her dress."

"Yeah, but where?" Sarah Beth insisted.

Lottie Mae shook her head. "That better than a year gone. How I gonna 'member that?"

Sarah Beth pointed to her friends sleeve, bodice and skirt. "Here, here and here…See that's how I remember stuff. I got pictures o' that day all up in my head, from the time I woke up til I went to bed." Sarah Beth tapped her temple. "Fact is, I got pictures of every day I ever lived up here and I call 'em up whenever I need t' remember somethin.'"

"Well, I ain't got no pictures up in my head, that's for sure." Lottie Mae gave her friend a sly grin. "Maw, she say sometime she don't think I got nothin' up there a'tall."

"Then how you remember stuff?" Sarah Beth asked.

"Simple. I 'member stuff…Well, I 'member stuff…What kind of question that be?…I 'member stuff with my head…But not with no pictures, that's for sure."

For the first time in her life, Sarah Beth sensed she might be different from other people. *Maybe one day them pictures'll just up and get.* The thought frightened her. She stood up and began looking on the ground around the tree trunk. Picking up small rocks, she asked Lottie Mae to help. When they each had a hand full, Sarah Beth put a stone on each nickel and penny mark. Then she picked up the nickel rocks and put them in her right pocket. "Every time I gets me a nickel, I'll put it in this here pocket and throw a rock out." She scooped up the penny rocks and dropped them in the left pocket of her coveralls. "Pennies go in here the same. When I gets me enough f' a nickel, I'll put 'em in the nickel pocket and pitch another rock out."

Her rudimentary accounting system settled, Sarah Beth applied herself to getting the money she needed.

"It's pickin' time. Maybe ya can picks," Lottie Mae suggested.

"Don't know nothin' 'bout pickin' cotton," Sarah Beth answered. "Paw never let me. Says it's nigger work."

"It be nigger work, that's for sure. The bending'll bust yo' backbone right out 'n', Lawd, yo' hands'll bleed for a month of Sundays. But you'll catch on t' it easy enough. Don't take but a pea-brain to get it right." As Lottie Mae spoke, she studied Sarah Beth's scratches in the dirt. "Girl, you sure is some smart. I gots t' 'member how t' do all like that with them scratches 'n' rocks. Bet it'll come in handy one day."

"Why, Lottie Mae? You fixin' t' run off, too?"

"Course not. Ain't got no reason. But I'll needs me some money, too, by 'n' by. One day I 'spect a fella'll ax me t' marry up with him." Lottie Mae held out her skirt. "Can't marry up with nobody in this here ol' thing."

The sweet, innocent laughter of the two girls echoed through the fields as they sat arm in arm, each dreaming their own version of the good things to come.

SARAH BETH SPENT THE NEXT four weeks picking cotton for a penny a pound. She hid her scratched and bloody hands from her father, shoving them in her pockets whenever he was around. In the process, she discovered something curious. Whenever she fingered her rocks, or the coins that gradually replaced them, and looked at him, she felt a strange power over him. The more her resources increased, the greater her feeling of dominion. She grew reckless and took to spending time around him, basking in her new-found power, which almost became her undoing.

One Friday, her paw heard the coins jingling in her pocket and demanded to know how she had gotten money. She took out a hand full of stones and told a tall tale about collecting lucky rocks. After that she kept her money tied in a piece of old rag so its clinking would not do her in.

WHEN SARAH BETH WAS TWO nickel rocks short of her seventy-cents goal, she almost became rich. Mid-morning one Sunday found her in the outhouse hurrying nature and trying to block out the hateful sounds from the cabin.

Suddenly, her ten-year-old brother—a short, nondescript boy with limp brown hair and immense, haunted brown eyes—ran on to the shack's sway-back porch.

"Wait, Jeremy," Sarah Beth called. "Remember what momma and me said 'bout staying shuck o' paw when he's full o' 'shine."

The boy yelled at his sister, defiance chiseled onto his face, "I'm hungry!"

"Okay, Little Man, gimme time t' finish here and I'll see if–."

"I'm hungry *now!*" Jeremy turned and ran through the cabin door.

The child ran out almost as soon as he ran in, his paw chasing after him. Naked, clutching his breeches in one hand, the man lashed his son with a belt as if the poor child was a mule in harness. Only a mule would have been treated better. The man beat the boy with the metal buckle.

As Sarah Beth desperately tried to pull up her clothes and help her brother, a mote of justice found its way to their squalid existence. The moonshine and porch steps conspired to make her paw fumble-footed, pitching him forward in a rag-doll tumble of flailing arms and legs, a fall that would have broken the neck of a sober man. But, as usual, in

Sarah Beth's world, fairness went wanting. Her paw survived, unin-jured, and stood his drunken self up unsteadily in a beige haze of dry delta dirt.

As Jeremy ran past the empty chicken coop toward the woods, his paw cursed him and threw his belt after the boy. Then, smearing the dust on his sweat-soaked body into muddy smudges as he tried to clean himself off, the man picked up his pants, retrieved his belt and stormed onto the porch. At the cabin door he yelled, "Goddamn it, woman, why ya don't teach them kids some manners! Now *you* gonna get the lickin' I should've gived that Goddamn son of your'n!"

Leather slapped skin repeatedly and did not stop until her mother pleas for mercy became incoherent screams of pain.

Sarah Beth wanted to run into the woods, find her brother, help him, hide, do anything to escape the awful sounds coming from the cabin. Instead, she crept towards the porch steps.

Watching her paw stumble and cart-wheel in slow motion, praying for him to die when he hit the ground, Sarah Beth saw silver glints fly from his pants and land close to the bottom step. Now she approached cautiously and found a fortune half covered by dirt. Two quarters. She knew each coin was valuable, contained several nickels, but had no idea how many. She scooped them into her pocket and ran as fast as she could to find her brother.

JEREMY SAT IN HIS SPECIAL place, a blackberry thicket with no discernable entrance—unless you knew exactly where to look for a pas-sage so small neither he nor Sarah Beth could crawl through on their hands and knees. They had to lay flat and pull themselves in by their elbows, dragging their legs behind.

Sarah Beth wormed her way into the brambles. Her brother sat with his knees drawn up to his chest. Hugging his legs, he shook from silent sobs.

"He get you?" Sarah Beth gently touched Jeremy's shoulder.

The boy winced and pulled away, glaring at his sister.

"Here, lemme see," Sarah Beth said with tender insistence.

Jeremy recoiled further. "Lemme alone!"

"Aw, come on." Sarah Beth made the sweet eyes and googly faces that always made him laugh. "Ya gotta lemme help ya."

The boy hissed at his sister like a baby cottonmouth. "Don't want none o' *your* help!"

"Why ya like that, Little Man? I just wanna–."

"*DON'T WANT NONE OF YA HELP! YOU CAUSE IT! WHY I WANT YA HELP WHEN IT'S ALL YA FAULT!*"

Sarah Beth gaped at her brother, flabbergasted. "How can ya say that?"

"'Cause it's true!" Jeremy leveled his sister a hateful glare. "If ya'd go t' him when he wants, everything'd be all right! But ya won't! So he beats me 'n' momma! I hate ya, Sarah Beth! *I HATE YA!*"

How could she reason with the wild animal her little brother had become? "But Momma told me t' stay shuck o' him when he's like that, just like she told you."

"I hate ya for that, too! Momma loves *you* best! She don't love me none a'tall. If she did, she'd let ya go t' him!"

Sarah Beth began to protest but stopped as her brother squirmed his way out of the blackberry patch.

Jeremy turned back to the briers, red-eyed, teeth bared. "*I HATE YA, SARAH BETH! IHATEYA, IHATEYA, IHATEYA!*" he screamed and ran off into the woods.

Sarah Beth sat motionless for a long time. Jeremy's loathing deeply disturbed her. She thought to find him, tell him of her plans to run away and send for him when she could. No. He was too young. He might let on to paw. Her brother would find out how much she loved him soon enough.

Sarah Beth finally slithered from the blackberry patch as the sky glowed mauve, then ambled back to the clearing where their cabin stood. She found her momma sitting on the porch's tumbledown steps holding her head in her hands. By this time on Sunday evening Sarah Beth knew her paw was passed-out drunk inside. "How's Jeremy?"

Her momma's head jerked up and Sarah Beth gasped at the sight of the bruises on the woman's face.

"Ya surprised me, Honey Girl. Didn't hear ya come up." Her momma sighed. "Little Man's alright. Your paw only got him once, right here." The woman reached around and held the back of her right shoulder. "It'll swell up right bad, though."

Sarah Beth told her momma what had happened.

"Don't let it bother ya none, Honey Girl," her momma said, the words mechanical. "He's just a little tyke and don't mean nothin'. He'll come around...Just wait."

Sarah Beth sensed an unusual melancholy about her momma and touched her arm. "What's wrong?"

"Nothin'." The woman's voice sounded distant, her eyes looked vacant.

"Now, Momma." Sarah Beth drew out the words, making them a gentle accusation.

The woman sighed again. "Ya paw done right good huntin' the other day and had money left over from his 'shine. I heared it jingle in his britches. Can't find it nowheres now. I looked but it's gone. I thought...Well, maybe, if they was enough, we'd get us some eats or some such. Now...."

Sarah Beth took the two quarters from her pocket. "Here, Momma." She held out her hand, palm up. "I seed 'em fly out his britches when he fell."

The woman looked down at her daughter's outstretched hand, the coins dim against the child's white skin in the failing light, then raised her gaze. Comprehension slowly filtered into her eyes and, in the silent understanding that passed between them, Sarah Beth knew her momma approved her plan.

"You keep that there money, Honey Girl." Tenderly her momma folded Sarah Beth's fingers back around the coins.

"No, Momma," Sarah Beth said, her voice just above a whisper. "I just about got what I need. You take 'em. Get stuff for you and Jeremy…Food and such, like ya said." She laid the money in her momma's hand.

The woman looked at the coins, then at her daughter. Knotting her gnarled, twice-broken hand into a fist so not to lose the treasure, she hugged Sarah Beth to her. "Oh, how I love ya, Honey Girl! I love ya so much!" Tears overflowed her eyes. "I wish there was more I could do for ya!"

"Ya done more than a body should already." Sarah Beth hugged her momma, but not too tight knowing what her paw had done to her.

Regardless of how dreadful her momma's existence, Sarah Beth knew the woman tried her best to make life tolerable for her children, and not just in the beatings she took for them. Her momma kept their clothes clean even if they looked more like patchwork quilts than shirts and britches. The cabin presented greater difficulties. Unbearably hot in summer shut tight against the bugs, miserably cold in winter with frigid wind whistling through chinks in the clap boards, her momma worked tirelessly to keep it clean. And to stave off the winter cold, each fall she and her children covered the inside of the shack with old newspapers.

This wall covering had sown the all-consuming desire for school in Sarah Beth. Everywhere she looked, incomprehensible words surrounded her. Like whispers that faded just beyond her ears, she could not make out their meaning. But, unlike whispers, the words on the walls did not fade. The paper turned yellow and brittle, but the words remained crisp and black; taunting her; marching around the cabin walls; badgering her mind like the flies and mosquitoes of summer tormented her body. To make the words stop torturing her, Sarah Beth knew she had to understand them, absorb them, comprehend their magic and mystery.

In the comfort of each other's embrace, mother and daughter swayed slowly back and forth on the porch steps as the chirp and chatter of the night rose around them. After a while Sarah Beth looked deeply into her momma's eyes. "Tell little Jeremy good-bye f' me. Tell him I love him a whole bunch, too. He don't think I do."

"He knows, Honey Girl, he knows. He's just hurtin' right now 'n'–."

"No, he don't, Momma. He don't know a'tall."

"Then I'll tell him, Honey Girl. I surely will."

CHAPTER 4

ANOTHER SATURDAY FOUND SARAH BETH huddled at the edge of the woods, this time marshaling the pluck to do what she must. After a while she heard her paw's loud demand, "Where's my woman!" In a few minutes he would call for Sarah Beth herself. The relentless cycle continued.

Can't tarry no more.

Slowly Sarah Beth merged into the thicket, the voices from the cabin fading, the ritual scenes reverberating in her mind as clearly as if her eyes saw them.

Me and momma been all through this, Sarah Beth thought as she pushed her way through the undergrowth. *Ain't no other way. If there was, she'da told me. Gotta leave 'em...Up t' me t' save 'em both...Wish I could send for 'em t'gether, but momma's right. Little Jeremy's got t' come first. Then momma...First thing, got t' get me a job...Cookin' or cleanin' or some such...How much t' charge? Shoulda asked Elona. She done cleanin' before. She'd know. Too late...Maybe not. Could swing by her place and paw'd never be the wiser. Elona'd never tell.*

Sarah Beth changed directions and headed for the road leading passed the Talbot farm.

Gotta find me a place t' stay near a school, get me some learnin' and not scrub floors all m' whole life...Be a teacher ma'be. Need t' start school right off. Wonder how long it takes a body t' learn readin' and writin'? Don't matter none. Get me a place close t' school 'n'...Damn! Didn't figure in no money for a place to stay...Likely I can find me a boardin' house...For ten cents a day? Not hardly. Them places is dear. Could bunch up my money, pay more a day...Double Damn! Better find me some work quick. Better—

Deep in thought, Sarah Beth stepped from the woods directly into the path of an on-coming carriage.

"*Whoa!*" the driver shouted, jerking on the reins.

Frightened, the horse reared, neighing wildly. Sarah Beth threw her arms up to shield her face from slashing, iron-shod hooves.

"Git out o' there, boy!" the driver yelled.

Bedlam. Rearing horse. Clattering traces. Groaning, tottering wagon. Yelling people. Dust and noise. Sarah Beth ran.

When the horse settle down, she stopped and called, "I-I'm sorry. I-Is everythin' okay? Didn't mean no harm, ya know. Just didn't heared ya is all."

"Come here, boy," the man sitting behind the driver demanded.

Sarah Beth approached timidly. "I-I'm real sorry, mister. Didn't mean no—."

"Sorry don't get shit, boy," the man spat. "You nearly knocked this here wagon over, you know that?"

"I-I truly am sorry."

"Not near as sorry as I've a mind to make you...Gimme that." He reached up to snatch the whip from the driver.

"Jeb," the woman sitting next to him scolded in a slow, thick Southern drawl, "don't be in such an all-fired hurry to beat a body. No harm done." She appraised Sarah Beth with a practiced eye. "Ya'll come closer."

Hesitant, Sarah Beth came within touching distance of the carriage. She cowered under the man's scowl, the inquisitive assessment of the woman, the unusual, sympathetic look of the driver.

"On what was ya thinkin' so hard that ya don't hear a horse and buggy?" the woman asked, not unkindly, as her obvious appraisal continued.

"T-Thinkin' I needed t' get me s-some work."

"Oh. And where'd that be?" the woman asked.

"Baton Rouge," Sarah Beth said, awed by the woman's fine jewelry and clothes.

Jeb resettled himself, straightening his coat and adjusting his shirt cuffs so precisely an inch of white showed at his wrist. Clearly annoyed he demanded, "Can we go now, Inez?" as he dusted himself with a handkerchief.

Inez put her hand intimately on Jeb's thigh. "In a minute. Don't be in such a huff when there's money t' be made." Rubbing Jeb's leg, Inez said to Sarah Beth, "Baton Rouge is a long ways off. Got family there?"

Sarah Beth looked down at the dusty road. "N-No, ma'am," she whispered.

Inez raised an eyebrow. "Wouldn't be runnin' away from home, now would ya?"

Sarah Beth reasoned she had her momma's permission. "No, ma'am." Head bowed, she peeked up to see if the woman believed her.

"Take that hat off!" Inez commanded.

Stunned by the sharp suddenness of the order, Sarah Beth obeyed without thinking, her scarlet-gold mane cascading below her shoulders, shimmering and sparkling in the sun.

Jeb leered. "Well, now. Ain't that a fine how-do-ya-do."

"Keep them pants buttoned," Inez snapped. To Sarah Beth she said, "Here," and patted the seat. "Come sit by me and tell me all about it."

Jeb helped Sarah Beth into the carriage and gave her a good fondling in the process, the child not realizing what had happened or why Inez slapped Jeb's hand.

Ignoring the reprimand Jeb smiled. "Got us a real fine one here. If she's still–."

"Shut up and we might find out." Inez scooted to the middle of the seat settling Sarah Beth next to her and away from her lecherous companion. Shooing the driver with a wave of her hand, Inez said, "Go on, Jethro," then asked Sarah Beth, "What's ya'll's name?"

Eyes wide with the thrill of her first carriage ride, the horse racing them along in full canter, the child replied, "Sarah Beth LaBranche."

"So, Sarah, where's–."

"Mostly folks call me Sarah Beth."

"Well, I declare. I surely am sorry." Inez gave the child an unctuous smile. "But tell me now, where *are* all these folks that call ya'll Sarah Beth?"

"Got no family." Sarah Beth stared down at her baggy pants, then up at the woman to see if the latest lie passed muster.

"An orphan?" Inez seemed flustered, as if the thought of such tragedy offended her tender sensibilities to the point of fainting. "Oh, you poor child you. So ya'll weren't runnin' away from home."

"Oh, no, ma'am," Sarah Beth said.

"And how did such an awful thing happen?" Inez asked, her tone conveying great concern.

"What?…Oh, they, ah, got caught up with the fever…Or maybe it was the influenza. I guess I don't rightly know. One day they just keeled over…Dead…All of 'em."

"So now ya'll alone in the world," Inez said, the inflection of her voice showing her sympathy. "Oh, my dear, sweet girl, that's just too terrible. But know what? It's terrible in a strange and wonderful way."

Sarah Beth's expression clearly said she did not understand.

"Here's why. This here is Jeb Winthrope. And I'm Inez Breaux, of the Mobile Breauxs. Maybe ya'll heard of us."

"Can't rightly say, ma'am," Sarah Beth answered.

Inez compressed her lips as if to say, *Anybody who is anybody knows the Mobile Breauxs.* "No matter…We run a home for girls…In New Orleans. Now don't ya'll see? That's the wonderful part. For us to come so far and find someone who needs us." She smiled at Sarah Beth. "Understand? God meant us to get together."

"Why you folks so far up-river from New Orleans?" Sarah Beth asked.

Before Inez could answer, Jeb leaned over and said, with a mocking smile, "God told us to come up and collect money a man owed us."

Inez scowled at him, then turned an angelic face to the girl. "Jeb's right. A very fine, southern gentleman promised us a donation for our orphanage, but left town before he made good. So, we come to remind him he owed us the money and fetch it. Donations are how we help the poor young children that need us."

Sarah Beth became excited. "Oh, can my brother—."

"Thought you said *all* your folks was dead." Jeb glared at the girl.

"Th-they is, m-mister. Th-There's just me 'n' my brother left. Ah…H-He's stayin' with my aunt, ya see. But…ah…She ain't got enough for the both of us. So I left."

"That's so, so terrible." Inez seemed heartbroken. "And I know how much ya'll'd like to help him. We'd like to help him, too, but, see, we run the orphanage for *girls*." Inez brightened. "Know what, though? I know the people who run the orphanage for *boys* down in New Orleans. When we get back home I'll ask if they got room for ya brother. How'd that be?"

"You'd do that? Oh, thank you kindly, Miss Inez. Thank you so much…But…."

"But what?" Inez asked.

"I heared them orphanages is awful places."

Inez wilted, her face a charade of sweet sadness. "Now do I look like the kind of person who'd run an awful place?"

"No, ma'am." Sarah Beth blushed.

"Well, I should think not!" Inez said in her haughty best. "Our orphanage is a wonderful place. Soft beds. Good food. Pretty clothes. Wonderful neigh—."

"Oh, Miss Inez, do you got a school?"

The woman looked into the child's expectant face. "Ah…Why, ah…Yes. Course we do. A wonderful school. Can't turn out no stupid girls, now can we?"

"Can I…Do ya think…Could I please go?"

"Course ya'll can."

"Then I can learn me t' read 'n' write 'n' cipher?" Sarah Beth's enthusiasm soared. "How long ya think it'll take, Miss Inez? I mean, t' learn me all that school stuff." Sarah Beth bounced on the seat more than the bumpy ride required.

The woman pursed her lips and rubbed her chin. "For a smart girl like ya'll? I should think no more than what, Jeb?…Two, three weeks outside."

"In two weeks," Jeb said as he leered at the girl, "she'll know everything she'll ever need."

Inez filled the ride to town with stories of her orphanage that numbed the sugar-plum fantasies of Christmas. Arriving at the St. Francisville landing about dusk, they met the packet boat on which Jeb and Inez had booked passage as husband and wife. The captain objected to the extra passenger until Inez told him Sarah Beth would sleep on the floor in their cabin and still pay full passage.

Exhausted, all three ate quickly and retired.

Sarah Beth wiggled and squirmed on the familiar hardness of the wooden floor, sleep competing with the myth of her soon-to-be wonderful life. At dawn, through a porthole, she watched the birth of the morning star, an omen of her own new beginning, of poverty and abuse's suffocating cocoon unraveled, of her most cherished hopes and dreams no more than a wish away.

A POOR NIGHT'S SLEEP LEFT Sarah Beth listless. She spent the morning lounging on deck, occasionally dozing, Inez Breaux never far away. The woman's closeness gave Sarah Beth great comfort, as if her guardian angel hovered near by.

When Sarah Beth first imagined life away from home, she pictured a lonely, peril-filled ordeal. Her new-found patron, her protector, allayed her concern, convincing her she had concocted danger from fancy rather than substance. Her faith in Inez Breaux, content and secure, Sarah Beth watched the willows along the banks of the Mississippi slowly drift by.

Around noon the packet landed in Baton Rouge. Sarah Beth watched passengers and cargo discharged and replacements come aboard. Underway again, the breeze and the young girl freshened; she from a morning of rest and the satisfying meals she had eaten since meeting her benefactor. Sunset found Sarah Beth at the rail, a steady breeze tingling her face as she watched the shoreline fade to purple and lights twinkle on in the houses and small towns scattered along the river.

With the faint glow of an orange sunset stippling distant clouds, the packet sailed past a great white house with balconies supported by gigantic columns, a long driveway and a huge, arched gate facing the river. The main building had two unsymmetrical wings. The upriver expansion resembled the portico of the White House. Sarah Beth had once seen a picture of the mansion where the President of the whole United States stayed and that picture lived in vivid detail in her memory with the rest of her life's experiences. The downriver extension looked like a cottage appended to the rest of the structure. The bright glow of the sky just before nightfall magically back-lit the scene. Slowly, the lights came on and lit the plantation's many windows like the opening of a lover's faceted eyes; as if the beautiful mansion saw Sarah Beth and instantly loved her as much as she loved it.

"Ohhhh. That's soooo pretty!...Mister," she called to a deck hand working close by, "ya know anythin' 'bout that house over there?"

The man looked at the child, blew his nose in his hand, wiped it on his shirt and continued coiling a rope next to one of the boat's cleats.

"Please, mister, can't ya just tell me?"

The crewman fixed his good eye on Sarah Beth. The milky one stared up and out over the rail. He looked and smelled part weasel, part river pirate; more inclined to eat the child than answer her question.

Sarah Beth beamed at him. Her two newest friends had taught her to trust strangers. Standing in a halo of light cast by a porthole, she radiated that faith and a wholesome, fresh innocence. Gold and scarlet hair, washed, sun-dried and wind-combed, framed her exquisite face like a lion's mane.

"Go on back by ya maw 'n' paw 'n' leave a body t' work," the annoyed deck hand said.

"Got none."

"Well, now, who's them people I seed ya with?"

"Oh, them? They takin' me t' an orphanage down t' New Orleans."

"You, too, huh?" The child's flawless beauty, her angelic green eyes, her guileless smile, her similarity to the orphan he had once been, something about Sarah Beth found the kernel of humanity in the river rat. His lips curled into the caricature of a smile, exposing gaps in tobacco stained teeth. "That's Nottoway," he said and leaned on the rail next to her.

"Nottoway." Sarah Beth exhaled the word with breathless wonder. "It's so beautiful…Likely the most beautiful thing I ever did see. It's how I dreamed a fairy-tale castle'd look."

"T' some it is," the boatman said. "The White Castle of Louisiana they calls it."

Sarah Beth made small, happy sounds, too thrilled to speak.

"There's a town a little ways downstream, White Castle, named after it…The house was built afore The War. In one of them top corners, under all that fancy wood stuff…Can you see where I'm talkin' about, little lady?" he asked as he pointed.

Sarah Beth shook her head.

"Maybe it's too dark, but there's a lot of frilly woodwork up nigh on t' the roof…Anyways, the story's told of how there's a cannon ball stuck up in that there corner."

"Did them damn Yankees charge 'em?" Sarah Beth asked, dismayed.

"Not if I heared the right of it. The shot come from a Yankee gunboat. After Spoons took N'Awlins–."

"Who's Spoons?"

"Spoons Butler, the Yankee general what run N'Awlins after the North took her. Anyhow, he sent gunboats upriver. And when they got here, they commenced to cannonize the place. But the story's told how a Yankee officer on board had once upon a time been t' some shindig up t' the big house there. They say he begged the captain t' leave Nottoway be. Done a good job, too, 'cause thar she stands."

The mystique of the beautiful mansion grew deeper for Sarah Beth. Not only had she seen a real fairy-tale castle with her own eyes, but learned its story, one designed to stir the heart of any soon-to-be thirteen-year-old girl.

The packet slipped silently on down the Mississippi's banks and the sight of that wonderful white castle became another of the permanent pictures in Sarah Beth's mind, another star in the firmament of her ambition, a new beacon to guide the direction of her life. She would rescue her mother and brother, go to school and, one day, live in a house like Nottoway.

Sarah Beth stayed at the rail until the mansion melted into the darkness and she could only see the jewel-like windows set against the black-velvet night. Those, too, vanished as the packet rounded a bend.

Back in the cabin, the dazzling sight of Nottoway shimmered inside Sarah Beth's eye lids and kept her awake–that and the sounds from Jeb and Inez's bunk.

The night before the couple had gone to sleep almost instantly, spent from a long day traveling. Now rested, tonight they giggled under the bed linen like Sarah Beth's parents did on Tuesday night. Several times they ooooo-ed and ahhhhhh-ed together, having first made strange shapes under the bed sheet.

"Get the kid over here," Sarah Beth heard Jeb say as she wafted on the edge of sleep.

"Not on ya life. That's too much money to be a-wasting. 'Sides, people 'round here might not cotton t' the idea."

"C'mon, Inez," Jeb wheedled. "Let's have us some real fun. We can have her fixed later. Them old geezers never know the difference anyway. Just a night or two. You know you'd like it as much as me."

"No," Inez snapped. "There's too damn much money at stake!"

"Then what I'm gonna do with *this*?" Jeb demanded.

Inez giggled. "I'll take care of *that*." She slid under the covers.

"Ummmmmmmmm," Jeb moaned.

"See...told ya...I'd take care of it," Inez said. "And I'll get us...another one...I promise...Just...not this one...Okay?"

"UMMMMMMMMM," Jeb groaned louder.

Ain't that nice, Sarah Beth thought as sleep enfolded her completely. *They want a baby...A girl like me.*

CHAPTER 5

SARAH BETH TREMBLED WITH A fine excitement. As tug boats spewing thick, black smoke nudged the packet into berth at New Orleans, she gorged her eyes on the sights and sounds ashore. Everywhere she looked she saw people, a lifetime's worth for a poor country girl. Whistles blew and workmen yelled. Huge piles of cargo attracted swarms of men like flies to a cow patty. Bales of cotton came to the levee in endless streams of wagons while countless other wagons took sacks of coffee away. Teamsters cursed their mules, roustabouts cursed each other and some men seemed to curse just so they wouldn't lose the hang of it.

The boat's crew heaved thick ropes to waiting line-handlers and the packet took its place in the endless file of masts and smoke stacks along the levee. Inez found her prize and led her down the gangplank into the seething maelstrom, Sarah Beth holding tight to the woman's hand. Faces—black, brown, beige, tan and white—flashed before her. The tongues of Babel assaulted her ears. Bare-chested men—thin and flat-bellied with muscles like wire rope or fat and smooth with arms as big as tree trunks—hefted crates, toted bales and carried sacks. Occasionally, someone noticed the woman-child and stopped to admire her, captivated by her magnificent scarlet-gold mane or her sweet, beautiful, innocent face. Tromping around piles of cargo, dodging wagons, stepping over stinking mounds of fresh mule and horse manure, Inez and Sarah Beth picked their way across the levee to the street.

"Where's Mr. Jeb," the child asked as Inez pulled her from the trailing edge of the vortex toward a waiting carriage.

"Had stuff to do. He'll catch up with us in the District, ah, at the orphanage, I mean." Inez climbed into the gig with Sarah Beth following.

"Alex," Inez said to the driver, "take us…home. I've told the captain ya'll'd come back for the luggage later. Right now I need to get me somewheres quiet."

"Yes, 'um."

"Miss Inez," Sarah Beth said, exuberant, "can I set up there next to Alex? I could see lots better."

"Suit yourself." The woman leaned back and opened her parasol against the sun.

Sarah Beth scrambled on to the driver's seat. "Hi there, Alex, I'm Sarah Beth. What's the horse's name?"

"Jimbo," the Negro said, looking at the girl with the expression he saved for friends in coffins.

"He's beautiful."

"Miss Inez do love her horses, little missy." Alex flicked the rains and the chestnut gelding began to prance; neck arched, hooves snapping, almost as if he knew how much Sarah Beth admired him.

Alex coaxed the carriage along the crowded street for several blocks, driving parallel to the levee's unbroken mountains of cargo and bustling army of workers. Then they turned left, down a broad avenue with a wide median full of electric trolleys.

Sarah Beth saw buildings with four and five rows of windows stretching up their facades, tall enough for a flat-land country girl to think they could scrape fleece from passing clouds. The monolithic, grey Customs House took up a whole square and defined the word "huge" for her. Shops and businesses filled the buildings lining the boulevard–a vast thoroughfare teaming with people, wagons, carriages and trolleys.

If the activity on the levee overwhelmed her, the throng on the wide concourse completely dumbfounded the naive Sarah Beth. Cringing and moving closer to Alex for protection, she shouted over the din, "I-Is it always like this?"

"I should say so, little missy." Alex threaded their way through the confusion with whip and rein. "This here be Canal Street, the mostest big street in the whole gul-darn city with all them stores and such and everybody coming on downtown to do they business."

As she took in the tableau, smelled air tinged with the scent of horses and coffee and the sweat of a thousand souls, Sarah Beth felt more than apprehension. The milieu quickened the life in her, accelerated her blood, increased the pace of her innards to a new and exciting speed. She inspected shop windows as they passed, dazzled by the diverse merchandise offered—especially the beautiful gowns. Enthralled by one particularly striking dress she said, "Look, oh, look, Miss Inez, ain't that just the most beautiful thing ya ever did see?"

Inez, always interested in the latest fashion, sat up. "Oh, that old thing." She leaned back and dismissed the gown with a flip of her hand. "I got one just like it back at Vestal House. Ya'll can wear it, if ya want. It's maroon–."

"Oh, *thank* ya *so* much, Miss Inez!" Sarah Beth gushed. "I surely never dreamed…A dress like that…And f' me."

"Course, it'll take some altering. I *am* much bigger than ya'll." Inez expanded her chest to make her point.

"What's Ve-Venal House?" Sarah Beth asked.

"Vestal House, and it's the name of our orphanage. Hadn't I ever told ya'll that before?"

"No, ma'am," Sarah Beth said from her seat next to Alex, who stared dispassionately down Canal Street. "But it's a right pretty name. It mean somethin'?"

"Young girl." Fangs would have made Inez's sneer complete.

"Bet I'll learn me all kinds o' stuff like that when I get schoolin.'"
Sarah Beth bounced on the driver's seat with the exhilaration running
through her.

"School starts soon, m' dear," Inez drawled. "Tonight maybe, tomorrow night latest."

At the train station on Basin Street, the carriage turned right and
drove the block to Customhouse Street. In front of Tom Anderson's
saloon, Alex turned left. Wherever Sarah Beth looked she saw women in
windows talking to men on the *banquette*.

"People are so gul-darn friendly 'round here," Sarah Beth said, taken
by the congeniality of New Orleans' infamous shutter girls, denizens of
the city's notorious Tenderloin District–Storyville. "Ain't nothin' a'tall
like I thunk up a big city t' be."

Alex stopped in front of a three-story Victorian mansion. Sarah
Beth's heart strained at the thought of living there. "It's beautiful! Just so
out 'n' out beautiful!"

Inez dispatched the driver back to the wharf for the baggage, then
hurried her young companion up the massive front steps. The door
opened before they reached it and Sarah Beth found herself in a foyer of
unbounded grandeur, though more refined tastes would have called it
gaudy.

"Thelma, take our newest, ah…arrival, here, and clean her up good,"
Inez said to the uniformed colored woman who had opened the door.
"She'll need a dress, maybe tonight. That maroon one I bought a few
months back, the one with the ruffled neck and sleeves."

Thelma nodded.

"Course, the bodice needs to be tucked." Looking at Sarah Beth, Inez
gave the child her most indulgent smile. "Remember the one in the
store window?"

Sarah Beth barely had time to nod her appreciation before Inez
blustered more instructions.

"And, Thelma, make sure she's rested…Sarah Beth, I want ya'll to wait and meet the other girls later. Tomorrow maybe, or the day after…Oh, and, Thelma, send somebody to find Skinny Will. I need him to run an errand…Now ya'll go with Thelma, Sarah Beth. Do everything she tells ya…Thelma, I'll be in m' sittin' room. Send Skinny Will in when he comes…Oh, and make sure the Spanish Parlor is ready for tonight…About nine o'clock, I think. I want our newest little arrival, here, to meet Judge Watson as soon as he can make it…He's one of our benefactors," Inez explained to Sarah Beth. "That's how we…support the orphanage. I told ya'll that, didn't I?…Anyway, Judge Watson is a very, very important man. He's got lots of pull in this city and he's very fond of the girls here…'Specially the brand new ones." Inez's grin lost its meaning on Sarah Beth. "I think he'll want to meet ya'll 'fore anybody else does. Now go on, both of ya, shoo…I'll be up in my sittin' room writin' the Judge a note, Thelma. Be sure to send in Skinny Will soon as he gets here."

Thelma took Sarah Beth to the kitchen. On the way they passed rooms of different color and motif–the French Empire Red Parlor, the Edwardian English Blue Parlor. Sarah Beth sighed. Never had she seen such splendor.

The kitchen, warm and filled with the aroma of baking bread, seemed larger than Sarah Beth's whole cabin back home. A huge stove dominated the room. Thelma explained that feeding and providing hot water for twenty or so people required the large apparatus. An immense vat built into the right side of the device produced the steaming water the maid poured by the bucket-full into a tin tub in the middle of the room. Buckets of tepid water from a cistern in the backyard brought the bath to a temperature barely less than scalding. The maid helped Sarah Beth undress, then gave her a vigorous scrubbing and washed her hair.

Several girls between twelve and fifteen years old wandered in and out of the kitchen. Some smiled. One giggled and pointed, saying to her companion, "Fresh meat." Others gave guarded waves and sad looks.

None of them spoke to Sarah Beth and, remembering Inez's instructions, she did not talk to any of them—except to smile or giggle or wave back.

Her head wrapped in one large towel, her body in another, Thelma took the child to a third floor bedroom and fitted her for the maroon dress Inez promised Sarah Beth could wear. Inez had sent word that Sarah Beth should not eat until after her interview with Judge Watson, but by five o'clock the child was ravenous. Thelma sneaked her two apples to blunt her hunger, then laid her in bed to rest.

Sarah Beth could not sleep on the mattress. Bunching the bed linen on the floor, she tossed for a while and was surprised three hours later when the maid woke her. Sarah Beth thought she had not slept at all.

Thelma helped the young girl dress. First came a thin, frilly camisole, then the gown, which had been altered while Sarah Beth slept. The colored woman sat her charge down at a mirrored dressing table and tortured the rats' nests out of Sarah Beth's disheveled mop, producing magnificent results. Wispy, scarlet-gold ringlets outlined Sarah Beth's cheeks and brow. Pulled back from her face and caught with mother-of-pearl combs, the rest of her hair fell like a great, curled plume below her shoulders, the darker crimson highlights accentuated by the maroon dress. A necklace of dark green stones completed the transformation of a young girl into a gorgeous woman.

"Come here," Thelma said leading Sarah Beth to the window, "ya need some lil' color." The maid moved the curtain back, spit on the wallpaper, rubbed her thumb on a damp red rose and dolled each of Sarah Beth's cheeks with a bright circle, using the same color to turn the child's lips crimson. Spitting on a leaf, Thelma applied green under Sarah Beth's eyes. "There. Go see what ya think of ya'self now."

"That can't be me I'm seein'," Sarah Beth said, looking in the mirror.

"Sho nuf is." The maid showed a big, toothy grin.

"But...But...." Sarah Beth spun around on her low stool. "Thelma, ya turned me out beautiful."

The maid's laugh came in big, hearty bellows. "Ain't me, chil', it's you. Alls I done was a touch here and there. No, siree. Ain't me a'tall. Ya got to be the most prettiest white gal I ever did see." Abruptly Thelma gave Sarah Beth a regretful look. "And that sho nuf be the shame of it."

Sarah Beth had been looking over her shoulder, straining to admire the back of her dress and her hair. "What? What's the shame of it?" When her question went unanswered, she looked up at the maid.

"Nothin'." Thelma avoided the girl's eyes. "Nothin' a'tall. 'Cept you sho is beautiful. Why, you don't even look like no little girl. You's a woman. Look here, you's even got a bosom." The colored woman added, almost to herself, "That's right. You's a woman...And us womans gotta do what we gotta do. Me, I gotta fend f' m'self...Just like you."

Sarah Beth looked down at the low, scooped neckline of the dress and noticed for the first time her breasts had a soft rise. She spun to the mirror to see the full effect. "Oh, Thelma, ya right. I *am* a woman!"

"Ain't all it's cracked up t' be."

SARAH BETH ENTERED THE PARLOR where Inez sat waiting for her. The room, wallpapered in gold, reflected the *demimonde's* gaudy notion of a Spanish hacienda—wrought-iron candelabra and sconces, tinny crossed swords on the wall, ornately carved chairs and tables, intricately hewn cabinets. Dominating it all, a sense of too much furniture stuffed in too small a space.

"Just look at how fine ya'll done up...What!" Inez scowled at the maid. "Thelma, ya'll been spittin' on my hand painted wallpaper again, ain't ya?"

"B-B-But, Miss Inez—"

"Didn't I say t' cut it out. Makes 'em looked spoiled already and the customers—." Inez saw the quizzical look on Sarah Beth's face. She pointed a finger at the maid. "Don't do it no more."

Thelma lowered her head. "Yes, 'um."

"Sarah Beth, come set next to me so I can see how good ya'll look." Inez patted the cushion of the chaise. "Oh, yes. Ya'll do nicely…Right nicely, soon as I get this junk off ya face." Inez wet her handkerchief on the tip of her tongue and rubbed the color from Sarah Beth's cheeks, lips and under her eyes, nodding approvingly at the faint traces that remained. "Nervous?" she asked the child.

Sarah Beth nodded. "And hungry enough t' chew down a horse."

"This'll help both." Inez poured *Mariani*, a wine steeped in coca leaves, into a tumbler, added sugar and handed it to the girl.

Sarah Beth sipped the sweet, fruity-tasting liquid tentatively, smiled and drained the glass.

"Have another." As Inez mixed the drink she said, "I know ya'll's worried about meeting Judge Watson, but, really, ya'll shouldn't be. He's a very important man, and our most important client, that's true, but there's nothing t' worry 'bout. Just remember t' be nice t' him, no matter what."

"How?" Sarah Beth had finished the second glass of wine and, for some inexplicable reason, the question made her giggle.

Inez laughed with her and refilled the glass. "Well, if the Judge says sing, sing. If he says play the piano–."

Bubbles of laughter burst from Sarah Beth unbidden. "I can't play no piano. Don't even know where it's at." She tried to dam up her mirth with her hand only to snicker around her fingers.

"Ya'll won't have to play the piano, I promise. But understand me good, now. Ya'll do whatever the Judge wants. If he wants t' kiss ya–."

"Kiss me!" More peals of laughter. Sarah Beth threw her head back and drained the wine glass. "How he gonna kiss me? I'll be out looking for that damn piano." She laughed so hard she rolled on her side.

"Be serious now." Inez tried to frown, but smiled in spite of herself. "The money Judge Watson gives us keeps a roof over our heads and feeds us. Ya'll like t' eat, don't ya?"

"Don't know. Been so dad-gum long since I ate, m' damn belly thinks m' throat's been cut." Sarah Beth's joke bent her over laughing again and she almost fell off the chaise.

Inez took the empty glass. "This here is serious business now. Whatever the Judge wants–." A knock interrupted her. "Yes."

Thelma opened the door just wide enough to be seen. "Judge Watson's here."

"Don't just stand there looking stupid, show him in." Inez rose to meet her guest.

The maid disappeared. In her place a short, portly man in a frock coat and vest stood in the doorway. "Inez, my dear, how are you?" He smoothed wisps of gray hair over the moles and wrinkles on his bald dome, plumped his muttonchops into place, and rolled his hands together like a miser contemplating money. "I came as soon as I could after getting your note. Where–."

Inez swirled theatrically and pointed to the chaise on which Sarah Beth half sat, half sprawled.

"My word! She *is* gorgeous! But is she still–."

"Course, but don't take my word for it. Have Doc Jessup–."

"That old humbug. For a cut of your exorbitant price, he'd bed his grandmother then swear she was still intact. No, Inez, this is far too important to me…Much beyond the money. I have a reputation, a wife, a family. I must be absolutely certain. I must be cured."

"Don't I know how much this means? Would I pass off used goods on a man of–." The judge's cynical expression cut Inez off. "Well, then, ask her yourself. She's got enough Mariani in her to answer truthful…Come here, Sarah Beth."

The girl stood unsteadily and attempted to walk with poise, but her feet shied away from the idea. She tottered to Inez and the judge took her hand, kissing it gallantly. Sarah Beth beamed. Men only kissed the hands of very great ladies.

The judge, not much taller than Sarah Beth, looked deep into her eyes. "Have you ever, ah, slept with a man, my dear?"

"No, sir." Sarah Beth's tongue felt thicker than she remembered. "Only a boy."

The judge's face tinted crimson and he flung Sarah Beth's hand away. "Who?" Inez demanded.

"M' brother." Sarah Beth gave Inez a lopsided, drunken smile.

Inez visibly calmed. "How old's ya'll's brother?"

"Ten."

Inez smiled triumphantly at the judge.

"My dear Inez, I'm sure you understand that I must be certain beyond a reasonable doubt. This is my health we're talking about…Perhaps my very life." Turning to Sarah Beth, his honor continued his cross-examination. "Has a man ever…Mmmm…Or a boy…ah…been intimate–."

"What's that mean?" Sarah Beth asked.

Impatient, Inez demanded, "Has man or boy ever stuck his tallywacker betwixt ya'll's legs?"

Sarah Beth slurred her protest. "No, ma'am! Why would–."

"See, Judge, she's perfect," Inez said, ignoring Sarah Beth. "Never been tampered with."

"Perfect? She's beyond perfect! Just look at her, Inez. She's absolutely, positively–."

"Then we have–."

"Oh my, yes!" The judge took Sarah Beth's hand again and pulled her close, putting his arm possessively around her waist. "Oh, yes, indeed. We have an agreement, we certainly do."

"And the price?"

"Yes, yes…Just as in your note." The judge's reply came quick and breathless as he ogled the delicate rise of Sarah Beth's breasts. "Seven hundred dollars." He flicked the madam away with his hand. "Leave us."

Inez inclined her head obsequiously, gave the judge a half curtsey and left, closing the door gently behind her.

"Here, sit with me, my dear." The judge supported the unsteady girl, guiding her to the chaise. "You are unbelievably beautiful, you know."

Sarah Beth, her mind addlepated by the coca wine, enjoyed the attention and reassurance of her newly discovered beauty.

Seated next to her, the judge's pudgy hand moved up Sarah Beth's arm to her shoulder, then her neck. He ran the back of fat fingers across her collar bone, dawdled with the soft, ripening mounds on her chest and explored the shallow crevice between them. Tugging at the sleeves of her dress, the lecher pulled down her bodice. A rabid froth of spittle bubbled in the corners of his mouth as he rolled down the thin straps of her camisole.

Ya'll do whatever the Judge wants. If he wants to kiss... Ya'll do whatever the Judge wants... Ya'll do whatever... Ya'll do... Inez's words echoed in Sarah Beth's drugged and drunken brain. *Ya'll do whatever the Judge wants. If he wants to kiss you...*

She let him.

Ya'll do whatever the Judge wants.

He wanted to fondle her.

Ya'll do whatever the Judge wants.

He wanted to raise her skirt.

Ya'll do whatever the Judge wants.

He wanted to corrupt her innocence, steal her future and destroy any chance Sarah Beth might ever have to be happy.

Ya'll do whatever the Judge wants.

CHAPTER 6

AT THE END OF HER fourth month in Storyville, Sarah Beth sat on a mound of garbage trying to summon the courage to ram the jagged edge of a broken bottle into her wrists, to gouge her arm until the sharp points found arteries and veins, to pour out her anguish and remorse in streams of her own blood. But she could only drag the makeshift blade lightly across her skin, leaving a stuttering trail of red dots and dashes, the Morse-encoded plea of a tormented soul: *Momma, I'm lost. Jeremy, I can't save you. God, oh, God, I'm so, so sorry!* As she tried again to make the ragged blade pierce the tender skin of her wrist, her vivid memory brought her back to the last time she had seen Inez Breaux.

AFTER TWO WEEKS AT VESTAL House, the credibility of Sarah Beth's innocence wore thin. About 5 a.m. one morning, Sarah Beth's last customer left and she dragged herself up the stairs to the attic dormitory where the experienced girls slept. Thelma had taken the beautiful gown and chemise Sarah Beth wore to entertain and the child shivered in the damp, unheated garret as she scrambled to find the shirt and coveralls she wore the day she arrived.

Inez threw open the attic door and rampaged into the room. Rushing up to Sarah Beth, she demanded, "What ya'll done! Mr. Butler won't pay! Says if I make a fuss he'll tell everybody I cheated him!" She grabbed Sarah Beth by the shoulders and shook her. "Tell me what happened!"

"I...I...." The child's eyes grew wide with fear.

"Tell me, damn it! What ya done!" Without warning, Inez punched Sarah Beth, her fist slamming into the child's stomach just below the breast bone.

Still naked, Sarah Beth crumbled to her knees trying to catch her breath. Slowly, she bent forward until her forehead touched the floor and she looked like a supplicant begging the whore-monger for mercy. The point of Inez's shoe smashed into Sarah Beth's shoulder and rolled her onto the floor. The child curled into a ball, gasping, tears streaming down her face, terror in her eyes.

Glaring at the other girls who had sat up on their sleeping pallets, Inez yelled, "Ya'll want some o' this!" and watched their heads duck under their bed sheets.

Inez prodded Sarah Beth with her toe. "Tell me what happened or I'll give ya more of the same."

"I'm...I'm sorry...Miss Inez." Sarah Beth choked on the air she needed so desperately. "He come in 'fore I was ready."

"And?" Inez, her hands on her hips, glared down at the girl. "What happened?"

"He seen me." With great effort Sarah Beth sat up and leaned against the wall, her right hand holding her stomach, her left arm across her bare breasts trying to preserve some shred of dignity.

"What was ya'll doin'?"

"Puttin' the sponge dipped in chicken blood inside me," Sarah Beth gasped.

"Goddamn it!" Inez's kick caught Sarah Beth in the jaw and the child lost consciousness.

When Sarah Beth woke, she found herself, still naked, being carried down the huge stone stairs of Vestal House. Jethro deposited her on the *banquette* as gently as he could, laid her shirt and coveralls on the sidewalk next to her, then retreated up the massive staircase. Sarah Beth scrambled into her clothes looking after him.

Inez stood at the top of the stairs, arms folded across her chest. "Now git. Don't lemme see ya'll 'round here again."

Still weak, Sarah Beth leaned on the hand-rail of the stairs. "Ya can't just throw me out. Not after all I done f' ya. Ya made good money off me. Ya gotta give me some. I got nowheres t' stay, nothin' t' eat."

"I taught ya'll a trade," Inez said with a smile that never reached her eyes, "use it," and stormed into the house.

"But ya can't just leave me like this." Painfully, Sarah Beth climbed the stairs. "I done everythin' ya wanted, everythin' *they* wanted, anythin' they wanted...Please, Miss Inez, don't send me off." She reached the front door and began pounding on it with the massive knocker. "Please. Please! PLEASE! Ya can't just leave me like this! I don't know where t' go!"

The heavy door held fast against her pleas; immutable, a silent, stoic portal to sin and degradation, immune to the child's pain, her grief, her hopelessness.

Sarah Beth slid down the varnished, wooden panel into a small, pathetic heap. "Ya just gotta let me in," she sobbed. "I don't know what t' do. Oh, God, ya just gotta let me in!"

The torrent of scalding water splashed down on Sarah Beth without warning. She scrambled away from the door and tumbled down the steps screaming.

From an upper window, Inez yelled, "Told ya'll t' git. Now go on. Ain't nothing for ya'll here no more."

Alone and terrified, Sarah Beth stumbled down the dark street. Two drunks, arm in arm and singing a bawdy barroom ballad, came toward her. She smoothed the matted tangle of her wet hair, put on her best smile and said the first thing that came into her panic-stricken mind as they staggered passed her. "Got any work I could do? I work real good, ya know. Anythin' a'tall. Cookin', scrubbin', mendin'. I work fast and ya don't have t' pay me much."

They only laughed and teetered past her.

Sarah Beth turned, hesitated, then turned back. There was nothing left for her to do. "You two sure could put the curl in *my* hair," she said loudly, mimicking the spiel of a shutter girl calling customers from her crib window. "Take me home with ya. I'll be good to ya both, I really will."

"Well, Jimmy, this has possibilities," the taller one said as he pivoted his companion around to face Sarah Beth.

"Who wants a drowned cat?" Jimmy slurred.

In the dim light from the saloon across the street, Sarah Beth saw they were both young men. *Rich boys carousing,* she thought as she saddled up to Jimmy. "I dry up real nice. C'mon, take me home, why don'tcha."

"Capital idea, Ralph." Jimmy hiccuped. "Take her home. But, hic, I don't think mother will let us keep her. He-he, he-he, he-he."

"Get away." Ralph—tall and dark and looking nothing like his brother—pushed Sarah Beth into the gutter.

"Check your wallet, hic, Ralph, 'cause she mighta took it."

"Oh, no," Sarah Beth said, running up to them. "I'd never do nothin' like that." She caught Ralph by the sleeve. "D-d-don't go. Please, don't leave me. If ya can't take me with ya, we can...There's gotta be somewheres 'round here we can go."

"How much?" Ralph demanded.

"A dollar," Sarah Beth answered, then added quickly, "f' the both of ya, that is."

"Don't have a dollar," Ralph said.

"Fifty cents, then. Two bits apiece."

"More like two bits a piece." Jimmy giggled.

"Nope," Ralph said.

"Then what? Tell me how much ya willin' t' pay," Sarah Beth begged.

Swaying, Ralph turned his pants' pockets inside out. "I'm afraid Lizette and her friends cleaned me out. How about you, Jimmy?"

"Me, too, hic," Jimmy said as he rummaged through his clothes looking for change.

Ralph steadied himself on a light pole and examined Sarah Beth closely. "Don't suppose you give credit?"

"What's that?" Sarah Beth asked, guarded optimism creeping into her voice.

"Do it on account," Ralph explained.

"Don't know as I ever done it like that." Sarah Beth looked around. "But if ya can find one o' them accounts, we can do it on it."

"No, no. Do it on account, on account of we don't have any money right now." Ralph laughed at his joke. "You be the jolly good fellow we know you are and we'll come back later and pay you."

"How much?"

Ralph considered. "Fifty cents."

"How I know you gonna come back?" Sarah Beth asked.

"Because you have my word as a gentleman," Ralph feigned offense at Sarah Beth's implied slander of his character, then bowed with all the tottering chivalry he could muster.

"A dollar, then. Gentlemen's got money."

"For whatever we want?"

Sarah Beth nodded.

Ralph and Jimmy each put an arm around the child and marched her down the street, steering her into the first alley they came to. They stumbled over broken boxes and wagon wheels until Ralph plopped down on an abandoned sofa with its ticking hanging out and most of its springs stuck through the upholstery.

Sarah Beth thought she would vomit as the stench of rotting cabbage and potato peels churned her empty stomach.

"Get undressed." As Ralph unbuttoned his pants, he admired the child's enchanting form in the paltry light of the approaching dawn."Come here."

With Sarah Beth standing between his splayed legs, Ralph roughly explored every nook and cranny of her body.

She flinched, but endured by focusing her mind on the money she had been promised.

Ralph grabbed her hair and shoved her face into his crotch. As she groveled before one drunken sot, she felt the other's hands on her buttocks. He tugged upward and she stood, bent at the waist, her head still buried between Ralph's legs. Jimmy pushed himself roughly inside her more painfully than she could bear. "Ow! That hurts. Ain't the right spot, nohow."

"It's, hic, the one I want. You'll like it, too. Just wait."

To banish the agony of her tender flesh ripping apart, to fight off the utter shame of her double degradation, Sarah Beth tried to imagine the gleaming silver dollar she would have; watched it tilt and turn; concentrated on the bright glints leaping from its polished surface. But nothing diminished the torture and she squeezed her eyes shut against the tears.

As the two scions of New Orleans' gentry debased her, Sarah Beth realized Inez had been right. She had a trade. She had apprenticed as a whore and learned the wiles of the scarlet sisterhood. She knew what these men expected and that to satisfy them, to earn their money, she must feed their vile conceit. From somewhere deep inside her, she found the strength to moan passionately.

"See, hic," Jimmy said. "I knew you'd like it."

As soon as the brothers finished with her, Sarah Beth ceased to exist for them. Making themselves presentable, they discussed which Sarah Beth had liked the most, talking as if she suddenly disappeared from the seedy alley in which they had plundered her body and soul. Stumbling down the alley toward the street, they whispered and laughed, slapping each other on the back.

Sarah Beth clutched her clothes to her body in a pathetic attempt to regain some smidgen of humanity. "That was real fine," she called after them. "Ya'll come back soon, hear? And don't forget my money. I'll wait right by the train station for ya. Don't be too long, now. And bring another dollar, if you've a mind."

Ralph's laugh echoed back to her.

Sarah Beth spent the day, hungry and alone, on the corner of Canal and Basin Streets, listening to the huff and screech of trains arrive and depart. A chill, damp wind sliced through her thin shirt and raised bumps on her flesh. She constantly scanned the faces streaming passed her, looking for Ralph or Jimmy, making her plans. *Need t' get me on back home. Don't care if paw beats me. Can't be no worse than this. Don't know the fare for a packet t' St. Francisville, though. After them two fellas pay me, I'll get me on down t' the levee and see if I can find out. Then I'll get me some work and earn the price.*

Her feet ached and twice Sarah Beth tried sitting on the curb. The pain from the torture inflicted on her the night before made it impossible. To slake her thirst when it became unbearable, she reluctantly dipped her hand in the green water of a horse trough. All day she shivered and waited, trusting Ralph and Jimmy to make good on their promise. By sundown, she realized they had never intended to pay her. Ashamed of how stupid she had been, exhausted, ravenous, Sarah Beth looked for a kind face in the crowd. The women turned away when she caught their eye, the men leered at her. Finally she found the courage to speak to a man rushing from the train station. "Please, mister, can ya spare me some change. I ain't ate since yesterday and got no place t' stay."

"Well, little darlin', we might could arrange something like that, but what's in it for me?" the man said as he appraised the child.

Sarah Beth knew the look. She had no choice. The door to hell had slammed shut with her inside. Now the bolt rammed home.

"Well? What's in it for me?" he asked again.

"Whatever ya want, mister," she said as tears glazed her eyes. "Whatever ya want."

Over the next days and weeks and months Sarah Beth spiraled down the descending circles of the abyss, taking the grand tour of each. Earlier that day she had tarried on the cusp of the lowest. Desperate to support herself, she approached Emma Johnson for work. Emma, reputedly the most loathsome virago in the Tenderloin, offered the child a part in the excruciatingly obscene circus she presented nightly in the spectacle hall of her huge bordello on Basin Street. Emma offered to let Sarah Beth bed the pony. *THE PONY!*

AS THE GRAY, OVERCAST SKY molted into afternoon, Sarah Beth collected the last gossamer shreds of her humanity and chose the comfort of the bottle's jagged edge slashing into her flesh rather than the final, black depravity Emma had offered her earlier that day. But courage would not come.

There's gotta be a way. Sarah Beth spied two dilapidated wooden crates. Dragging them together, she wedged the bottle, broken end up, between the cartons and knelt in front of it. If she raised her arm and closed her eyes, maybe in a fleeting second she could find the mettle to slam her wrist onto the jagged points. Sarah Beth stretched out her arm, her hand balled into a white-knuckled fist, then raised and lowered it a few times over the sharp spine of barbed glass, getting the feel of the swing. Her eyes squeezed shut, her fist raised high over her head, she thought, *I can do it. I can do it. I CAN DO IT! I GOTTA DO IT! I GOTTA—.*

Someone caught her arm.

Sarah Beth instinctively grabbed for the bottle to defend herself and spun to face her attacker. As she turned, she had the impression of a building falling on her as a giant bent and scooped her up in his arms, leaving the bottle behind.

"It can't be as bad as all that," a woman's voice said from the shadows behind Sarah Beth.

The young girl squirmed around in the arms of the giant and found a tall, stately, middle-aged woman looking at her. From the woman's plumed hat, to her kid gloves and shoes, she radiated a grandeur not typical of the *demimonde*, a dignity recognizable even by someone as unsophisticated as Sarah Beth. "Ain't none o' your affair."

"It is when you kill yourself in my alley." The woman brought a handkerchief to her mouth, stifling a cough. Tall and thin, her beauty faded by time, her appearance told of a vital spirit trapped in an infirm body.

"Then I'll take me someplace else," Sarah Beth said, surprised such a refined woman had a house in the District.

"Not until we've had a chance to talk," the woman replied, not unkindly. "Ty, bring her along."

A voice like rolling thunder spoke close to Sarah Beth's ear. "Yaz, 'um."

The child squirmed around again and looked into the face that modeled Michelangelo's David–chiseled nose, fine mouth, strong chin, high cheeks, glistening ringlets on his head. But while Michelangelo worked in pure, white marble, the face Sarah Beth saw had been hewn from the blackness at the center of the earth. "Ty...Tyrone?"

"No, li'l missy, I ain't no Tyrone. I's Titan. But calls me Ty. Everybody do." The smooth onyx of his skin creased into a smile.

"Titan, p-please put me d-down."

"Not on yo' life. Miz Myda, she say she want ya t' the big house and that's just where I's gonna put ya...Now ya don't go fussin' and wigglin' 'round like that. A little tyke like you don't got no chance a'tall gettin' way from ol' Titan. Ya'll just settle down and 'joy the ride."

Sarah Beth saw the uselessness in struggling against the giant; guile might work better. "Titan. Never met up with no man named that before."

"Ain't likely. Ain't likely ya ever met up with one it fits before, neither."

Sarah Beth twisted a bit. "My leg pains me." She looked for a opening. If she could just get him to release his grip a little. "Powerful strange name. Mean somethin', do it?"

"Big." Titan shifted the child to make her more comfortable, keeping her tight in his arms. "When I was born on Miz Myda's daddy's plantation, I weighed me thirteen pounds. Ol' Marse Pepé, that's Miz Myda daddy. The ol' Marse godfathered me for the baptizin' and gived me my name. That's the way it was done back then, 'fore the War and all. Knowin' all that like I did, I just grewed me up right into that name. Grewed me up seven feet tall and t'ree hund'ed pounds. He-he. That's me. I's a Titan all right."

Distracting the girl with his chatter, the colossus carried Sarah Beth into the kitchen of a large Victorian manor and sat her in a chair at the table. Her eyes shifted like a rat in daylight looking for a place to hide.

Titan walked casually to the back door, cutting off one avenue of escape. "Now what, Miz Myda?"

"What's your name, my dear?" Myda appeared a bit spent.

"Sarah Beth." She tried to guess where the other two doors from the kitchen led. One was likely a pantry, the other might lead to the front of the house and away from her captors.

Myda walked to the icebox and took out a platter of sliced ham. "You look like you could do with something to eat, Sarah Beth...?"

"LaBranche."

The child had decided which door might allow her to escape when it swung open and in scurried a very round, very short, very black woman. "Miz Myda, don't ya be doin' all like that," she said, wagging her finger and taking the platter from her mistress. "Ya know what the doctor done said...And you, Ty, what ya let her do it for? With your big old man self lazing by the back door."

"Woman, don't ya be startin' up with me."

Titan's grin and the look of great love that passed between him and the woman put Sarah Beth more at ease. The bond between the two reminded her of the love Elona and Josh Talbot radiated for each other. Perhaps she could rest here, but just for a little while.

"Lou Belle," Myda said, "surely the doctor would let me fix a sandwich for a hungry little girl."

Lou Belle turned to Sarah Beth and looked her over without a word, then turned back to her mistress. "I's the hungry-little-girl-sandwich fixer 'round here. Go on now. Sit youself down and find out how come she got so hungry in the first place." Lou Belle shepherded her mistress to a chair across from Sarah Beth, grumbling about folks doing other folks' work.

"Well, Sarah Beth, you heard Lou Belle," Myda said with a bemused smile. "How did you get so hungry?"

"Ain't ate in a spell. That'll make a body hungry every time."

"Sassy little thing, ain't she?" Lou Belle spun the sandwich plate in front of Sarah Beth to show her disapproval. "Ain't no call for sass when Miss Myda's doin' kindly and tryin' t' help."

"I'd be helped a damn sight more if Miss Myda minded her own business." The aroma of the ham, the nearness of the thick, crusty French bread further blunted Sarah Beth's need to escape. She hesitated. She could always run away later. She began to gobble down the sandwich.

"If I minded my own business, you might be dead now," Myda said.

"Dead? *Dead!*" Lou Belle came to the table, wiping her hands on her apron.

"Ty and I found her in the alley trying to cut her wrists."

Lou Belle put her hand tenderly on the knotted tangle of Sarah Beth's hair. "Lawd, Lawd, child, ain't nothin' so bad as t' kill yaself for."

"How you know?" Sarah Beth mumbled, her mouth so full, slivers of ham hung out.

"I knows, child, believe you-I-me, I knows." Lou Belle looked at Myda. "What we gonna do with her now?"

"Clean her up a bit, I think. With a full stomach and a hot bath, things may look better to her."

"Don't need no bath." Sarah Beth remembered how her fall into damnation had begun.

"Miz Myda say bath so bath you is gonna get." Lou Belle jabbed her hands on her hips for emphasis. "Ty, haul that bath tub in here and set it up. Then fills it with hot water. But not too hot. No need t' go scaldin' the poor child none."

SARAH BETH SAT IN A mass of flower-scented bubbles as Lou Belle gently washed her hair. The similarity between her introduction to Myda's house and Inez Breaux's chilled her, but her native wit and the wisdom acquired in the back alleys of Storyville told her of the difference between the two. Besides, she no longer had her virginity to lose, a realization that came as an unexpected comfort. Like it or not, she was a whore and this was a whorehouse. Though she refused to bed Emma Johnson's pony, she had lived on the streets for months, supporting herself by satisfying men's lust. Surely she could do the same here–in a lot more comfort and style.

"Rinse ya hair while I pour." Lou Belle dipped a pitcher into a bucket of clear water.

"Ya'll been in business here long?" Sarah Beth ran her fingers through the wet maroon tangle, trying to get the soap out.

"Since the District started. 'Bout six months back, I reckon." Lou Belle raised her voice. "Ty, get me some mo' water. This here child's gots mo' hair than a chicken gots feathers…'Fore that, we had us a 'hoe house uptown. 'Fore that, a long time ago, we ain't come t' N'Awlins yet."

"How come ya moved ya place?"

"'Cause the gov'ment made us."

"How come?"

"Ya ain't been down t' N'Awlins long, is ya?"

"Since right after pickin'."

Pouring more water on Sarah beth's hair, Lou Belle said, "Guess that 'splains it. See, child, back a while ago the gov'ment made all the 'hoes and the 'hoe houses move t' the District. Storyville, folks calls it 'cause a gov'ment man, Marse Story, come up with the idea. The righteous folk didn't like livin' next to 'hoe houses and them places was poppin' up all over. The righteous folk grumbled and griped and the newspapers, they grumbled and griped, too, 'bout it being such a shame and all that good people got t' live next t' 'hoes. Marse Story, he pass hisself 'round the whole whirl seein' how they done with they 'hoes. Then he come back t'

N'Awlins and say t' herd up all the 'hoes in one place and everybody'll get happy. So, that's jus' what they done. Then ol' Marse Story got the shivers 'n' the moans when folks started callin' the place they put the 'hoes after him—Storyville."

"Where was ya'll from before ya come to N'Awlins?" Sarah Beth asked.

"Plum Nearly."

"Where's that?"

"Plum out the parish, nearly out the state." Lou Belle laughed. "That was a long time ago. 'Fore we come t' N'Awlins we lived on Miz Myda's daddy's plantation." Lou Belle answered the knock at the door and brought in two more buckets of water. "Don't take your worthless self nowheres, Ty. I's gonna gived ya these here empty buckets and I's want ya fill 'em, case I needs 'em again." At the tub, she poured more water on Sarah Beth's hair. "Rinse till it squeaks, Honey. Then you knows all the soap's out."

"Did Miss Myda have a big, white house?"

"Lawd, yes, child. The biggest, whitest house ya ever did see. With front galleries upstairs and down. And another downstairs gallery in the back. I 'member when I was a little girl settin' on that back gallery by the bells. I was a house girl and all the rooms inside had a bell 'tached to it and them bells tinkled different so ya knowed where someone was what wanted ya."

"It must have been beautiful. Was it as pretty as Nottoway?"

"Don't know nothin' 'bout no Nottoway." Lou Belle ran her fingers through Sarah Beth's hair. "I just knows 'bout Whitewood Hall."

"Why'd you all leave?"

"Them goddamn, good-for-nothin', cur-dog Yankees burnt it down. But not before they chased them Johnny Rebs up one side the cane and down the other. Beat the new plantin' back down int' the dirt." Lou Belle kneaded the girl's hair roughly, exhibiting a bitterness that had not dissipated in forty years. "Damn near killed old Marse Pepé t' lose everythin' he ever had. Iffen he knowed all what happened, I reckon it would have killed him outright 'stead of him pinin' away like he done."

"What he didn't know?"

Lou Belle stopped rinsing the girl's hair and her eyes misted. "Them Yankees got drunk after they beat off the Rebs and raped up on every woman they could find, Miz Myda, too."

Sarah Beth's eyes filled. At least her flower had been gently spirited from her, not violently snatched away. "W-What happened?"

"Nary woman or girl, black nor white, they didn't find. I was luckier than Miz Myda. I come t' season and knew 'bout them things. She be two years younger and didn't know nothin'. But that didn't stop them damn Yankees. Two gots her 'fore they Cap'n made 'em stop. My, my, what a good man he was. Shot one of his own men. Killed him dead. Then stared down a whole big bunch of drunk soldiers on the front gallery waitin' they turn for Miz Myda, her bein' a young white gal and all."

"And you?"

"Honey, didn't nobody worry for us colored gals. Them damn Yankees had us as much as they wanted. Like as not that's why Ty and me never had us no chil'ens."

"You and Titan are married?" Despite the horror of the story, Sarah Beth could not help but smile at the monumental mismatch of Lou Belle and Titan.

"Never got 'round t' jumpin' the broom stick, 'ficial like, but we been together a long, long time." Lou Belle finished the girl's hair. "Me and Ty was born at Whitewood, raised up with Miz Myda. T'ree of us chil'ens all played together. Lawdy be, I still 'member her way back when. Jus' like you, full o' spunk, climbing trees, wearin' britches when she could sneak out in 'em, ridin' her horse like a boy. Lawd, Lawd, it was a good life. Leastwise, started out t' be."

Sarah Beth wanted to comfort the woman, but did not know how.

"Stand up and wash you own self now." Lou Belle handed the girl a wash cloth and soap. Sarah Beth lathered the cloth and applied it to her haunch.

"No, no, no. Ain't nobody ever learned ya t' wash. Don't never wash ya ass 'fore ya face. Ain't no sense to it." Lou Belle took the cloth and scrubbed Sarah Beth in proper order, saying, "My, my, my," sadly as she worked on the child's stomach and groin. Rinsing away the soap, she said, "There's two towels on that stool," and inclined her head to the foot of the tub. "One f' ya hair and one for the rest. Dry youself good while I gets some clothes f' ya t' wear." Lou Belle picked up the filthy rags Sarah Beth arrived in. "These I's gonna burn! Look all them cooties. Wouldn't surprise me none iffen I gots t' wash ya all over again jus' t' make sure the bugs is out ya hair."

"Wait." Sarah Beth jumped out of the tub and grabbed her clothes.

"Don't drip ya naked self all over this clean floor. I gots t' mop it now."

Sarah Beth rushed back to the tub and stood in a mound of bubbles almost knee deep. "I'm sorry. It's just…." She had no place to hide the knotted rag she rescued from her tattered coveralls, so she clutched it to her breast and looked defiantly at the housekeeper.

"Ain't nobody gonna steal you few pennies. We all knowed what you done to get that little money." With compassion Lou Belle took the child's face in her leathery, black hands. "Honey, ain't nobody here gonna do ya nothin' or hurt ya none or take you stuff. It ain't like outside." She nodded toward the window and the Tenderloin District beyond. "Miz Myda don't 'llow it…Now, gimme that grubbed up old rag."

Sarah Beth was reluctant to part with her hoard and Lou Belle had to pry it from her hand. The housekeeper untied the knot and dumped the coins into her hand. "Look-a-here now." She took a clean, white handkerchief from her skirt. "I's gonna put it all in here like that. Then I's tie it up real good." She knotted the handkerchief around a nickel and three pennies. "It'll be waitin' for ya right here." Lou Belle placed the handkerchief on the kitchen table behind Sarah Beth. "Now I's goin' t' find ya somethin' nice t' wear." Before leaving she hugged the girl to her ample bosom. "Ain't nobody here gonna hurt ya, child. 'Member that real good. Nobody."

Sarah Beth felt the unqualified love in Lou Belle's embrace and hugged her in return. The young girl had not known such affection since the last time her mother held her...back when she was a child...so very long ago.

CHAPTER 7

SARAH BETH ENTERED MYDA'S DOWNSTAIRS dining parlor about four o'clock in the afternoon to find a dozen women lingering over coffee and dessert. The *demimonde* in a parlor house slept late–a demand of their profession–which delayed both breakfast and lunch. That much Sarah Beth had learned during her short stay with Inez Breaux.

All conversation stopped when the child entered the room. Sarah Beth heard whispers of "beautiful" and "absolutely gorgeous." She stood a little straighter, hearing the judgement she had passed on herself a few minutes ago confirmed. She thought she looked much lovelier than that first, terrible night at Vestal House. Lou Belle had brought her a pale lime-green dress with a demure scooped neckline trimmed in white lace and an empire waist to camouflage her bulging stomach. The dress' emerald trim and the matching ribbon around Sarah Beth's neck accentuated her sea-foam green eyes, made them limpid. But the crowning adornment was her scarlet-gold hair. Lou Belle had trimmed her bangs and curled them so they framed her face. A great mass of gold-on-fire cascaded down her back, save two thin wisps twisting along her cheeks. The final touches, a few pinches to flush her face, a bite or two on the lips to make them a deeper red, gave the woman-child a rare, almost other-worldly beauty.

Myda DuBoisblanc sat regally at the head of a large, mahogany, pedestal dining table. "Ladies…Ladies." She called the second time a bit louder. "I would like you to meet Miss Sarah Beth LaBranche."

"Hello," Sarah Beth said from the doorway. She was immediately confounded by a chorus of hellos and names and a litany of compliments, each of which she tried to acknowledge with a polite smile and "Thank ya."

"My dear, I know this is all very bewildering right now. You'll have a chance to meet everyone again later. For the time being, come sit here." Myda indicated an empty chair to her left. "Ladies, would you please excuse us. Sarah Beth and I have some matters to discuss."

The *demimonde* nodded among themselves. Each had the house rules explained to her when she first arrived, too. Exchanging looks, some appearing jealous of the new and ravishing competition, they left in groups of twos and threes, whispering among themselves. At the door, each dropped a quarter in a bowl on the breakfront and five dollars in a second dish as they filed out.

Sarah Beth sat down before a baffling assortment of porcelain dishes, cut-glass tumblers and glistening silver utensils. Eating had never seemed so complicated before.

"Would you care for something?" Myda asked.

"I ain't hung–. No, thank ya kindly, ma'am, I ain't hungry. That sandwich done me fine."

"Would you at least care for coffee and dessert? Tilda, our cook, makes a wonderful bread pudding and we're having some today. Would you care to try it?"

Sarah Beth appreciated how Myda spoke to her, as if she were a friend's daughter rather than as the person Sarah Beth thought herself to be, the vilest tenant of the Tenderloin. Looking uncertain, she said, "That'd be right nice."

Myda inclined her head toward Lou Belle, who stood several paces behind Sarah Beth. Lou Belle went into the kitchen and, as the door swung closed, Sarah Beth heard the housekeeper say, "Tilda. Til-*DA* Get me another bowl o' that puddin."

The hush in the room became suffocating until Myda finally said, "I hope you enjoyed…." She paused as Lou Belle set the bread pudding in front of Sarah Beth. "As I was saying, I hope you enjoyed your bath. You look very pretty in that dress, gorgeous, in fact."

"Pretty ain't all it's cracked up t' be," Sarah Beth replied absently, trying to decide which of several spoons to use. She chose the soup spoon and began eating–hunched over, her arms spread on the table.

"How so?" Myda's expression clearly forgave the girl's bad table manners.

"Gets a body int' more trouble than they bargained for," Sarah Beth said through a mouth full of pudding. She licked a drop of whiskey sauce from her chin and remarked, "Ya right, Miss Myda, this here stuff's real good."

"And how bad *is* your trouble?" Myda directed her question more to Lou Belle than Sarah Beth.

"Bad as bad can be." Lou Belle put her arm tenderly around Sarah Beth's shoulders. "She's three months along, if ya ask me."

Sarah Beth finished her dessert and the spoon slipped out of her hand as she tried to put it down. The clatter heightened her self-consciousness, already sharpened by her sumptuous surroundings.

"My dear." Myda took the girl's hand. "Tell me exactly how you came to the District and what happened once you arrived. Be truthful. I can only help you if you tell the truth."

Sarah Beth looked deep in Myda's eyes. She saw none of the malevolence she had ultimately discovered in Inez Breaux's. *Should I tell? Workin' a parlor house'd be a damn site better than what I been up t' these past few months, and a heap better than Emma Johnson and her Goddamn pony. I could save me up some money and head on back to St. Francisville lickety-split.* "I run away from home and–."

"Why?" Myda asked. Before Sarah Beth could answer, Myda added, "Did your father bed you?"

"What an awful thing t' even think! Course he ain't–." Suddenly overwhelmed, Sarah Beth slumped back in the chair. *So that's what it was all about! All them times paw called after me, he didn't wanna beat me. He wanted t'...* It was all so clear to her now. *Oh, Momma, I knowed ya was takin' them beatin's f' me, but I didn't know why. How could I be so damn stupid? Oh, Momma, I'm so, so sorry. You done all that f' me and now look what I gone and done. I'm just what ya didn't want me t' be.*

Her wickedness so utterly inexcusable, Sarah Beth knew she could never see her momma again. She had lost forever the comfort of those arms protecting her, the sound of that sweet voice, the sight of that woman whose benediction of blood and broken bones she had debased. With this understanding came tears and an unalterable resolve. *I'll lay in the bed I made f' m'self, but, I swear before God, Momma, ya won't never know. And you'll never want for nothin', not if I can help it. Little Jeremy, neither.*

Myda watched the wash of emotions cross Sarah Beth's face and the tears begin. The older woman said, with great compassion as she squeezed Sarah Beth's hand, "It's all right. It happens to many–."

"That ain't it." Tears coursed down Sarah Beth's cheeks but her voice remained firm and unwavering. "I know now that's what he was a'fixin' t' do. But momma, she wouldn't let him. She took all them beatin's...It was her said I should go. So that's what I done. That's when I met up with Inez."

"I knew it," Lou Belle wailed, wringing her hands in her calico apron. "They done used this here po' child f' the cure. Bad enough if she catched it regular. Lawd, Lawd, why You don't strike down that Breaux woman dead?"

"What cure?" Sarah Beth looked from Myda to Lou Belle and back, wiping her nose on the back of her hand as she did. "Who's sick?"

Myda exhaled slowly, a great sadness on her face. "There are terrible diseases you can get when you bed a man. Some so terrible they can kill you or make you blind. Usually, they can't be–."

"That's what she got alright." Lou Belle continued wringing her hands. "A dose o' Big Casino. I seed enough o' it t' know."

Myda glowered at her long-time friend and housekeeper, her eyes telling Lou Belle to be quiet. "As I was saying, usually these sicknesses can't be cured. Though every pharmacy seems to have their own patient medicine for the diseases, none of them work. So desperate men do desperate things and many believe bedding a virgin will cure them. There are people in the District who specialize in finding virgins for men with syphilis. Inez Breaux is one of them. How long were you at Vestal House?"

"Two weeks," Sarah Beth replied, dismayed and terrified. "Is that what I got, that siffy stuff? I thought I just catched me a rash."

"After the first time, what did she do to make it seem you were still intact?" Myda asked.

"In what?" Sarah Beth's face showed her confusion.

"How did she make it seem you were still a virgin?"

"She gave me a sponge soaked in chicken blood to put inside."

"No doctor? No operation?"

"N-No." Sarah Beth's voice began to tremble despite her best efforts to control it.

"Sometimes a doctor will sew sheep gut–." Myda stopped and thought. "Inez wouldn't go to the expense. A girl getting married will, if she's ruined herself, but it's not necessary just for the cure."

"Oh, God, Miss Myda," Sarah Beth wailed. "I ain't gonna die, am I?"

Before she could answer, Lou Belle, hugging the girl, said, "Miz Myda, this here child sure do needs our help."

"I know that," Myda snapped. To Sarah Beth she said, "No, child, you won't die. We'll–."

"You said there weren't no cure. You said it kills or blinds ya. Ohhhhh, I don't want to go blind neither."

"You won't die or go blind."

"But you said–."

"Hush, now." Myda squeezed Sarah Beth's hand. "There are ways to–."

"What ways?"

"Captain Willie can–."

Sarah Beth sniffled. "Who's Captain Willie?"

"Hush and I'll tell you," Myda said.

"Cap'n Willie the goodest old man you ever gonna meet," Lou Belle said with a broad smile. "Tell her, Miz Myda."

"I will, if you both just give me a chance." Myda sat back in her chair. Relaxing, she seemed more like a kindly grandmother than a stately lady. "Captain Willie is an old filibuster–."

"What's bustin' horses got to do with it?" Sarah Beth demanded.

"Horses?" Myda asked. "Who said anything about horses?"

"You did, damn it!" Sarah Beth's voice rose. "Ya just said Cap'n Willie was a filly buster."

Myda smiled. "Calm down, dear, and let me explain. I said 'filibuster.' Before the War, New Orleans was filled with hot-blooded men seeking their fortunes. Several empires were conceived and the armies to win them recruited in French Quarter coffee houses. Expeditions were launched against Texas, Cuba, Venezuela and more. The plotters were called filibusters because they talked far into the night making their schemes. Captain Willie went on several of these campaigns, none succeeded and no one ever became rich. All Captain Willie got for his trouble was a few minnie balls and saber cuts. When the War came, Captain Willie joined a regiment called the Louisiana Tigers. But we lost anyway and…." Myda's voice trailed off.

Sarah Beth watched as the older woman remembered her hurtful past. She saw the pain in Myda's eyes, etched in her face, her entire aspect. The loss of Whitewood Hall, the rape, the life she had been forced to live, all showed clearly. Sarah Beth squeezed the older woman's hand.

Myda smiled, a melancholy smile, a smile of kinship beyond blood, of sisterhood parented by the same malignant fate. "After the War, Captain Willie, like many other Confederate sympathizers, went to Brazil. He spent years in the jungle with the Indians and learned their ways. They have many strange medicines we don't know about. He brought some back with him. One cures syphilis. I've seen it work. We'll ask him if he'll help you."

"Oh, Miss Myda, that's grand!" Appreciation spilled from Sarah Beth's eyes and down her cheeks. "I don't rightly know just how t' say thanks, but if–."

"There *is* a price, my dear," Myda said.

Sarah Beth wilted. "I got no money t' speak of."

"Not in dollars," Myda said, "though, God knows, I wish it were. If it were only money, I would have paid it and said nothing to you." The older woman smiled sadly. "No, child, the cost is much dearer than that, I'm afraid. You see, Captain Willie, as old as he is, likes young girls. If he agrees to cure you, he'll expect–."

"I'll pay and be twice glad f' the price." Sarah Beth instinctively understood the payment required. "Glad once t' be cured and once t' know the cure worked. He ain't gonna bed me if I ain't cured. That's reason enough t' pay his askin'."

Myda's eyes widened. "It's unusual to find someone as young as you with such intelligence and such ability to reason."

Sarah Beth beamed at the compliment. "Thank you kindly, ma'am. Always been tolerable good at figurin'."

"Of course," Myda said, "we'll have to ask Captain Willie when is the best time to do it, before or after you have the baby."

"Ain't havin' this here baby." Both Sarah Beth's tone and expression emphasized her fierce determination.

"Unfortunately, your trouble happens quite often in the District, my Dear. The House of the Good Shepherd will take care of you and put the baby–."

"I ain't having this here baby!" Sarah Beth yelled.

"What ya 'spect t' do, child?" Lou Belle asked.

"But, Dear, the House of the Good Shepherd is a home for wayward–."

"*I DON'T CARE! I AIN'T HAVING THIS HERE BABY!*" Sarah Beth's defiance suddenly evaporated. She grabbed Myda's hand in one of hers and clutched Lou Belle's with the other. "Please, Miss Myda. Please. Can't ya help me with that, too. I knowed there's ways and I'll pay ya whatever it costs. Just as soon as it's gone and I'm cured, I'll start working and ya can take it out m' wages."

"And where do you plan to work? On the street again. How much have–."

"I ain't never goin' back on the street. I'll work right here."

"You can't work here."

"And just why the hell not?"

"Because you don't know how," Myda snapped.

"Don't know how? *DON'T KNOW HOW!*" Sarah Beth slapped the table so hard she set the china tinkling. "This here *is* a whore house, ain't it? I've been whorin' nigh on three months. Kneelin' a'fore man and boy in doorways and alleys, doin' them French for the price of a slice o' bread. Liftin' my skirt for any man with the notion. Lettin' his friends watch for free just so's my next meal ain't somebody else's garbage. Tell me I don't know how t' cook or sew or milk a Goddamn cow, but don't never, *ever* tell me I don't know how t' fu–."

"We don't talk trash like that here! That may be fine for Smokey Row," Myda said with great indignation, using the pre-Storyville term for a well-known area of colored prostitutes, "but not in this house!" She stopped and composed herself, taking several deep breaths. "Satisfying a man's lust doesn't take much talent, anyway. Most will bed a tree if he finds a notch with moss around it."

"Sorry I was up t' talkin' like that, Miss Myda. I truly am." Sarah Beth feared her outburst might have ruined her prospects.

"The Mansion is not a...a common parlor house." Myda's vehemence moderated even more, her voice became more controlled. "There are no strumpets here. The ladies you met are courtesans. They entertain a man's mind, as well as his body, with their intelligence, wit, talent and grace. All the things you don't have. Even in that beautiful gown, with that beautiful face of yours, you walk like a keel boat bully with sore feet and talk like a field hand. This is a twenty dollar house–. Don't interrupt. I know they say there hasn't been a twenty dollar house in New Orleans since those damn carpetbaggers were run off, but this one *is*. Josie Arlington can't charge that much, nor the Countess, Wille Piazza. Not even that other octoroon, Lulu White. They all run five dollar houses. Get the customer in and out as fast as you can, and steal as much of his money as possible in the process. Not here, though. Our ladies are cultured. For twenty dollars a man might play chess or mahjong, or listen to his favorite lady sing. He might meet friends, discuss business or plan a political campaign. We cater to the elite of the city. No, my Dear," Myda concluded, shaking her head, "you definitely do not fit in here. Why, your table manners are dreadful. You don't even know which spoon to use."

"Oh, Miss Myda, I could learn me all that, and about the spoons, too." Sarah Beth realized the opportunity before her and groveled. "It's all I ever wanted t' do, learn me stuff. And I can play chest with Marjorie, just show me how. And sing, even. You just said I was smart and pretty, no, beautiful, you said. All the rest, can't ya learn me?" She turned to Lou Belle, sensing an ally. "I bet *you* could learn me some of that stuff, 'specially 'bout the spoons and all. Please," she turned back to Myda, "please, learn me t' be one o' them corny-zones."

"My dear," Myda said, trying to keep a stern countenance in spite of the corners of her mouth turning up, "I really do think you'd be much better off in the House of the Good Shepherd. After you have the baby, they'll put it up for adopt–. Let me finish, *please*. What you want to do is dangerous. Women die during abortions."

"Women die bornin' babies," Sarah Beth countered.

"Miz Myda, I ain't never gone agin ya before and I surely ain't gonna start now," Lou Belle said. "But this here child need help. And the baby what's comin', too. Ain't nobody gonna 'dopt no baby with the Big Casino. What kind of life that po' thing gonna have? 'Specially if it's weak and sickly. It'll likely die in a year or two nohow." Lou Belle hugged Sarah Beth tightly to her. "Lemme call Voodoo Woman. She ain't lost nary a momma she 'bortioned."

"Please, Miss Myda," Sarah Beth begged, "I don't want no baby. I don't know what t' do with it. If it lives and nobody wants it, it'll have t' stay with me. What if it's a girl? What then? I knowed trick baby girls started whorin' when they was eight, workin' with they momma. That ain't no life t' bring a baby to. I'm beggin' ya, Miss Myda, please help me get rid of it."

The older woman looked from her housekeeper to the girl, misgivings apparent in her expression.

"She need help real bad, Miz Myda."

"They all need help," Myda said. "We can't help every one of them."

"I knows that, but can't we help just this one? I won't never ax again."

Myda's regal posture drooped and she leaned back in her chair. After several deep breaths she said, "Get a message to Voodoo Woman."

"Thank ya, Miss Myda," Sarah Beth said. "You won't never be sorry you done it." Then, solemnly, she walked to the breakfront near the door. "Them gals put money in these here bowls when they left. What for?"

"A quarter a day for the police and five dollars a day room and board," Myda explained.

Sarah Beth took the knotted handkerchief from the bodice of her dress and untied it. With the solemnity of a holy rite, she dropped her few coins into the dish with the dollar bills. "On account. It's all I got, but if ya keep tab how much I owe, I'll pay it back. Every cent. I swear. I'm gonna be the best damn, ah, 'scuse me. Best darn corny-zone ya'll ever did see."

VOODOO WOMAN–MIDWIFE, ABORTIONIST AND high priestess to the superstitious harlots of Storyville–arrived the next day. In a small bedroom on the third floor of Myda's establishment she met Sarah Beth, almost scaring the girl senseless. Tall with wild, dark-brown hair and crossed eyes, Voodoo Woman seemed more the brunt of terrible curses than their author. Only the greatest steadfastness kept Sarah Beth lying in bed with her legs splayed and her knees up as she watched the sorceress unpack her paraphernalia, including a long, ominous piece of flexible wire. Fear etched the girl's face, along with determination.

Lou Belle held Sarah Beth's hand and crooned, "It okay, Honey," and, "There, there, sweet child, it be all right."

Myda put a small vial to Sarah Beth's lips. "Here. Drink this. Laudanum. For the pain." The look she exchanged with Lou Belle added, *And for the fear.*

Voodoo Woman sat on a low stool at the foot of the bed. Looking at Sarah Beth over the child's swelling stomach, the priestess said, in a low, raspy voice, "Don't worry, I done this lots o' times and ain't hardly never lost a gal. That's 'cause of the magic." She held up a wide-mouth bottle with a cork stopper and two bloody lumps in the bottom. "Fresh horse testicles." Taking the hocus-pocus in her hand, she rubbed the grisly mass slowly on the long wire, mumbling to herself, then smeared gore on Sarah Beth's belly, groin and legs. With more incantations, Voodoo Woman formed the wire into a loop.

As Sarah Beth felt the noose pass into her body, she bit her lower lip until it bled, refusing to scream or cry. *Goddamn 'em. Goddamn 'em every one. Goddamn Inez Breaux for makin' me a whore. I'll get even with her if it's the last thing I ever do! Goddamn Judge Watson f' givin' me Big Casino. Try 'n' kill me, will ya. Gimme a Goddamn kid, t' boot. Not on ya Goddamn life. Don't worry, Mr. Judge, you ain't seen the last o' me yet! And all the rest o' ya. I don't know ya names, but—.*

A sharp pain pulled Sarah Beth down from the ceiling where the drug had put her. Myda's hand on her forehead, the vial against her lips, she swallowed and floated out of her body again.

The rest think they got clean away. They don't know I can call to mind the face of every man that used me. Months of mocking laughter reverberated in her brain. She saw every alley in which she had debased herself, the boots and clothes of each man she had begged to abuse her, heard their taunts as she complied with their perverted demands. But when she tried to remember their faces, nothing. They were only genitals to her, of every size and description, each puffed up with its own self-importance, each a weapon tyrannizing her and all womankind. *That's the worst of it all, ain't it? Women got t' play like it's so wonderful for 'em to stick us with their scrawny, crooked little tallywackers, the very thing that makes 'em think us women is lower than dirt under dog shit.* Suddenly Sarah Beth realized she had never looked at the face of any man she serviced. She had performed the degenerate contortions they demanded, satisfied their sordid, insatiable lust and saw not one person who defiled her. *Don't matter none. They'll be others and they're all alike. If they want sweets from this gal, it'll cost them more than the change in their pockets. So Goddamn much more, I swear t' God!*

FOUR WEEKS AFTER THE ABORTION Lou Belle still kept Sarah Beth a semi-invalid, hovering over her constantly like a hen with chicks in the nest, refusing to let her see Captain Willie for yet another two weeks. Myda spent as much time with Sarah Beth as her management of The Mansion allowed, and the other ladies of the house stopped in from time to time. Sarah Beth became fond of them all, but the housekeeper and the mistress of The Mansion earned singular stations in her heart. Lou Belle took the place of Elona Talbot, the wonderfully generous woman of Sarah Beth's long-ago youth, while the benevolence of genteel and august Myda DuBoisblanc partially filled the loss of the girl's cherished momma.

Sarah Beth did not waste her enforced idleness, asking–demand-ing–that her education begin immediately. Lou Belle took up Sarah Beth's tutorage with great gusto, serving every meal on complete place settings with a full complement of utensils. She instructed the girl in the proper use of each item, table manners and general decorum. At the same time Lou Belle demanded that Tilda stretch her culinary talents to the limits, exposing Sarah Beth to a wide range of cuisine. This led to two unexpected results.

First, Sarah Beth discovered an immense fondness for sweets, a fancy her impoverished parents could never indulge so it had remained dor-mant until now. She could have dined exclusively on bread pudding and *crème brûle*, a velvet-smooth custard with a crunchy, caramelized sugar top. Only immense self-control prevented Sarah Beth's body from turning to fat rather than blossoming into its preordained voluptuous proportions. Second, Tilda's kitchen wizardry earned The Mansion the reputation as an excellent restaurant as well as the finest *maison de joie* in the city. So much so that Myda's regular clients held business dinners there, even when not scheduled to visit their favorite paramour.

Lou Belle organized the other ladies of the house into a coaching staff, each sharing her particular area of expertise with Sarah Beth. Jocelyn, a tiny blonde of great beauty, had the best eye for clothes and color. Marie, a stunning brunette, lent her flair for music. Each of the other girls contributed, too. But Katee, a tall raven-haired girl in her early twenties, taught Sarah Beth to assimilate all of the separate instructions into a coherent whole and eventually produced the most accomplished courtesan New Orleans had ever known.

While Lou Belle and the *demimonde* of The Mansion developed Sarah Beth's charm, Myda addressed her literacy. The girl amazed the older woman with the facility of her young mind. Soon after their les-sons in reading, writing and arithmetic began, Myda realized the scope of Sarah Beth's prodigious intellect, powered by a memory that recalled the exact details of everything the girl had ever experienced.

One morning six weeks after the abortion, Myda announced, "Captain Willie will be here tonight."

For the rest of the day Sarah Beth fretted, worrying that Captain Willie might not find her appealing enough and, thus, would not help her. Lou Belle and Myda's assurances that the old man had already agreed did not settle the child. With the housekeeper's assistance, Sarah Beth tried on and discarded more dresses than most seamstresses had ever seen and arranged her scarlet-gold mane in more styles than any hair-dresser had ever imagined–always leaving two wispy curls dangling down the sides of her face in what had become her signature.

Shortly after two in the afternoon, Lou Belle exploded. "Child, ya done wore me to a frazzle. I ain't gettin' no mo' dresses and I ain't gettin' no mo' combs for that hair of yours. Ya can see Cap'n Willie nekked as a jay bird, for alls I care." She collapsed into an overstuffed chair in Sarah Beth's bedroom. "I ain't movin' *no mo'!*"

"Oh, but Lou Belle." Sarah Beth, with a coquettish pout, flopped into the housekeeper's ample lap. "What if he don't, ah, *doesn't* like me naked."

"I 'spect that's the way he'll like ya best."

"Not til I'm cured and I ain't...*I'm not* cured yet. Please," Sarah Beth wheedled. "I just thunk, ah, *thought* of that new dress Katee has. You know, the dark blue one with the light blue sash. She said I could use it whenever I wanted. But it's got, ah, it *needs* to be taken up. Pretty, pretty please. With sugar on top...And whipped cream...And nuts...And chocolate sauce...And–."

"Oh, all right." Lou Belle laughed and shook her finger at the girl in her lap. "But this here be the very last one."

"Maybe."

"Ain't no maybe nowheres 'round here. It be the last–."

"All right, all right, all right." Sarah Beth pouted, then smiled. "Maybe."

MYDA AND SARAH BETH WAITED for Captain Willie and their scheduled four o'clock lunch in one of the private parlors the ladies

used to entertain their paramours. When the old man came through the
door, Sarah Beth marveled at how he walked. His silver-handled cane,
feet, shins, thighs, hands, arms and shoulders all seemed bent on different destinations. It amazed and astonished her when all the separate
parts of his body arrived at his chair simultaneously.

Captain Willie was everything a world traveler, soldier-of-fortune
and profligate should be at ninety-four. Except for a few gray wisps on
his dome and above his eyes, he had no hair where he should and much
where he shouldn't. Thick, black tufts grew from inside his ears and
along their edges. Clumps of hair protruded from his nose. Curlicues
grew from all the moles on his head, face and neck. Those dark lumps
speckled his features, competing with a multitude of wrinkles and
smallpox scars for first prize in disfigurement. His nose hooked ponder-
ously over lips that had caved in when his teeth escaped and his rheumy
eyes appeared to hold all the tears he should have shed during his lifetime but never did.

Sarah Beth imagined the old man's face as a map of all the places he
had been: the blue veins against pink and white mottled skin were
rivers, the wrinkles and creases roads, the large moles cities, the smaller
ones villages. She thought if she carefully peeled away each layer of his
skin, she might explore his adventures and be left with the smooth-
faced child that had begun this almost endless life. She pictured the
infant Captain Willie in her mind, with knots of hair growing from his
ears and nose, and laughed out loud at the image, which earned her a
reproving glare from Myda.

Lou Belle served them each a plate of red beans and rice. Myda had
decided on soft cuisine, rather than one of Tilda's more substantial culinary delights, in deference to Captain Willie's lack of teeth. The plate
the housekeeper set before the old man lacked the ham seasoning and
sausage that Sarah Beth and Myda found in theirs, another concession
to his gums. Lou Belle had explained to Sarah Beth earlier that Captain

Willie's visits always started with gossip from the District, and he did not disappoint them.

"Heard about the other night?" Captain Willie spoke and chewed at the same time. Even after he swallowed he chewed. In fact, Captain Willie chewed most of the time.

"No," Myda said as Sarah Beth collected herself and sat in respectful silence, a huge grin on her face.

"Terrible. Girls fighting. Disgusting. Women shouldn't fight." Captain Willie's voice squeaked like a chair badly needing glue. "Remember the first one I saw. With Walker and Henry in Nicaragua. The first expedition. Ha, me, one of the 'Fifty-six Immortals'...Actually fifty-eight, you know. Immortals, that is. Everybody says fifty-six. Fifty-eight, though. I know, I was there. Ah, that Colonel Henry! Greatest filibuster of them all. How the man could fight! Sword in one hand." Captain Willie raised his fork. "Pistol in the other." He aimed his spoon at Myda. "Every manner of weapon imaginable stuck in his belt." He looked around for more utensils with which to arm himself.

"What about the fight?" Myda gently prodded.

"Eh? What say?"

"The fight," Myda repeated louder.

"Cantina. Grenada. After we took the city."

Sarah Beth giggled, covering her mouth with her hands, as Myda steered the old man in the right direction. "I meant here in the District."

Captain Willie helped himself to peas and carrots, mashed them with his fork and mixed them with his beans and rice. He saw Sarah Beth's uncertain expression. "Goes the same place. Gets jumbled up down there. He-he. Just saving my stomach some trouble. Ha-ha, ha-ha-ha." His laugh turned into a cough that almost strangled him. Red faced, he asked, "Where was I?"

"Telling us about girls fighting in the District," Myda said.

"Eh?"

Myda raised her voice to almost a shout. "The fight last night in the District."

"Yes. Of course." Captain Willie netted the thought as it flew by. "Cross-eyed Louise and Fightin' Mary. Love. Same fellow. Hog Jaw Something-or-other. Short *I*-talian. Pencil-line mustache. Know him?"

Myda nodded.

Captain Willie became more interested in the slurry of red beans, rice, peas and carrots than reporting the fight and Sarah Beth asked, "What happened?"

"To who?" Captain Willie wondered.

"Cross-eyed Louise and Fighting Mary," Sarah Beth said, a bit flustered.

"Had a fight," Captain Willie said as he gummed his food.

"Who won?" Sarah Beth asked.

"Eh?"

Sarah Beth giggled again. "Who won the fight last night?"

"Cross-eyed Louise got a new name. He-he. One-eyed Louise now."

Dinner continued with Captain Willie sharing smatterings of rumor and ninety-four years of accumulated memory in no particular chronological order. With the last raisin of his bread pudding eluding his spoon in a mighty chase around his bowl, Myda brought up the evening's business.

"Captain Willie, Sarah Beth is the girl we spoke of. She spent time in Vestal House and you know what that means."

"Tut-tut-tut." The old man's eyes became more liquid. "Sorry. Must've been awful. First time that way."

Sarah Beth inclined her head in appreciation, but said nothing.

"She was given as the cure to…Well, we just don't know how many men," Myda continued.

"How long she been gone from there?" Captain Willie addressed his question to Myda.

"Four or five months ago. When we–."

"Should've called me sooner. Gone on a while."

"She was pregnant."

The old man leaned over and caste his rheumy gaze at Sarah Beth's stomach. "Don't look it."

"I'm not any more." Sarah Beth flattened her dress across her abdomen.

"Want the cure, eh what?"

Both Myda and Sarah Beth nodded.

"Like to. Can't though."

"What!" Myda exclaimed. "Why didn't you–."

"Why?" Sarah Beth demanded.

"Out." When neither woman seemed to understand, the old man added, "Gone. Used up."

Both Myda and Sarah Beth slumped in their chairs, crestfallen.

Myda recovered first. "But why didn't you–."

"Ha-ha. Little joke. Bound to be some left. Run my finger around. Get a tad more." Captain Willie twirled his finger in the air, scooping out an imaginary bottle. "Should be just enough, what? Ha-ha."

Too relieved to strangle the old tease, Myda and Sarah Beth beamed.

Captain Willie gave them both a wide, toothless grin. Then, putting down his spoon, attacked the renegade raisin with his thumb and index finger. It defended itself valiantly, but ultimately lost. Captain Willie popped it into his mouth, then licked the whiskey sauce from his fingers. He sat across from Myda staring at her, smacking his gums together, waiting.

"She understands the payment. She agrees," Myda said.

Captain Willie looked at Sarah Beth, the skin where his eyebrows should have been rising.

"We got, ah, *have* a deal. No, we have an *agreement*," Sarah Beth said, "but only if I'm cured."

"*Ke*-rect. Wouldn't have it any other way." Captain Willie winked at her. "Too old, you know. Don't want Big Casino now." The old man stood unsteadily. "Need to examine her. Get to it. Here, the table's fine.

Clean it off." With his cane he began to move the plates and serving dishes.

"Wait," Lou Belle called from the corner where she had been standing. "I's get that. You just move on away."

"Take all this off." Captain Willie switched Sarah Beth's skirt with his cane.

"Just a minute now," Myda said. "There'll be none of that here. Sarah Beth, show Captain Willie to your bedroom."

With her clothes off, Captain Willie made Sarah Beth lie on her bed. Bringing his eyes close, he inspected her, jabbing and gouging her with his fingers.

Sarah Beth squeezed her eyes closed, shamed by the indignity, then opened them. This was the life she had made. She would live it, live it well and the devil take the hind most.

"Big Casino all right," Captain Willie declared. Reaching into his pocket, he produced a small bottle and a pouch. "Rub this on. Every day. Three times." He handed Sarah Beth the bottle.

From the pouch he took out a long piece of something brown and mottled, handed it to Sarah Beth and said, "Eat this. An inch every day."

"I ain't eatin' that!" Sarah Beth flushed. "'Scuse me, but I ain't eatin' nothin' that looks like it grew on a tree."

"Did. On the roots. Nice earthy taste, nutty."

"I can't eat it," Sarah Beth said, bringing the fungus as close to her nose as she dared. "It stinks."

"He-he. Nutty smell, too," Captain Willie said. "Eat or not, suit yourself. Don't eat it, though, and you're a goner."

Sarah Beth held the disgusting growth as far away as possible. "H-How you know this is gonna make me better?"

"Seen it work. You, too, sorta. Head hurts, chew willow bark, don'tcha?" Sarah Beth nodded.

"Ever look at willow bark? Ever smell it?" Captain Willie did not wait for an answer. "Disgusting, too. Almost as bad as this. Chew it though, don'tcha? Headache's gone, ain't it? Same here. Indians in Brazil know things white men never thought of. With plants and such. Like *wurali.* White man calls it curari. Comes from a plant. Kills a man like that." The old man tried to snap his fingers, but couldn't. "Cure with it, too. Strange. Same thing cures and kills. Seen their poultices, too. Awful looking. Awful smelling. On a bullet wound, sucks the minnie ball right out. Lots they know we don't. Go on, eat it. Inch a day. Don't miss. Have to start again, if ya do. If ya don't wanna, well, I warned ya."

For five weeks the old man came every third day. He poked and prodded Sarah Beth, examined her with watery eyes close to her skin, ran blue-veined hands over her entire body until she thought he had memorized the location of every pore. Finally, as she lay on the same bed where he first examined her, he pronounced her cured.

She sat up. Naked, she arched her back and posed as Katee had shown her, putting her budding physique to best advantage. "And the payment?"

"Eh?"

"What about the payment?" she asked louder.

"Now's fine." Captain Willie stared at Sarah Beth, wetting his lips with the tip of his tongue. "Later's fine, too."

"Now."

The old man ambled away and Sarah Beth marveled again that all of him arrived at the chaise in time for him to begin undressing.

"Chamber pot," he demanded.

Sarah Beth called Lou Belle and asked for the appliance. When the housekeeper returned, she handed Sarah Beth the porcelain bowl and said, "Give him it, then pass youself back here." When the girl returned, Lou Belle asked, "You ever been with a real old man before?"

"No."

"Then, Honey, let me gives ya some free advice. It take a heap o' time t' gets 'em ready. Once he be all set, don't you let him use that chamber pot again. No, siree. Iffen he do, ya gots t' start with him all over again."

"Thanks," Sarah Beth said and turned to Captain Willie.

He stood by the chaise, naked, his sagging skin looked five sizes too large for him.

"Miss Myda said ya was, ah, *you were* in Brazil a good many years." Sarah Beth spoke a notch or two louder than normal in deference to Captain Willie's inability to hear as well as he once could.

"Better 'n twenty."

"Bet you know Brazil-talk real good, don't you?" Sarah Beth suggested.

"Yep. Portuguese."

"Say something in…Whatcha call it? Pot-o'-geese? Then tell me what it means." Sarah Beth had vowed to make the men who used her pay more than money. Whatever premium she extracted would be eminently fair. Health. Knowledge. Their souls.

CHAPTER 8

DEAR MOMMA THE LETTER BEGAN in stilted, labored printing–the kind that requires the tip of the writer's tongue to stick out from the corner of her mouth.

I hope you are fine. ~~a~~*And that little Jeremy is fine too. I am fine too. I am very sorry that I* ~~ain't~~ *have not written to you before now. I truly am. But I wanted so much to write my own first letter to you and it took a while longer than I thought for me to learn how. But not* ~~two~~ *too much of a while I suppose. I left right after picking and here it is planting. The time sure does go by fast, does not it. I am fine. I have me a job now and as you can see I have me some schooling too. I am learning to write and read and cipher. They call ciphering arithmetic in school. I am doing real good at it too. It is real easy for me to learn stuff and my teacher says he* ~~ain't~~ *has never seen nobody catch on to stuff as easy as me. He says I will be reading big thick books in no time at all. He says I am a genius. That is a new word I learned that means really smart. And he says I am another new word. Prodigy. That means real smart and real young all at the same time. Sometimes he reads me from the big thick books. Momma they have such wonderful stuff inside them. About people that lived a long time ago and the great things they* ~~done~~ *did and the wonderful lifes they had and their castles and horses and all the fights they fought and all like that. And there is stuff called science too. All about things that happens all the time and why it does. Like how come you can see yourself in the mirror and why fish*

~~ain't~~ *are not really where they look to be when you see them in the water. And Momma I found out that grown ups play games just like kids do. They got this game called chess. It is like too armies fighting each other with kings and queens and all. I play it with my teacher all the time. And sometimes I win. I know you might think it is silly that I can win from a grown up man but I can. And I do not think it is just him letting me. He said with a little more practice I could get real good at it. He said I could be a accomplished player. Accomplished is just what he said. That means I could get real good at it. Does little Jeremy ever talk about me? I miss him a lot. I miss you too. A lot too. But I do not miss you ~~no~~ more then him nor him ~~no~~ more then you. I miss you both the same and I wish that I could see you both but I can not because of school and work and all. I did not tell you that I had a job. I am sorry I did not write about it before. I am a–.*

The paper puckered where her tears fell. She could not write *whore*, though her mind screamed the word so loud it echoed off the walls around her. She could not tell her beloved momma she whored for her room and board, whored for her clothes, whored for the knowledge filling her insatiable mind.

More tears.

She could not write, *murderer*, either. She could not write, *I killed your grandbaby*. Her momma would never understand that Sarah Beth could not love the child growing within her. Not *her* momma, not the woman who dearly loved the man that beat her senseless every week of her life.

Sobs racked Sarah Beth and she rested her head on her tablet, hugged the small Queen Anne desk on which her pad lay as if some minuscule comfort came from embracing the page with the word "momma" written on it. She willed the tears to stop. This was her life now, she reminded herself. She would live it, live it well, and the devil take the hind most.

Twirling her finger in the wisp of hair that hung at the side of her face, Sarah Beth finally wrote the word 'maid,' ending the sentence with the lie she had decided upon.

I work for a very nice lady who has a very big house. But not big enough for me to send for Jeremy. And I do not think the lady likes little boys. But she likes little girls and takes good care of me and feeds me ~~real~~ very good and I sleep in a very nice room at the very upstairs which is big but not big enough for Jeremy to stay here ~~two~~ too. I wish he could because I miss him so much and think of him every day. And I think of you ~~twoo~~. But no more then him and him no more then you. By now you must have found the money in the envelope. If you have not then you should look for it because it is in there. I put it there myself. ten dollars is not all that much so you should not fret that I ~~got~~ have no money for my own self. I do not need but a little bit and I have that so you keep the money I send you and by ~~stuff~~ things for you and Little Jeremy but do not let paw know you have money because he will spend it all on whiskey all the time and then there will never be ~~no~~ any good days at all ~~no~~ any more. I have to go now because it is almost time for my lessons. now that I know how to write I will write you every week and send you money too.

She signed the letter *Your loving honey girl daughter, Sarah Beth* and, though she had been taught to do so, did not print her return address on the envelope. Her momma would never know where to find her or the shame of what she had become.

MYDA HEARD SHOUTS AND THE crash of falling furniture in the parlor where Sarah Beth entertained her callers. The older woman rushed up the stairs, with Titan close behind. When she burst through the door she saw two overweight men in their fifties, using canes as swords, hacking at each other amid the battle-scarred carnage of over-turned chairs, lopsided tables, tilted paintings and broken vases.

Sarah Beth, her long green skirt flouncing, bounced and clapped, goading the combatants to greater fury. "Oh, Albright, you *do* care f' me…Jack, if ya want me, ya gotta win."

Incensed, hands on her hips, Myda demanded, "What is the meaning of this! Stop it! Stop it at once!"

The aging warriors ignored her. The taller of the two, Albright Hinton, whacked his opponent on the side of the head, sending Jacques Deleronde tumbling over the chaise. With his cane waving menacingly above his head, Hinton kicked the divan aside and moved in for the *coup de grace*.

Myda nodded to Titan.

So intent were the fighters on each other, neither saw the seven foot, three hundred pound Negro rush them. Titan caught the downward arching cane inches from Deleronde's face and yanked it from Hinton's hand.

Red-faced and puffing, Hinton lumbered around to confront the giant. "How dare you!"

"Stop it, I say!" Myda shouted.

Sarah Beth applauded loudly. "Oh, Albright, you were *soooo* wonderful."

With his adversary occupied, Jacques Deleronde rolled himself to his feet and aimed a two-handed swipe of his cane at the back of Albright Hinton's head. Titan shoved the intended victim to the ground and took the full force of the blow on his left forearm. Grabbing the weapon in one hand and Deleronde's arm in the other, the giant snatched the cane away and sent Jacques Deleronde sprawling on top of his opponent.

"Hooray, Jack," Sarah Beth cheered, "so brave, so very brave."

"Stop that this instant, young lady!" Myda commanded. "I'll have none of this in my establishment!…Titan, show these…these…*gentlemen* the front door."

The giant hooked a hand in the armpit of each man and hauled them to their feet. Jacques Deleronde felt all his pockets with his free hand as his gaze scoured the floor, obviously searching for something.

With Deleronde distracted, Sarah Beth ran to Albright Hinton and kissed him full on the mouth, then whispered, "Albright, you were *wonderful*. Where's your hat."

Hinton tried unsuccessfully to jerk his arm away from Titan. "You heard her, boy. I have to find it."

With Albright's attention on his bowler, Sarah Beth stole over to Jacques Deleronde and took his hand, rubbing it first briefly on her cheek, then her neck and, finally, against her bosom. "Oh, Jack, ya'll are coming back t' see me again, aren't ya?"

"Of course, my dear," Deleronde said, fondling her. Then, remembering his search, he asked, "You haven't seen my wallet by any chance, have you?"

"Why, no, Jack," Sarah Beth answered, the picture of innocence. "But if we find it, I'll bring it right over to your house."

Deleronde tried to protest, but Sarah Beth pulled Titan's head down, whispered something in the giant's ear, then skipped behind a overturned table–waving and smiling seductively to each of her paramours in turn.

Titan let go Jacques Deleronde's arm long enough to pull out a leather billfold partially protruding from Albright Hinton's outside coat pocket. "Look-a-here, Miz Sarah Bet'. This here what ya talkin' 'bout?"

Deleronde, who saw where his wallet came from, grabbed for it. "That's mine! The bastard stole it." He tried to punch Hinton, but Titan kept the two men apart.

"Thief!" Deleronde yelled.

"Scoundrel!" Hinton shrieked backed, as Titan jostled them into the hall.

Myda closed the door and, with her arms folded, turned to Sarah Beth. "What were those two men doing here *at the same time?*"

The young girl did not answer immediately. She righted one of the chairs knocked over during the fight, sat down and arranged her hands in her lap as she had been taught. "Well, you see, it's like this. Jack had to go out o' town on business, so he asked if he could come by t'day and I said yes."

"And why did you choose this particular time for him to call?" Myda tapped her foot on the oak floor. "You know full well Mr. Hinton calls this time every Wednesday evening to have *hors d'oeuvre* with you."

Sarah Beth, her sea-foam green eyes wide and innocent, answered, "I forgot."

Myda's foot tapped faster. "With that mind of yours, I hardly think so. You did this deliberately."

Sarah Beth bowed her head and fluttered fine, copper lashes against her cheek. "Oh, Aunt Myda, how could you think such a thing? I'd never do that."

Myda strode to the fireplace and stared into the coal grate. "And you picked Mr. Deleronde's pocket."

"Aunt Myda!" Sarah Beth's head popped up. "I never stole nothin', ah, anything from nobody…or is it anybody…or maybe somebody."

"I didn't say you stole anything." Myda turned her head to the girl and put her hand on the marble mantle. "You put Mr. Deleronde's wallet in Mr. Hinton's coat. Just for meanness, I think."

Sarah Beth bounced out of the chair. "Oh, did ya see the look on Jack's face! It was priceless, if ya ask me. And there wasn't nothin', ah, anything mean about it. Just a joke is all."

"A joke. Like making appointments with two men at the same time, I suppose." Myda's fingernails drummed the mantle.

Sarah Beth stood in front of the older woman trying to look like a chastened school girl, but she could not play the part. First her eyes sparkled, then the corners of her mouth turned up, then she bent over laughing. Staggering to the chair she had just vacated, she fell into it again.

"I fail to see the humor in all of this." Myda's voice lost none of its sternness as she waved her hand at the ransacked room. "Have you any idea how much it will cost to repair all this."

"It costs what it costs." Sarah Beth skipped to the door, opened it, then turned back to her mentor. "Don't be mad, Aunt Myda. It was just a little old joke. Nobody got hurt, 'cept a coupla old sticks of furniture and I'll pay for that. I got more money than I know what to do with anyhow. 'Sides, it's about time somebody gives them old geezers a taste of their own medicine, don'tcha think? C'mon now. A little smile won't crack ya face, will it?" She picked up her long, emerald skirt and hurried through the door, her voice trailing back, "I'll go find me a fella or two downstairs so there's no loss for the night."

"No you ain't." Lou Belle, a dustpan stuffed in her apron, pointed her broom handle at Sarah Beth as if a bayonet was attached to its end. The young girl, walking backwards through the doorway, looked like a spy caught behind enemy lines. "You just march yaself on over there and help clean up the mess ya made."

"Me?" Sarah Beth protested. "I didn't make the mess."

"Maybe not, but I gots me a feelin' you the one stirred up those that did…Here, hold this." Lou Belle handed Sarah Beth the dustpan. "Am I right, Miz Myda?"

Picking up a knocked-over chair and pushing shards of a broken porcelain vase into a little pile with her toe, Myda told Lou Belle what happened.

"Lawd, Lawd," Lou Belle said, looking down at Sarah Beth, who had stooped to hold the dust pan in front of a small mound of debris. "With you 'round, a body don't never have to know *what* happened to know who behind it."

"It was just a joke," Sarah Beth said, looking up at the housekeeper.

"Joke?" Lou Belle scolded. "That's what wrong with ya. Everythin' a joke, nothin' ya don't take serious. And Miz Myda, bless her soul, she don't deserve none o' this. Child, that woman treat ya like the little girl she ain't never had. Fact is, ya done wormed ya way int' her heart like ya done mine. *You is* the little girl ain't neither of us had. And this how ya say, 'Thank ya, ma'am' for all she done? Ya ought be ashamed."

Sarah Beth dropped the dustpan and ran to Myda. Hugging the older woman with her head on her mentor's chest, she sobbed, "Oh, I'm so sorry, Aunt Myda. And you, too, Lou Belle. I never thought they'd up and fight each other."

At first Myda held her arms away from the girl, but the contrition in Sarah Beth's voice won her over. She held the child she loved as her own and stroked her hair. "What did you think would happen?"

"They'd shout at each other. Maybe push each other around. But I never thought they'd come to beatin' one on the other with their canes." Sarah Beth lifted her head and said with a grin, "Lord, wasn't that a sight t' see?"

Myda could not keep the twinkle out of her eyes. She looked at Lou Belle, who swept and smiled to herself.

"But I'm awful sorry I done, ah, did it, Aunt Myda," Sarah Beth continued, serious again, "awful, *awful* sorry. And I swear, I'll never, *ever* do nothin', anything like that again. *Never!* I promise."

Myda wiped the tears from Sarah Beth's cheeks with her thumbs and rearranged the two wispy curls that hung down on either side of the child's face. "I know you mean that now. But I have a feeling I'm going to hear you say that again…and again…and again and again."

"Me, I ain't got no feelin'," Lou Belle said, leaning on her broom, "I knows it for a nat'l fact."

Part II

Spring 1905

CHAPTER 9

CLOP, CLOP, CLOP. SUNLIGHT SPARKLED through the huge canopy of oaks overhead as Sarah Beth's carriage drove passed the great mansions set back from the *banquettes* on St. Charles Avenue. As the estates slowly filed by, secure behind iron fences, immense lawns and flowered gardens, she thought, *Some people do find their Nottoways.*

Clop, clop, clop. The horse's hooves beat in time to her racing heart. Titan, proud and straight, towered above her in the driver's seat; his top hat adding to his height, his back so wide Sarah Beth imagined a whole bolt of broadcloth had been used for his black morning coat.

Spring in New Orleans can be beautiful, she thought. Four to six weeks of almost perfect weather occasionally interrupted by wind-shifts ushering storms through. That flawless April morning, clouds built to the west, heralds of thunder and rain in the offing. But not even the threat of a deluge could stifle Sarah Beth's excitement. "Are we almost there?"

"Yes, 'um, young missy." Titan used the old plantation term for the younger mistress of the manor. The master's wife was old missy, no matter how young. Old Missy's daughter was Young Missy, even when Old Missy was ninety and Young Missy seventy. "Right up the street a ways." He turned and smiled at her. "You sho in a hurry t'day."

"I've been working on this for months now, Ty, and I'm anxious to know what Professor Anderson thinks of it."

The enormous Richardsonian Romanesque building, Gibson Hall, with its arches, false turrets and rough stone facade—the centerpiece of Tulane University's campus—came into view. Sarah Beth knew the school had begun as the Medical College of Louisiana in 1834, but Paul Tulane's endowment twenty-one years ago, the year of her birth, gave it its present name.

Titan stopped the carriage in front of the middle set of three large stone stairways leading directly to the second floor. Sarah Beth waited for him to climb down, doff his hat and offer her his hand. Only then did she exit, a very fashionable lady clutching a thick folder of papers.

"Ty, would you please?" She pointed into the gig.

"F' sure." Titan leaned into the carriage and lifted a crate of books, a box large and heavy enough for two average men to strain themselves lifting. He slung the crate under one arm, leaving his other hand free to help Sarah Beth up the stairs as he towered over her.

Inside Gibson Hall, the mismatched pair stopped before an open door reaching halfway to the fifteen-foot ceiling. Above it, a large glass transom had been opened. High ceilings, transoms and floor-to-ceiling windows ventilated buildings in New Orleans against the insufferable heat that permeated the city much of the year.

Sarah Beth drew a deep breath and knocked.

Professor Philip Anderson looked up from his writing, his angular features and brown eyes softening when he saw his visitor. "Ah, my dear Sarah Beth." He glanced at the clock on his desk. "A bit early, aren't you?"

Sarah Beth took a step backwards. "I can wait in the carriage if there's something that needs your attention."

"Nonsense, my dear. Everything else pales before being with you. Please come in." Professor Anderson, just under six feet, came around the desk and held a chair for her.

Sarah Beth waved her hand toward her driver. "Philip, I think you've met Titan, haven't you? He has the books you lent me. Where shall he put them?"

"I'll take them." When Philip felt the weight of the box, he seemed to decide his slim physique was not up to the task at hand. "Ah, put them in the corner and I'll reshelve them later."

Sarah Beth scanned the room. Overstuffed bookcases reaching high up the walls visibly groaned under the weight of thick tomes, all neatly organized by subject. She smiled. "Dear, dear Philip. A place for everything, and everything in its place."

Teasing her back, he replied, "An ordered mind, an ordered life." He sat down behind the desk and looked pointedly at the folder she held. "You've finished the assignment?"

"Yes. All done." She handed him her manuscript.

Leaning forward, he whispered, "What, no foreplay?"

"Philip!" Her tone chided him; her expression, clearly displeased. Turning to the giant, she said, "Thank you, Titan. Please, wait for me in the carriage. I shan't be long."

Philip leaned back in his chair. "'A place for everything, and everything in its place' applies to you, too."

"It does. And this is neither the time *nor* the place." But her pique would not hold against her excitement. "Aren't you even going to look at it?"

"Hmmmm. Just another student project," he said with playful indifference. "Aren't you the early one this morning. It's hardly ten o'clock." He looked at her with a wry sideways glance. "Got to bed *and* to sleep at a decent hour last night?"

"In fact, I didn't. I was up very late putting the finishing touches on that." She pointed impatiently to the folder he held. "I can go to bed early tonight and sleep late tomorrow. I'm not receiving callers this week. Now, will you look at my work? If you keep me waiting much longer the anticipation will make me explode into a big, ugly mess all over your neat, orderly office."

"No callers? Not even *tomorrow* night?" Disappointment filled his voice.

"I'm afraid not. I'm sorry. Mother Nature has intervened."

"Just dinner, then."

"As you wish." If he wanted to spend his money on a platonic visit, she would let him.

He opened the folder and began skimming the text. She sat on the edge of her chair, fidgeting with her ring and watching his face intently.

"Ambitious project." He read the title aloud, "'An Analysis of the Variations between the Original and the Standard Editions of 'Les Chouans' by Honoré de Balzac.' Hmmmm. Beautiful penmanship. Don't ever use one of those infernal typewriting machines." He turned several pages. "Ha, you didn't trust Defauconpret's translation of 'The Last of the Mohicans,' the one likely available to Balzac, so you translated it yourself. No wonder this took so long...Yes...Yes...I agree with your translation here rather than his." He flipped several pages more. "Great Scott! You read Haas' comments in the original German!" He looked at her, awed. "French, German, how many languages do you have?"

"*Ich möchte aber zunächst noch zeigen, dass Balzac selbst die Abfassungszeit der Chouans in die Zeit von 1827.*" She continued to quote Haas extensively and ended by saying, "I speak, read and write French, German and Portuguese, plus English, of course."

He laid the folder on his desk and looked at her earnestly. "How on earth did you learn Portuguese?"

"I had a friend, a very dear old man, who spent years in Brazil. He taught me. I seemed blessed with a facility for language."

"And that quote from Haas, it's much more than you included in your paper. I could understand you remembering the portion you used, but...Was it accurate?" Professor Anderson appeared truly mystified.

"Yes. Another blessing. I remember exactly anything I've read. As if it's actually printed here." Sarah Beth tapped her temple.

"Simply amazing. And to think, such a wonderful intellect has been given to a–." His lips formed a hard line and dammed up the word as he looked away.

After a long, oppressive silence, Sarah Beth said, "The word you're looking for, dear Philip, is 'whore.'"

Philip looked at his books, as if he were browsing for one in particular.

"If I upset you, I'm sorry," Sarah Beth said. "Perhaps I should have said 'prostitute,' or 'Jezebel.' 'Jolly good fellow' would have sounded even better," she said, using the Victorian euphemism, then sang, "For she's a jolly good fellow, for she's a jolly good fellow, for she's a jolly good fel-l-low...Which nobody can deny."

"I'm sorry." He whispered, still not looking at her.

"Why?" she demanded

"Because...It was...Unkind."

"To say it or think it."

He hesitated. "Both."

"Why?" she demanded again.

He remained quiet and searched somewhat blankly for whatever book he pretended to need.

"You're the literature professor. Tell me, Philip, why are words like 'whore' and 'slut' so offensive and words like 'jolly good fellow' are not? Is it the number of syllables, do you suppose?"

"Don't do this to me, Sarah Beth. I said I was sorry. Let it go."

"I'm not doing anything to you, Philip. I'm truly interested in what you think."

He looked at her again. "Ask that Austrian fellow, what's-his-name? Freud?" He picked up her manuscript and thumbed through it. "It has more to do with the way people think than with literature."

"What do you think about my essay?" She deliberately changed the subject. "I guess that may be somewhat unfair, seeing as you've only glanced–."

"Your essay be damned! I want to talk about you, about us." He swung around in his chair and scrutinized her so intensely he seemed to be counting the scarlet hairs on her head.

"And *I* wish to talk about my essay." Sarah Beth stood and began to browse through his books.

"It's wonderful, stupendous–."

"No," she snapped. After fingering the spine of one of his volumes, tracing the gold lettering for a while, she asked, "What do you really think? Have you read enough to have an opinion? As if I were actually one of your students."

"Honestly, from the little I've seen, I'd say it's good, very good. Good enough for a master's thesis." He pinched the bridge of his nose. "Of course, I want to read it more closely and discuss–."

Glowing from his praise, she faced him."Do you really think so? You're being sincere, aren't you?"

"Yes. I wouldn't say it if I weren't...Damn it, Sarah Beth!" Jumping up from his desk, he swept her into his arms. "Please, my dearest darling, talk to me about your work later. Talk about us now."

She pushed him away. "Close the door, please." As he did, she walked to the window. "Philip," she said with her back to him when she heard the latch snap, "what is there to talk about? We are Thursday evening, early because you have an eight o'clock class on Friday." She faced him. "Tell me, exactly what else is there to talk about?"

He tried to take her in his arms again, but she gently fended him off.

"I love you." He bowed his head. "And I believe that you love me." He looked at her. "How else could you–. Oh, God! The thrill of it, Sarah Beth! The sheer joy when we're together! You just *can't* be like that when you're with other–." He hung his head again. "I truly love you. I want to take you away–."

Her laugh scorned him. "The correct version of that speech is, 'What's a nice girl–'. No, 'What's an intelligent–'. No, wait, here it is. 'What's a nice, intelligent girl like you doing in a place like that? Let me take you away from all this.' Is that what you're trying to say, Philip?"

"Don't mock me. Please, don't mock me."

She smiled somewhat kindly at him while inwardly she laughed. *How pathetic you are! And how sweet it is to see. You may buy me, but the payment is dear.* "I'm not mocking you," she lied. "I think it's lovely. If you want to see me more often, I can rearrange my schedule to make free a few hours on another night or two."

"No!"

"Then what?"

"A boarding house, a small allowance. If you love me, truly love me, it–."

"Why not just more time together?"

"I don't want to share you! Oh, God, Sarah Beth! The nights I've laid awake burning for you, knowing you were with…." He took her in his arms.

She did not resist, kissed his cheek and, with her mouth close to his ear, said in a husky whisper, "Surely, more time together would satisfy that scorching wick of yours."

He let her go and sat down at his desk, his head in his hands. "We have to be practical about this. I have a family, too. I'm sacrificing their well being right now to be with you. I can scarcely afford one evening a week as it is. I want us to be together more and this–."

"So it's less a matter of love and passion and more a matter of jealously and economics?"

"No!" He ran his fingers through the ringlets of his light brown hair. "But I must be, *we* must be practical about–."

"Then let's be eminently practical and get married."

"What!…Yes. Of course. Later though. I mean, the children and my wife, I-I do owe them something." His hands slid from his hair to his face. Then he brightened. "In the mean time, I could put you up in–."

"You won't marry me, Philip, ever." Sarah Beth's voice was flat, her tone matter-of-fact.

"Oh, but I will. Just give me some time." He looked up at her–his blue eyes rash, reckless.

"Don't lie to me, Philip. At least I deserve more than that." She walked to the window. "Perhaps I'm being unfair. I suppose you *do* think you'll divorce your wife, abandon your children, all for me."

"Yes. Yes!"

"To rescue me, I suppose. Save me from my wicked life."

He vaulted from his chair and took her by the shoulders from behind, awkwardly trying to kiss her neck around the wide brim and ostrich feathers of her hat. "Yes, my darling. Oh, yes!"

She shook him off and stepped closer to the window. Reaching her hand out, she gently touched the screen, plucking the wires with her fingernail as if they were harp strings. "How long have you had window screening?"

"What?…What does that have to do with–."

"Indulge me, Philip. How long?"

He walked away from her, running his fingers through the curls of his ginger hair again. "I don't know. Years, I guess."

"Ten, fifteen?"

"I don't know! What possible connection–."

"Window screening was invented in 1880. Did you know that? I researched it. Such a simple, elegant solution to a problem that has plagued mankind throughout history. Insects. Before window screening, there was mosquito netting. Someone must have thought, 'Instead of putting the netting over the bed, we should put it over the whole house.' Remarkable, don't you think?" She marveled at this hypothetical thought process as she described it. "Then whoever thought of it decided the netting did not have to go over the entire house, just the windows and doors."

"See here, Sarah Beth, I want to talk about us," Philip demanded.

"I am…When I was a child we had no window screening, no mosquito netting, either. So we kept the house closed up tight, even in summer, to keep the bugs out." Her voice had a distant ring to it, as though she were talking through time. "I remember summer nights laying in the cabin loft. I remember being so hot I thought I was a loaf of bread. I imagined myself in the oven and the sweat rolling off of me was melted butter giving me a rich, golden crust. We couldn't open the windows because the bugs and mosquitoes were so thick they'd carry off the cows. That was the choice, swelter or be eaten alive. The heat was the better of the two. At least you'd eventually fall asleep if the bugs weren't biting you."

"Sarah Beth, why are you telling me all this?" Philip insisted. "I lived without window screening when I was a child. I know what it was like."

She turned to face her adversary-lover. "Philip, you're thirty-five. You're remembering what it was like a quarter century ago. I'm telling you it's like that today. There are people this coming summer that will sleep in sweltering heat to avoid the bugs." She made a mental note, I must write and tell momma to buy window screening.

"But what could that possibly have to do with us!" Philip's tone clearly showed his exasperation.

"Everything, Philip, everything. I didn't know about window screening until I came to New Orleans. All I now know, all I have, all I am, is because of my life here. It's not the life I would have chosen for myself if I would have had an option." *And I was never given that choice,* she thought as she twisted one of the two long curls falling gracefully down the sides of her face. "But it's my life now." She stood next to him, touching her hand on his cheek in a satire of affection. "It's *so sweet* of you to want to save me, but I don't need rescue. Please understand. No matter what you may think of me or the life I lead, I've found my stand of grace." *Have I?* she wondered as she spun away from him and walked to the door, *Have I really?* She twirled back to face him, her long skirt swishing around and adding drama as she intended. "No, Philip, I'll not live my life tucked away in a room somewhere. I'll not spend my days and nights waiting for you. Call on me or not, as you wish. If you do, we'll be the same as ever. If not...." She shrugged, turned, then turned back. "Will you evaluate my essay?"

He nodded.

"Objectively?"

He nodded again, not looking at her.

A smile of triumph flashed across her face. *Call me a whore will you! Then watch me take my pound of flesh and the blood that goes with it, which is nothing less than I deserve.* "Thank you. By Thursday after next you should have had time to read it. We can discuss it over dinner."

"I don't know." Philip spread his arms, encompassing the papers strewn about his desk. "I have another test scheduled, plus all these to grade."

"And we have an agreement," Sarah Beth said sharply. Then her tone became gratingly solicitous. "With all that work ahead of you, perhaps you should spend *tomorrow* night grading papers."

His head bounced up, a doleful expression on his face. "No!"

"Then we'll discuss my essay at dinner a week from tomorrow, *before* you have your dessert."

Staring deep into Sarah Beth's eyes, Philip nodded.

She blew him a kiss and gaily skipped out the door.

CHAPTER 10

AGLOW FROM PHILIP ANDERSON'S PRAISE of her essay, Sarah Beth stepped from the carriage on to the *banquette* in front of The Mansion. Lou Belle stood, hands on hips, negotiating with Zozo LaBrique, who wore her customary red bandanna and calico apron. Brick dust was a staple in the Tenderloin. Scrubbed onto the front and back steps of a house, it warded off hexes and evil *gris-gris*. Regardless of their original baptism, voodoo was the religion of the *demimonde*, and its practitioners amassed fortunes catering to their disciples.

"Lou Belle," Sarah Beth called, "Aunt Myda doesn't want you using that silly–."

"I knows. But she stayed upstairs in the bed this morning with a weakness and I ain't takin' no chances. 'Sides, it clean the stoops good, too."

In the foyer, Sarah Beth took the long pins from her hat and asked Lou Belle,"Has the meeting started yet?"

"Indeed it ain't. It can't till you gets there. Not with the Old Missy up in the bed."

"I want to talk to Aunt Myda first." Sarah Beth started for the stairs.

"That's okay by me, but all them folk in the parlor might could get some antsy."

Sarah Beth, her hand on the newel post, called over her shoulder, "It will only take a minute. There's a thing or two I want to talk to Aunt Myda about. They can wait–."

"You just sayin' all that," Lou Belle scolded. "What ya means is ya wants t' make sure Miz Myda be all right. And, honey, she is. But maybe she won't be iffen ya goes up there. Ya knows how she like everything on time and all. It might make her worser iffen she knowed all them people is waitin.'"

Recently Myda had been having weak spells more often and her general health seemed to be deteriorating, raising Sarah Beth's concern. Being permanently exiled from her mother and brother, Sarah Beth had focused all the love she would have given them on Myda DuBoisblanc. But Lou Belle was right. Going upstairs might distress Myda more.

With Myda's health in decline, Sarah Beth had assumed more of the administration of the business. Last night, the two of them had discussed today's program at great length. Though Myda planned to attend, Sarah Beth was to conduct the meeting. *If anything was wrong, Sarah Beth reassured herself, Lou Belle would tell me.*

Sliding the two massive doors of the main downstairs parlor into their wall pockets, Sarah Beth entered a room with more feathers than an aviary and more blossoms than a garden. The aristocrats and peasantry of the scarlet sisterhood packed the room sipping tea, with some unmistakably disappointed by the lack of more potent refreshments. The first of the *demimonde* to catch Sarah Beth's eye was Josie Arlington, one of the madams Sarah Beth thought of as the Four Queens of the District, the one Sarah Beth nicknamed the Queen of Clubs.

Josie, whose real name was Mary Deubler, started on the turf at seventeen and soon developed a reputation as a rough and tumble bawd. Sarah Beth had heard stories of the famous fight between Josie and Beulah Ripley, a Negro harlot and one of Josie's competitors. The brawl took place on Burgundy Street where Beulah snatched out most of Josie's hair and Josie bit off half of Beulah's ear and most of her lower lip.

Over the years, Josie continued her fighting ways and populated her establishment with viragos, mannish women apparently very popular with the opposite sex based on the success of her business. Four years after her fight with Beulah, in November of 1890, Josie's fancy man, Philip Lobrano, shot Josie's brother, Peter Deubler, during a fight in Josie's establishment—a fight that included Josie, all her girls and everyone else in the building. Shooting Josie's brother cost Lobrano his mooching rights and caused Josie to reform. Thereafter, she worked hard at being the most high-toned madam in New Orleans.

Josie sipped tea and chatted with Lulu White, Emma Johnson and Countess Willie Piazza. Together the four were the high royalty, the ruling sovereigns of the Tenderloin.

Lulu White, a short, fat, ugly octoroon with heavy negroid features and a ridiculous red wig, was the most outlandish of the Storyville madams. Her considerable business skills and the beautiful octoroons that worked in Mahogany Hall, her fashionable parlor house on Basin Street, made her establishment a favorite of the New Orleans gentry. Her most ingenious marketing ploy was the use of discount coupons. She sold books of fifteen tickets, each depicting a different carnal act and entitling the bearer to the delights displayed on it.

What Lulu lacked in beauty, she made up for with ostentation, which earned her the nickname Sarah Beth gave her: the Queen of Diamonds. Today Lulu wore full regalia: formal gown, diamond rings on each finger and both thumbs, numerous jeweled bracelets on both arms, a diamond necklace and emerald alligator broach. Only her famous diamond tiara was missing. *Too garish, perhaps, for afternoon tea*, Sarah Beth thought as Lulu smiled her ever-sparkling smile—diamonds capped in all her front teeth—at the woman next to her, Emma Johnson.

Sarah Beth considered tall, thin Emma the closest thing to pure evil on earth, the Queen of Spades. Unprincipled, lacking any human emotion, Emma sold young boys and girls into sex slavery and held awesome power over numerous women both in and out of the District, many of whom were her lovers. A gourmet of perversion, she exploited the most depraved forms of sadomasochism, fetishism and voyeurism for profit, having starred in many vile performances in her early career to compensate for her total lack of beauty. Though the elite of New Orleans would have no physical contact with her or her thespians, they paid handsomely to watch the inconceivably libidinous exhibitions in the theater-ballroom of her Basin Street bordello.

The fame of one of Emma's employees, Cawzi, almost surpassed her own. A short, starved-looking man, Cawzi performed ten shows a week in which he repeatedly demonstrated his vast sexual prowess. He tripled his one hundred-fifty dollar a week salary consulting with aging philanderers and selling them his vitality elixir, guaranteed to make them as potent as he.

Standing next to Emma was the last of the four queens, the beautiful octoroon, Countess Willie Piazza, whom Sarah Beth had dubbed the Queen of Hearts.

Unlike Lulu, Willie could have passed for white. The most cultured of the District's landladies, she spoke fluent English, French, Spanish, Dutch, Basque and Portuguese and maintained a large personal library that included an unabridged version of *1001 Arabian Nights*, *The Anatomy of Melancholy* by Robert Burton, and many of the works of Alphonse Daudet–her favorite author. Willie, a kind and generous woman, had given Sarah Beth complete run of her library whenever the girl chose.

Perhaps the first madam to recognize the different quality of musicians that played in the District, Willie's appreciation for the "professors" that "manipulated" pianos in the parlor houses partly led to today's meeting of the Society of Venus and Bacchus.

Sarah Beth took the place Myda would have normally occupied at a table in front of an auditorium arrangement of chairs. "Ladies…Ladies…If we all take our places, we can begin."

After some refilling of tea cups and choosing of chairs, the members settled into their seats.

"Ladies," Sarah Beth began, "I'm sorry to say that Miss DuBoisblanc cannot join us today. She's not feeling well and asked me to take her place. If there are no object–."

"Who ya'll are?" someone called from the back of the room.

"Excuse me," Sarah Beth replied.

A woman in the last row stood up. "I said, 'Who ya'll are?' It's okay if we know that, ain't it?" She nodded to several woman close by, and sat down again.

Sarah Beth's wits momentarily left her. How could the woman who ruined her life, who banished her from the two dearest people she would ever know, how could Inez Breaux not remember her? "I, ah...I...I...."

"Come on, out with it, pretty," Inez shouted. "Tell us ya'll's name. We ain't got all day, ya know," and the lower class *demimonde* around her giggled.

"My name is Sarah Beth LaBranche." She said it flat, without emotion, scrutinizing Inez closely. The gossips said Inez had deteriorated terribly since Jeb Winthrop deserted her, taking all her money and a beautiful young girl Inez had planned to sell. Rumor had Inez working in one of the low-class cribs close to Smokey Row, the colored red-light district behind Storyville. Inez's bloodshot eyes, red nose and worn clothes confirmed the reports that she had become a querulous twenty-five cent whore who drank away her earnings at the Pig Ankle Cabaret.

"If there are no other objections," Sarah Beth began again.

"That wasn't no objection," Inez called. "I was just asking ya'll a question like I got a right to."

"If there are no more *questions*, then," Sarah Beth said, "we'll get on with the meeting...The first item on this afternoon's agenda is the complaint about Countess Willie paying more than the agreed-upon wages to the professors."

The crowd nodded and buzzed.

"Does anyone have anything to add?" When no one responded Sarah Beth said, "Perhaps the Countess will be good enough to explain what she has done."

Truly a *grande dame*, Willie Piazza secured her monocle in place before she rose and faced the audience. Where the other *demimonde*, queens and subjects alike, chose the most gaudy clothes, Willie dressed elegantly. New Orleans' most aristocratic matrons, seamstresses in tow, flocked to the Fair Grounds race track on opening day to copy the gowns worn by the Countess and her boarders.

"Ladies," Willie said, fitting a Russian cigarette into a two-foot ivory, gold and diamond holder, "we agreed last year to pay the professors a dollar a night for performing." With a flair for the theatrical, she struck a match and lit her cigarette. "I've haven't raised their wages any higher." A murmur rose and the Countess waited until the crowd quieted. "What I *have* done is merely given them a guarantee on their tips."

Someone called, "What's the difference?"

"The difference is, my dear, that their wages have not gone up." The Countess puffed on her cigarette holder, then let the smoke stream from her mouth and across her upper lip as she inhaled it into her nostrils. "A good professor can make twenty dollars a night in tips. I've seen exceptional cases where they've made much, much more, but that's rare. I've also seen times when they've made no tips at all. It depends on the crowd. So I've simply promised them a minimum of five dollars a night between their wages and tips."

"Ain't that just the same as raising up their wages?" Grace Lloyd, who's operated a parlor house on Conti Street around the corner from the Countess', asked to a chorus of, "Yeah" and "That's right."

"No, it's not." The Countess aimed her sparkling cigarette holder at Grace. "Wages are what I *have* to pay them. The guarantee is something I only make good on sometimes. And not very often, I might add."

The women had arranged themselves according to their hierarchy. Josie, Lulu, Emma and the Countess occupied the first row, in front of

Sarah Beth, with lesser notables like Julia Dean, Josephine Icebox and "Queen" Gertie Livingston, next to them and in the two rows behind. It was this group, the landladies of the two to five dollar sporting houses, that objected to Willie's scheme. The rest of the crowd, the common harlots that boarded in the parlor houses or worked in the cribs that filled the District, unattended by musicians and lavish surroundings, had come to the meeting because of the other subjects on the agenda—confining the ensuing argument to the first few rows.

After the brouhaha had gone on for several minutes, Josie Arlington settled the issue by agreeing with the Countess. No one seemed interested in testing Josie's resolve to remain a refined and genteel madam. She had become very moody since the recent fire in her parlor house, which almost killed her and forced her and her boarders into residence above Tom Anderson's famous saloon on the corner of Basin and Iberville Streets. Some said her skirmish with death caused her to realize her own mortality and profoundly affected her. Sarah Beth agreed with that analysis.

With the discussion over, Countess Willie sat down, mumbling, "What do they know? They don't even keep their damn pianos in tune."

"The next item to discuss is the French Balls," Sarah Beth said, referring to the prostitutes' Mardi Gras galas.

Inez Breaux jumped up. "Talk about that later! Right now we wanna talk about voodoo!"

The women in the back rows yelled their agreement. "Yeah!" "That's right!" "Let's talk about that now!" "Why wait?" "Do it now!"

Sarah Beth considered the *demimonde's* fanatical belief in voodoo ridiculous. Yet, true believers all, the women on the turf in Storyville believed beyond contradiction in the power of *Gèdé Nimbo*, the powerful ruler of the graveyard spirits. They accepted as scientific fact that Voodoo Woman could cause venereal disease—using goat testicles for gonorrhea and wasp blood for syphilis—and induce pregnancy. Abnormal children born in the attics of Storyville's sporting houses were believed to have been sired by her spells rather than earthly fathers. Her feared "sealing power" reputedly closed up a *demimonde*, putting her out of business. Lala, another voodoo priestess, claimed to increase the business of any woman who smeared Lala's powder on her legs–red powder on one, green on the other. Many of the *demimonde* swore this particular *gris-gris* worked for them. Eulalie Echo, godmother of Jelly Roll Martin, one of the first famous professors, practiced "good" voodoo. The madams, bartenders and girls of the District all consulted her on any matter important to them.

"Very well." Sarah Beth sighed. "We'll take that subject up now. Perhaps Miss Breaux can explain–."

"Ya damn right I will," Inez shouted. "Somebody hexed me. Ya'll damn well know it and I do, too. That's why Jeb left me. Ya'll agreed. No black *gris-gris*. But–."

"What happened, dearie, did Voodoo Woman seal ya up?" a woman at the end of Inez's row asked to a burst of laughter.

The same old argument and, in Sarah Beth's mind, one that would never be satisfactorily settled. A year ago, May Spencer, one of the more respected members of the Society of Venus and Bacchus, had argued for the *demimonde* to stop using the weapons of Voodoo Woman and Lala against each other. She insisted that the government would close the District if the use of black magic did not stop. May's arguments had forged a flimsy armistice for a while. But Sarah Beth had foreseen the truce would not last. Today proved her something of a oracle.

"Nobody sealed me up. I can still–."

"Don't make no never mind," a woman who billed herself as Tiki-Tiki the Polynesian Princess stood and said. "Everybody knows that ain't the way Inez makes her money. But if somebody put the *gris-gris* on her and made her man leave, then it ain't right. We agreed not to use the black voodoo again' each other. We agreed, damn it!"

"Who done it, dearie?" someone called to Inez. "Do ya know?"

"Her!" Inez pointed to a woman two rows in front of her. "Gypsy Blue!"

Gypsy vaulted from her chair and faced her accuser. "I ain't never done ya nothin', bitch!"

"Please, ladies," Sarah Beth called, "can't we–."

"Bitch?" Inez screamed. "Me a bitch! Ya'll's the bitch! Ya'll wanted her, that girl I was saving for a gentleman who offered–."

"You ain't never knowed a gentleman in ya whole miserable, Goddamn life," Gypsy yelled.

Inez, climbing over chairs and spectators, grabbed at her nemesis.

A Sicilian knife appeared in Gypsy's hand, the gleaming blade springing from the black grip at the touch of a button.

"No! Stop that! Do your fighting outside!" Sarah Beth ran to the back door of the parlor. "Titan! Lou Belle! Anybody! Come quick!" She ran to the front door and called again.

Titan and the handy man, Joe, ran in the rear door to find Inez and Gypsy Blue circling each other. Gypsy crouched, the knife weaving in front of her like the single, gleaming fang of a viper. Inez cocked a chair high above her head. A ring of onlookers had formed and betting money was out.

Titan, his seven-foot frame towering over the women around him, bullied his way through the mob. He grabbed Gypsy's knife hand and, at the same time, seized a leg of Inez's chair. Both women fought against the giant Negro. Titan's huge paw locked tighter around Gypsy's arm. He forced the knife upward and bent her arm back. Cursing and yelling, Gypsy struggled to sink the blade into his hand.

With Titan preoccupied with Gypsy's knife, Sarah Beth feared Inez might wrest the chair from him. She pushed her way through the pack and, putting all her hate and venom into the punch, delivered a round-house that knocked Inez Breaux out.

Just as Inez crashed to the floor, the knife fell from Gypsy's hand.

"Joe," Titan said, "you dump that one out the back door and me, I's carry this one out the front. If they meets up again outside, then that be they own doin'."

Joe dragged Gypsy Blue to the rear parlor door, the woman screaming threats at her unconscious opponent.

Titan tucked the limp form of Inez Breaux under one arm and hauled her, nose dripping blood, in the opposite direction.

"Wait," called Deanie Jean, billed in the District as America's Suicide Queen because of the number of times she had tried to kill herself.

Deanie held smelling salts under Inez's nose and smiled apologetically to the crowd. "Only fair. If Gypsy Blue finds her out cold, she'll kill Inez. Leastwise oughtta be a fair fight."

Sarah Beth saw no reason to be fair to Inez Breaux.

"I's got more hot tea here, ladies." Lou Belle, in a effort to pacify the now riotous mob, brought in several steaming pots on a silver tray.

A sudden controversy flared over the outcome of the fight. The bettors backing Gypsy claimed they had won because Inez had been knocked out. Inez's backers called the match a draw because Sarah Beth had knocked Inez out and no one had money on her.

"All bets are off," Sarah Beth declared, trying to avert the free-for-all she saw coming. Titan and Joe reappeared to enforce her decision. To settle the crowd, Sarah Beth shouted above the hubbub, "Have more tea, ladies, while we tidy up."

After a few minutes the crowd became as decorous as bawds could be and Sarah Beth again sat at the head table, flexing the hand she had hit Inez Breaux with, trying to stop its throbbing. She knew Inez and Gypsy's confrontation would not end a meeting in the District where a man laying dead on a barroom floor hardly attracted any notice.

"I think we'll save further discussion on the voodoo issue for a later meeting," Sarah Beth said. "Our last agenda item is the French Balls...I think we all know the complaint. Over the years the uptown ladies have become interested in our Mardi Gras celebrations–."

"'Cause theirs is run by stuffed shirts," Minnie White yelled.

"Yeah," Jessie Brown called. "Who wants t' see Rex and Comus!"

"That ain't the point," Hilda Burt said. "They look down their noses at us. All gussied up, wearin' masks and such. Ya'll seen 'em. Like when they take the grand tour of the parlor houses on Mardi Gras day." Hilda assumed a squeaky voice, "Oh, Buford. I say, Buford, didja see that woman over there. Is *she* one of them jolly good fellows? I say, Miss, can ya tell me what it's really like to do, well, ya know, *that* with *all* them men. Ain't it perfectly horrible? How ya can stand it?" Hilda spread a cheap fan and fluttered it, pretending she might faint.

"I even seen 'em looking 'tween the shutters of the cribs," Dolorous Fry shouted. "Ain't they never seen a nekked woman before? Let 'em come 'round when I'm working! I'll give 'em an eyeful, I will…With they own boyfriend, too!"

"Eyeful hell! Claw them's eyes *out*! That'll put the stop to it," Babbette yelled, scratching at the air.

Sarah Beth tried to regain control of the meeting. "Ladies. Ladies! *LADIES!*"

No one paid attention to her.

Lou Belle rushed in to help, but no one wanted more tea either.

Just as another riot appeared in the offing, Josie Arlington stood up. "All right. That's enough. *THAT'S ENOUGH!*" When the mob quieted down, she said, "We all know the problem. What we gonna do about it?"

"Don't let them int' the ball," suggested someone.

"Can't keep them out," Josie said. "Ours ain't like them uptown carnival balls. People buy tickets to ours. For Rex and Comus and all, they got personal invites and they don't let nobody in without their name on the invite."

Josephine Icebox suggested, "Let's us have invites, too. Leastwise, put names on the tickets." Miss Icebox earned her name being the most passionless whore in the District. "Queen" Gertie Livingston, Josephine's madam, had a standing reward for any man who could thaw her.

"That ain't going to work," Josie said.

Minnie Ha-Ha recommended, "Let's just tear the hair out of a few of them snotty bitches. That'll make 'em stop comin'."

"And get us all thrown in jail," Josie said.

"Since when you been worried 'bout goin' t' jail, honey," Deanie Jean, the Suicide Queen, said. "You been to the hoosegow more times then I've tried to kill myself."

"If you'd buy better rope, maybe it wouldn't break and you'd get the job done," Kitty Lala commented dryly, referring to Deanie's recent unsuccessful attempt to hang herself.

"And don't buy cheap bullets neither," Lilian Blodgett added, reminding the crowd of the time all of the bullets in Deanie's gun had misfired.

Deanie ignored her critics. "That ain't the point. Josie don't never stay in jail. And I hear tell her fines ain't all that much, if a'tall."

Josie chuckled. "I do alright. But a fight might just bring more o' them hoity-toity bitches back next year."

Deanie said, "Well, if you're so smart, Josie, what do *you* think we should do?"

Josie gave her audience a wry smile. "I'll tell you what I think. I think we should do 'em the worst they can think of."

"Yeah, what's that?" someone called.

"Get all their names in the newspaper." Josie knew the Victorian gentry abhorred appearing in the news, even for their good works. "That'll get some daddies getting switches out."

"And how we gonna do that?" Nettie Griffin asked.

"We all got city licenses to work, right?" When everybody nodded, Josie explained her plan and the crowd endorsed her idea.

"How you gonna fix all that up?" Alice Schwartz asked.

"Don't worry, I'll get it done," Josie said and, after a bit more discussion, the meeting adjourned.

"WELL, THAT GOT A LITTLE loud downstairs," Myda observed as her young protégée entered her room. "What happened?"

With her sprained hand in a sling, Sarah Beth sat on the edge of the older woman's bed and recounted the meeting.

"I'm sorry, my dear," Myda said. "I didn't mean to throw you to the lions like that."

"Nonsense." Sarah Beth cradled her injured hand. "I was glad to do it. I'm concerned about you, though. We all are. These weak spells have been getting more frequent. Shouldn't you see a doctor?"

"We'll talk about that later. Right now you should be off. You have an appointment this afternoon, don't you?"

"Aunt Myda, I, ah…." Sarah Beth resettled herself on the bed, smoothing the linen and plucking at some imagined lint. "With you feeling poorly and all, I, ah…Well, I just don't think it's such a good idea for me to be, well, you know, away from here."

"Nonsense, child." Myda took Sarah Beth's uninjured hand. "I'll be fine. I have Lou Belle and Ty to look after me. If I need you, I can always send for you."

"It really would be easier for me to stay here, now that I'm helping so much with the business. More convenient, too. There'd be much less running back and forth."

"Dear." Myda took Sarah Beth's chin and turned the girl's face to her. "You've been a very great help. As well you should. When I die–." Myda pressed her finger against Sarah Beth's lips as the younger woman began to protest. "Shush, we all have to die sooner or later and when I do, the business will be yours and you must know how to operate it. The house is paid for and so is the furniture. It will all be yours. You're the only family I have, Sarah Beth, and I want you to have it, along with the money I've saved, then keep the business or sell it, whatever you prefer. You'll be a rich woman. And young. Use the money to find your Nottoway."

"When that day comes, and I hope with all my heart it's far in the future, I'll keep The Mansion," Sarah Beth said with the fervor of an oath. "It's all the life I want." *And the only one I deserve*, she thought as she laid her head gently on the older woman's breast. "There's nothing for me beyond the District. I'll live and die on the turf. It's the only thing I know."

Myda drew her hand tenderly down Sarah Beth's cheek.

"How I love you, Aunt Myda! You've been so very, very good to me. But I don't want you to talk like that. I don't want to lose you, too."

"That can't be helped, child." Myda tenderly rubbed Sarah Beth's back. "Whatever happens, happens. But do take my advice. Go look at the room. I think it's best for you. I wish I would have done it years ago when I had the chance. Get away from here for a while, my beautiful Sarah Beth. Expand that wonderful mind of yours. Meet new people."

Sarah Beth sat up and fidgeted with one of the wispy curls at the side of her face. "Humph! New people. To humiliate me when they find out what I am. It doesn't seem worth–."

"It is, dear. It really is. And you may find you can keep your secret."

Sarah Beth smiled a weary smile. "Not in this city. Not with the men who've called on me or seen me here. The Mansion is the most fashionable house in the District. Important men come here. I can have no secrets in New Orleans."

"Then, perhaps, another city." Myda's oft-repeated suggestion was more a gentle urging. "But even if you never leave New Orleans, even if you operate The Mansion for the rest of your life, a room to yourself and away from here will do wonders for you. You'll see. Now go."

"I can't. I'll be arrested. It's illegal for a lewd and abandoned woman to be outside the District."

Myda stroked Sarah Beth's scarlet-gold hair. "I know you're afraid, but stop making excuses."

"It's not an excuse. The law says–."

"I know what the law says and you know it doesn't work like that." Myda gently nudged Sarah Beth from the bed. "There are bordellos outside the District and house girls walk down the *banquette* in the best neighborhoods. Josie Arlington owns a home on Esplanade Avenue, and she's one of the most notorious bawds in the city. You know very well that when a woman in the life gets arrested outside the District, it's because she's caused more trouble than she can bribe her way out of. To see you, talk to you, anyone would think you're exactly what you appear, a refined and beautiful lady. That is, when you behave, which I certainly hope will be more often now that you're grown. Besides, you need to get away."

"What exactly do you mean by 'behave' myself?" Sarah Beth asked.

"You know what I mean. You've changed, you need to change back."

"I haven't changed," Sarah Beth said.

"Yes, you have, my Dear. I've seen it. I'm a student of faces."

"I know," Sarah Beth said, "I've watched you watch people."

"And do you know what I look for?" Myda asked.

"Not exactly."

"I study people's faces at rest, when they're staring out the window or standing on the corner waiting for someone." Myda fluffed her pillow. "Have you ever done that?"

"Sometimes," Sarah Beth said.

"Have you noticed the differences?"

"I'm not sure I know what you mean."

"You can tell a person's true self watching their face at rest." Satisfied her pillow had been puffed up sufficiently, Myda put it behind her and leaned back. "Some are bland, some scowl. A few, rare faces are happy at rest–smiling, eyes bright. That's how I tell what kind of person someone is, by their face at rest. When I first met you, dear, you were happy. Your face rested in a smile, your eyes shown with a happy glow. Lord knows, you had every reason to be unhappy, but you weren't. Over the years that's changed. I've watched it. At first, your expression became neutral. Now the corners of your mouth turn down at times. This life is wearing on you. So is your guilt and your need to avenge yourself on men for what they've done to you. If you're to change back, you need to get away from here."

"Guilt for what?" Sarah Beth twisted the curl at the side of her face so tight that the tip of her index finger turned white. "Being in the life? True, I wouldn't have chosen–."

"No." Myda spoke in a soft, low voice. "The guilt of having betrayed your mother."

Sarah Beth's face turned ashen, her expression hard. "There's no guilt, except, perhaps, for being so incredibly stupid, incredibly naive." She turned from Myda and looked out the window. "People say how smart I am. Ha, what a joke! How could I not see what paw was up to, what momma did to stop him?" In her mind Sarah Beth saw herself and her brother huddled in the blackberry brier the day her paw fell off the porch, heard Jeremy scream he hated her because she would not go to paw when he called. "Even little Jeremy, two years younger than I, saw it. He knew, why didn't I? I watched momma and paw. I knew what men and women did together. You would've thought I could add two and two when he called me, 'Come here, gal, your old paw's got something sweet for you, something real sweet.' Oh, Aunt Myda," Sarah Beth sobbed, "how could I not see what was going on? Then I let that bitch, Inez Breaux, use me. I should've–."

"There, there," Myda crooned, "I know you blame yourself for what happened, but you shouldn't. There was nothing in your experience to tell you that a man might bed his own daughter. Had it happened to any of your friends?"

Sarah Beth thought of Lottie Mae and her family, of the love and kindness that dwelled only a mile from the hell where she had lived. "No." Sarah Beth wiped her cheeks with her uninjured hand.

Myda turned the younger woman so they faced each other again. "That proves my point. Yes, you were incredibly naive, but you had every right to be. You knew what husbands and wives did together. For you, it was nature running its course. And as for Inez Breaux, in her day she could charm the claws from a cat. But all that's in the past. You must stop punishing yourself for your imagined sins."

"This is the life I made for myself," came Sarah Beth's rote reply, "I'll live it and–."

"Yes, yes, I know all that." Myda dismissed her ward's credo with a wave of her hand. "Poppycock, if you ask me."

"I didn't," Sarah Beth snapped and immediately became apologetic. "I'm so sorry, Aunt Myda. I didn't mean–."

"I'll forgive you on one condition."

"What's that?" The wary tone of Sarah Beth's voice said she knew the answer.

"Go look at the room."

"If I promise to smile more when I'm staring out the window, do I still have to see the room?"

"Yes."

"But–."

"No more excuses, young lady." Myda nudged Sarah Beth from the bed. "Off you go."

CHAPTER 11

AFTER THE UNITED STATES PURCHASED Louisiana in 1803, more Americans than ever inundated New Orleans. The native Creoles hated these *Kaintucks*, an insult first hurled at the hard drinking, incorrigible flat-boatmen that visited the city from the upper Mississippi River. As more and more Yankee invaders arrived, a fierce rivalry developed for control of the city, its wealth, its politics, and its future.

For a while, the Creoles competed to a dead heat. The Americans built their mansions on St. Charles Avenue—in what became the Garden District—and their own town square across from Gallier Hall. The Creoles raised beautiful manors on Esplanade Avenue, once a part of the deMarginy plantation that formed the eastern border of the French Quarter. Their town square, the *Place d'Arms*, later renamed Jackson Square, already stood in front of St. Louis Cathedral, facing the river. But over the years the ferocious aggressiveness of the invading Yankee entrepreneurs routed the haughty, lethargic descendants of the original French and Spanish settlers, wresting control of the Creoles' homeland from them.

Titan stopped the carriage in front of a stately, old Creole estate on Esplanade Avenue. The house stood in frayed grandeur; an aloof dowager queen, her fortunes in decline. The gardens needed weeding and the bushes pruning. Shutters hung at odd angles. Mildewed white paint had tenuous hold on the building, patches of weathered gray wood showing where its grip completely lapsed.

From the *banquette* Sarah Beth looked at the house for a long moment. Despite a threadbare facade, its essential majesty remained. The graciousness of its architecture, the elegance of its columns, the welcoming sweep of the front galleries were both spectacular and pathetic. Sarah Beth immediately loved the old house. Here was her Nottoway; not the mansion of her dreams but one that suited what she had become. Standing on the sidewalk, unbidden tears crept down her cheeks. She shook them off, refusing to pine for either the house or herself.

A creaky iron gate complained of her passing and the uneven, moss-dappled brick walk played pranks on her feet. At the front door an old, uniformed colored woman answered her knock, then, with knees that groaned in sympathy with the ancient staircase, led her to the second floor. At the door to a solarium in back of the house, the maid stopped and called to a shawl-wrapped elderly woman dozing in a ladder-back rocker, "Some lady 'bout the room."

The maid's voice wrenched the old woman from her afternoon nap.

"That there Miz Annadette," the maid said to Sarah Beth.

The solarium, typical of the rooms in most New Orleans homes, had thirteen-foot ceilings, giving it an airy, spacious feel. The woman and her rocker filled most of a burnished rectangle the late afternoon sun cast through one of the large windows.

Gathering her wits about her, the old woman adjusted the ivory, open-weave shawl around the shoulders of her black blouse and smoothed her charcoal-gray skirt. Then her hands fluttered to her head making sure her tight bun of silver hair was presentable. "Please come in, my dear," she said, beckoning Sarah Beth with a fragile, porcelain hand, adding "Sit here," and patted another rocker close to hers.

When Sarah Beth had settled, her hostess said, "I'm Annadette Cheramie." Noticing Sarah Beth's bulky bandage, she added, "Oh, my. What happened to your hand?"

"Ah, a sprain…This morning…Getting out of the carriage…Clumsy me fell." Sarah Beth added a timid, embarrassed laugh to give credence to her lie.

"I'm sorry. I do hope it's not too painful," Annadette said. "Have you seen a doctor?"

Sarah Beth shook her head. "It's nothing serious."

"You should see a doctor. Perhaps if…Well, we'll see. Would you care for coffee?" Annadette asked.

"Yes, please…Oh, and my name is Sarah Beth LaBranche."

Annadette nodded to the maid, who left to fetch the refreshments. "I don't know quite what to do now. You see, I've never let a room before."

Sarah Beth smiled. "Then we'll find out together. I've never taken one before."

"Splendid." Annadette clapped her hands. "Shall we begin our little game by learning something about each other?"

"Fine," Sarah Beth said, suddenly more than a bit ambivalent.

"Are you from here?" Annadette asked the perennial first question of a Creole, which translated to, *Do I know anyone who knows you?* Creole culture placed great import on positioning a stranger in proper social context.

"No, St. Francisville," Sarah Beth said.

"Oh." Annadette sounded disappointed. "I don't know anyone from there. But then, you must be *German* French," she added, smiling at her little joke.

Sarah Beth nodded.

As the maid placed the china coffee service on the table between the two women, Annadette asked, "Do you mind helping yourself? I don't trust these old hands not to make a mess."

"May I pour yours?" Sarah Beth asked.

"Yes, thank you," Annadette said. "Do you know how Germans came to have French names?"

Sarah Beth knew but shook her head as she filled the two cups, wanting Annadette Cheramie to talk about anything except her potential lodger's background.

"The Germans came to Louisiana in the 1720's. That scoundrel John Law lied to them, promised them gold and silver waiting to be picked up from the ground. They settled upriver of New Orleans. We French came to call it the German Coast. The story's told of a German trying to make a French customs official understand his name. The German broke a twig from a tree, shook it at the Frenchman and said, 'Zweig! Zweig!' The customs inspector said, 'Aha, LaBranche.' That's how you got your name." Annadette sipped her coffee. "You come from wonderful stock, my dear. Hard working. Salt of the earth. We Creoles even have a saying about you Germans. When there's something particularly hard to be done, we French say, 'It takes a German to do it.'" Annadette nodded, with a wink for punctuation.

Considering her life, Sarah Beth thought, *How appropriate.*

"But enough of that," Annadette said, "what brings you to New Orleans, my dear?"

"I work here."

"For whom…And what do you do?"

Sarah Beth squirmed in her rocker. Had she known she would have to give a autobiography just to get a room, she would never have come. "I, ah…For a lady uptown…As her, ah, secretary." Sarah Beth looked for someplace to put her cup and saucer. She had to escape before Annadette became more inquisitive.

"'*Méricain coquin?*" the old woman asked.

Sarah Beth gave a curt nodded, a weak smile and recited in the sing-song French patois of the Creoles, "'*Méricain coquin, 'Billé en nanquin, Voleur di pain Chez Miché d'Aquin,*" as she began to gather her things to leave.

Annadette chuckled. "I haven't heard anyone say that for years. When I was a child, my friends and I used to sing that when we caught one of those *Kaintucks* in the French Quarter...We lived there, you know...American rogues stealing bread from the baker," Annadette said a bit wistfully, translating the gist of the verse. "My, my, that certainly brings back memories. *Parlez-vous français?*"

"*Mais oui, madame.*" Sarah Beth hoped the conversation's new direction meant an end to the inquest, and she settled back in the rocker. "*Et Espagnol et Portugais.*" Sarah Beth realized if the conversation ever turned back to her employer, the game would surely be afoot.

Annadette continued speaking in French. "Do you read and write Spanish and Portuguese as well as speak them?"

"But of course, madame." Sarah Beth continued the conversation in a language as natural to her as English.

"How wonderful! And how did you learn?"

"Ah...Friends. I have friends who taught me. Languages come easily to me."

"Well, I suppose you want to know a little about us," Annadette said.

Sarah Beth nodded, delighted to talk about anything but herself.

"We live here alone, my grandson, Cyprian, and I. And the servants. Of course, I shouldn't say servants. There's only one left. Our maid, Mary. This has been my family's home since we moved from the French Quarter when I was a child. Cyprian is a doctor and would do quite well if...But I'm afraid I'm boring you, dear. There are just the two of us in this big house and I thought we should share some of what we have with others. There are not many places in the city where a respectable lady like yourself can lodge."

Sarah Beth winced inwardly.

"Come." Annadette levitated herself from the rocker. "I'm sure you want to see the room before you decide."

Sarah Beth followed the old woman up a flight of stairs to the third floor. Annadette climbed the steps one at a time, straightening each knee with her hands to mount them. Sarah Beth tried to help, but the old woman waved her away. At the top landing Annadette held tight to the newel post catching her breath, then shuffled toward the front of the house.

"Here we are, my dear." Annadette threw open wide double doors.

Sarah Beth caught her breath. The room seemed almost as large as the cabin of her youth, with high ceilings and abundant, beautifully crafted furniture scaled to the apartment's gigantic proportions. Long drapes hung from the windows and puddled on the floor, the excess material apparently wasted in the antebellum fashion that displayed the owner's wealth. *Oh, wouldn't momma love to see this*, Sarah Beth thought.

"This was my parents's room," Annadette said. "After they passed away, I occupied it for years. But the stairs have become too much for me. Do you like it, my dear?"

"Like it? How could I *not* like it?" Sarah Beth ran her fingers lightly on the finely veined marble top of the dressing table. "It's...It's absolutely beautiful."

"I'm so glad you approve," Annadette said. "We've several rooms to let, but I love this one best. Not just because my dear parents lived here, but because it's so–." She swept her cane around the room as if it were a scepter. "Just look at this furniture. This bed." Annadette ran her hands along the carved foot board of the massive half teaster. "It was fashioned by Monsieur Mallard, one of the most famous of the New Orleans cabinet makers. It's made of *palissandre*, violet ebony. And the craftsmanship is unequaled."

As she listened, Sarah Beth noticed the sparkle in Annadette's clear, brown eyes. These were not the eyes of an aged woman, but those of a vibrant, lively spirit who quaffed life in great gulps, with zeal and relish.

"See here." Madame Cheramie raised one of the two carved and hand-rubbed finials on the foot board of the bed. It came out attached to a long dowel. The old woman took a smaller dowel hidden in the base of the post below the finial and put it through a hole in the longer dowel that appeared as the finial was raised. The smaller dowel, perpendicular and protruding on either side of the larger one, positioned the decorative finial almost at the level of the teaster. Annadette explained the device. "That's how my parents slept before they had the house done with window screening. They would drape the mosquito netting from the teaster over these finials and raise them. Then they could sleep comfortably and pest free." The old woman lowered the finial. "Monsieur Mallard made the matching armoire over there, too." Annadette stood a little straighter as she inspected her reflection in the full-length mirror on the chiffonnier's front door. "The dressing table you admired is also from Mallard's shop. And this desk and chair," she said, hobbling to the window, "was made by François Seignouret, another of the city's famous cabinetmakers. Over there, that small table next to the fireplace–."

A loud boom, like a cannon shot, reverberated through the house as a door slammed somewhere far off.

"I wonder if that's Cyprian," Annadette said. "I'd like you to meet him." The old woman swayed her way out of the room and called down the stairwell in French, "Cyprian…Oh, Cyprian! Is that you?"

"*Oui, Gamé,*" a basso voice called back, using the Creole French diminutive for grandmother.

"Come up here. I want you to meet our new boarder."

Sarah Beth piqued at the old woman's presumptuousness as the heavy strides of a man taking two risers at a time tattooed up the stairwell. "Madam Cheramie, I made no–."

"Nonsense, dear girl." Annadette's blue-veined hand waved aside Sarah Beth's objection as she hobbled back into the room. "You said you loved the room, didn't you? And I pride myself on being an excellent judge of character. You're just the type of boarder we want. Now, about the rent. Do you think–."

Cyprian Cheramie strode into the room. In his early thirties, tall and commanding with black, wavy hair and thick raven eyebrows, he was, by far, the most handsome man Sarah Beth had ever met.

"Ah, this is the grandson I told you about. Cyprian, this is Mademoiselle LaBranche" Annadette continued, speaking in French.

"Please call me Frank." Dr. Cheramie spoke the same Creole patois as his grandmother. "Cyprian François is much too pretentious, do you not think, Mademoiselle LaBranche?"

Whatever he chose to call himself, this was the most captivating, the most perfect man Sarah Beth had ever encountered—broad shouldered, with dark, strange, penetrating eyes. Jaded by the scores of men she had known, Sarah Beth never expected to meet one who could have such an immediate and spellbinding effect on her.

In three brisk and powerful strides Frank Cheramie stood next to Sarah Beth, bowed and reached to kiss her hand. His gallantry stopped when he noticed the bandage. "What have we here?"

"Mademoiselle sprained her hand," Annadette explained.

"How?"

"She fell getting out of her carriage."

Sarah Beth let the old woman speak for her, too befuddled to answer for herself.

"May I see it?" Frank gently lifted Sarah Beth's forearm.

Sarah Beth said nothing, even more flustered by the man's touch than his presence. *This can't be happening, not to a woman like me!*

"Let him look at it, my dear," Annadette said. "As I mentioned, he's a doctor…Though you might not know it from the way things are around here."

"*Gamé!*" Frank frowned at his grandmother as he unwrapped Sarah Beth's hand. "Can you move your fingers, Mademoiselle?"

She did.

"Good, now bend your wrist for me."

Sarah Beth flinched slightly but managed to follow his instructions.

"Hmmmm. No contusions and good movement, though a bit sore. There will be a nasty bruise before long. Nothing seems to be broken.

Strange, I would have guessed the bruise came from…No matter. The diagnosis is correct. Who made it?"

"I-I did." Sarah Beth found her voice and a fraction of her wits. "It seemed…obvious."

Smiling, the doctor asked, "And where did you study medicine?"

Sarah Beth found herself captured by his extraordinary eyes. "I-I didn't…I've studied many…But not medicine."

"Just my little joke, Mademoiselle."

"I-I'm sorry…I-I didn't…" Sarah Beth forced herself to stand straighter in an attempt to gather her wits. "Forgive me, please. I'm usually not so foolish. Really I'm not."

"We don't think you're foolish at all, do we, Cyprian?" Annadette said. "It's only natural to be a bit confused. You come to see about a room for let and end up being examined by one of the city's finest doctors, not that we can eat on his reputation," Annadette grumbled, plainly the latest barb in an on-going argument.

"*Gamé*, there is no need to air any of that now. I am sure Mademoiselle is not interested in our–."

"It's of no great concern whether Mademoiselle finds out now or later," Annadette said sharply. "She can't live here and not know." The old woman turned to Sarah Beth. "My grandson is a wonderful doctor. I didn't exaggerate when I said he was among the finest in the city. But that's all he does. He doesn't often send out bills and, when he does, he forgets to collect them. I'm sure *you* understand, Mademoiselle LaBranche. Someone in your position, the secretary of an eminent lady, must know the importance of being organized. And, *mon Dieu*, those 'Méricain coquin never miss a chance to get more money. Do you think I would have allowed my parents' beautiful home to run down so–."

"*Gamé*, that is quite enough. Please." Frank gave his grandmother a stern look. "Mademoiselle LaBranche did not come here to hear about–."

"Bah!" Annadette did her best to storm from the room, but the years had stolen the bluster from her walk.

Frank turned to Sarah Beth. "Please forgive grandmother, Mademoiselle. She is old and sometimes–."

"There is no need to apologize for her, *Monsieur le Docteur*." Sarah Beth liked Annadette Cheramie, sensing a vein of iron deep within the old woman, though cloaked in parchment skin and crowned with silver hair. "I think she's wonderful and I'm sure at her age you or I would speak our mind exactly as she does. That's part of her charm. At least I think so."

"That is very gracious of you."

"Not at all."

They stared at each other and Sarah Beth tried to discover what fascinated her about Frank's eyes, then she looked away. He held her hand far past the needs of his examination and, reluctantly, she withdrew it.

"*Gamé* does not realize how time-consuming my patients and my research are. I have no time to send out bills." Frank looked at Sarah Beth earnestly. "We know so little about curing the sick and there is so much to learn. I guess at *Gamé's* age the comfort money brings is important. But the time spent sending bills can be put to much better use. There are so many patients." Frank leaned close and whispered. "If *Gamé* knew how many could not pay even if I sent a bill, she would be apoplectic. But they all must be treated. Just because a man has no money, or is colored, does not mean he and his family should not get medical care. And the more patients I treat, the more it helps with my research."

Annadette hobbled back into the room. "Don't think I don't know how many of your patients can't pay, Cyprian."

Astounded, Frank said, "*Gamé*, you were listening outside the door?"

"Nonsense." Annadette gave her grandson a sharp look. "I don't eavesdrop!" She turned to Sarah Beth. "You see the tomfoolery I must put up with, Mademoiselle?"

Laughter bubbled up behind the hand Sarah Beth put to her mouth.

"If only my poor, charitable, disorganized grandson had someone to help him," Annadette said.

Sarah Beth caught the hint, and something else, too. She saw the glint of the matchmaker in Annadette's eyes. *If she only knew,* Sarah Beth thought, *perhaps she wouldn't be so anxious to pair her grandson with me.*

"We never did discuss the rent," Annadette added. "I had imagined five dollars a month would be fair…And another five dollars if you took most of your meals with us. Will you be eating with us often?"

"No, madame…Ah, most evenings I take dinner with my, ah, employer. In fact," Sarah Beth rushed the words, "most evenings I spend at the lady's home…I-I only wanted a room of my own for, ah, when she goes to, ah, Biloxi."

"Oh?"

In one syllable, Annadette demanded an explanation Sarah Beth was not prepared to give. "S-She has, ah, relatives in Bay St. Louis that she visits. Ah, about once a month."

"I thought you said Biloxi, dear," Annadette said.

"Did I? Of course I did." Sarah Beth's eyes went round with fear. *Leave before they find you out!* she thought. But Frank Cheramie still gazed intently at her, binding her inextricably to the room, the house and the people in it. She blathered on, stuttering and stammering, hoping to find her way through the labyrinth of lies she had fabricated. "Yes, of course. You see, ah, she has relatives in both Biloxi *and* Bay St. Louis."

"And who exactly is your employer," Annadette asked.

"An American lady–."

"I know, I know," Annadette insisted. "But what's her name, dear?"

"Name?" Sarah Beth twisted the curl at the side of her cheek. "Name. Yes, her name. Her name is, ah–."

"Surely you know the name of the woman you work for," Annadette demanded.

"I am sure she does," Frank said. "But not in the face of your inquisition, *Gamé.* Can you not see how distraught you have made Mademoiselle

LaBranche. She injured herself earlier and I would not be surprised if she were still suffering from mild shock. Now all these questions. It is enough to make anyone forget."

Annadette looked at her grandson, then at Sarah Beth. "I suppose Cyprian's right, my dear," she finally said with a warm smile. "I hope I haven't set back your recovery."

Sarah Beth sighed. "Of course not."

"See to her hand, Cyprian. Then see Mademoiselle to her carriage," Annadette instructed. With another warm smile for Sarah Beth, she asked, "Mademoiselle, when will you be taking up residence?"

"I-In a day or two, I suppose, madame."

"Very good. I shall look forward to seeing you again." As Annadette shuffled from the room, she slapped her grandson playfully on the arm. "Don't call me old, and don't deny you said it, either. I heard you whispering when I was out of the room. And don't whisper. I know all about the patients who can't pay." She slapped him again. As she limped from the room she called over her shoulder, "Never whisper. It's hard enough as it is to hear when you're my age."

Frank Cheramie smiled affectionately after his grandmother. In English he said, "She is such a character. And so headstrong since she has gotten older."

From the hall Annadette called, "I just told you I'm not old."

Both Frank and Sarah Beth laughed.

Sarah Beth leaned close to Frank's ear. "How old is she?"

"No whispering goes for you, too, young lady," Annadette called in English as her head bobbed slowly down the stairs. "Eighty-five," she added, her voice raised so she could be heard. "Not that it's any of your business."

Sarah Beth chuckled. "Doctor Cheramie, didn't she just say she was hard of hearing."

"I lied," Annadette called, her voice faint and far away.

"She is such a darling," Sarah Beth said. "I'm quite fond of her already."

"With all of grandmother's foolishness we never did settle on the rent. Is five dollars a month acceptable?

"Quite," Sarah Beth said.

Smiling, Frank re-wrapped her injured hand. "Then I shall look forward to the pleasure of seeing you from time to time. Perhaps I could show you my clinic one day. It is downstairs, in the back of the house." Intense black eyes looked deep into Sarah Beth's. "I would so much enjoy showing it to you."

"And I would enjoy seeing it, Doctor Cheramie." *Those eyes*, she thought, *what is it about his eyes?*

"Tut-tut. Call me Frank, please."

Sarah Beth lowered her head and copper lashes fluttered against her cheeks. "We've only just met, Doctor Cheramie. But I *would* enjoy seeing your clinic sometime."

"THIS WHERE YOU BE STAYIN', Miz Sarah Bet'?" Titan asked as the carriage drove away.

Sarah Beth sat waving back at the weathered house and Frank Cheramie standing at the old, iron gate. There was something magical about the man. As much as she wanted him to be like every other man she had known, Sarah Beth sank deeper under his spell the more she thought of him, of his touch, of his dark, enchanting eyes. What did she find so fascinating about his eyes? She had not allowed herself to study them for fear of becoming lost in their mystery. *Eyes are eyes*, she told her self; still something about his bewitched her.

"Miz Sarah Bet'?…Miz Sarah Bet'!"

"What?…I'm sorry, Ty. Did you say something?" Sarah Beth looked up absently at the giant Negro towering above her in the driver's seat.

"Yaz, 'um. I axed if this be where you gonna stay."

"Oh, yes, Ty! It's a wonderful house, don't you think? And the family's wonderful, too," Sarah Beth gushed, animated by the memory of Frank Cheramie. "The lady of the house is a wonderful old woman, eighty-five and still going strong and this was her family's house when she was young and she needs the money from borders to make ends meet because her grandson's a doctor, but he's too busy with his patients and research to send out bills. Isn't that exciting?"

Titan studied his mistress for a moment giving the horse its head. "Yaz, 'um."

"Ty," Sarah Beth called.

"Yaz, 'um."

"Go home by way of the French Quarter, please."

The giant turned and look down at his mistress. "What ya wanna do that for?"

From the bastion of legendary Creole culture in the early nineteenth century, the French Quarter had degenerated into squalid dock-worker slums. The dialects of Rome and Palermo filled streets where taunts of *'Méricain coquin* once were heard.

"I love the old buildings and like to see them sometimes." Sarah Beth would not admit, even to herself, that she wanted to bask in the history of Frank Cheramie, to find a trace of him somewhere high up in the cornices of the buildings or in the rusted, iron-lace that trimmed the balconies.

Titan grumbled and turned the buggy on Royal Street.

Sarah Beth thought of the other *demimonde* and their fancy men. Until now, she had questioned how any woman involved in commercial love could aspire to its romantic version. How could the decadent heart conceive the most hallowed promise of the chaste? Then she chided herself for including Frank Cheramie in the same musings with *demimonde* and fancy men. He was nothing like the toughs and leaches who attracted Storyville's women. He was good and kind and considerate and honest and just and moral and pure and…far beyond the range of her sullied heart.

Sarah Beth refused to grieve for what might have been, what could have been, what, perhaps, should have been. She had made this life. She would live it, live it well and the devil take the hind most. But what harm could it do to allow her life to converge ever-so-slightly with Frank Cheramie's?

CHAPTER 12

IN THE WEEKS THAT FOLLOWED, Sarah Beth made a habit of returning from the Cheramie's to The Mansion via the French Quarter. From the *Veaux Carré*, Titan turned the carriage on to Canal Street and drove to Basin Street, then turned again and drove between Krauss' Department Store and the Southern Railroad Depot toward Storyville.

On one of those days, the piercing cry of a train whistle yanked Sarah Beth from her ruminations and, half a block ahead, she noticed a woman, small valise in hand, drag a much younger woman from the train station across the street toward the Tenderloin. When the carriage came abreast of the pair, the woman stood in front of the Terminal Saloon deep in conversation with a ferret of a man and still holding the girl tightly by the wrist.

"Stop the carriage please, Ty."

When the gestures of the man and woman confirmed her suspicions, Sarah Beth climbed down to confront the pair, determined to stop the tragedy taking place.

The young girl cried hysterically and struggled to pull away. "Oh, Momma, please don't! I'm sorry, Momma! So sorry! Really I am! I didn't mean for it to happen! Oh, Momma! Please! Please! I love you, Momma! Please give me another chance! I'll do better! I'll be good! Oh, Momma, please don't! Please! *PLEASE DON'T!*"

The woman spun and slapped the girl in the face. "Shut up, you hussy!" she yelled and turned back to the man. "That doesn't seem like much."

"It's all you gonna git for her, lady," the ferret said. "Look about. All we got 'round here is women."

"But she's young. Men like girls young as her," the woman protested. "And she's…never been touched."

"Even if three men on camels and a star comes with her, forty-five dollars is m' last offer." The ferret shoved a handful of bills at the woman.

"Chicken Dick," Sarah Beth shouted as she approached, "look at the girl. She's not cut out for the life. In a month or two she'll try to kill her–."

"By then, it won't be no concern o' mine, jus' like this ain't none o' yours now," Chicken Dick said eyeing Sarah Beth. "Now git."

Sarah Beth made it her concern. "She's so young and–."

"You're breakin' my heart. But, like I always say, if a gal's old enough to bleed, she's old enough to breed. Now git on about ya own business and stay outta mine." Turning to the girl's mother, Chicken Dick repeated, "Forty-five dollar's m' final–."

"Your *final* offer, Chicken Dick?" Sarah Beth asked. "Or every cent you have?"

"Stay out o' this!" The ferret tried harder to force his money into the woman's hand.

Sarah Beth asked the girl's mother, "Would it make a difference if he was offering you all his money? It would to me. It would mean she's worth a lot more than he can pay."

"I…I…." The woman's eyes darted from Sarah Beth to Chicken Dick and back. She held tightly to the girl whose struggles had degenerated into tormented sobs.

"He offered you forty-five dollars," Sarah Beth said. "I'll give you fifty."

"Ain't no fair. We struck the deal," Chicken Dick shouted. "Fifty-five, but that's m'–."

"See," Sarah Beth said to the woman, "you can't trust a man named Chicken Dick Charlie." Sarah Beth turned to the ferret, "By the way, I've been meaning to ask. Is Chicken Dick a name or a description? I'll give her sixty dollars."

"Fuck you 'n' the horse ya come t' town on!" Chicken Dick yelled. "You'll get outta here if ya know what's good for ya! Sixty-five is my fi–."

"See." Sarah Beth spoke to the woman, but her eyes did not leave her opponent. "He lies all the time. He said fifty-five dollars was his final offer. I wonder if he has the money. You can't trust a man like him." Sarah Beth decided to end the bidding. "*TWO HUNDRED DOLLARS!*"

"*GODDAMN YOU!*" A knife flashed in Chicken Dick's hand.

Titan thundered, "Hold on," and jumped from the carriage. Before he could effect Sarah Beth's rescue, a pearl-handled derringer came from somewhere in the folds of her dress and she fired.

Chicken Dick screamed, dropped the knife and grabbed his upper left thigh. "*Jesus Christ, woman!* You almost shot off m'–."

"That's what I was aiming for." Sarah Beth cocked the hammer of the silver plated gun and aimed carefully at Chicken Dick's crotch. "Damn thing never does shoot straight."

Chicken Dick scrambled backwards. "Oh, no ya don't!" he shouted, covering his groin with his hands. "Take her. There'll be other times! When ya don't expect it! When ya ain't got ya gun or ya giant-ass nigger with ya! Just ya wait, bitch! This ain't over!" He limped off down the street, hurling curses over his shoulder.

The derringer disappeared and Sarah Beth turned to the woman, speaking in a very calm and reasonable tone. "Now don't you want to reconsider? You don't really want to sell your own daughter, do you?"

"Yes," the woman said. "Oh, yes, indeed I do! And good riddance!"

"You're overwrought. Perhaps if we discuss the matter, you'll see–."

"No! We had an agreement! Two hundred dollars. That's what I want. Every penny of it or I'll sell her to that Chicken fellow."

"Alright, if you insist." Sarah Beth counted out the price in twenty dollar bills she took from her purse. The woman grabbed the money, snatched up her valise and stormed off toward the train station.

Sarah Beth put her arms around the girl's trembling shoulders. "There, there, dear. It's all right. What's your name?"

The girl, sobbing uncontrollably, could not speak.

"I promise," Sarah Beth said gently, "nothing bad is going to happen to you. Tell me your name."

"F-F-Frances."

"Frances what?"

The girl muttered something Sarah Beth did not understand. "What?"

"Kay," Frances sobbed louder.

"Well, Miss Frances Kay, lets sit in the carriage and see if we can sort this out." Sarah Beth led the young woman to the buggy and, when they were settled, asked, "Would you care to tell me what that was all about?"

The understanding in Sarah Beth's voice seemed to win Frances over. "Momma don't want me no more," she sobbed.

"Why?"

"'Cause of Jiiiiiiiiimyyyyyyyy!" Frances fell into Sarah Beth's arms, crying uncontrollably again.

Sarah Beth petted Frances until the girl calmed down again. "Who's Jimmy?"

"My little brother." Frances sat up, wiped the tears from her cheeks and sniffled.

"What happened to him?"

Frances sat motionless. Then tremors took hold of her body and her face seemed as if it would explode. When the tears came, they burst forth with such force they splashed on to Sarah Beth's hands folded in her lap. Frances shrieked and collapsed again into Sarah Beth's arms.

Sarah Beth stroked the girl's hair and gently massaged her shoulders. "There, there," she said. "You'll make yourself sick from crying so hard. Why don't you try to stop, dry your eyes and tell me what happened. Sometimes just talking about something makes you feel better. What do you say?"

Frances' head remained buried hard against Sarah Beth's chest, but, by degrees, the heart-rending sobs diminished. She lifted her head and wiped sheets of tears from her cheeks with the back of her hand.

"What happened?" Sarah Beth prompted.

Frances sniffled and stared at Sarah Beth. The younger woman's mouth formed a hard line and her eyes held a defiant glare.

The cause can wait, Sarah Beth decided, *now's the time for the cure.* "Let's find someplace for you to stay. After a nice dinner and a good night's rest, things will look better and we can get you on a train back home."

"*NO!*" The vehemence in Frances' voice startled Sarah Beth. "I'll never go back there!" Frances vowed, folding her arms across her chest. "She ain't never loved me, never a'tall!"

"You're over reacting," Sarah Beth said sternly.

"Oh, no, I ain't. She ain't never loved me. It was always *Jimmy!*" Frances said her brother's name more passionately than an oath. "Jimmy this and Jimmy that, Jimmy the next thing. Always him. Never me. Well, I'll show her. If she don't want me, at least you do. You paid good cash money for me. That's more than she ever done...Besides, it's a wonderful life here, ain't it? Men always wanting to be with you and all. Music. Fun. Laughing all the time. Dancing. Pretty clothes. Yes. *Oh, yes!* I'll do what I gotta." Frances spoke with great determination as she leaned forward in her seat. "If Momma thinks I'm a whore, then that's what I'll be. And one day I'll go back home and show all her friends what she done me. I'll go to church and tell 'em how she sold me. I'll–."

"It's not the wonderful life you think it is," Sarah Beth said. "For most of the people here, it's wretched."

"Then why you here, huh? And why'd you buy me?" Frances demanded. "Two hundred dollars is a lot of money. You ain't gonna spend that much money for nothing."

Sarah Beth raised her hands in exasperation. "I didn't *buy* you. I gave your mother the money to save you from Chicken Dick Charlie. He would have used you, then put you on the turf, unless he could have auctioned you. You *are* a virgin, aren't you?"

"That's a terrible question to—."

Sarcastically, Sarah Beth interrupted. "What's terrible about asking a girl who wants to be a whore if she's a virgin?"

Frances wilted. Eyes cast down, she whispered, "Yes."

"Then, for a girl as young and pretty as you…How old are you?" Sarah Beth demanded.

"Seventeen."

Sarah Beth wondered why, at twenty-one, she considered seventeen so young. *Life in the District, I suppose,* she thought, then said, her voice soft and kindly again. "Anyway, Chicken Dick could have gotten seven or eight hundred dollars for you."

Amazed, Frances said, "I didn't know I was worth *that* much. Is that why you spent—."

"I told you, I didn't buy you. You're free to go." Sarah Beth reached for the handle of the carriage door.

Francis looked desolate. "Got no place to go if you don't want me."

"It's not a question of wanting you or not," Sarah Beth said. "And you have a place to go, The House of the Good Shepherd."

"What's that? The poor house?"

"No, a place for girls that need help."

"A home for wayward girls, ain't it? Well, I ain't wayward. Not yet, at least."

Sarah Beth smiled. "The nuns will take you anyway."

"No!" The gloss of revenge crept back into Frances' eyes. "Momma says I'm wicked so that's just what I'll be. The most wicked whore ever there was. Then I'll go home and whore with all the men in town and tell 'em it was momma put me up to it. And all the church ladies will talk about her till she can't show her face on the front porch. That's what I'll do, all right. I'll fix *her!*"

"And fix yourself, too" Sarah Beth said. "Is worth it? You don't know what life on the turf is like."

"Yes, I do!" Frances insisted, vengeance obviously controlling her judgement.

Thinking about her own momma, how the sainted woman had protected her daughter, Sarah Beth could not imagine anything so terrible as to make a mother and daughter hate each other as much as Frances and her mother did.

"Besides, God wouldn't have sent me here if He didn't want me to stay," Frances added. "When He wants me out, He'll get me."

"Wonderful!" Sarah Beth slapped her hand on the seat. "Just what the world needs, another whore waiting for Jesus! That's what most of the women in the District are, you know. Magdalenes. Each one waiting for Christ to come around the corner and save her." Fingering the wisp of curl next to her cheek, Sarah Beth decided Frances needed a good dose of reality. "So you want to work in the District. Do you know how to check a man?"

Frances frowned. "For what?"

"Big and Little Casino. Syphilis and gonorrhea. Some men can give you terrible diseases if you bed them. You can go blind or die." Sarah Beth took a small mirror from her purse. She touched her hair in several places and adjusted her wide-brimmed hat, taking her time so Frances could absorb the information. "So, before you bed a man, wash him. Wash him very good and check him closely. They think you're doing it because they like it, but it's really for your own protection. If he has any sores, don't bed him. He might have Big Casino. Oh, and when you first start to wash him, check for Little Casino. Gonorrhea, gleet some people call it. Do it immediately, before he gets too soapy or stiff."

Frances fell against the back of the seat, fingers covering trembling lips. "You don't know how to check a man, do you?"

The girl shook her head.

"Can you milk a cow?"

Frances nodded.

"That's how you check for Little Casino. Grab his tallywacker like the tit on a cow's udder." Sarah Beth reached into the air and demonstrated. "Pull down and squeeze at the same time. Just imagine the milk pail underneath him and you'll get it right. If puss comes out, he's got gleet. Don't bed a man with gleet and never forget to check every john so you don't get sick. Even if he's a regular customer. You don't know who he's been with since the last time you saw him. Oh, and be careful when you drink with a man. Some of them think it's fun to shoo-fly a girl."

"What's that?"

"Putting something into a girl's drink to make her sick. Some men have a grand old time watching a woman vomit." Sarah Beth pointed at a boy talking to a man in front of the Fewclothes Cabaret. "See that little fellow? He's trying to sell the man a copy of the *Hell-o* book. It's a guide to the District listing all the girls and where they work, sort of the Tenderloin's city directory. There's another one called the Blue Book. You'll want your name in both so the johns that favor you can find you as you move around. And, believe me, you'll move around."

"Why do they call it Fewclothes Cabaret?" Frances asked. "Do the people dance naked?"

Sarah Beth chuckled. "George Foucault runs it but no one can pronounce his last name. So they call him Fewclothes...Look. The boy didn't make the sale. Watch. I'll bet he–. There, did you see what he did?"

"He flicked something off his arm," Frances said.

"He flicked cooties on the man because he wouldn't buy a book," Sarah Beth said. "Cootie flicking is considered great fun in the District, too."

Frances looked disgusted and Sarah Beth smiled.

A group of young white boys began milling around Fewclothes Cabaret. Shabbily dressed and bare footed, several carried strange-looking musical instruments.

"Who are they?" Frances asked.

"The Razzy Dazzy Spasm Band, the only white musicians in the District." Sarah Beth did not tell Frances about the music and musicians of Storyville; of the colored "professors" like Jelly-Roll Morton and Tony Johnson who manipulated pianos in the parlor houses; or of "King" Oliver who played trumpet in Pete Lala's Café and coached a young boy called Satchmo. To do so might add to Frances' romantic vision of the Tenderloin. "The Spasm Band plays in the street and passes the hat." Sarah Beth named each member–the leader, Stalebread Lacombe and his homemade, cigar-box violin; Harry, who sang through a section of rain spout; Whiskey; Cajun and his harmonica; the brothers Willie and Monk; Warm Gravy; Chinee, who played a bass fiddle made from a piano crate; and Family Haircut, the scat-singer. Theirs was a new kind of music, spirited and sprightly, and Sarah Beth liked it very much. It was new and different and people called it by a new and different name, jazz. But Sarah Beth told Frances, "They hardly make any money at all, poor kids."

Sarah Beth tapped Titan on the back. "Drive around the District, slowly, please, Ty."

The carriage lurched forward, moving on "Down the Line" as the first two blocks of the District on Basin Street were called.

"Those houses there are called cribs." Sarah Beth pointed to the buildings between Fewclothes Cabaret and the corner. "You might consider getting one. This is a choice spot. Girls here charge a dollar a trick. Back there," Sarah Beth nodded toward Claiborne Avenue, "they charge as little as a dime. White girls, too."

They came to the first cross street.

"This is Iberville. Until last year it was called Customhouse Street." Anticipating Frances' question, Sarah Beth added, "Don't ask me why the name changed because I don't know."

They passed a saloon on the corner of Basin and Iberville. "That's Tom Anderson's place, The Anderson, billed as the first electrified saloon in America." As Sarah Beth spoke, the lights went on to ward off the impending dusk. "Tom Anderson's the most powerful man in the District. Sort of the king around here...A member of the state legislature, too."

They drove passed Hilma Burt's parlor house on Basin Street and Frances found the next establishment, Diana and Norma's, a bit curious. "Why are those women sitting in the windows sucking their thumbs?"

"That's a French house." When Frances did not seem to understand, Sarah Beth explained. "They're showing the men coming in on the trains what they do."

Frances snickered. "A man will pay to have his thumb sucked?"

Sarah Beth raised an eyebrow and stared at the girl.

"Oh," Frances said after considering the matter. "*OH, MY!*"

"You should think about working there," Sarah Beth suggested.

"But why?" Frances demanded, obviously taken aback.

"To establish you're a virgin," Sarah Beth said. "Then make a deal with Emma Johnson. She'll auction you as one of the attractions at her circus. Emma will want half, of course."

"A circus?"

"Not the kind you're thinking of." Sarah Beth described the loathsome, degenerate performances involving women–the younger and prettier, the better–and various animals. Frances gagged her disgust.

They drove past Lulu White's Mahogany Hall, Countess Willie V. Piazza's octoroon brothel, Emma Johnson's Studio, the Hook and Ladder Company and turned down Conti Street, riding along the side of St. Louis Cemetery No. 1, where Marie Leveau, the Voodoo Queen of

New Orleans was buried. On Robertson and Conti, Sarah Beth pointed out a street light and said, "They call that the laughing lamp post."

"Why?" Frances asked as Sarah Beth knew she would.

"Last Fourth of July some white boys caught a colored girl from Smoky Row." Sarah Beth aimed her finger across Claiborne Avenue at the area of colored cribs. "They tied her, naked, to that lamp post, shoved big fire crackers into her, front and back, lit long fuses and stood around laughing while she begged and screamed and pleaded for help."

"Someone helped her, huh?" Frances asked, her voice expectant. "Nobody's that mean, are they?"

"No one helped her." Sarah Beth kept her own voice flat and passionless. "The onlookers thought it a great joke. The boys had taken all the gunpowder out of the firecrackers. They were just teasing her. Having a little fun."

"Oh, my God! People are so cruel."

"Cruel, and crazy," Sarah Beth noted. "Some men come to the District and hire two women, one to strangle him while the other beds him or does him French."

Frances gasped. "Why would anyone do that?"

"Some say sex is better when you're almost dead."

"Is it?"

"I don't know," Sarah Beth said. "And I have no intentions of finding out."

"Is there ever, you know, an accident?"

"What do you think?" Sarah Beth's tone answered the question.

They rode down Robertson toward Canal Street, passing two of the three city squares that make up St. Louis Cemetery No. 2, the rear boundary of the white section of the District. At Iberville they turned back toward Basin Street. Sarah Beth continued acting as tour guide until they reached the corner of Marais.

"Ain't she the sweetest looking little thing you ever did see," Frances remarked of a golden-haired girl about eight riding a pony. "Wonder what she and that pretty little horse is doing down *here*?"

"She works here."

"Oh, God, no!" Frances fairly shrieked. "Not that beautiful little girl!"

"Yes. With her momma." Sarah Beth relentlessly pounded reality into Frances' brain. "When she was five, her momma started letting her wash the tricks. Last week I heard her momma lets her do the French now. When she's old enough, her momma will auction her virginity at Emma's. She'll get a high price, too, because everyone will know she's a virgin…Oh, and that cute little pony performs with the girl's momma every night at Emma's. The child probably watches. Imagine what it must be like to have a pet pony that beds your momma."

Sarah Beth's commentary had its intended effect. Frances leaned over the side of the carriage and retched, a sight not uncommon on Marais and Iberville Streets near Tournier's Saloon. Sarah Beth dabbed the remains from Frances' mouth with a white handkerchief when the girl had finished.

Sick of soul and body, Frances huddled next to Sarah Beth. "Oh, Miss LaBranche! This here's such a terrible place. Not like I thought at all."

"Dear, sweet Frances, I'm sorry if I was hard on you. But I don't think you would have believed me any other way. This is a terrible place, even more terrible than you imagine based on what little you've seen. The District is not full of sin and corruption because the people here enjoy being wicked or because being wicked is so much fun. Only one word explains the Tenderloin." Sarah Beth paused for effect. "Greed. In Storyville, greed pressures the piston and runs the engine. Look at those houses." Sarah Beth pointed down a block of single story, two family dwellings. "Anywhere else in the city a family would live in each side, paying six to ten dollars a month in rent. The owner makes twelve to twenty dollars on his investment. But families don't live in the houses here. They're partitioned into cribs, a dozen, or so, to a side and rented for three dollars a night. Think of it, Frances. That's seventy-two dollars a *night*, over two thousand dollars a month, compared to twelve or twenty. Some of the best families in the city own property down here. It's a wonderful investment. And the French houses. Why just entertain men in French?" Sarah Beth proved her question rhetorical by answering it. "Because it's quick and can be done in a space much smaller than a crib. More girls needing less room can turn more tricks. That equals more money. And even when a girl beds a man, the idea is to get him finished as soon as possible. One girl I know brags she can have any man done in two minutes. But before you take them to the bedroom or the French parlor, make them spend all their money on wine and champagne because the landlady gives you a commission. Then take them upstairs and finish them quickly so you can come back down and charm another john. And if a john still has money when you've finished him, give a wink to the boys at the door. They'll follow him outside and relieve him of it." Pausing and leaning back in the carriage seat, Sarah Beth asked, "Frances, is this the life you want for yourself? Is this how you want to get even with your mother?"

"Oh, no, Miss LaBranche. B-But what should I do?"

Sarah Beth thought back to the day, so many years ago, when Myda had tried to steer her away from the life. Sarah Beth had been too stubborn to listen and, when communing with her most private self, admitted her mistake. Now a new sorrow had been added. If she had taken Myda's advice perhaps she would have met Frank Cheramie under different circumstances. Sarah Beth took the despondent Frances' hand in hers. "Go to the House of the Good Shepherd. They'll take very good care of you."

"W-Will you visit me? I-I don't know anybody around here and I'll be so lonely."

"Of course I'll visit." Sarah Beth hugged the desolate girl. "Of course I will."

"Oh, Lord," Frances said suddenly dismayed. "I got no cash money to pay back what you spent on me." She began to sob again. "But I'll find me some work. Good, clean, honest work, even if I got to scrub floors. I promise. And I'll pay it all back, every copper cent, a little at a time. I swear."

"The money's not important, Frances," Sarah Beth said. "What's important is that the sisters at Good Shepherd will take care of you."

AFTER PLACING FRANCES IN THE protective custody of the nuns, Sarah Beth returned to The Mansion. She and Myda ate and talked in Myda's private suite, recounting the day's excitement. When she mentioned Frank Cheramie, Sarah Beth was as miserable as she had made Frances earlier. Myda empathized with her protégée, but the commiseration did nothing to cheer Sarah Beth.

After telling Lou Belle she would not be receiving callers, Sarah Beth retired to her attic bedroom. In her night gown, she brushed and braided her hair absently, thinking about Frank Cheramie and the possibilities that could never be hers. At the window, she held aside the lace curtains and stared in the direction of the Cheramie house. Tomorrow, perhaps, she would see him. In bed, her last thought was of him, as it had been each night since they met. As she drifted to sleep, she wondered how a man, any man, could effect a woman like her the way Frank Cheramie did.

CHAPTER 13

SPRING BECAME SUMMER BY DEGREES Fahrenheit. Each day the tropical sun boosted the temperature closer to the boiling point. In New Orleans, a city surrounded by water–Lake Pontchartrain, the river and the interminable swamp–the humidity made life almost unbearable, congealing the air like gumbo thickened with *filé*. The Crescent City stewed as it did every year from May through September.

Sarah Beth hardly noticed the disagreeable climate so absorbed had she become in her new life outside the District. She spent as much time as possible at the Cheramie's or with her new friend, Frances. At one time, Myda's rule requiring her boarders to take holiday during their "moon blood," as Lou Belle called it, rankled Sarah Beth because of the enforced idleness, made bearable only by her studies. Now she looked forward to spending the time at the old house on Esplanade Avenue and was glad she had explained her hiatus to Annadette during their first meeting.

Life outside the District provided Sarah Beth with a new interest, one she did not know she had until she took up residence with the Cheramies. At first, she viewed gardening as a diversion. Soon it became a way to spruce up the faded grandeur of the old house she had come to love so much. After her voracious mind absorbed several books on the subject, she attacked the flower beds in the back yard for practice. Satisfied with the result, she began working on the front yard.

Late one afternoon, Annadette found Sarah Beth sketching the front of the house, her first step in planning the new gardens.

"What are you doing now?" Annadette called from the porch.

Sarah Beth told her and the old woman shuffled to the front steps, stopping at the railing.

"Has Cyprian ever shown you his clinic as he promised?"

Sarah Beth looked up from her pad and recalled, *She had disappeared down the stairwell when he said that.* She chuckled to herself. *Hard of hearing is she?* "No, he hasn't had the time. He's always working. If he's not seeing patients here, he's making house calls."

"Sometimes I think he'd forget to eat if I didn't send Mary after him." Annadette rapped her cane on the floorboards. "It's past five o'clock. His patients should all be gone. Why don't we go see?"

Sarah Beth saw the same matchmaker's look in Annadette's eyes that she had seen on several other occasions. Knowing the old woman's intent, Sarah Beth still let herself be persuaded. She wanted to know more about the only man she had ever met that held such fascination for her.

They found Frank in the kitchen sterilizing his instruments.

"Cyprian, you–."

"Not now, please, *Gamé*. Ask Mary to keep dinner warm. I have too much–."

"Cyprian, where are your manners? You have a guest."

Frank turned from the pot in which his instruments boiled. "Ah, Miss LaBranche. What a pleasure."

Sarah Beth smiled and inclined her head. "Thank you, Doctor."

"And to what do I owe it?" Frank asked.

"Your bad manners," Annadette said. "I distinctly remember you offering to show Miss LaBranche your clinic and, when I asked, she said you hadn't."

"I *am* sorry." Frank stirred his instruments with a long, metal spoon that grated against the sides of the porcelain pot. "When might be a good time, Miss LaBranche?"

"Now," Annadette said for her.

Amused, Sarah Beth watched the play between matchmaker and victim.

Looking at Sarah Beth, Frank said, "I wish I could, but I have so much to do just now. Perhaps–."

"And what could possibly be important enough to make you so impolite to our guest?" Annadette insisted.

"Not guest," Sarah Beth interrupted, "boarder. There's a difference."

"Don't encourage him, dear." Annadette patted Sarah Beth's arm. Turning to her grandson, she asked, "Well?"

"*Gamé*, I have reams of research to review," Frank said. "Oh, and I, ah, I had intended work on my accounts this evening," he added. "Send out some of those bills you so often chide me about."

"What are you researching?" Sarah Beth asked.

"An eye disease." The steam from the pot added to the summer heat and popped droplets of perspiration on Frank's forehead.

"Don't distract him, dear," Annadette said. "I had him talking about his bills. Though, if I were you, I'd be insulted. Seems he'd prefer to spend time with his accounts rather than you."

"I did not say that, *Gamé*. You are putting words in my mouth." Frank appeared more than a little flustered as he glanced from his grandmother to Sarah Beth and back.

Sarah Beth found the scene adorable. Whenever she had seen Frank before, his tall, imposing presence had always been the essence of poise and refinement. To see the little boy in him unsettled by his old grandmother made him more human and quite endearing. *Or is he flustered because of me?* She brushed the thought away. *That's ridiculous. I mean nothing to him.*

"What he needs is a good secretary," Annadette suggested pointedly. "Someone who'll make him do his work in proper order. See his patients, send his bills *and then* he works on his treatment journals. Better yet, he needs someone to send out his bills for him."

"Perhaps I might help," Sarah Beth found herself saying.

"I certainly could not allow *that*," Frank said.

"Why not?" Annadette asked. "She's bright enough. You said so yourself, Cyprian."

He talks about me? For the first time she could remember Sarah Beth felt the heat of a blush on her cheeks. "Thank you, Doctor."

"I, ah, one night at dinner, we, ah…" Frank suddenly gave his pot of instruments much more attention than necessary.

"It wouldn't be too much of an imposition, would it, dear?" Annadette asked.

"Not at all. You know how much I enjoy keeping busy, what with the garden and all." Sarah Beth found the idea intriguing, even though she recognized that Annadette played matchmaker and business manager at the same time. "And arithmetic is such a wonderful mental exercise. I'll have the accounts in order in no time."

"Wonderful!" Annadette exclaimed.

"If you must be pressed into service, I would much prefer if it were as my research assistant." With long metal tongs Frank took his instruments out of the pot and set them on a clean, white cloth. "At least there you would feel a sense of accomplishment, a sense of fulfillment, knowing you–."

"Perhaps I could do both," Sarah Beth suggested.

"Nonsense. That is much too much of a burden," Frank said.

"But I have some free time back at The–, ah, at my employer's. If I'm reviewing treatment journals, I could take them with me and work at odd moments."

"Fine, fine." Annadette linked arms with Frank and Sarah Beth, guiding them to the door. "Show her your clinic, Cyprian, and tell her about your accounts. Remember, my dear," she said to Sarah Beth, "bills first."

As Sarah Beth and Frank walked down the hall toward the back of the house, Sarah Beth turned and caught a brief glimpse of the matchmaker's twinkle in Annadette's eye. She turned back to Frank smiling and asked, "What are you researching, Dr. Cheramie?"

"A particularly debilitating eye disease, *phlyctenular ophthalmia.*" Frank led Sarah Beth into his waiting room, a smallish, spartan area filled with rows of straight-back chairs. "The disease tenders itself as minute nodules, very small pimples, in the conjunctiva. The nodes appear singularly or multiply, varying in size from a very small grain of sand to the head of a pin. When in mass, they often congeal into what appears to be a single area of infiltration tenanting the whole of the conjunctiva that may be seen when the eye lid is open."

Though others might find Frank's speech stilted, Sarah Beth considered it complimentary. He spoke to her as an equal.

"The affliction seems to repeat itself in the same patient year after year and sometimes causes blindness if not treated properly," he added.

Frank and Sarah Beth walked through a small examining area and into a larger room that served as his office and library. The room had a faint antiseptic smell, an aroma Sarah Beth would forever associate with the man standing next to her.

"The condition seems less prevalent and severe in whites than Negroes, which I attribute to their generally more squalid living conditions." From a cabinet above his roll-top desk, Frank took several thick books. "These are my treatment journals for the past ten years. Buried in all this data are the various regimens I have used. But I have never had the time to properly analyze them, to determine scientifically if there is one best treatment. Of course, I have an idea which might be the best. But the practice of medicine cannot be based on intuition. We need facts. That is what you can do, if you would be so kind. Get the facts from these." Frank tapped the journals.

"And your accounts, Doctor?" Sarah Beth asked with a teasing lilt in her voice. "I trust they are as detailed as your treatment journals."

"Well, ah, you see, actually, ah, though I have always meant to, ah, I have not had the time to sit down and, with pen and paper, create what one would call–."

"You have no ledgers, do you, Doctor?" Sarah Beth asked, still baiting him.

Dispirited, Frank said, "Yes."

"Yes, you *do* have ledgers or yes, you *don't* have ledgers?"

"Yes, I do not have ledgers," he sighed.

"And does *Gamé* know of this total lack of business acumen on your part?" Sarah Beth continued her game.

"No," the beleaguered doctor answered, "and I hope, no, I trust, she will not learn from you, dear Mademoiselle." He took Sarah Beth's hand and looked deep into her eyes.

All the banter left her and Sarah Beth found herself, once again, under the spell of his enchanting eyes. "O-Of course not. I would never–."

"Then it shall be our little secret. You will not tell *Gamé* what a terrible businessman I am?"

She tried to look away, but couldn't, captured by eyes indefinably unique. She swallowed and managed to say, almost breathlessly, "Our little secret."

"Remember, we Cheramies are very good at keeping secrets. Keep this one and, perhaps, we can consider you a Cheramie, too." Frank eyes sparkled.

Sarah Beth somehow found her composure and returned his teasing. "Why, *Monsieur le Docteur*, is that an offer to be dear friends?" she asked, playing on the literal English translation of his family name, "or a proposal of marriage?"

Frank's remarkable eyes became serious. "Only time will tell."

THE ASSAULT ON FRANK CHERAMIE'S accounts became Sarah Beth's first task and her approach would have made Rockefeller and Vanderbilt proud. She compared his appointment book to his bank statement to determine who had and had not paid. Then, knowing many patients were charity cases, she caught him at odd moments to inquire.

"Baker," she would ask.

"Which one?"

"Richard, a growth on the i.r.f. Right foot?" she added tentatively, "but what's the *I*? Inside?"

"Instep. You are a wonderful administrator, you know, Miss LaBranche." Frank looked down the throat of a small boy held immobile by his mother. "Not only can you decipher my handwriting, which is poor by any standards, but you understand the abbreviations." He tossed the tongue depressor into the waste can and leaned close to her ear. "Send the old welch a bill for two dollars."

Sarah Beth soon discovered many of Doctor Cheramie's poorer patients paid more promptly than those better off.

"Ezekiel Adams? His daughter had an inflamed eye," she said, going to the next name on her long list.

"Hmmm. No bill. Zeke is a smith and shod our horse a week or so later." Frank used a long, thin, cotton-tipped wooden swab to coat the boy's throat with a yellow, sticky paste. "By the way, have you had time to review my treatment journals on *phlyctenular ophthalmia*? That is what Ezekiel's daughter, what's-her-name, had."

"Marie," Sarah Beth reminded him, "and, no, not yet, Doctor. I've been working on the bills."

"Blast the bills, Nurse." Frank smiled at her as he lifted the boy from the treatment table. "I need to know which of those therapies is best."

"I'm not sure *Gamé* Annadette would agree," she called teasingly over her shoulder as she left.

But that evening Sarah Beth began an analysis of Frank's treatment journals in his office-library on the ground floor in the rear of the house. Reviewing ten years of records written in a pinched, hurried hand would take time and she decided to devote at least an hour a day to the project.

Frank Cheramie's research carried forward a rich tradition in New Orleans. One of the foremost medical centers in the United States, the city supported two medical colleges and several widely read medical journals. Even a French-language journal, *L'Union Médicale de la Louisiane*, flourished for a while. Perhaps it was all in self-defense. The Queen City of the South was widely regarded as the domain of the Third Horseman and his spawn: yellow fever, cholera, malaria, measles and most every other infestation evil could propagate.

For such a daunting project, Sarah Beth made several false starts. Finally, she decided to review Frank's journals chronologically. Abstracting the information into tabular form, she listed the date, race and age of the patient, the treatment–hydrogen chloride wash, borax-boracic wash, enzymol, or any of a number of other remedies–noted the proportions, strength of medication and frequency of application. She recorded severity using the numerals 1 to 5 from the most mild to the most severe. At first Frank had to classify the cases for her, but soon she learned to classify them herself. To determine the most effective therapy, she logged the time it took for the various remedies to counter the disease. Having annotated the first half-year, she summarized it into a short table giving the treatment used according to race and showing the average time to cure each class of patients.

When she showed her work covering January to June 1895 to Frank, his praise and promise to include her as co-author of the article he intended to write brightened her soul and dreams. Wanting more of his approbation, Sarah Beth re-doubled her efforts and by mid-May, when her fictitious employer made another imaginary trip to the Mississippi coast, she had finished the first three years of his journals.

Sarah Beth began her time off with Frank's records for January, 1898, and devoted herself to the project exclusively, taking her meals in the cluttered library next to his clinic, listening and smelling the practice of medicine just outside the door. By late evening of the third day her beloved doctor's handwriting took on a life of its own. The strokes of his pen began to wiggle on the page like so many squashed ants. The heat from the kerosene lamp compounded the hot summer air and sucked much of the enthusiasm out of her. Her eyes burned.

Pushing away from the desk, Sarah Beth stretched cramped arms and legs in a most unladylike fashion and hooked the hair from one of her cheek curls under her nose. "I wonder what I'd look like with a mustache?" she said out loud to herself. Then she quickly assumed a more genteel pose before anyone walked in on her, thinking, *I'm going daft. The man's handwriting is enough to drive anyone stark, raving mad. And blind, too.*

The shelves of Frank's library, each jammed to groaning, attracted her attention and she stood to browse, hoping to discover more about the man who had so quickly become central to her life.

She learned no more than she already knew. Every book, every pamphlet, every magazine concerned medicine. She looked carefully and found not one work of fiction, not even the most deserving: Balzac, Hugo, Dickens, Shakespeare.

She had surrendered all hope of discovering anything new about Frank when she reached the back wall of the library and found an entire section devoted to yellow fever. While Frank had organized the other books systematically, this portion of his collection was a hodgepodge, and obviously well used.

To divert her mind from visions of eyes dusted by calomel powder and swathed in yellow oxide salve, Sarah Beth began organizing the books and articles, some torn from journals and held together with pins. She piled them on the table behind her, glancing through them as she did and her phenomenal photographic memory absorbed for future reference pages she barely saw. With her back to the door, she reached up high for a thin pamphlet folded and, apparently, accidentally stuffed behind several large volumes. The title, which she could see, intrigued her: *Statstique des Vaccinations, Partiquées avec la culture atténuée du microbe de la fievre jaune.* She had never heard of a yellow fever vaccine.

"Please do not do that," Frank said from behind her.

Startled, Sarah Beth came off her toes and stumbled backwards, bumping into the table. "My goodness." Her hand went to her throat.

"I am sorry. I did not mean to frighten you. But I do wish you would leave those books alone."

"I was only organizing them as you had already done the others." Sarah Beth's eyes begged for an explanation.

Obviously, his had been a tiring day, too. He sat heavily in the chair by the roll-top desk, idly scanning Sarah Beth's notes. Finally he said, "No man wants his failures exposed, especially to someone important to him."

Again, Sarah Beth's question, "Failures?" came from her eyes.

Frank looked at her and took a very deep breath. "I became a doctor so I could find a cure for yellow fever. In the '78 epidemic, I lost my entire family. My father was a doctor, too. Part of the material you were looking through, some dating back to 1850, was his. He was obsessed with finding a cure for yellow fever, also. But the disease took him. And my mother and younger brother. Gone, all gone. I was only eight and did not understand why I was spared, even though I lived in the same house. Funny, I have never contracted the disease."

"Be careful what you wish for, Doctor," Sarah Beth admonished with a smile.

Frank nodded and smiled back wistfully. "Gradually, my child's mind decided God had let me live to complete my father's work."

"Now with Reed and Carroll proving Finlay's mosquito theory correct, you feel you've lost your purpose?" Sarah Beth's compassion was obvious as her subconscious prompted her with facts from the material she had just scanned.

Frank arched thick, black eyebrows. "You certainly are well read. But loss of purpose is not the problem. We know how the disease propagates, but have no cure for it. I could still discover…No, it is the waste, the tragic waste of lives that bothers me most. Imagine, if you will, Miss LaBranche, the precision required of a yellow fever epidemic. A victim can only infect a mosquito during the first three days he has the fever. The disease incubates for twelve days in the insect and only then can that mosquito infect another human, who infects other mosquitos that infect other humans, and so on. Had all that been known in '78, perhaps my family would not have died. Had we known it in '97, perhaps the panic that year would not have been so bad. All that misery, all that suffering, all brought on by an infinitesimal bug, the mosquito *stegomyia calopus*."

Sarah Beth thought back to the months just before she ran away from home. "I remember I was very, very sick late in the summer of '97. Momma said it was Yellow Jack."

"What were the symptoms?"

"At breakfast I was fine as a fiddle. Then I went out on the porch with my brother and got the worst headache I've ever had. It came on so suddenly. My whole body hurt. My arms, my legs, my back." Total recall allowed Sarah Beth perfect memory of the pain and she shivered. "I couldn't keep anything down. Momma kept me in wet sheets and fanned me to bring the fever down."

"It sounds as if you had yellow fever." Frank's voice had a far-away, detached quality as he continued pining the loss of his family. "You are lucky, Miss LaBranche. Once you have had the disease, you are immune for life."

"With all we know now, it should make no difference."

"But it does. We have no cure and–."

"What about that French pamphlet–."

"I do not read French."

"What!" Sarah Beth showed him her brightest smile trying to boost him from his melancholy. She came up behind him and reached out to touch him. Unsure, she pulled her hand back quickly. With the same teasing lilt in her voice she said, "Cyprian François Cheramie speaks French but doesn't read it. Does *Gamé* know?"

"Yes." Frank's smile was a tired one. "I speak it because when I first came to live with her, she would not speak to me in English. That was right after my family…."

"Oh, Frank." For the first time Sarah Beth addressed him in familiar terms. "You mustn't let yourself be so depressed. I know you'd like to go back, do everything over, change the things that caused your parents'–."

"Of course I would," he snapped. "But that is not what distresses me most. Our troubles with that blasted fever are not yet over! We do not know what causes yellow fever, we have no cure and the mosquito theory is just that, a theory. Half the people do not accept it. And the ones in charge, the politicians, the bureaucrats, the leaders that should be directing the rest of us, have done nothing. Why?" Frank aimed a finger at Sarah Beth for emphasis. "Because it costs money and spending it leaves less for them to steal. And, of course, it is bad for business. But knowing what we know, have we done anything to prevent another outbreak?" Controlling himself once again, Frank answered his own question, in loving, gentle tones looking at Sarah Beth. "In a word, my dear, *dear* Sarah Beth, no. The city has spent no money to clean its open gutters. Every house in New Orleans has a cistern, but there has been no campaign to cover them. People do not realize that *stegomyia* is a house mosquito. They do not have a great flying range. And they lay their eggs in standing water." Frank's temper flared again. "This whole blasted city is nothing but blasted containers of blasted standing water!" He rubbed his eyes with his thumb and forefinger. In command of his temper again, he said, "No, my dear, we have not seen the last of Yellow Jack. He is waiting for us out there somewhere. It is only a question of time. I assure you, he will be back."

The telephone in the next room rang. Sarah Beth stood in the doorway, listening as Frank answered, "Hello...Yes, this is Doctor Cheramie... Good evening, Profess–...Yes, I know Doctor Grander...Yes...Yes...I see...Yes...How long has she been–...Nothing stays down?...Any temperature?...I'll be there as soon...Within the hour...Yes, as fast as I can. Goodbye, Professor."

"Are you a prophet, Frank?" Sarah Beth asked.

"What?"

"The poor woman can keep nothing down. She has a fever. You just said that Yellow Jack would be back. Does she–."

"*Doctor* LaBranche," he teased, "you should eavesdrop on *both* sides of the conversation before making your diagnosis. The poor lady is, ah, with child and her, ah, condition is very discomforting."

"I see." Sarah Beth recognized Frank's reluctance to discuss such an indelicate subject with a woman and sulked her way back into the library. *Typical male*, she fumed to herself and sat down at the desk as Frank came in.

"I say, Sarah Beth could you...You know, it *is* good to call you by your given name. Thank you."

She smiled, placated a bit by his warmth. *Perhaps I shouldn't be so hard on him. After all, his condescending attitude is typical. He can't help being a product of his time. He'll change, though,* Sarah Beth promised herself, *I'll see to that.*

"I was wondering," Frank continued, "if I might impose on you?"

Sarah Beth looked down at his terrible penmanship and wondered what further imposition he had in mind.

"You see, the poor lady I just spoke of on the telephone is very, very ill. She has not been able to keep anything on her stomach for three days. That Doctor Grander I mentioned has attended her over the years but is unavailable tonight and recommended me. I have studied his technique in these cases. It's quite a remarkable advance. You see, Doctor Grander has found that–."

"Get to the point, Frank," Sarah Beth urged, "you have a sick patient waiting."

"Well, I was wondering, if it is not too much trouble, could you possibly see your way clear to assist me? I would not ask except the device requires two people to handle it. From the sound of the woman's husband, he is in no condition to be of any use and, I expect, neither is she. I know this is an imposition and may offend your tender sensibilities to see–."

Sarah Beth stood roughly, glaring at Frank, her hands on her hips. Leaning forward on the balls of her feet, she would let the him know, despite his proper Victorian upbringing, he could not patronize her. "Exactly which tender sensibility would that be, Frank!"

"Why, you know, your tender, *female* sensibilities."

"Yes, Frank," Sarah Beth stalked toward him, "but exactly which one! The one making that poor woman go through hell to give her husband a child!"

Frank took a step backwards, clearly shocked by Sarah Beth's unladylike language.

"Or perhaps the tender sensibility that allowed women to face wild Indians and bury their children in unmarked graves in order to populate this country!" She continued forcing his retreat toward the bookshelves. "Or is it the tender sensibility that lets women wash and scrub and cook and clean all day every day for their families with no rest and no time for themselves!" Pinning him against the bookcase, she demanded, "Exactly *which* of these tender, *female* sensibilities are you talking about!"

Taken back by the unexpected vehemence of her attack, Frank stammered, "I-I *am* sorry. I-I did not mean to offend you. N-Nor did I realize you were one of those, ah, suffragettes."

"Frank!" Sarah Beth snapped, part in exasperation, part in disgust. "Ohhhhhhhh…Let me get my hat!"

AS THE CARRIAGE WOUND ITS way uptown, Frank explained the procedure he intended to use to a very irate assistant. On his lap he held a stiff leather case with the instrument inside. On the seat next to him lay a container of twenty extra batteries. Sarah Beth sat with her arms folded, glaring at him.

"This is the rheostat." He moved a small brass handle on the device. "It controls the amount of current delivered to the patient." He tapped a short, brass cylinder with a glass cover. "This gauge tells how much current is being applied. Your help is needed for the electrodes. They plug in here." He showed Sarah Beth two holes in the side of the box. "The electrodes have to be in contact with the patients skin when the current is applied. Otherwise, she could be shocked and her skin cauterized. That is where you come in. As you can see, it takes more hands than I have to properly work the galvanometer. Usually I will ask the husband for help if the patient is too sick, but this man is too upset, almost hysterical."

"So despite my tender sensibilities...."

"I have said I was sorry several times now. Can you not find it in your heart to forgive me? Please?"

Sarah Beth's heart could find anything Frank wanted. She smiled in the darkness. "You're forgiven." She unfolded her arms. "But what's wrong with being a suffragette?"

"Not now, Nurse," he said in playful indignation. "I have more instructions for you."

Frank continued explaining the treatment plan until they reached a three-story Victorian house on First Street, uptown in the Garden District–the old American quarter.

A very distraught husband answered their knock. "Doctor? Thank heaven you're here! Maggie's been–." Professor Philip Anderson stopped in mid-sentence and stared at Sarah Beth.

She gawked back, just as bewildered. What had begun as a great adventure with her beloved doctor quickly became an impending disaster. If Philip said anything, her time with Frank Cheramie would end immediately in disgrace. Sarah Beth knew she always ran the risk of Frank discovering the truth about her and denouncing her as the pariah she was. She accepted that, but had not expected it to happen so soon. Suddenly she realized her life would be a series of near-catastrophes until Frank finally discovered who and what she was. *But please, not tonight*, she silently begged the malignant fate that, thus far, had guided her life.

Philip Anderson seemed to have taken root in the doorway. Bleary eyed and disheveled, he looked from nurse to doctor and back, but, thankfully, did nothing to indicate he and Sarah Beth knew each other.

"Could you show us to the patient?" Frank asked, unaware of the drama taking place around him and looking past Philip into the house. "Where is she?"

"Wh-What…Oh, of course." Philip tore his gaze from Sarah Beth. "Th-This way."

They found Maggie Anderson upstairs lying in the middle of a four-poster bed, both her and the room in greater disarray than her husband. As they entered, she moaned loudly, "Philip, is the doctor here yet?"

"Yes, Maggie, he's right–."

Just then a spasm churned through her. Her husband raced to the bed as she leaned over and greeted her guests with a thin stream of bile gagged into a bucket on the floor. "Thank God," she said when she flopped back against the pillows.

Sarah Beth noticed the rancid smell in the room. She looked into the bucket and turned away, her nose crinkled in disgust. "Professor… Anderson, is it?"

Philip nodded, clearly not understanding why Sarah Beth treated him as a stranger.

"That bucket desperately needs a good cleaning. Could you see to it?" Sarah Beth looked to Frank for confirmation.

Frank nodded and Philip Anderson mechanically took the bucket from the room.

"A good cleaning," Sarah Beth called after him. "Lots of lye soap." Relief flooded through her at the sight of Philip's back going down the hall. At least she might have this one chance to serve her cherished doctor. Then–. She pushed the future from her mind.

Frank stood over his patient. "Madam, is this your first child?"

"Please, doctor," Maggie Anderson begged, "can we talk later? Right now all I want is for my stomach to let me be. If you can do that–."

"I have to be sure the treatment I have in mind is correct," Frank explained. "I'll be as quick as I can." He questioned Maggie Anderson to eliminate disease and neurotic tendencies as possible causes of her distress and concluded, "I think we have a classic case here of uterine reflex vomiting. Turn over on your stomach, please, Mrs. Anderson. I believe galvanization will help. Miss LaBranche, please help Mrs. Anderson raise her night clothes. I need her bare back exposed. Cover her, her…." Frank waved his hand, indicating the patient's buttocks, his professionalism clashing with Victorian etiquette. "Use the bed linen."

"No, Doctor," Maggie Anderson protested. "I'll not have a woman–."

Frank winced.

Sarah Beth read the pained expression on his face and mouthed, "Don't worry. I'll behave."

"Mrs. Anderson, I brought Miss LaBranche with me because I need her help," Frank explained. "A nurse, if you will. Normally, I would have the patient herself assist me if possible. If not, I would ask her husband. But, frankly, madam, in his condition, I would not let your husband assist with last rites for a cat. I know many women feel as you about being attended by another woman, but, you see, don't you, if you could help me, and you are a woman, then Miss LaBranche–."

"All right, all right." Maggie Anderson waved her hands. "Just get on with it."

Frank prepared the galvanometer as Sarah Beth readied the patient. He placed the two electrodes against indentations in Maggie Anderson's spine. "Here, Miss LaBranche, hold these like this. Now, Mrs. Anderson, you may feel a tingling, but that is normal. Please tell me when the nausea lessens." He turned the rheostat. "Hold the electrodes tight against her spine, Miss LaBranche. Any better, Mrs. Anderson?"

With her face buried in a feather pillow, Maggie Anderson shook her head.

Frank turned up the rheostat. "How about now?"

"No," came the muffled reply.

The doctor moved the lever a little more to the right. "Now?"

Another muffled, "No!"

Frank watched the gauge. "Almost fifteen milliamperes," he muttered. "Any better?"

"No. Wait. Yes. I do think my stomach is behaving better," Maggie said.

"Good." Frank reduced the current a bit.

For ten minutes Frank and Sarah Beth galvanized Maggie Anderson. Sarah Beth's hands began to cramp from holding the electrodes and Frank relieved her so she could work the kinks from her fingers.

"Do you feel as if you will vomit again?" Frank asked.

"No, Doctor." A relieved Maggie Anderson spoke into the pillow. "This is the best I've felt in days."

Looking at Sarah Beth, Frank said, "Miss LaBranche, please find Professor Anderson and get Mrs. Anderson something to eat." To his patient he asked, "What seemed to make you the most nauseous?"

"Just the thought of roast beef."

"Then see if you can find some roast beef, Miss LaBranche."

"But, doctor," Maggie protested, her voice muffled, "if roast beef makes me sick why–."

"The best way to cure you," Frank explained, "is to make your stomach tolerate that which makes it the sickest. Trust me. You will eat the roast beef while we are here. If you feel nauseous, we will galvanize you until you feel better."

Sarah Beth went slowly, reluctantly from the room. "Professor Anderson," she called treading slowly down the stairs, holding tight to the dark, varnished banister and dreading the inescapable confrontation with her obsessed paramour. Yet, this might be her only opportunity to assist Frank in the actual practice of medicine. She would risk everything for that chance. "Professor Anderson, where are you? We need roast beef for your wife...Professor Anderson?" Her voice bounced back to her from empty rooms. At the bottom of the staircase she turned toward the rear of the house, assuming the kitchen to be in that direction. "Professor Anderson? Can you hear me?"

She walked down a hall, looking into vacant rooms. Finding the pantry, she went in and through a second door into the kitchen.

Suddenly grabbed from behind and spun around, Sarah Beth's hand instinctively reached for her derringer.

"What are you doing with *him*?" Philip hissed.

"Trying to help your wife." She released the small gun and pushed against his chest with both hands. "Let me go. We, the doctor wants some roast beef for–."

"Not before you tell me what you're doing with *him*!" Philip shook her.

Sarah Beth pushed against her captor with all her strength and the frazzled man, worn out from three days tending his wife, lost his hold on her.

Sarah Beth stepped back, straightening her dress. "I told you, I'm here to help with your wife. Nothing more. Now, is there any roast beef in this house?"

"Roast beef be damned! I want to know–."

"Keep your voice down and listen to me, Philip!" Sarah Beth commanded in a harsh whisper. "Your wife is upstairs puking her insides out to give you a child! Whatever you have to say to me can wait until after we've taken care of that poor woman! Now move!" She pushed him aside and demanded, "Where's the ice box?"

Philip's knees buckled and he crumpled into a chair next to the kitchen table.

Frank called, "If you have to cook the roast beef, Miss LaBranche, never mind. Find something else. Lamb, pork, just get some meat!"

"Where *is* the ice box, Philip?" Sarah Beth insisted in hushed tones.

"On the back porch," he said despondently, then added, "It leaks."

Sarah Beth returned from the porch with a large, cooked roast on a platter and some butter. "Find me a frying pan," she ordered as she rummaged through drawers for a carving knife. Then, trying to relieve the tension with small talk, she asked, "Where are your children?"

Not moving from the chair, Philip said in a vacuous tone of voice, "At a neighbor's."

"Philip, the frying pan."

Frank called again. "Nurse! Where is the food?!"

Sarah Beth went to the door. "I'm heating it up, Doctor!" and mumbled to herself, "Defending my honor in the process," then thought, *Ha! What honor?*

She turned to find Philip Anderson with the large carving knife clenched tightly in his hand.

"Do you know what you've done to me?" he demanded.

"Ph-Philip, I-I tried to be your friend and confidant when you needed one." Sarah Beth fumbled for her gun as she spoke.

"You've made me into a madman." He attacked the roast, slicing it into thick slabs. "I burn for you...I inhale you...I sweat you. I think of nothing but you...Not my wife...Not my children...Not my students... Only you."

Sarah Beth picked up the roast platter and took the knife carefully from Philip, claiming to need it to cook. He had put the frying pan on the stove. The pat of butter sizzled and splattered when she dropped it in and, for a time, was the only sound in the room.

"Your hot wick has done a lot of damage to that poor woman upstairs," Sarah Beth said after a while. "Shouldn't it be cooled down by now?"

"You're the cause," he said as Sarah Beth fried the meat.

"Me? I suppose *I* made her pregnant."

"In a way." Philip collapsed into a chair again. He sat holding his head in his hands and resting his elbows on the table. "I can't afford to…to be with you as much as I need, so I go to her. If you would only agree to my proposal, I could–."

"Philip." Sarah Beth turned, holding a plate of roast beef and utensils. "I simply will not live my life like that."

"You love him, don't you?" Philip asked, his voice devoid of all emotion.

Sarah Beth stopped as she reached the door. "Wh-Who?" But she knew her heart had betrayed her and the entire world could see her feelings for Frank Cheramie.

"Your doctor, who else? And he loves you, too. It's very clear to me. It's written all over you both. Have you taken him to your–."

"Indeed not! I'm just a boarder at his, at his grandmother's house. And, and he needed my help tonight with a very difficult case so I–."

"Where is the damned food!" Frank's voice boomed through the house.

"Coming," Sarah Beth called back. To her despondent lover she said, "Philip, perhaps we should stop–."

"Sarah Beth," he said, a strange fierceness in his eyes and voice, "if I can't have you, I don't know what I'll do."

"You'll be sensible, Philip."

"Will I?"

UPSTAIRS MRS. ANDERSON BECAME NAUSEOUS as soon as she smelled the food. Frank and Sarah Beth galvanized her until her stomach quieted, then the doctor made her eat. As soon as she became sick again he administered another treatment.

"I thought doctors made people well," Maggie said, her spirits improved enough to joke. "So far, Doctor Cheramie, you've spent the evening making me ill."

"Your condition has trained your stomach to reject whatever is put in it," Frank explained. "We have to retrain it. I will be back tomorrow morning and, perhaps, again tomorrow night to give you more treatments."

"Is that really necessary, doctor?" Maggie asked. "I feel so much improved. And, of course, I don't want to impose on your kindness."

Or run up your bill, Sarah Beth added to herself.

"Mrs. Anderson, I am not quite sure you understand just how sick you were," Frank said. "I do not wish to alarm you because it is very rare, but death has resulted from your condition. And all that upheaval cannot be good for that blessed little child. But if it is the bill you are worried about I can—."

"Oh, no. If it's necessary, then, by all means, I'll see you tomorrow."

But, heavens to Betsy, don't call me cheap, Sarah Beth thought and immediately felt ashamed. She, herself, caused the woman's financial trouble. But she knew the remedy. Tomorrow, she would send Philip a note refusing to see him anymore. Maggie Anderson had enough to fret about without added money worries.

"Will you be needing me tomorrow, doctor?" Sarah Beth asked.

"I think not," Frank said. "Either Mrs. Anderson or her husband should be able to help with the electrodes."

"Then it was very nice meeting you, Mrs. Anderson." Sarah Beth gathered up her hat and bag. "I hope you feel better and I know your baby will be just beautiful."

Philip, more haggard than when Sarah Beth first saw him that night, showed her and Frank to the door. As the doctor instructed Philip to call if his wife's condition worsened, relief overwhelmed Sarah Beth. *What a sweet dear he is,* she thought looking at Frank. *Too absorbed in his patient to see anything strange in Philip's behavior, save that of a distraught husband.*

In the carriage, Frank said, "Thank you for not taking insult when Mrs. Anderson objected to you helping me."

"I suppose she's entitled to her opinion, though I'm sure it comes from her being taught that women are somehow unworthy–."

"There are two sides to that." Frank placed the galvanometer on the seat next to him. "Some women refuse to be treated by male doctors. Several I know have died for want of medical treatment. That attitude comes from their upbringing, too. Curious, is it not?" he observed.

For the rest of the ride home, Frank and Sarah Beth enjoyed a companionable silence, both of them exhausted and elated. The exciting, shared experience of saving Maggie Anderson from a life-threatening crisis drew them close.

But a pall hovered over Sarah Beth as well. Philip Anderson's obsessive behavior frightened her. Was tonight the beginning of the end of her time with Frank Cheramie?

CHAPTER 14

AT HER WRITING DESK THE next morning, Sarah Beth began composing the letter to Philip Anderson soon after she woke. *Dear Philip*, it began in a beautiful cursive script, a blend of art and communication, *considering your behavior last night and the present needs of your wife, I believe it best if we no longer–*.

A knock at the door interrupted her and she turned the letter face down. "Who is it?"

"Annadette."

Sarah Beth opened the door and smiled. "Good morning. And what a pleasant surprise, Frances. Learning your way around?"

"Did we disturb you?" Annadette asked, seeing Sarah Beth still in her bed clothes. "It's almost eleven and I thought you would be–."

"Not at all." Sarah Beth stepped back, inviting them in. "I helped Doctor Cheramie with a patient last night and we returned rather late. With all the excitement, I couldn't fall asleep right away. I'm afraid I slept much later this morning than I planned. But do come in."

The three settled into chairs Sarah Beth had grouped by a large window overlooking the backyard and carriage house with the old slave quarters above it.

"It's so delightful having another boarder." Annadette patted Frances' hand. "I just wanted to stop by and thank you for bringing her to us. I've already told her how you help with Frank's accounts and his research.

Now I find you're his nurse, too. That's wonderful. But it makes me feel so guilty charging you rent."

"Nonsense, *Gamé*. I enjoy doing it." To Frances, Sarah Beth asked, "Did you sleep well?"

"Lots better than at that orphanage. All the girls moaning and snoring. 'Preciate you puttin' me up here, Miss Sarah Beth. Money out of your own pocket and all." Silently mouthing the words, Frances said, "I'll pay back every last cent."

Sarah Beth shook her head, smiled and mouthed back, "No, you won't."

Annadette levitated her frail body slowly out of the chair. "I'm sure you young folks have a lot to talk about, and I've a boarding house to run. Shall I have Mary bring coffee?"

Sarah Beth and Frances nodded, the older woman left and the conversation centered on Frances' move to the Cheramie's and settling in until the maid arrived.

"What will you do now?" Sarah Beth asked after her first sip, "Work? Attend school?"

"Don't rightly know yet. But don'tcha think I'm a mite old for school?" Frances asked as Mary closed the door. "I peeked in the class at Good Shepherd 'n' its nothing but little kids. Well, not exactly, I guess. Couple older girls in there, too, but they stuck out like sore thumbs."

"You'd be embarrassed?"

Frances looked down into her cup and nodded.

"So?"

"I could get me a job, maybe work in one of the stores on Canal Street."

"Then what?" Sarah Beth asked.

"Haven't thought much past that."

"Really?"

"Course I'd like to get married," Frances giggled in a very self-depreciating fashion, "but who'd marry me?"

"Any man with decent eyesight and his right mind," Sarah Beth said. "You're a beautiful young woman with great native wit. But it's more common sense than actual knowledge. That's why I think you should go to school. A man wants a wife he can hold an intelligent conversation with, one who can run his household for him. You can't do that if you don't know whether the grocer has given you the correct change."

"I guess. But–."

"I'll make a deal with you," Sarah Beth said. "You go to school and I'll help you as much as I can. That way you'll get out faster."

"I can't let you do that, too. You done so much already." Frances set her empty coffee cup on the small table next to her chair. "You saved me from that terrible man, got me into Good Shepherd, now you're paying for me to stay here. I–."

"I couldn't let you stay at the orphanage." Not wanting to tell Frances the real reason, Sarah Beth lied. "I saw how unhappy you were."

"Didn't mean to let on about it."

Sarah Beth shook her finger playfully at her young friend. "I know you tried to hide it, but I saw right through your tricks."

"Still can't let you do nothing else for me. You done enough already. 'N' you're so busy what with, ah, your, ah, work in the, ah…well, your work. Then there's everything you do 'round here, helping Dr. Cheramie and all. There's just so many hours in the day, Miss Sarah Beth. You can't go round using them up for everybody else. You got to have *some* time for ya'self."

Sarah Beth took Frances' hand. "We all have something we enjoy doing, something that gives us so much pleasure we look forward to it after our regular work is finished. Reading, sewing. You understand, don't you?"

Frances nodded.

"That's how I feel about helping Dr. Cheramie and teaching you," Sarah Beth said. "Both are things I very much enjoy doing. In the little time I have available, it would give me the greatest pleasure to lead you into the world of books, of science and mathematics and geography and all the wonders there are in this great universe, a cosmos full of incredible things, chocked full of mysteries we can solve together." She gently squeezed Frances' hand. "Would you give me that happiness, please?"

Frances smiled and nodded. "Thank you. Thank you so much. You're the most wonderful person I've ever known." She stood. "Excuse me, will ya? Still got some stuff of mine to put away."

"Frances," Sarah Beth said as the younger woman reached for the door knob. "You never did tell me why your mother brought you to the District."

The expression on Frances' face—the agony, the tears filling her eyes—all said the ordeal was still too painful for her to discuss.

"I'm sorry," Sarah Beth began, "I shouldn't have—."

"After all you done for me, you got a right to know. It's just that right now I—." Emotion closed Frances' throat.

"I'm sorry I asked. But, if one day you want to talk about it, I'm here to listen."

"Thank you." Frances closed the door gently.

Sarah Beth finished her coffee looking out at the back yard blooming in its summertime glory. Frank had used some of the money from her rent and accounting to repair the property. New paint on the out buildings and her work in the garden turned a once ramshackle, overgrown plot of a back yard into a lovely view. It pleased Sarah Beth to have helped the family she had come to love so much, and she looked forward to helping Frances, too.

Then she remembered the unpleasant duty that began the day and returned to her writing desk, sighing as she picked up the pen.

HER WEEK LEAVE FROM THE Mansion over the following day, Sarah Beth spent the first part of her last free day working on Frank's accounts, then turned to his research. The doctor's passion for scientifically determining the best cure for *phlyctenular ophthalmia* had infected her, too. How could it not when she constantly read case histories of people left sightless, or nearly so, by the disease? But something else motivated her, too; something that had nothing to do with altruism and everything to do with Frank Cheramie.

For the first time in her life, Sarah Beth felt a strange and exciting texture to her relationship with a man. From Philip Anderson and her other consorts, she wrested all she could, vengeance sealing their liaison. From Frank, she wanted nothing more than the opportunity to serve him. In a life filled with more men than wind-blown leaves in a storm, he alone called forth the goodness pent up in her withering soul; he alone among men held claim to her munificence, rather than lay heir to her malice.

But, despite her zeal to help him, summarizing Frank's research frustrated her. No treatment or combination seemed best, though the feeling that something escaped her notice nagged at her. She trudged on, hoping Frank's medical training would give him an insight she lacked.

When the afternoon became evening and the doctor's scrawl began worming its way across the pages of his journal again, Sarah Beth knew she had to get away from the treatment records for a while. With Frank out on a call, she decided to continue her investigation of the yellow fever material in the rear of the library–this time without interruption. She carefully memorized the position of each book and article to return it to its proper place, not wanting to upset Frank again. Despite his reluctance to let her into this painful part of his life, she needed to know about anything of such great importance to him.

She quickly put aside the articles already committed to her prodigious memory. Discovering new material, she browsed it, her eyes acting like camera lenses imprinting the images on her brain. Some material seemed out of place. Doctor Samuel Choppin's report on the first authenticated blood transfusions in the United States, performed at New Orleans' Charity Hospital on a cholera patient in June of 1854, intrigued her. *But how does this apply to yellow fever?* she wondered.

Her curiosity piqued, she read more, knowing Frank would not keep Choppin's article in this section of the library unless it somehow related to the disease that took his family. She soon confirmed this judgement. In a clipping from the *New Orleans Medical News and Hospital Gazette*, Sarah Beth discovered Dr. N. D. Benedict transfused a yellow fever patient, his own sister, in 1858.

For twelve days Dr. Benedict had watched the woman progress through the classic stages of the disease. On the thirteenth day she appeared to recover, but late in the afternoon relapsed. For another night and day she worsened until, as her brother wrote, "…her mortal restlessness increased, the pulse became the merest flutter…" and he estimated she had no more than four hours to live.

Benedict and the other attending physicians decided only heroic intervention would save the woman's life. Knowing people who recover from yellow fever never contract it again, Doctor Benedict theorized something in the blood of a living fever survivor might help his sister. He selected as a donor a young man who had endured the disease in 1853, recovered and now enjoyed excellent health. Through a two-inch incision, the doctors prepared the median vein of the patient's left arm to receive the transfusion. The lengthy surgery worked and the woman recovered completely, despite the difficulty in preventing the donor's blood from clotting during the procedure.

Yet other studies in Frank's collection reported mixed success with blood transfusions. Patients sometimes improved, sometimes died with no consistency of results, much the same as in Frank's *phlyctenular ophthalmia* investigation. Some authorities claimed that in many cases the transfusion itself caused the patients' death. But, throughout the 1800s, no one knew why. Current articles showed blood transfusions were still hazardous. Recipients died or not and the reason eluded medical science.

But one of Frank's articles held such promise even medically untrained Sarah Beth could see it. Karl Landsteiner wrote of his discovery, in 1900, of two agglutinogens which, after further research, might be used to match a donor's blood with that of the recipient.

Another study which seemed out of place concerned whooping cough vaccinations. Its inclusion made no sense until Sarah Beth discovered several articles on yellow fever vaccines, none of which had proven effective. Then she remembered the French report and the promise of its title. Standing on her toes to retrieve the slim pamphlet from behind a thick book, she felt someone staring at her and spun around.

Frances stood in the doorway, her cream-colored blouse accenting her dark hair and eyes.

Sarah Beth's hand went to her heart to stay its pounding. "You gave me quite a start."

"Sorry, didn't mean to. Thought if you weren't busy, well, ya said you'd teach me t' read and write and I thought, maybe, this'd be a good time. Will I read as fast as you when I get good at it?"

How long had she been standing there without me noticing, Sarah Beth wondered. "I don't think so," she replied, noting how the girl's taste in clothes had improved. "Most people read much slower than I. My eyes and mind seem to act like one of Mr. Eastman's little Kodak cameras. Only I don't have to send my head to him to have the film taken out and developed, or have new film put in." She smiled at her joke. "And my pictures aren't round like his, either. I remember things just as I see them. So, I don't actually read. I store pictures of the pages in my head and remember them. Don't ask me how because I don't know. Whenever I want to remember something, it just pops up. It's truly a blessing." Sarah Beth thought of the images from her childhood of her mother's bruised and battered face that a word or sound or smell could suddenly conjure in her mind. *At least a blessing most of the time*, she added to herself.

"Guess you're blessed in lots of ways," Frances said, still standing in the doorway.

"Whatever do you mean?"

"Takes a blind man not to see you're just about the prettiest woman ever was or will be." Frances sounded a tad jealous. "And you dress so pretty and got a mind that takes pictures and all. What else could a body want?"

A different life, Sarah Beth thought. "You'll have blessings, too. You'll learn to read and write. And we can talk more about clothes, how to walk, how to run a household, how to act, what forks to use." Sarah Beth remembered Lou Belle tutoring her in the social graces and smiled. "That was the hardest part for me. I was young and stubborn and refused to understand why eating had to be so complicated. But I learned and so will you."

"You're so good to me." Frances gushed. "You're the big sister I've always wanted, the momma–." She looked mournfully down at the large table filling the center of Frank's library. "How come you do all this for me?"

Could Sarah Beth explain? Why, cynic she thought herself to be, had she decided to make Frances' future radically different from her own? Why did she feel that she and Frances, two human motes aimlessly adrift in time, were somehow connected? Sarah Beth felt the same affinity for Frank Cheramie; yet, with him, the linkage had an altogether different weave. She knew now she loved him desperately, her bond to him stretching into the future. Her nexus with Frances came, inexplicably, from the past. Could her union with her new friend traverse some past life, or was her attachment to the young woman the same sentimentality quarried up by lost kittens and stray puppies?

"Why?" Frances asked again when Sarah Beth did not answer.

Idly winding one of her cheek curls around her finger, Sarah Beth answered, "Because those that can should."

Frances seemed satisfied. "Could we start right–. I mean, when do ya think ya might have the time?"

"What about now?"

Frances bounced on her toes and clapped her hands. "Oh! That'd be wonderful." She faced the wall of books and threw her arms open wide. "Which one of 'em first?"

"None, I'm afraid."

"Oh, but why not?" Frances asked, crestfallen, "Is there stuff in 'em I shouldn't read?"

"No." Sarah Beth found her young friend's child-like exuberance contagious and spoke with an enthusiasm that matched Frances'. "These are all medical books. Quite boring, I'm afraid. Besides, you're not ready for books yet, boring *or* otherwise. We have to start with the alphabet." When Frances seemed not to understand, Sarah Beth added, "The a-b-c's."

"Can ya at least tell me what you was reading when I come in? Never know, maybe someday I'll read up on medical stuff."

We'll work on grammar and diction, too, Sarah Beth thought, then told Frances about yellow fever.

THE REMAINDER OF MAY PASSED quickly, as did June and the first three weeks of July. Sarah Beth helped Myda with the administration of The Mansion, entertained her callers, assisted Frank with his accounts and research, and taught Frances to read, all of which increased the pace of her life to a full gallop.

Yet, the sheer velocity helped her, kept at bay the dread always lurking close by, the fear that her beloved doctor would find out the truth about her and banish her forever from his life. Frank Cheramie had become the epicenter of her universe, incessantly on the cusp of her thoughts. Even when she sold herself to other men, his lips kissed her, his hands caressed her, his arms held her. Locked in another man's embrace, she stared adoringly up into Frank Cheramie's dark, mysterious eyes and gave herself to him willingly...wantonly.

Philip Anderson's erratic behavior gave credence to Sarah Beth's morbid, irrational dread that Frank would one day soon discover the truth about her. Philip had come to The Mansion several time since receiving Sarah Beth's letter, only to be turned away, each time with more difficulty and a vow to return. *If he really wanted to destroy me, he would have told Frank about me weeks ago. No, Philip merely wants to plead his case,* she concluded and refused to see him. *He has a pregnant wife to look after.*

Sarah Beth successfully avoided any confrontation with her jilted suitor until late in July. She, Myda and their boarders had finished afternoon lunch. Sarah Beth planned to visit the Cheramies for an hour or two before her first caller and had just told Myda her plans when they heard a ruckus in the foyer. Disturbances were frequent in the District and, from time to time, some lout accidently found his way into The Mansion. Over the years Myda had learned to let Titan handle these unpleasantries. Usually, one look at the three hundred pound ebony giant and troublemakers decided they were in the wrong place. True to this strategy, the *demimonde* remained at the dining room table, conversation and dessert forgotten as they strained to hear what was happening.

At first unintelligible, the voices in the foyer became louder until Sarah Beth heard Philip Anderson yell, "I swear before God I'll do it right here if she refuses to see me!"

The door opened and Titan stepped half into the dining room. Looking back into the foyer, he said, "Don't ya try none t' come on in here. Iffen ya does, ya gonna wish ya pulled that there trigger by the time I gets finished wit' ya." Titan looked at Sarah Beth, then back into the foyer and continued glancing back and forth as he spoke. "Miz Sarah Bet'…it's that Professor fellow…He gots hisself a gun…Holdin' it to hims head…Says iffen ya don't sees him…he gonna blast hims brains all over the wall…Now, iffen ya ax me…I says let him and be shuck o' the man…He ain't nothin' but trouble…But then I gots to thinkin'…maybe *you* might feel different…What's ya wants I should do wit' him, Miz Sarah Bet'?"

Sarah Beth laid her napkin next to her dessert dish. "I'll talk to him, Ty. Thank you."

"You wants I should stay wit' ya?"

"No, thank you." Sarah Beth started through the door and paused. "But don't go too far away, either," she whispered over her shoulder.

In the foyer Sarah Beth faced a thin, haggard caricature of the man Philip Anderson had once been. Most of the sanity had escaped his bleary eyes, now set in a drawn, gaunt face. His clothes, obviously worn for days, reeked of whiskey. His cheeks had not seen a razor, his hair a brush nor his body a bath since last he dressed. Rocking unsteadily back and forth, the only unwavering aspect of the man was the revolver thrust firmly against his temple.

"Philip," Sarah Beth said with mild reproval, "put that down."

"I had to do it. It was the only way I could get to see you. I have to, you know. See you, that is. It's like a disease. I have a sickness. *Sarahbethalitus.* There's no cure. None. Not at all. Like yellow fever. And I'm dying from it. Oh, God, I'm dying from it." As Philip spoke the remaining glimmer of reason in his eyes dimmed. "So I may as well die like this. It's faster and better in its own strange way." He cocked the gun's hammer.

"I thought you would only shoot yourself if you couldn't see me, Philip. Now that you see me, you may put the gun down." Sarah Beth spoke like a school teacher to a recalcitrant six year old.

"No. Now that *you* see *me* I can kill myself!"

"Why?" Sarah Beth asked, bargaining for time.

"So you'll know what you've done."

"What have I done, Philip?" Sarah Beth kept her voice calm as she took a step forward.

"Don't! Don't come any closer. I'll do it. I swear! I really will."

Sarah Beth heard his desperation, saw the tincture of insanity in his eyes. "What if I agree to see you again, Philip?"

"How often?"

"How often would you like?" Sarah Beth asked.

"Always. Never leave my side."

"What about your wife?"

"Blast my wife!"

"And the child she carries, too, I suppose." Sarah Beth's voice began to rise. "What about your other children? Do you really want to desert them? They're so young, Philip. What will they do without their father?"

"But I need you so mu—." The whites shown all around his eyes and he smiled the smile of a lunatic. "That's it! *You* could be their mother... *You* be the momma and *I'll* be the papa" he said in a sing-song voice. "That's how it should have been, you know. They should be our children. Really, they should."

"But they're not, Philip. They'll miss their mother."

"They'll forget her. In a matter of days. No, in hours. And we'll be together. All of us. Forever."

"All right, Philip, if that's what you want."

He looked at her dubiously. "You're only saying that so I'll put away this gun. You don't mean it." He took the pistol from his temple and looked at it, shaking it to make his point. "This is the only way."

Sarah Beth abandoned logic as useless on a man in Philip's condition. Before he could return the gun to his head, she took one of her derringers from the folds of her dress and pressed it to her own temple. "Then I'll kill myself first. Throughout eternity you'll know you killed me, that it was your fault."

"Wonderful." Philip's eyes glowed with a manic light, "we'll spend eternity together."

"No," she countered, "God will punish you for making me kill myself." Sarah Beth barbed her words, deliberately making them harsh, and shouted, "We'll be in separate parts of hell!"

Hers was a desperate ploy. Philip Anderson had clearly lost the capacity for rational thought. Irrationality seemed to her to be the only answer.

He began to raise his gun.

"Don't! If you kill yourself, so will I."

"No you won't, you've too much to live for." Tears filled his eyes.

"And what exactly is that?" Sarah Beth demanded. "Why would I want to live knowing I stole Maggie's husband, that I caused you to abandon your children, one not yet born. Tell me, Philip," she insisted in her most caustic tone, "what do I have to live for?"

"You'd do it, too, wouldn't you?" he said, his near-insanity giving credence to Sarah Beth's desperate ploy. "You'd kill yourself just to torture me…To think I adored you. And thought I couldn't live without you. But really I can. I could even kill you myself." He leveled the revolver at her and smiled a wicked, evil smile, squeezing his left eye closed and looking at her over the pistol's sights. Her life depended on where his shaking hand pointed the gun when he fired.

Damn! What a stupid thing to do! Sarah Beth surreptitiously slipped her left hand into the folds of her skirt in search of her other derringer.

The pistol roared, but a huge black hand had flashed from behind Philip and yanked the revolver upward just as it fired.

With the gunshot reverberating off the foyer walls, Sarah Beth felt her knees go weak.

Philip shriveled, as if his life-force had been discharged by the gun. He would have collapsed on the floor had Titan not caught him. A rag doll in giant black arms, some of his strength returned as venom. "Whore! Slut! Harlot! Trollop! Whore!" His voice trailed off as Titan carried him out the front door.

"Sarah Beth!" Myda cried from behind her ward. "Oh, dear, are you alright?" Discovering the younger woman had not been harmed, Myda's anguish turned to anger. "I've seen you do some stupid things in your life, Sarah Elizabeth LaBranche, but that one takes the cake! If Ty hadn't the presence of mind to…Well, I'd just hate to think what would have happened."

Sarah Beth held up the second derringer. "I would have been forced to shoot him."

"He shot first!" Myda led Sarah Beth to one of the small parlors where the *demimonde* entertained their guests. Shoving a glass of brandy into the younger woman's hand, she continued to fume. "Why do you continually put yourself in such jeopardy! The very first time I laid eyes on you, you were trying to kill yourself. Headstrong. Willful. Damn it, Sarah Beth, do you really want to destroy yourself? First, you condemn yourself to life in the District because of what you imagine you've done to your mother. Then you convince me to let you stay here and proceed to put me through hell! Horse races down Canal Street. Intrigues. Lovers played one against the other. Grown men with families fighting over you. I thought I'd never live through it. Then you take a room outside the District and suddenly become a lady." As Myda caught her breath she poured herself a brandy. "I've never seen such a change in a person! I thought, finally…Now this!" Myda aimed an angry finger at her protégée. "You had better get over your guilt or one day, young lady, you'll get yourself killed and have no one to blame but yourself."

"Guilt?" Sarah Beth paused with her glass halfway to her mouth. "Guilt has nothing to do with it." She took a large gulp and winced as the brandy burned its way down her throat. Clearing her voice, she said, "You know how I feel about these men after what they've done to me. I take their money and whatever knowledge they can give and that's it. I don't have feelings for any of them. And I certainly don't feel *guilty* about anything!"

"Everything you've done is because of guilt. You stayed in the District because you blame yourself for becoming exactly what your mother tried to prevent. And did you hear yourself in the foyer?" Myda demanded, her hand shaking so hard she almost sloughed the amber liquid in her glass onto the rug. "Going on about his wife and children, how you had nothing to live for if you made him desert them."

Sarah Beth rolled her eyes. "Drivel. I had to say something to make him reconsider." She sipped the brandy now, letting it soothe nerves rubbed raw by the closeness of death.

"Then why didn't you let Ty handle him in the first place?" Myda sat across from her protégée, a modicum of control coming from her glass of brandy. "Or badger him into shooting himself...Or shoot him yourself...No, Sarah Beth," the older woman shook her head, "you're playing tricks on your own mind if you don't admit you acted out of guilt."

"Aunt Myda, that's ridiculous. I was merely–." Sarah Beth thought back to the day, brief months ago, when she brought her essay on Balzac to Philip. He had been irrational then, too; jealous, possessive. How he infuriated her! After what he did this afternoon, she should feel the same way. But, strangely, she did not. What had changed? What had happened to her? All she felt now was pity for him and–.

Her memory flashed an image of Maggie Anderson writhing in her bed. No one deserved to suffer so much. What abysmal pain she endured to give her lunatic husband a child, a child he would abandon, along with her, just to–. *I am responsible for that. And God knows what else? I've ruined seven lives so far. Momma's, Jeremy's and the five Andersons, counting that poor, unborn child...No. There must be dozens, hundreds more I don't know about. I've always said I lived the life I chose, lived it well, but without any concern for how it affected others. I thought I was the only one who paid for what I'd become. But that's not true, is it? I'm like a stone skipping endlessly across an endless pond, spiraling out ripples, inundating lives I can't even imagine.*

Sarah Beth looked across the room at the woman as dear to her as her own momma. "Perhaps...Perhaps you're right, Aunt Myda. Maybe it was guilt. Maybe...maybe I did deny it because...because...."

"Because you finally realize the mistake you made staying here." Myda put her hand gently on Sarah Beth's cheek. "That motto of yours, 'Live the life I've made, live it well and the devil take the hind most,' is all hogwash, you know. False bravado. You're a sensitive, intelligent, caring woman. You can't help but see the mistake you made staying in the Dis–. Shhh, let me finish. And if you couldn't see it by yourself, then your feelings for that doctor of yours would have told you. And if not him, then that girl you've taken under your wing would have made you realize it. Can't you see how you're living your other life through her, the life you should have had, making sure she doesn't make the same mistakes you did." Myda rose from her chair and Sarah Beth followed.

"Aunt Myda, do you really think–."

"Yes, dear, I do." Myda took Sarah Beth by the arm and led her to the door. "But you've had enough excitement for one day. And enough to think about, too. Why don't you spend the evening upstairs? I'll explain to your callers when they arrive. Perhaps one or two of the other girls can fill in for you."

"I'll be all right," Sarah Beth said. "We have a business to run. I'm no shrinking violet, retiring after every little thing."

"I would hardly call attempted murder a little thing," Myda said.

"Be that as it may, I'm fine. But I don't think I'll have time to visit the Cheramies." Sarah Beth twirled one of her silky, scarlet cheek curls. "I should get them a message, though. They're expecting me and might worry when I don't arrive."

"Why not send Ty?" Myda suggested.

"I don't think so. I'd like to tell them myself." If she could not see Frank, Sarah Beth at least wanted to hear his voice. "I'll use the telephone at Tom Anderson's."

"Think about what I said, won't you?"

"I will," Sarah Beth promised.

Myda looked deep into her young friend's eyes. "Think about something else, too. You really can't be taken seriously when you hold yourself hostage." A broad smile spread across Myda's face. "That was the most ridiculous exhibition I've ever seen."

Sarah Beth laughed and shrugged. "It's all that came to mind. I didn't want to shoot him. What if the *Mascot* or the *Sunday Sun* found out?"

Sarah Beth asked, referring to the local newspapers that focused exclusively on doings in the District. "It might have gotten back to people at Tulane. Philip could have lost his job. He has a wife, two children and another on the way. I couldn't risk–."

"Doesn't that prove my point?" Myda gently prodded.

Sarah Beth looked thoughtfully at her dearest friend and played idly with the red ringlet falling down the side of her face. Could Myda be correct? Had guilt been Sarah Beth's motivation all these years?

But Myda was wrong about one thing. The most stupid thing Sarah Beth had ever done was failing to understand her paw's intent so long ago and becoming, by her own inaction, an accomplice to her momma's beatings. Sarah Beth asked herself, *If Myda's right about the guilt, maybe that's where it comes from…Or maybe because I didn't shoot my bastard paw when I had the chance.*

THE NEIGHBORHOOD TELEPHONE WAS IN Tom Anderson's office above his saloon, two blocks from The Mansion. Myda insisted Titan drive Sarah Beth in case Philip Anderson still prowled the District.

Sarah Beth returned to The Mansion twenty minutes later–blanched, eyes white-ringed with fear.

"Goodness, what's wrong?" Myda rushed to her ward, seeing the panic on the younger woman's face. "Did that horrid man–."

Sarah Beth shook her head and her wide eyes searched her mentor's face. "Worse than that, Aunt Myda, much worse. Oh, God!" As if relaying some sinister secret, Sarah Beth whispered low and hoarse, "It's in the city."

Myda eyebrows arched. "What is, dear?"

"Yellow fever!"

CHAPTER 15

"HOW THE BLASTED FEVER GOT into the city is a matter of considerable debate." Frank answered Sarah Beth's question as he measured the room in strides. "The available evidence indicates it arrived, as usual, on one of the South American fruit boats. Probably around mid-May."

The doctor, his grandmother and their two boarders sat in the downstairs front parlor of the house on Esplanade Avenue.

"What makes you say that, Dr. Cheramie?" Frances asked. "We're almost at the end of July. If it come in two months back, wouldn't somebody know before now?"

Frank stopped pacing and plopped into one of the overstuffed chairs. "We should have. By the time the Health Authorities became wary, after two or three suspicious deaths came to their attention, all dock workers or their families, it was too late. You know these Italians, clannish, secretive, crushed together in the slums of the French Quarter, illiterate in both English and their mother tongue, so poor they only seek medical help in dire emergencies. And when they do, they want their countrymen to treat them, the worst thing that could have possibly happened. Italian doctors know nothing of yellow fever." Frank picked at the chintz antimacassar on the arm of the chair. "Though the outside world did not hear of the fever until now, we suspect word-of-mouth spread the story of strange deaths through the tenements and people fled to other parts of the city, taking the disease with them. Some have surely gone to other cities. We have one foci of infection in the French Quarter and I am sure we will have others, starting, I am afraid, in the poorer sections."

"So what do we do now?" Frances asked, after a whispered conversation in which Sarah Beth explained *foci* to her. "How we stop the fomites from getting around and making everybody sick?"

"First," Frank said, looking at Frances as if she were a truant schoolgirl, "you and everyone else must forget what you think you know about yellow fever. There are no fomites! Despite what everyone thinks." He gave the doily a good plucking, then continued. "Fever patients do not exude anything that causes the contagion. One cannot contract yellow fever from these imagined motes in a patient's breathe or clothes or blown around in the wind. One contracts yellow fever from the stegomyia mosquito. To stop the fever, or at least control it, we must destroy those blasted insects, stop them from breeding."

"How?" Annadette asked.

"By immediately improving the city's sanitary conditions." Frank jumped out of the chair and began pacing again. "Many of our neighbors think those of us who can do for themselves should. I agree. The authorities will have trouble enough raising funds to screen and oil the poorer sections of the city. So, I have consented to be named Chairman of our ward's Fever Committee. I have already appointed a Finance Committee to raise funds. We will hire workmen, buy supplies, hire wagons, do the necessary to protect our section of the city. With whatever funds we have left over, we can help others."

Sarah Beth knew what fighting the fever meant. *All* standing water in the city must be eliminated. With New Orleans' many cisterns, privies and open gutters, the task would be arduous. And the old myths about the disease had to be fought, too. The fables of fomite transmission and the fever springing spontaneously from the miasma of the swamps surrounding the city had to be countered with the truth of mosquito propagation. Every responsible citizen had to do her part. Every responsible citizen had to help the man she loved overcome his demon, even if it meant risking–. "Frank, what about the poorer sections? Shouldn't someone–."

"As I said, the Health Authorities will organize–."

"Based on what priority?"

Frank stopped pacing, frowned, then shook his head. "I have no idea. Probably some notion of where the next foci will likely be, I expect. Why?"

Sarah Beth looked down at her hands folded in her lap. "I…Someone must consider…Many of the lower classes frequent…." She forced herself to say it. "Storyville." Having said the dreaded word, she rushed out the rest of her thought before anyone could interrupt her. "If Storyville becomes a foci, the fever could quickly spread to the rest of the city. Even to better class neighborhoods because the, ah, clientele are gentlemen, or some of them are…Or so I'm told. And don't you think we must–."

"That is exactly what I would expect from a person like *you*," Frank said.

Sarah Beth heard the words but not the soft, loving tone that robbed them of their harshness. *How did he find out? Philip! How long has he known?* she wondered. "W-What do you mean, Frank? I-I'm at a loss to…." *Don't deny it. That only make's it worse. Just go.* She struggled to her feet, most of the strength drained from her body.

Frank took her hands in his and helped her up. "I mean only that a person as good and decent and kind and strong as you would naturally have for her charity the worst kind of people. You *are* a very strong woman, Sarah Beth LaBranche. I have known that ever since the night we visited Professor Anderson's wife. I am not surprised to find you working among the city's most wretched and despicable characters." He beamed his admiration at her. "In fact, I admire you all the more for it."

Relief inundated Sarah Beth as she flinched inwardly from the sting of Frank's reference to "the worst kind of people."

More unexpected praise came from Annadette. "We may abhor what those people do, the life they live, and we must stop their evil from propagating, but, as Christians, we do not hate the people themselves. As you well know, Sarah Beth, Frank treats them on occasion without charge, making certain *adjustments*, shall we say, to those kinds of girls in the orphanages when he can. But still, they're human. No matter how much we despise their way of life, we have a Christian duty to help them. And never forget," she added, "in protecting them from the fever, we protect ourselves."

Sarah Beth sat heavily in her chair and looked at Frances, who had followed the exchange with great interest.

For Sarah Beth, the crisis had passed. Temporarily. Now she faced a more difficult one: Fighting mosquitos in the District without Frank finding out about her. More lies. More deceit. How could she continue duping the only man she would ever love? What choice did she have?

"What do you propose?" Frank asked.

"A-A fever committee, I suppose," Sarah Beth said. "Like the one you've formed."

"Splendid," Frank said.

"Wonderful!" Annadette exclaimed. "Just like the old days. The Cheramies were always leaders during times of crisis. I remember when the Yankees took New Orleans. Cyprian, your father and grandfather were both on the ramparts at Fort Jackson. When Farragut broke through, many of the Confederate soldiers deserted, spiking the cannons. But your father and grand–."

"Please excuse me, *Gamé*," Frank interrupted. "I've a great deal of work ahead of me. You do understand, don't you?" With a smile for Sarah Beth he hurried from the parlor.

Sarah Beth and Frances followed Frank's lead and heard Annadette exclaim as they left the room, "Well, I declare!"

SARAH BETH PUT THE LAST, long hat pin in place as she heard a gentle knock. Through the half-opened door she saw Frances standing in the hall outside her bedroom. "Come in."

"Where you fixin' to go?" Frances strolled around the room, absently running her fingertips over a glossy marble table top and lightly touching the *bric-a-brac* on it.

"To the District. There's so much to do." Looking in the mirror, Sarah Beth made a minor adjustment to the angle of her hat. "I must start organizing the Fever Committee."

"I wanna help. Can I come?"

"If you'd like. But I don't think there'll be much for you to do just now. You might want to stay here instead and practice your penmanship. It's coming along quite nicely, you know."

"Thank you," Frances said absently.

"Is there something wrong?"

"Not exactly. I was just wondering about something Miss Annadette said." Frances continued her pointless ambling around Sarah Beth's bedroom.

"What's that?"

"Well, you remember what she said about Dr. Cheramie making *adjustments* to the girls in the orphanage?"

Sarah Beth nodded.

Frances looked directly at Sarah Beth. "What did she mean by that?"

Sarah Beth looked at her young friend for a long moment, then led her to the sitting area by the window overlooking the back yard. "In order to help the world become a better place, people like Frank and *Gamé* Annadette believe they must do things that you and I may disagree with."

"Like what?"

"Well, for instance, those adjustments *Gamé* Annadette spoke of."

Frances looked at her lap, arranging her hands for sitting as Sarah Beth had taught her. When she was settled she asked, "Exactly what does she mean by *adjustments* anyhow?"

"Changes."

"What kind of changes? What's Dr. Cheramie do to the girls?"

Sarah Beth looked out into the garden. How could she explain to Frances that Frank and Gamé did what they thought best no matter how terrible it might sound? She decided to be candid. "He sterilizes them."

Frances frowned. "What's that?"

"Fixes them so they can't have babies."

"That's the most awful thing I ever heard of!" Frances gasped. "Nobody's got the right to say who can and can't have babies." More calmly she added, "Anyway, I don't think Dr. Cheramie would do nothing like that. He's too good a man."

"Frances, try to understand. Frank and his grandmother think they're doing the right thing. They're good people–."

"I know Dr. Cheramie's good, about the best man I ever met. But he wouldn't be if he took a woman's babies from her before they was even born." Frances' eyes took on a warm glow. "I don't believe Dr. Cheramie could ever do that. No sir. Not him."

"He thinks he's helping the world."

Frances shot out of her chair and yelled, "How the hell could anybody think–."

"Shhh. Keep your voice down." Sarah Beth glanced toward the door.

Frances resettled herself in the chair and visibly took control of her temper. "How can anybody, 'specially somebody wonderful as Dr. Cheramie, think taking babies that ain't even born yet could help the world?"

Sarah Beth knew the explanation would take time. She walked over to her dressing table collecting her thoughts. Removing the pins from her hat, she said, "The year 1809 was very curious. Perhaps no other year in history has given the world as many great men."

"What's that got to do with stopping people from having babies?"

"I'll get to that." Sarah Beth put her hat on her dressing table and fluffed the feathers. "Right now, consider this part of your education." Turning to Frances she said, "Remember, a husband wants a wife he can talk to. This could well be a topic of conversation." Walking to the tasseled cord hanging next to her bed, Sarah Beth asked, "Coffee?"

Frances nodded.

Sarah Beth rang for the maid. Sitting across from her young friend again, she asked, "Where was I?"

"Way back in eighteen-ought-nine, but, for the life of me, I don't know why."

"Some of the great people born that year were William Ewart Gladstone, Alfred Lord Tennyson, Edgar Allen Poe, Oliver Wendell Holmes, Elizabeth Barrett Browning, Felix Mendelssohn, Abraham Lincoln and Charles Darwin."

Frances crinkled her nose. "Ain't never heard of any of 'em but Lincoln."

"Lincoln and the man I want to tell you about, Charles Darwin, were born on the very same day that year, almost at the same time."

Mary, the Cheramie's maid, brought coffee as Sarah Beth told Frances about Darwin's voyage on the *U.S.S. Beagle* and his theory of evolution, developed during his circumnavigation and propounded in his book, *Origin of the Species.*

Completely rejecting the notion that she was descended from monkeys, Frances still wanted to know, "What's all that got to do with fixing girls so they can't have babies?"

"Darwin's theory says only the fit survive. The weak die before they have a chance to breed. People like Frank and *Gamé* accept Darwin's theory and see themselves helping along the process of natural selection." Sarah Beth took a sip of her coffee. "They believe it's their duty to insure principled people survive and the corrupt become extinct. By doing so, they see themselves as making the world a better place." Sarah

Beth held up her hand to stop Frances from interrupting. "Please don't judge them too harshly. Many, many people believe as they do. The Cheramies are very good people doing what they think is right and helping the needy as much as they can. Frank gives medical treatment to the poor even when he knows they can't pay. In her day, *Gamé* fought, and still fights, to stop young children from having to work so that they can attend school. They give money, food and clothes to the poor and help them find a place to live. Frank and *Gamé* may be Social Darwinists, you and I may disagree with some or all of what they believe, but no one can say that they have not done a great deal of good. And still do, for that matter."

"*You* don't believe in that Social whatcha-ma-call-it stuff, do you?" Frances asked. "Can't people better themselves if somebody gives 'em a chance, shows 'em how? It ain't true, is it? People ain't born what they are and can't change?"

Sarah Beth had grappled with the question often. She thought back to her early life, her momma and her brother, Jeremy. What would have happened if she had started on her odyssey to save them from her paw two minutes later? What if she had crossed that road in the dust of Inez's Breaux's carriage rather than in front of it? What would her life be like now if she had been given the chance to fully reach her potential? "No," she said slowly, sadly. "Life is mostly what a person makes of it, good or bad. They do it deliberately or by mistake, but they do it themselves all the same." *Just as I have*, she added to herself.

"What about luck?" Frances asked. "Ain't luck got a lot to do with it?"

Sarah Beth slumped a bit in her chair. "I don't know. Sometimes, years later, you still don't know if something happened to you because of good luck or bad." *What kind of luck was it that Myda and Titan found me in the alley that day?* "What is luck anyway? If a man works hard and gets rich, is he lucky or diligent? Who's to say? But," she added, pulling herself out of her melancholia and the chair at the same time, "for now we'll just have to think about that. I have a Fever Committee to organize."

Sarah Beth had her hat back on and was about to leave when Frances asked, "That's why you took me out the orphanage, ain't it? So something like that wouldn't happen to me. So I'd have a chance to make whatever life I could for myself. So somebody didn't make no *adjustments* to me."

Sarah Beth turned. With one hand resting lightly on the door frame and the other on the knob, she nodded.

As Sarah Beth walked down the hall, Frances called after her. "Still, if Dr. Cheramie thinks that way, maybe there's something to it."

Preparing to descend the stairs, Sarah Beth paused and lifted the hem of her skirt. Glancing back at Frances, she saw her young friend's tender look, the same doe-eyed expression Frances had whenever she spoke of Frank. *As far as she's concerned, he can do no wrong.* That thought led to another. *Perhaps Gamé won't be the only matchmaker in this house.*

"BUT IT'S SO UTTERLY FRUSTRATING, Frank!" Sarah Beth slammed her hand on his roll-top desk for emphasis. "Not one person believed me!"

"Not unexpected," Frank said. "We are battling ignorance as well as disease and mosquitos."

When Sarah Beth told Frank she addressed a meeting of the Society of Venus and Bacchus, the smirk he could not quite hide said, *That certainly gives new meaning to the phrase* **social aid and pleasure club**. Seeing that humor only made her madder, he had been serious ever since. "What to do now? I know." He snapped his fingers. "Dr. Kohnke's lantern slides. You get together a small group, the leaders, you know, the religious, ah, civic…The politicians! That place must be swarming with politicians. Most were sired in the Dis–. Pardon me. Pay no mind to what I just said. But can you get a group like that together? Perhaps a doctor might convince them. One armed with all the latest medical science, along with an optical presentation."

Frank, the *demimonde* and her all in the same room! Such thoughts fueled Sarah Beth's nightmares. "I-I just don't know. These people are so very different. A-Are you sure you want–."

"Nonsense, my dear." He waved away her objection. "I think they are not so very different from you and I."

Sarah Beth winced at the half truth.

"We'll do it in the front parlor," he decided.

"*Here!*"

"Of course," Frank said. "What better way to show respect for those people and win them over. We will do it as soon as you can make the arrangements. Ten, or so, of the top people. The generals and generalettes, if I might call them that. By the way, what *do* they call themselves?"

"Madams, landladies, queens. Collectively, they call themselves the *demimonde.*"

"How quaint." Frank literally translated the French. "The *little world*, the *half world.*"

Sarah Beth trembled at the thought of such a meeting. When she volunteered to fight the fever in the District, she knew the undertaking had risks. But her heart craved to helped Frank find his own stand of grace, to atone for being his family's only survivor of the '78 epidemic. *Perhaps when he knows how terrible this was for me, he'll be more forgiving.* She pushed the thought away. There would be no forgiveness. *This is the life I made, I'll live it, live it well, and the devil take the hind most. Which, in this case, will probably be me.*

SARAH BETH TWISTED THE CURL at the side of her face and wondered how she would get through the evening. Fifteen denizens of the *half world* led by Tom Anderson sat in the Cheramie's front room. Christened Thomas Christopher Anderson forty-eight years earlier, the tsar of Storyville had sprung from the New Orleans ghetto known as the Irish Channel. Drawn early to the *demimonde*, he was an accomplished newsboy, police informer and drug runner by age twelve. With his connections on both sides of the law and some shrewd investments, soon after the Board of Aldermen created Storyville, it became "Anderson County." His longtime association with whores greatly prepared him for a career in politics, and he was eventually sent to the state's biggest bordello, the Louisiana House of Representatives. Reddish-blonde hair tipped with silver, eyes bright blue and clear, a prodigious handlebar mustache neatly trimmed and waxed, Tom Anderson's presence filled the Cheramie's front parlor despite his merely average stature and build.

Attending with Anderson was his adjutant, Billy Struve, along with Josie Arlington, Lulu White, Emma Johnson, Countess Willie Piazza, Myda DuBoisblanc and several of the Tenderloin's lesser notables. *Gamé* Annadette and Frances sat in the parlor, too; the older woman out of curiosity, the younger to fill her need to be near Frank Cheramie.

Sarah Beth knew if Frank could convince Tom Anderson of the mosquito doctrine's truth, the District would cooperate. But could she watch him do it without her heart stopping? Every time someone looked at her, she feared her secret would be out.

After a few opening remarks, Frank showed the lantern slides, commenting as he began that he had borrowed them from Dr. Quitman Kohnke.

"Who's that?" someone in the back row called.

Turning like a monarch on his throne, Tom Anderson said, "Dr. Kohnke is the head of the New Orleans Board of Health. A very knowledgeable and honorable gentleman." To Frank, he asked, "If these are Dr. Kohnke's slides, I presume he agrees with you."

Frank nodded.

Tom Anderson turned to the crowd again. "I know Dr. Kohnke *personally*. Worked with him on several public health matters in the Legislature. I have great respect for the man. If he's convinced this mosquito business is true, then so am I." He turned back to Frank. "What must we do, Dr. Cheramie?"

"The most important thing is to remain calm. Most of you may remember the epidemic of '97." Frank looked at Sarah Beth and smiled. "Though some of you were only children then."

Hesitant, Sarah Beth returned his smile as she thought back to that summer and all the summers before and since, wondering if she had ever been a child.

Frank continued. "The epidemic of '97 was strange—very, very strange indeed. The fever did not even enter the city in the usual way, from the river. It came from Ocean Springs, that small resort town on the Mississippi Gulf Coast."

"How did it get there?" someone asked.

"Conjecture, of course, but the Public Health Officials from New Orleans concluded it probably came in through Ship Island, the quarantine station for Cuban refugees on the Mississippi Coast, or through Mobile. Mobile's quarantine is notoriously lax because they are trying to steal the South American steamship trade from New Orleans. We are only sure of one thing. When the summer residents of Oceans Springs discovered the fever, they came home to New Orleans and brought it with them. But that is not the point."

"What's the point?" Tom Anderson prompted.

"The differences between the Great Epidemic of '78 and the epidemic of '97. In '78 we had the most terrible outbreak of the Saffron Scourge ever to invade the United States. One hundred-twenty thousand cases, twenty-thousand deaths. Four thousand dead in New Orleans alone. It was absolutely the most terrible thing that has ever happened to this city. Then the disease abated for almost a generation. Just went away. Poof! There were sporadic cases here and there, but no epidemic. In '97 the plague was mild, but everyone panicked. Officials in New Orleans tried to keep it quiet, but how could they with the telegraph. New York knew what went on in New Orleans the day after it happened. With such tremendous communication advances, there are no secrets anymore. Here in the city there was hysteria, pandemonium.

The sick placed under house quarantine, yellow and black flags hung on their homes and seven hundred Sanitary Officers employed by the city to enforce the quarantines. But there was a great debate over taking away people's freedom to leave their homes, especially those in the family who were not sick. People snuck out of quarantine and were arrested. And, of course, those who did not have the disease favored the quarantines and did not want sick people around them. When we tried to establish a yellow fever sanatorium at the Marine Hospital on Tulane Avenue, a mob over a thousand strong stopped us. Then we tried to use the Beauregard School Building on Canal Street as a yellow fever hospital for the poor. Another mob prevented us. I was there, along with doctors from Charity Hospital and the Sisters of Charity. About midnight we evacuated the building in an attempt to placate the crowd. And a good thing, too. The mob set the school on fire and cut the hoses when the fire brigade tried to put it out."

"Are you afraid of another panic?" Anderson asked.

"Yes, but it is hard to predict exactly what will happen." Frank paced, holding a long, wooden pointer across his chest. "In '97 the plague was mild. But everyone remembered or had heard so many horrible stories about the Great Epidemic of '78, they panicked. We had mild outbreaks in '98 and '99 without panic. Who knows what will happen this time? Will there be a panic? Or worse, will people remember the mild outbreaks at the end of the century and become so apathetic they ignore this outbreak? Of one thing I am sure. We have more to fight than just the disease. We must be prepared to fight apathy, panic and ignorance. Which is why it is so important that you, the leaders of the Dis–, ah, ward be familiar with these slides. So, if I may continue."

Tom Anderson granted permission with a sovereign wave of his hand. "By all means."

Frank gave the entire presentation, including specially-prepared glass containers of wiggle tails, live mosquito larvae and pupae. His audience laughed at the antics of the insects projected on to the bed sheet hung against the wall.

"While they may seem harmless, even darling, as some of the ladies might say, they are our deadly enemy." Frank struck the enlarged larvae twitching on the sheet with his pointer. "We must protect our cisterns, our privies, our gutters and all other standing water from the female. Use wire gauze to keep her out so she cannot lay her eggs, oil standing water where she has laid them already. Oil kills the larvae."

"You said the female carries the fever from person to person, didn't you?" one of the *demimonde* asked.

Frank nodded.

"And the female of the species is more deadly than the male," another in the back of the room quoted.

Tom Anderson turned to the audience. "Hell, Queenie, we knew that already."

"What do you propose, Doctor?" The octoroon fashion plate, Countess Willie Piazza, led the group back to business.

"A committee should be formed to raise money and go about screening and oiling in, ah, your, ah, neighborhood."

Sarah Beth had cringed all during the presentation at Frank's obtuse attempts to be politic and did so again at his latest attack of diplomacy.

"Then, ladies and gentlemen," Frank continued, "when all the cisterns have been covered, when all the privy vaults and gutters have been treated, when every old barrel stave that can hold a teacup full of water has been thrown out, you must do it again. You can never rest. There must be constant re-inspection, a never-ending hunt for standing water, a continual search for victims so their homes can be fumigated and screened to keep mosquitos away from them. You must stay eternally vigilant until the threat of plague is completely passed."

"I agree with Doctor Cheramie," Tom Anderson proclaimed. "And as Chairman of this screening committee, I open for fifty dollars. Who'll call?"

"I'll see your fifty and bump it fifty," Countess Willie said, waving her two-foot, diamond-crusted cigarette holder.

"I call your raise," Anderson bellowed back. "Who else?"

Josie Arlington, flouncing her new-found refinement in the form of ostentatious charity, raised her voice, "I'll match the pot. Two hundred dollars."

"Just a minute," Frank said. "That's all very generous, but you should have someone qualified to head your committee."

Indignant, Tom Anderson demanded, "Are you saying *I'm* not qualified?"

"What I am saying, Mr. Anderson, is that someone familiar with medicine should–."

"Enough said, my dear Doctor." Tom Anderson's tone was forgiving, the hand he waved magnanimous. "Your point is well taken. I defer to you, sir."

"No. You do not understand. I have already accepted the chairmanship of one committee. Another would be too much. I could not do both jobs properly."

"Then who do you suggest?" Anderson asked.

"I was thinking of Miss LaBranche. You all know her and–."

"*I'm* not qualified but a *woman* is?" Anderson's cheeks reddened.

"I did not mean it that way. Well, perhaps I did." Frank had reached the limits of his diplomatic ability. "See here, Anderson. You must understand. Medical knowledge is important in this endeavor. Miss LaBranche has been assisting me for some time now. She is quite studied in yellow fever, having read extensively on–. And the fact that she is a woman is of no consequence. Mrs. Dr. Kohnke prepared all these wiggle-tail slides. And quite well, I might add. We each should be happy doing what we do best."

Bedlam broke out. Voices raised. Fists waved. People stood. Fingers shook. The crowd split in their opinion; the majority supporting Tom Anderson as Committee Chairman.

Sarah Beth knew there would be no screening, no money, no coopera-
tion without the Tsar of Storyville. She raised her voice above the hubbub.
"I agree with Mr. Anderson. Please. Please listen to me…Thank you…I
think Mr. Anderson should be Committee Chairman." The group settled
down. "I think his organizational abilities and vast experience qualifies
him, much more than I, to serve as Chairman. I would be happy, however,
to assist him in whatever way possible." She gave Anderson her most
enchanting smile. "That is, if he thinks it appropriate."

"Completely appropriate." Tom Anderson gave Sarah Beth a small
but courtly bow.

"If you, Mr. Anderson, raise the money," Sarah Beth said, looking
from Anderson to Frank to the crowd, "handle all the finances, arrange
for the supplies and pay the bills, I'll be happy to do the rest, which is
nothing more than giving the District a good spring cleaning. And, after
all, cleaning is surely woman's work."

Everyone laughed.

"Now that's settled, I think my able assistant and I should retire to
my office to map out plans." Tom Anderson extended a hand to Sarah
Beth.

"Just let me get my hat," she said.

The group began to leave, with "Thank yous" and "Good nights" all
around. Frank caught Sarah Beth by the elbow and steered her into a
small sitting room off the parlor. Before he could speak, Tom Anderson
entered.

"Doctor, a word in private, if I might?"

Sarah Beth started to leave.

"Not you, my dear." Anderson winked at Sarah Beth. "I would never
exclude my able and, if I may say so, beautiful assistant. I'm just concerned that Lulu and the Countess don't overhear."

"What is it?" Frank's face and tone showed his clear annoyance at the
way Anderson flirted with Sarah Beth.

"I'd like your opinion on a somewhat delicate matter, Doctor." Frank nodded and Tom Anderson continued. "Well, it's like this. There's our section of town, the District, and then there's the section for all the nigger gals behind us, sort of like the old Smokey Row used to be. Anyway, everybody knows niggers don't get Yellow Jack, so I was wondering, why spend money on Smoky Row? Mind you now, if niggers got the fever, I wouldn't be saying this."

Sarah Beth saw Frank's dark, mysterious eyes begin to smolder. She felt the same anger. Equating human suffering to money made her furious. But before she could tell Tom Anderson what she thought of him and his proposal, Frank spoke, and, surprisingly, very calmly, too.

"Mr. Anderson, what you propose would be a sensible allocation of scarce resources if your assumption was true. Coloreds and whites have the same incidence of yellow fever. The difference is morbidity."

Tom Anderson looked at the doctor askance.

"Morbidity...death rate," Frank explained. "About twenty percent of white fever victims die, whereas only one-half to three percent of coloreds die. And coloreds get much milder cases. I have seen colored laborers dig ditches suffering from the fever while a white man, flat on his back, can scarcely raise his hand. Now I have a theory about–."

Sarah Beth had often chided Frank for his infuriating habit of digressing. "Get to the point, Frank."

"The point, my dear Mr. Anderson," Frank said, smiling at Sarah Beth and their private joke, "is that a colored man who *will not* die from the fever can transmit the disease to a mosquito, which, in turn, may infect a white man who *will* die from it. In protecting the coloreds, we protect ourselves."

"Aha! Excellent point, Dr. Cheramie. Well taken. My able assistant, here, and I will take the necessary steps in Smokey Row, too...And I think it best to play down this death rate business, don't you? You know how the niggers are. Never met one who didn't favor killing off a white man or two if he got the chance. They'll get sick just to pass it on to us."

Tom Anderson put on his gloves, tapped his bowler into place and said to Sarah Beth, "See you at my office in a few minutes, Beautiful and Able Assistant."

"That was quite an impressive performance, Dr. Cheramie," Sarah Beth said, smiling her approval after Tom Anderson left. "Though I thought for a minute you might hand him his head in a box."

"Just a song from your hymn book, Miss LaBranche. 'Cleaning house is surely women's work.'" Frank smiled, then added, playfully, "Though I must say, you are very confusing. One minute you staunchly defend women's rights and the next you act like that awful man's sniveling charwoman. If I would have depreciated women like he did, I would have likely found my own head in a box."

"Politics, Frank, that and knowing how to handle men," she teased.

"Oh, and I suppose I do not require handling. You can just bully me around any way you choose."

Sarah Beth took a step toward the door. "I have to catch up with the others. And, no, Dr. Cheramie, you don't require handling, you require a leash, a whip and a chair." Impulsively, she blew him a kiss.

He pantomimed catching it and held it to his heart.

Oh, God, she thought. *Now look what I've done. I must never lead him on like that! Especially if he's to marry Frances.*

CHAPTER 16

TOM ANDERSON'S OFFICE REFLECTED THE character of the man; walls covered with raised mahogany panels, populated with soft leather sofas and chairs and a huge roll-top desk, scented with the aroma of expensive Havana cigars. Sarah Beth saw no fussy antimacassars, no chintz, no bisque statuary resting on crocheted doilies. The room was obviously the lair of a man accustomed to power and money. She took a seat near Anderson's desk, the soft light from the gasolier and shaded kerosene lamps enhancing her beauty–adding more sea-green to her eyes, picking out the highlights in her golden-red mane.

"We must be related, you and me," Tom Anderson said. "We have the same color hair. Though I must admit, mine has seen the frost more than yours." He smiled warmly. "When this fuss is over, would you consider working for me, or, perhaps, with me? I own several businesses in the District and I'm always on the lookout for good managers. I have a particular establishment in mind, a boarding house you might say, that should suit you very well."

"I'm flattered, Mr. Anderson," Sarah Beth said, knowing the strings that came along with the offer. "Might I suggest we see how well we work together on the fever project before we make further commitments to each other?"

"As a politician, my dear, I enjoy a tactful parry almost as much as a beautiful woman. When the two are combined, I find the blend irresistible."

When he smiled, the ends of his handlebar mustache moved up. "I'll remember your suggestion. Be sure of it. But now to business. What equipment will we need?"

Neither knew, so they set about oiling and screening imaginary cisterns, privies and gutters to develop a bill of materials: wire gauze, hammers, tacks, extension ladders, funnels and the like.

With the equipment decided, Tom Anderson handed her a slip of paper. "These merchants will honor your orders for supplies. The invoices will be sent to me."

"Shouldn't they come to me first to check the quantities billed against the amounts ordered and received?" Sarah Beth asked.

"Under ordinary conditions that would be good business." Tom Anderson's voice carried an undertone of oily, solicitous condescension. "But these are extraordinary times. The invoices will come to me. Simply a question of efficiency."

Sarah Beth nodded and thought, *Efficient graft.*

"How many work gangs will your spring cleaning need?" Anderson asked.

They discussed the matter and, at Anderson's suggestion, settled on four crews, an oiling gang, two cistern screening gangs and one combination house screening and fumigation gang. The latter would act as a flying squad, dispatched quickly to screen and fumigate any house where the fever was discovered. Because they had not considered fumigation when developing their list of materials, they added sulphur and the necessary fumigation equipment to their needed supplies.

"Now, where should the headquarters for this operation be?" Anderson asked.

"I've given that some thought," Sarah Beth said, "and I suggest the fire house between Emma Johnson's Studio and Willie Barrera's place. With the fire wagon out, oh, we'll need wagons, don't you think? About three, I should say."

"Capital idea about the fire house, my dear. And you may have just found one of your wagons, unless someone decides to burn down the city instead of save it." Then Anderson bellowed, "Billy!"

When his assistant, Billy Struve, stuck his head in the door, Anderson told him, "Tell the captain of the Hook and Ladder Company we'll need his fire house as a base of operations, and his fire wagon, too. If he gives you any guff, send him to me. And on your way out, send in the men I chose as foremen for the work gangs."

"*You* chose, Mr. Anderson?" Sarah Beth's eyebrows rose. "Shouldn't *I* select my own house cleaners?"

"Matters like selecting foremen require a great deal of discretion. Whether you admit it or not, this plague is part blessing in disguise."

"*That* statement certainly needs explaining," Sarah Beth replied.

"It's the work, you see," Anderson said, leaning back in his chair and folding his hands over his paunch. "I'm sure you took no notice in '97, too young, but the fever brought New Orleans to its knees. The commerce of the city was paralyzed. Shotgun quarantine. Armed mobs stopped trains from New Orleans. Railroad bridges were burned. Freight, mail, passengers, anything from New Orleans was stopped. Business fell off and there was no work for anyone. But this time it's different, you see. We've plenty of work fighting these blasted mosquitos and we must make sure–."

"That your friends get it." Sarah Beth smiled sweetly as she insulted her host. "I believe it's called patronage in polite circles. But some might not be so polite and call it cronyism."

Tom Anderson leaned farther back from his rolled-top desk and his chair squeaked. Rather than taking offense, he smiled. "You're very smart for one so young and beautiful. Are you sure you don't want to work for–."

His proposition interrupted by a knock, Anderson waved four men into his office, introducing each as they entered. The first, John Griswold, was a shaggy, treacherous-looking, grizzly bear of a man, a month or so past his last bath and shave. He lumbered into the room, gave Sarah Beth a belligerent glance and said, "Evenin', Mr. Anderson."

Next came William Ryan. A boyishly handsome young man, Sarah Beth guessed he was four or five years older than she–making him twenty-five or six. A head shorter than Griswold still put him well over six feet, with a physique that made him a fair match to stop a runaway train bare-handed. He doffed his newsboy cap, exposing unruly, tallow-colored hair, and said in a thick brogue, "Aye, and a very good evening to ya, Mr. Anderson. You, too, mum. And all the lads call me Liam. Sure and I'd be proud if the two of you would do likewise."

The third man, Athanasisos Iliolakis, tipped his hat and gave Sarah Beth a warm Mediterranean smile. Short, rotund, nondescript and middle-aged, he shook his finger at her and admonished, "You call me Ike. No Mr. Iliolakis. No Mr. T'omas. None like dat. Ike. 'Cause I like you so much from the first time I see you right now."

Anderson chuckled. "Ike, you like everybody the first time you see them."

"Yeah, dat's me." Beaming, Ike stepped a pace or two behind the other men, his hat obsequiously in hand.

When the last of the four entered the room, Sarah Beth said, "I can't work with this man, Mr. Anderson."

"Miss LaBranche, certainly you can give him a chance," Anderson said reasonably. "You're judging him on–."

"The last chance I gave him, he pulled a razor on me."

"Yeah?" Chicken Dick shouted. "Well, the bitch shot me in me leg! After she stole a little chippie I was dickerin' for." Chicken Dick glanced quickly at John Griswold, then at Tom Anderson. "I seed the chippie first and almost had the deal struck with her ma when, damn, if this bitch don't come along and stick her nose where it don't belong! Damn if I didn't pull out me–."

Tom Anderson silenced Chicken Dick with a pointed finger. "Miss LaBranche, I'll vouch for each of these men, even Chicken Dick. They're good men. Respectable men. Honest, hard working men. We have to select our foreman very carefully. Paying a man three dollars a day–."

"Three dollars a day! *THREE DOLLARS!* Are you mad?" Sarah Beth exclaimed. "The going rate in the rest of the city can't be more than seventy-five cents for foreman and four bits for laborers. If you pay foremen three dollars, I can't imagine what you're paying common workers!"

"Two dollars a day," Anderson said.

Sarah Beth gave the Tzar of Storyville an incredulous look.

"Miss LaBranche, to do this work properly we need the best craftsmen available," Anderson explained. "And we *must* pay them for the hazards they encounter. After all, they're exposing themselves to the fever for the benefit of the city. There has to be some compensation for *that.*"

"What happens when we run out of money?" Sarah Beth asked.

Anderson leaned back in his creaky chair and lit a cigar. "We raise more," he said between puffs. The smoke wafted gently over the chimney of the kerosene lamp on his desk, forming a gossamer, swirling column in the light above.

Sarah Beth realized she negotiated with a master. She also knew, to be successful, haggling had to produce something for both sides. Her adversary would know that, too, so she made her bid. "I'd sooner see the *good* men get another fifty cents a day than give a job to a weasel like him." She nodded toward Chicken Dick.

"Done!" Anderson straightened in his chair and slapped the desk top. "Sorry, Charlie. Maybe I'll have something else for you later."

"Bitch!" Chicken Dick shook his fist at Sarah Beth. "Just 'cause you're a twenty dollar lay don't mean you got gold betwixt ya legs and can do a man any way ya like! This ain't over, whore. Not by a long–."

With one huge hand, Liam grabbed Chicken Dick by the hair and lifted him to the tips of his toes. "Sure and ya won't be talking to no lady like that while I'm around." Letting go the man's hair, his fist smashed Chicken Dick in the face, sending him stumbling backwards.

Ike, the affable Greek, took a sock filled with sand from his inside coat pocket and, smiling all the while, walloped Chicken Dick on top of his head. With a dull thud, the brigand fell to his knees.

"You don't should talk to nice lady like that no more, you hear?" Ike back-handed the sock across Chicken Dick's jaw, sending him sprawling. "Talk nice to nice lady. You don't, you don't talk some any good no more." Looking at Sarah Beth, Ike smiled. "He talk nice now."

"Little rough on Charlie, weren't you two?" Anderson asked.

The Greek shrugged. "He don't talk nice."

"Sure and I'm sorry if I bloodied up ya rug on account of the likes of him, Mr. Anderson. But he's got no call goin' on like that to Miss LaBranche."

"Thank you, Ike," Sarah Beth said. "And you, too, Mr. Ryan."

"Liam, if ya please, mum." The huge Irishman stared at the floor twisting his cap in his hands. Sarah Beth's smile brightened him and he pushed his cap confidently into his back pocket.

"Billy!" Anderson bellowed. When Billy Struve came to the door, Anderson pointed to Chicken Dick Charlie's unconscious body. "Get him outta here." Then, looking at the group assembled in his office, he said, "Now we need another foreman."

Liam stepped forward quickly. "Got me a brother would make a damn fine foreman, Mr. Anderson. Sure and he could be using the work, too, with a family and all."

"I don't know." Anderson scratched his head with the hand that held his cigar. "I know you, Liam, but not this brother of yours."

"Sure and I'll back him, sir. He's a fine, good man, he is."

"We don't need any drinking men," Sarah Beth said.

"Oh, no, mum." Liam turned to her. "Us Ryans stay sober as church mice till sundown."

"But do you come to work the next morning?" she asked.

"Aye, mum. Sure and a wee dram of whiskey ain't never kept good Irishers like me and Timmy down yet."

Tom Anderson nodded to Sarah Beth to make the decision.

"Have your brother at the Hook and Ladder Company tomorrow morning. Seven sharp. Any man late for work is out of a job."

"Aye, and I'll be thanking ya kindly, mum. You, too, Mr. Anderson." Liam rushed out the door.

"He ain't mad, Miss Nice Lady," Ike said, explaining Liam's behavior as he followed after the Irishman and urged Griswold to do the same. "He just no want for you should change up you mind is all."

After the foremen left, Sarah Beth asked, "What about the workmen? Do we interview them now?"

"Miss LaBranche," Anderson said, his tone patronizing again, "I believe a foreman should always pick his workers."

"But the manager shouldn't pick her foremen," Sarah Beth said. "How quaint. Oh, and I just realized what a perceptive man you are, Mr. Anderson. You knew we would need four foremen before we even discussed it. Amazing." She smiled sweetly and stood to go.

Tom Anderson escorted her to the door, beaming his appreciation for this astute and ravishing young woman. "I'm indeed sorry I haven't had the pleasure of your acquaintance before. I've seen you round about the District, but–. At any rate, I look forward to working with you on this *and* future projects. By the by, it was very fortunate for us that one of your callers was a doctor so familiar with yellow fever."

"He's not a caller." Sarah Beth spoke too quickly.

"Hmmm. Then how did you come to know him?"

"A-A room. I-I've taken a room at his, ah, at his grandmother's house."

Of average height, Tom Anderson was only a few inches taller than Sarah Beth and they looked each other in the eye. "Then should I assume the good doctor doesn't know your, ah, occupation?"

"I didn't say that." Haste exposed her lie. Sarah Beth coiled one of the wispy curls framing her face around her index finger. *Damn! I've only half a brain.* She had given Tom Anderson a trump he would not hesitate to play.

CHAPTER 17

THE MORNING FOLLOWING HER MEETING with Tom Anderson found Sarah Beth and Frances in the fire house of Hook and Ladder Company No. 4 on Basin Street. By 7 a.m., they had an inventory of equipment and supplies to buy from the list of merchants Tom Anderson had given Sarah Beth the night before. She divided the purchases as equally as possible among the several businesses as she knew Anderson would want. Hating the graft and corruption that had wormed its way into Frank's noble project, she accepted it as a truth of human nature. The very same thing would be done by ward-healers around the city. There would be some volunteer groups, like Frank's, that would operate for the greater good, but, with politicians, greed greased the axle.

The workers arrived and Liam introduced Sarah Beth to his brother. A year or two older than Liam, dark-haired and quite a bit shorter, Tim Ryan had the same honest, open look as his younger brother. Sarah Beth liked them both. Each brought three men of similar ilk, and Sarah Beth decided the Irishers would be good crews, probably her best. Ike brought three Mediterranean men very much like himself and Sarah Beth predicted to Frances they would be a good crew, too.

Liam, Tim and Ike's men showed Sarah Beth the truth in the birds-of-a-feather adage. The two rogues John Griswold brought with him confirmed it.

After some discussion, Sarah Beth and her foremen settled on the work assignments. Griswold and his men would function as the oiling gang. Liam and Tim would screen cisterns. Ike's men would be the flying squad, fumigating infected houses, cleaning gutters and resupplying the other gangs as needed.

With the men off buying supplies, Sarah Beth and Frances tackled the second project scheduled for that morning, explaining to Titan and Lou Belle what had to be done in the colored section of the District. "So," Sarah Beth concluded, "I need both of you to talk to the girls in Smokey Row. The oiling and screening gangs will be there as soon as they finish here."

"But, Miz Sarah Bet', them gals don't gots t' bother none and neither do you," Titan said. "Everybody know colored folk's 'mune t' Yellow Jack."

"No, they're *not*, Ty! Please understand that," Sarah Beth pleaded. "I've read the reports. Coloreds die from the fever just like whites. Oh, please, Lou Belle, Ty, convince your people to kill the mosquitos just like the rest of us. Will you do that for me?"

"Yaz, 'um," Titan said.

"I'll try, Miz Sarah Beth," Lou Belle added, "I surely will."

For an instant Sarah Beth heard the echo of her momma in Lou Belle's answer. How long ago was it? *Several lifetimes, by now,* Sarah Beth thought. *I asked momma to make sure Jeremy knew I loved him and she said, "I'll tell him, Honey Girl. I surely will."* Briefly she pictured her momma's face. *I love you, momma. And I miss you so much.*

Frances came up from behind, her voice pulling Sarah Beth back to the present. "Here's the map you wanted."

"Put it on that table over there, please." Sarah Beth dabbed her eyes with her handkerchief. "Let's see how we can keep track of the gangs' progress."

At 10 o'clock, Sarah Beth had her first emergency. When his gang returned with supplies, Liam told Sarah Beth, "Ain't no wire gauze to be had in the whole city, mum. Sure and everybody's after buyin' it up just as fast as they can. The little we got ain't gonna stretch nowhere close to what we need for all the work to be done. Faith, if we ain't needin' a good idea, and right fast, too."

Sarah Beth fingered the curls running down the side of her face. "What can we cover cisterns with that's just as good as wire gauze?"

"Cheesecloth," Frances suggested, "a good, heavy cheesecloth. It should lay right and tack down easy enough."

Sarah Beth seized her friend's hand. "That's a wonderful idea! Liam, go to the Maginnis Mills on, on…Ohhhh! I can't think of the street now!"

"'Tain't much of a problem, mum, seeing as I knowed the place ya after."

"Good. Go to Maginnis and get us some cheesecloth."

"And how much will I be wantin', mum?"

"We were going to start with sixteen bales of wire gauze so get sixteen bolts of cloth."

"Aye. And how will I be payin' for it, mum? Maginnis ain't one of the places givin' us credit." Liam shuffled his feet, obviously not used to asking a woman for money.

Sarah Beth reached into her purse. "Here." She handed him a twenty dollar bill. "Wait, take more." She handed him another. "Be sure to get a receipt so Mr. Anderson can reimburse me." She turned and called, "Mr. Griswold."

"Yeah?"

"And you, too, Ike."

"What Ike can do for Miss Nice Lady?"

"There's no reason for your crews to wait for the Ryans. You and your men don't need screening or cheesecloth. Let's get started oiling. Ike, help Mr. Griswold's crew set out their supplies. Then start your gang on the gutters, Ike."

Sarah Beth, Frances, Griswold and Ike laid out the working schedule on a map of the District. Starting from the Hook and Ladder Company, the gangs would work back and forth from Canal Street, the western boundary of Storyville, to St. Louis Cemetery No. 1 on the east. Moving across its width, the gangs would work the District from front to back, starting at Basin Street and working toward Smokey Row. Griswold's crew would oil the cisterns and privies; Ike's gang would clean and oil the gutters; the Ryans' men would follow, covering the cisterns and re-oiling them.

Before the workmen left, Sarah Beth had Frances make up a list of the supplies and tools they took with them. If Tom Anderson was determined to pad the expenses of the operation, Sarah Beth could do nothing about it. But she could make sure no one stole their equipment. The men would check out their gear each morning and check it back in each evening. "Broken or damaged tools must be returned, along with empty oil cans and such. Anything you can't account for will be deducted from your wages. Does everyone understand?"

The men nodded and Sarah Beth sent them to work.

"Did you see how Mr. Griswold looked at you?" Frances asked Sarah Beth after the crews left.

"Yes."

"I don't think he likes you."

"That might be part of it," Sarah Beth said, "but I think he mainly doesn't like taking orders from a woman."

"What will you do?"

"Nothing right now. We'll wait and see what happens."

Sarah Beth set up double-entry ledgers on everything that could be counted: yards of cheesecloth used, feet of gutters cleaned, number of cisterns covered, cases of fever encountered, gallons of oil consumed—endless statistics.

"I want you to keep the accounts," Sarah Beth told Frances when she completed the format of the books. "It's good practice for your sums and excellent practice for a wife in keeping household accounts. Who knows," Sarah Beth said, hinting her plan to Frances for the first time, "one day you may keep the household accounts for Frank."

Frances blushed, then said, excitedly, "Do you think so?" Suddenly forlorn, she added, "No, that could never be, no matter how much I…" She sighed. "It just could never be."

Sarah Beth looked directly at her young friend. "Stranger things have happened, Frances. Remember, never say never."

Work in the fire house settled into the beginnings of a routine. Sarah Beth and Frances scribbled out innumerable lists and file folders, commandeering the wall-hooks for the firemen's clothes to hang their myriad clipboards. At noon Sarah Beth sent one of the firemen for sandwiches.

Titan and Lou Belle returned from Smokey Row at one o'clock, just as Liam, Tim and their men arrived with the cheesecloth.

"Frances, will you please enter the supplies in the ledger while I talk to Ty and Lou Belle." Sarah Beth walked over to the mismatched pair. "Can we count on your people to work with us?"

"Well, t' tell the trut', Miz Sarah Bet', it's a little bit *comme-ce, comme-ça*." Titan wiggled his hand to show a chancy outcome.

"What's wrong?" Sarah Beth asked.

Lou Belle answered for her husband. "Them colored 'hoes took lots o' talkin' 'fore they believed the fever ain't just a white man's sickness. But we's told 'em all like ya said, Miz Sarah Beth, and they finally believed it up. Then they say it's like everythin' else. Coloreds gets the last of it. If it so 'po'tant for the gals in Smokey Row t' do the screenin' and oilin' and all like that there for the fever, they axed why the white folk ain't doin' nothin' now, 'stead o' when they gets 'round to it? What me and Ty oughtta tell them, Miz Sarah Beth? We *gots* t' tell them somethin' 'cause they ain't gonna do nothin' 'bout the fever till they finds out."

Sarah Beth spun one of her cheek curls around her finger. "Tell them…Tell them…Tell them an oiling gang will start in Smokey Row tomorrow. Tell them Ty's the foreman, if that's alright with you, Titan."

"Sho' nuff, Miz Sarah Bet." Titan stood proud, to the full extent of his awesome height.

"Can you get a gang, no, two gangs to work with you, Ty?" Sarah Beth asked. "It should be easy, the money's so good. You get three dollars and fifty cents a day as foreman and your workers get two dollars and fifty cents. With pay like that, men should fall all over themselves to work for us."

As the three continued discussing their plans for Smokey Row, Sarah Beth heard an angry murmur behind her. She turned just as someone pushed the tallow-haired Irishman toward her and said, "If ya ain't after tellin' her ya'self, Liam Ryan, then I'll be doin' it meself."

"Tell me what, Mr. Ryan?" Sarah Beth asked.

"That it ain't no fair, mum." Liam staggered to a stop a few feet in front of Sarah Beth. "A white man's always paid more than a nigger. Aye. And if ya go on payin' them the same as us, well…." He turned and looked at his men, then back at Sarah Beth. "Well, we ain't gonna work for ya no more."

Sarah Beth knew the intense rivalry between the Irish and coloreds in New Orleans went back to just after the Civil War. Freed slaves worked for less than the Irish longshoremen and gradually drove the Sons of Eire from the docks. Yet, she could not believe old animosities could divide people in a time of crisis. "There's a plague to be fought, Mr. Ryan! How can you talk about quitting? And even if there were no yellow fever, you'd turn down more money for a day's work than you normally make in a week just because I agreed to pay–."

"Sure and it ain't the money, mum." Liam looked at the floor and twisted his newsboy cap. "'Tis the idea of it. Ain't no Irisher gonna work for the same wage as a nigger." He looked directly at Sarah Beth. "Aye. We've had just about enough of 'em takin' work from us. Bad enough ya usin' niggers to do Irisher work. But to pay 'em the same. No, mum. We'll not be standin' for it. So ya'll just have to be makin' up ya mind.

Pay us what's fair or ya've lost the two best screenin' gangs ya'll likely ever get."

And Tom Anderson's support, Sarah Beth thought.

Liam got backing from an unexpected source. "That there fella's right, Miz Sarah Bet," Titan said. "Coloreds don't never make the same as whites."

"Do you hear what you're saying, Ty?" Sarah Beth demanded.

"Sure and ya should be listenin' to ya own nigger, mum," Liam advised. "He knows more about this than you, and makes a lot o' sense, he does."

Sarah Beth began to protest. "But–."

Titan shook his head. "T'ings be the way they be and that's all they is to it."

"All right!" Sarah Beth threw up her hands. "It's not fair and I don't like it, but all right. The colored gangs get a dollar a day less than the white gangs. Does that make you happy, Mr. Ryan?"

Liam turned to his men. They huddled together, whispered among themselves, then nodded.

"Sure and 'tis a fine judgment ya made, mum," Liam said, "and ya'll be gettin' no more argument from us."

"So how much does we get 'xactly, Miz Sarah Bet," Titan asked.

"A dollar fifty a day for the workmen and two fifty for the foremen."

Titan's face brightened. "That sure is good pay, Miz Sarah Bet'. Thank ya kindly."

Sarah Beth shook her head and looked to the god of the fire house ceiling for patience and understanding.

OVER THE NEXT TWO DAYS, though Frank never strayed far from her thoughts, Sarah Beth saw very little of him. The demands of the mosquito war had them both laboring from before sunrise to late night. Their brief visits, mostly tired smiles and weary looks, replenished their souls with the sight of the other.

Neither had Sarah Beth found time to write her mother or meet with Tom Anderson, and she had much to discuss with him. With Frances and the work gangs settled into a rhythm, she decided the time had come to pay the Tzar of Storyville a visit. She had reached the fire house door when a carriage stopping interrupted her errand.

Willie Piazza, looking her most chic, called, "Sarah Beth, may I have a word with you?"

Sarah Beth put a gloved hand above her eyes to shield them from the glare of the morning sun. When she recognized her friend, she said, "Of course, Countess. Won't you come in?"

"The subject is somewhat delicate." Willie opened the carriage door. "Perhaps you could join me."

With Sarah Beth settled, the gig pulled off down the dusty street and Sarah Beth asked, "What can I do for you?"

Sarah Beth and the beautiful octoroon had been friends almost as long as Sarah Beth had been at the Mansion. The Countess had sealed the bond between them by giving Sarah Beth the use of her extensive library, contributing significantly to Sarah Beth's education.

"At your doctor-friend's the other night," Willie explained, "I thought we were making donations rather than an investment. Now that I understand I have a stake in this venture, I was wondering who I should discuss my share with, you or Tom?"

"Investment?" Sarah Beth asked, perplexed. "Venture? Returns? I'm afraid I haven't the foggiest notion of what you're talking about."

"You're either very good or incredibly naive," the Countess said. "We've been friends too long for you to deliberately deceive me, so I have to believe you don't know what's going on."

"I beg your pardon."

"Look, Sarah Beth." Willie spoke patiently. "Your crews are charging a dollar per crib to screen cisterns. I don't mind contributing to a worthwhile cause, but, when it turns out to be a money-maker, I want my share."

"What!"

The Countess leaned back against the padded leather backrest of the carriage seat and smiled. "Incredibly naive. You don't know anything about this, do you?"

"I most certainly do not! This is a charitable project, not a business! At least that's what it's *supposed* to be." Sarah Beth slumped a bit. "I can't believe people would corrupt such a noble effort. Why–. Never mind, I should know better. I just didn't expect it to happen now, when everyone is in so much danger." Sarah Beth looked steadily at the Queen of Hearts. "Believe me, Willie, I'll get to the bottom of this."

The Countess put her hand gently on Sarah Beth's arm. "Be careful, my dear. You don't know who's involved."

Sarah Beth covered Willie's hand with her own. "Thank you, but if Tom Anderson sanctioned this, I'll quit and expose him."

"How can I help?" the Countess asked.

"Have your driver ride down Liberty Street. I have to locate my screening gangs and find out first hand what's going on." Sarah Beth squeezed her eyes closed as if she were in pain.

"What's wrong?" the Countess asked. "Are you ill?"

"Sick at heart." Sarah Beth pinched the bridge of her nose. "I didn't expect this from Liam."

CHAPTER 18

SARAH BETH KEPT TRACK OF her crews with a map hung on the firehouse wall. When Griswold finished oiling a city block, she put a blue "X" through it and wrote the date in the same color. When Liam and Tim completed screening that square, she put a red circle around it and dated the completion. She recorded Ike's progress in oiling gutters with a green line around the perimeter of the block and a date when he finished the block.

Knowing where the crews worked, Sarah Beth instructed the Countess' driver where to go and they found screening equipment on the *banquette* several doors from Groshell's Dance Hall on the corner of Liberty and Iberville Street just as Sarah Beth expected.

"What else can I do?" the Countess asked as the carriage stopped.

"Nothing, thank you." Sarah Beth opened the carriage door. "I'll handle it from here."

The houses in the District were built close together, separated by narrow alleys and high, weathered, wooden fences. Sarah Beth went down one of these confined walkways, stepping over small piles of trash, edging around old crates and tumbled-down furniture. She found a rusted washtub canted against the fence with a small quantity of water in the bottom, filled with mosquito larvae. Tipping the water out, Sarah Beth thought, *They should be cleaning this up, too.* In the backyard, she found high weeds and more trash, but no workmen. Voices in a yard two houses to her left told her where the gang worked. She chided herself for assuming the men would be working where their equipment was. Liam had explained his methods to her. The crew placed their extra provisions ahead of where they worked and moved from yard to yard using their ladders to climb the fences separating them.

In front of the house where the screening gang worked, a large pile of trash stood neatly stacked on the sidewalk. *I should have known where to find them from this.*

Going down the alley she saw it had been cleaned thoroughly, in contrast to the first house she had inspected. *They do good work*, she thought, and became even madder at Liam for extorting money from the crib girls.

In the back yard, where the weeds had been cut and the rubbish hauled away, Sarah Beth found the screening crew on extension ladders laying cheesecloth over the top of a cistern and tacking it down. From the ground Liam supervised the work.

"Mr. Ryan," Sarah Beth called, barely containing her fury. "I'd like a word with you."

"And a good morning t' ya, mum." Liam tipped his cap. "Out inspecting the troops, are ya now?"

"Where's that brother of yours?"

"Over there." Liam pointed behind Sarah Beth. "If ya'd like, I'd be after gettin' him for ya."

The sound of hammering on the opposite side of the block told Sarah Beth the two gangs were working both sets of backyards on the square. Tim Ryan and his gang had the buildings facing Marais Street while Liam and his men worked the houses on the Liberty Street side.

"That won't be necessary." Sarah Beth assumed her most rigid posture. "What I have to say can be said to you alone. By whose authority are you charging for the screening?"

Liam looked down at the cap in his hands. "Aye. I was wonderin' meself how long it would take f' ya t' hear about that."

Sarah Beth remained severe. "Not very damn long at all, as you can see. But that doesn't answer my question. Who told you to do it?"

"Sure and ya've got it all wrong, mum." Liam ventured a quick look at Sarah Beth's angry face. "T'ain't me and Timmy. Aye. Me and him is gettin' paid more than fair for the work. We wouldn't be doin' nothin' like that."

"Then who?" Sarah Beth demanded.

Liam continued examining his newsboy cap.

"Griswold!?"

"Sure and we told him t'ain't right and, don't ya know, he told me and Timmy to mind our own damn business, he did."

"This *is* Tom Anderson's doing!" Sarah Beth balled her hands into fists. "I should have known he was up to no good when he wanted to hire that weasel, Chicken Dick!"

"Faith, mum, keep ya voice down." Liam leaned close to Sarah Beth. "And ya got that all wrong, too. I don't think Mr. Anderson knows nothin' about it either, leastwise not unless he heard it 'round, like you."

"I'm truly sorry for accusing you and your brother wrongly, Mr. Ryan," Sarah Beth began, then became angry again. "But how could you let that scoundrel extort money for what we're doing? Why didn't you tell me? It's terrible…It's…It's just wrong!"

"Aye, Miss. Wrong is one thing. Bein' a stool pigeon is somethin' else again."

"So you'd let Griswold–."

"Me and Timmy figured ya'd come to it soon enough. Just like ya done."

Sarah Beth clenched her teeth. "When I find Griswold–."

"I expect he's oiling down in Eclipse Alley, behind St. Louis Number One," Liam volunteered.

"Yes, I know. Thank you." Sarah Beth turned to leave.

"Will ya be talkin' to him now?" Liam asked.

"There'll be no talking," Sarah Beth said, "I'm going to fire him."

"Sure and ya got ya big nigger with ya, too, don't ya?"

"Titan's working in Smokey Row," Sarah Beth said.

"Aye. But if I could be sayin' so, mum, a wee slip of a gal like yaself ain't no match for a hunk of man like John Griswold. And he's a mean one, too, he is. If I was you, mum, I'd be after takin' me nigger."

"Well, you're not me, Mr. Ryan, are you?" Sarah Beth turned to leave.

"Beggin' your pardon, mum, but while you're here, there's a thing or two I'd like to be talkin' to ya about."

Sarah Beth gave the handsome Irishman a wry smile and answered him in his own thick brogue. "This wouldn't be some o' ya blarney, now would it, Liam Ryan? An excuse to be keepin' me here till I calm down and reconsider your advice about Titan."

"Faith, mum, an honest Irisher like me wouldn't be doin' nothin' like that." Liam smiled, endearingly boyish. "Aye. Ya've got me confused with a Brit."

As he twisted his cap and refused to look Sarah Beth in the eye, he confirmed her guess, but she let him lead her to the cistern anyway.

"Sure and if you'll be lookin' there, where Sean's tackin' down the cheesecloth, mum." Liam pointed to the top of the cistern. "Many's the time–. See, it's after doin' it now. The head of the tack's too small to be holdin' when we pull the cloth tight. The coverin' tears and comes off the tack."

"Then we should get tacks with bigger heads."

"They don't make 'em, mum. But me and the boys been thinkin'. Aye. If we had us some heavy pasteboard squares, an inch by an inch, I'd guess. We could be puttin' the tacks through the middle and they'd be holdin' better. What do ya say to that?"

"Wouldn't that slow the work?" Sarah Beth asked.

"Aye, and we thought about that, too. Beggin' your pardon, mum, but the girls 'round here ain't doin' much but layin' about, business bein' off like it is with the plague and all. Sure and if some of 'em would be after cuttin' out the squares in their spare time and others shovin' the tacks through, why, we'd have us a supply and the work wouldn't go no slower than now."

"A very good idea, Mr. Ryan," Sarah Beth said, "ingenious, in fact. I'll see what I can do to get the girls working on it." Sarah Beth walked around the cistern, inspecting it like a general examining breastworks before a battle. "Look there, Mr. Ryan. Your men aren't bringing the cloth down far enough."

"Sure and I don't know what ya mean. We're after coverin' all the top."

"That's not enough. Here, I'll show you." Sarah Beth called to the man on the ladder, "Come down from there, please," and climbed up in his place.

Liam looked respectfully up at Sarah Beth, but Sean could not resist a peek at the small patch of stocking-covered calf that showed between Sarah Beth's high-top shoes and the hem of her dress. Liam caught the workman staring at Sarah Beth's leg and cuffed him.

"Here." Sarah Beth ran her finger down a crack in the cistern. "See how the staves have split. Mosquitos can get in through these tiny crevices, lay their eggs and all your work is for nothing. You should bring the cheesecloth down to here," she said pointing two feet from the top of the cistern.

"Aye. But ain't it a big waste o' cloth?" Liam asked.

"No." Sarah Beth climbed down the ladder. "You've got to cover every opening bigger than a sixteenth of an inch. If not, you're wasting the material and your time. The way you've done it, you've left chinks big enough for the mosquitoes to get through."

"Sure and I'm sorry for not thinkin' about that me own self. We've done many a job just like this one. What do ya say t' me sendin' Tim and his gang back t' the ones we've finished. He can add an extra band of cloth 'round the sides to cover up the holes we've missed. Aye, and re-oil them t' boot."

"I noticed most of your oiling equipment on the *banquette* a few doors down. Why?" Sarah Beth asked.

"'Cause none of it works," Liam explained. "Sure and I'm more likely t' be after pourin' oil on me own self than in the cistern with such as we got. The eaves make them big oil cans useless."

"How do you oil the cisterns then?" Sarah Beth asked.

"An old beer bottle, a wine bottle or an empty bottle of good Irisher whiskey, sacrilege though it may be."

Sarah Beth smiled her approval. "There's certainly enough of those around here." She had decided earlier that Liam and Tim would be her best workers, and the ingenious way they solved problems proved her intuition correct. She turned and walked toward the alley.

Liam trotted after her. "Ah, mum. Sure and another thing I'd like ya to be seein'. Could ya be comin' over here with me?" He pointed to the side of the house.

Sarah Beth, realizing Liam still tried to delay her, did as he asked.

As a defense against the flooding that often inundated a city on average six feet *below* sea level, New Orleanians raised their houses on brick piers. Liam bent down and pointed under the house. Sarah Beth gathered her skirt and stooped to look, too.

"See there," Liam said. "That circle o' brick work is the top of an old well. Sure and when we found this one, I sent one o' the boys back t' check some of the houses we already done. And, don't ya know, he found a lot of old wells that ain't covered and oiled. He poked around a little more and found some old cisterns inside sheds, too. Ain't none of them covered nor oiled. Aye. And one o' the girls showed him a cistern inside the house where she worked. It weren't covered, neither. Likely there's many more like that. Sure and I'm thinkin' Tim and his gang ought t' look around all the houses we done while he's addin' the cheesecloth. Him and the boys can take care of anythin' like that he finds, and add to the cisterns we done, too. In the evenin' when we come in, he can tell ya where all the hidden cisterns and wells are at. If ya mark 'em on that map o' yours, we won't be missin' 'em when we go back t' re-oil."

Sarah Beth stood and straightened her dress. "It won't do any good to cover the outside cisterns and oil the privies if the mosquitos can breed in old wells and cisterns we didn't find. This is an important discovery, Mr. Ryan. You and your brother are doing a wonderful job. I'm going to ask Mr. Anderson to give each of you a two dollar bonus." She turned to go.

"So now, I guess, you'll be after takin' yaself back to the Hook and Ladder Company to get us some tacks with pasteboard covers and spread the word about the hidden wells."

"Sure and ya'd be wrong if ya thought that, Liam Ryan." Sarah Beth gave the Irishman his blarney right back to him. "Now I'll be after takin' that no-good John Griswold off the job. Ya tacks can wait a wee bit longer."

Sarah Beth walked out the yard and down the narrow alley to the street with Liam looking after her, twisting his cap anxiously in his hands.

ECLIPSE ALLEY RAN ONE BLOCK between Liberty and Marais Streets, perpendicular to the rear wall of St. Louis Cemetery No. 1, cutting what otherwise would have been one square into two. The sidewalks in this dingy section of the District lived up to the name *banquettes*–little benches. Made of wood like pedestrian walkways from the city's Creole past, they lined both sides of the mud street from gutter to building. Sarah Beth turned into the Alley, her heels drumming on the planks, looking and listening for signs of the oiling crew.

Halfway down the street, Griswold's laugh came from a dilapidated crib-house as she passed. Following the sound, Sarah Beth stepped unobtrusively on to an oddly-canted porch that ran down the side of the house. She found the huge man in one of the cribs, his back to the door, talking to a naked woman huddled on a squalid, thin mattress. The scene evoked a remembered image of her paw hulking over her momma that flashed, unbidden, through Sarah Beth's mind.

The room's only furnishings were a small chest with one drawer missing, a chipped porcelain pitcher and bowel, a lopsided chair and the overpowering stench of stale beer and urine. White chalk had been used to decorate the bare, planked walls with crudely drawn pictures of various carnal acts.

"Pay up or spread ya legs, girlie. We take trade," Griswold said as Sarah Beth walked into the shabby stall.

"You'll do neither," she said from behind him.

When Griswold spun to face her, Sarah Beth saw Chicken Dick Charlie, who had been hidden by Griswold's bulk when she first entered into the room.

"What's he doing here?" Sarah Beth demanded, pointing at Chicken Dick.

"Him? He works f' me," Griswold sneered. "What's it t' ya?"

Sarah Beth looked from one man to the other. "Griswold, you're fired."

"Ha! I don't works for *you*, chippie, I works for Tom Anderson. He's the only one can fire me. So you just skedaddle back to the firehouse and play like you're doing somethin' important."

"Griswold, you're fired," Sarah Beth repeated. "And if you appeal my decision to Mr. Anderson, be sure to tell him you're extorting money and sex from the people you're supposed to be helping."

"Anderson don't need to know." Griswold took a threatening step toward Sarah Beth.

Chicken Dick's straight razor flashed in his hand. "I've had me just about enough of this bitch, Johnny. We can't afford her saying nothin' to Anderson. I'm gonna carve her up in itsy, bitsy pieces. Ain't nobody gonna have the nerve t' tell Anderson nothin' after that."

The derringer appeared in Sarah Beth's hand and she aimed at Chicken Dick's head. "You have a short memory."

Griswold stepped between the gun and his confederate. "That little pea shooter don't scare me none, chippie. And I got me a better idea,

Chicken Dick. Ya said back at Anderson's place the bitch thinks she's got gold betwixt her legs. What say we each sink a shaft and find out?" Griswold chuckled and took another step toward Sarah Beth.

She cocked the derringer.

"Told ya that don't scare me none, chippie."

"Perhaps this will." Sarah Beth aimed the small gun at the huge man's crotch.

Griswold covered himself with two hands as big as hams and continued to inch toward her.

"How about your right eye?" Sarah Beth asked as she aimed.

"Don't worry, Johnny," Chicken Dick said, hiding behind his enormous co-conspirator. "She shot me a'fore and said them little guns don't shoot straight. She'll never hit your eye. Go on, Johnny-boy, get her."

Sarah Beth backed toward the door. "Brave friend you've got there, Griswold." She reached into the folds of her dress for her other derringer, realizing she should have taken Liam's advice and brought Titan.

Before she could draw the other gun, Chicken Dick pushed Griswold into her and slashed at her from around the big man's chest. Griswold grabbed her gun. Sarah Beth fired harmlessly into the air, but close enough to powder-burn Griswold's eyes.

Roaring in pain, Griswold's momentum pushed him against Sarah Beth and the two tumbled out of the door with Chicken Dick, still slashing, close behind. The razor sliced the bodice of Sarah Beth's dress, barely missing flesh and bone. Griswold rubbed his eyes and cursed as his huge body pressed Sarah Beth hard against the porch's rickety railing.

"Look out, Johnny," Chicken Dick yelled as he tried to hold two men at bay with his razor. A lead pipe found Chicken Dick's shoulder and he screamed, dropping his weapon. Then the pipe hit him in the jaw, spraying blood on Sarah Beth's face and clothes.

A large timber crashed down on Griswold's head and he fell against Sarah Beth, pressing her so hard against the porch railing she thought her spine would snap. Someone yanked Griswold away and a powerful hand grabbed Sarah Beth's arm, pulling her from the melee.

Sarah Beth suddenly found herself looking up at Liam Ryan's smiling face, then at John Griswold's fist as it pounded the smile away.

The Irishman staggered backwards. Finding his balance, he charged with his head down, slamming his adversary against the wall. Liam threw his head up and hit Griswold's jaw so hard his teeth collided loudly. Liam shot a left hook to the side of Griswold's face, a right cross and another left. Griswold's guard faltered and Liam pounded his midsection, each powerful uppercut picking Griswold off his feet. The next mighty right to Griswold's jaw dropped him to his knees, the one following sprawled him on the floor.

Liam, breathing hard and staggering a bit, walked up to Sarah Beth. "Now wouldn't ya say a few Irisher lads is as good as a big nigger any day?"

Sarah Beth could only stare at him.

Liam turned to his brother and waved his hand at Griswold and Chicken Dick. "What about them two, lad? Will they be up t' mischief any time soon?"

"Not hardly, little brother." Tim stood over Chicken Dick brandishing the lead pipe he used earlier.

Liam bent down and picked up Griswold's head by the hair. "Wake up, man." When there was no answer, Liam shook Griswold's head. "Can ya hear me, man?"

Griswold still said nothing, so Liam slammed his face into the porch's wooden floorboards a few times. "Can ya hear me yet, man?"

Griswold opened his eyes and moaned.

"If you can hear me, man, say somethin'." Liam let go of the man's hair. Griswold's head stayed up and he croaked, "Yeah."

"Sure and ya best be listenin' to me now, John Griswold, and payin' me mind, too. And ya friend over there with ya. Can ya still hear me?" When Griswold nodded, Liam continued. "Mind yaself, man, 'tis over.

Do ya understand what I'm sayin'? 'Tis over and done. You and ya friend, there, best be gettin' any idea o' revenge against this lady out from ya heads. And ya best be knowin' that if anythin' happens to her, anythin' a'tall, ya'll be after findin' ya nuts stuffed up your nose."

Griswold nodded, then his eyes rolled back and he passed out.

Liam stood up and said to Sarah Beth, "Beggin' ya pardon, mum, but, with a man the likes o' him, I've got t' be choosin' me words careful." He looked at Tim and the other men he had brought with him from the oiling gang. "Pack 'em up, lads, and go dump 'em somewhere."

Sarah Beth's wits had returned and she asked, "Do they still have the money they stole?"

Liam checked Griswold and Chicken Dick's pockets. From each he took a thick roll of bills. Handing the cash to Sarah Beth he said, "Enough to choke a horse or two, mum."

Sarah Beth pushed the money back to Liam. "Please return it to the people they stole it from, Mr. Ryan."

"Aye. And ya'd trust me t' do that now, would ya? Thank ya, mum." Liam looked at Sarah Beth's dress and quickly turned his head. "Cover yaself, mum," he said and waved his hand in front of her chest.

Sarah Beth look down and saw the gash the razor had made in her dress and chemise, exposing part of her breast. She pulled the rip closed. "I'm repaired now, Mr. Ryan. Thank you"

"Oh, no, mum." Liam took off his shirt. "Ya can't be goin' 'round like that. Here, use this."

As she buttoned his shirt around her, Sarah Beth studied the Irishman: strong arms, muscular shoulders, a powerful chest that tapered to a small waist, tallow hair and boyish good looks. *A very, very attractive man,* she thought and imagined him with Frances. *No, Frances needs someone more like Frank. And Frank needs someone like her, or, at least, someone like she'll become. Still, this Irishman is quite attractive. And a gentleman, too, even with a woman like me. He'll be a catch for someone.* "All covered up now, Mr. Ryan. You can turn around."

When he did, Sarah Beth noticed a dribble of blood running from the corner of his mouth. She took a handkerchief from her sleeve and dabbed his lip.

"No need t' dirty such pretty lace on the likes o' me." Liam reached up and took Sarah Beth's hand.

"It's the least I can do for the man who rescued me."

"A damsel in distress, eh, mum?" Liam's broad smile showed almost perfect white teeth.

"Most of the time, this damsel's distress seems to be self-inflicted," Sarah Beth quipped.

Liam became serious and Sarah Beth noticed a flush building from his neck onto his cheeks.

"Sure and there's somethin' I like to be askin' ya, mum."

"Yes."

"Well, mum, ya see it's like this, I, ah…Since that night when I first seen ya in Mr. Anderson's office I been wantin' to ask ya. And, well, there ain't no other way t' say it but straight out, so here goes. Mum, I'd like your permission t' come by." Liam seemed out of breath when he finished talking.

Sarah Beth took her hand from his and continued wiping the blood from his mouth. "Of course, Mr. Ryan. We can arrange a time for you to call at the Mansion."

"Oh, no, mum, I didn't mean *that*. I meant a sit-in-the-parlor-and-talk kinda keepin' company. Later on, in a month or two maybe, if ya've a mind, I could rent us a buggy and we'd go on a picnic or some such."

The appalling New Orleans' summer heat and the exertion of the fight caused streams of sweat to run down Liam's face, which Sarah Beth began gently wiping away. "Mr. Ryan, am I to understand you're asking permission to court me?"

"Oh, no, mum. 'Tis too soon, though it could come t' that later on."

Sarah Beth wiped his brow. "Do you know what I am, Mr. Ryan?"

"*What* ya are ain't near as important as *who* ya are. A man'd have t' be deaf, dumb and blind not t' see you're a strong and good woman with a streak of kindness in ya that runs from the top of ya head to the soles of ya feet. Why else would ya be comin' after the likes of John Griswold by yaself? And what for, I'm askin'? 'Cause he ain't done right by women who'd pay his price in trade as soon as look at 'im? No, mum. 'Tis 'cause what he done ain't right no matter who he done it to. Aye. What a woman ya are! One I'd like to be keepin' company with."

Sarah Beth had seen the look in Liam's eyes often in the past, but only after a man had discovered the ecstasy of her boudoir. But, while similar, Liam's look was different, too, lacking the carnal cast of the other men who wanted to possess her.

What a tempting offer from such a tempting man, she thought. *Will I ever find another one who knows my past and still accepts me?* Liam's interest gave her a brief, faint ray of hope. *Perhaps Frank, too, could forgive–. No, not prim and proper Frank.*

Sarah Beth's thoughts of Frank decided Liam's fate. In fairness, knowing how the Irishman felt about her, Sarah Beth could not agree to Liam's proposal when Frank would always own her heart. Surprisingly, the decision saddened her. *Of course I'm bound to have a certain fondness for him. After all, he did save my life.*

"Mr. Ryan–."

Liam put his fingers on Sarah Beth's lips. "No need to say it, mum. Ya eyes spoke for ya." He took the handkerchief from her hand. "If ya don't mind, though, I'd be after keepin' this for me own self."

"Why?"

"I rescued a damsel in distress. Aye. That makes me a knight and everybody knows a knight must have a token of his lady fair." Liam folded the handkerchief into a neat square and put it in his pants' pocket.

"Mr. Ryan, I'd feel dishonest if I gave you the impression you have anything more than my gratitude."

"Well said, mum, and I understand. But I know, too, many's the lass who's had a change of heart when it comes t' matters such as this. So don't be surprised if the day comes when I'm askin' ya again."

Sarah Beth walked to the porch railing. "You won't forget to return the money, will you?"

"Aye, mum. And if there's any left over 'cause I can't find the lass it's owing to, it'll find it's way t' the poor box in St. Patrick's Church."

"Thank you."

Liam tipped his cap and strode off down the porch.

Entwining the curl next to her cheek around her fingers, Sarah Beth waited until he had almost reached the street before looking after him. Ignoring the wretched summer heat, she pulled his shirt close around her and found it very comforting. Despite her overpowering love for Frank, she could not help but feel a bit saddened as she watched the massive back of the splendid Celtic giant disappear. *He'll certainly be quite a catch for somebody.*

CHAPTER 19

AT THE MANSION, SARAH BETH changed the dress Chicken Dick slashed and set out on the errand she had originally intended earlier that morning.

"Do come in and have a seat, my dear," Tom Anderson said when Billy Struve, Anderson's lieutenant, led her into the politician's lair. "Something to drink? Coffee? Brandy, perhaps?"

"No, thank you," she said.

"You know, I've been meaning to pay you a little visit," Anderson said, "but there's so much work. So, tell me, how goes our little war?"

Anderson's welcome seemed overly gracious to Sarah Beth, honeyed to cover some deceit. "Those of us actually doing the fighting are quite busy, too."

"There now, don't be so cross." Anderson lit a large cigar, puffing on it until the tip glowed bright red. "Wars have to be financed, my dear. The men who raised money for the Confederacy played a role just as important as our brave fighting boys. Look how well I've done, too." He pointed to several rows of mason jars filling his roll-top desk. "We have these collection boxes in every establishment in the District. And look what else. I've made arrangements with the Mayor to get all of the Board of Health advisories." He thumped a stack of papers on a table next to his desk. "We give these out at the Anderson and the Arlington. I'm going to make sure all the establishments in the District give them out, too. Free. It's our duty to make sure everyone knows how to fend off the great tragedy threatening our wonderful city."

Sarah Beth nodded.

"Oh, and look here. These are being worn everywhere." He handed her a lapel button, similar to the kind worn during political campaigns. In the middle was the picture of a mosquito and around the edges the legend, *My cisterns are all right. How are yours?* "We're giving these out at all my establishments, as well as a free drink, to anyone who can proved he's screened his cisterns." Anderson smiled roguishly. "I wonder what else could be free in return for a man screening his cistern?"

Sarah Beth was not even mildly amused, and the look on her face showed that fact clearly.

Anderson studied his guest through a thick haze of cigar smoke, then asked, somewhat petulant, "Well, what can I do for you?"

Not knowing what Anderson was up to, Sarah Beth decided to proceed cautiously. She handed him the bill for the cheesecloth she had bought and explained why she had done it. "I didn't know if we have *arrangements* with any of the cloth factories. We'll be needing more, so if you tell me where I should get it–."

"Of course." Anderson reached into the desk's lowest side drawer, took out a metal box, counted out some bills and handed them to Sarah Beth. Pointing to the mason jars and answering the question in her eyes, he said, "That hasn't been counted yet. I'll give you the name of a cheesecloth supplier as soon as the proper agreement has been reached."

After counting her reimbursement, Sarah Beth said, "You've given me too much."

"How so?"

"The bill was thirty-three dollars. You gave me thirty-six dollars and thirty cents."

"Your purchasing commission." Anderson smiled.

"Oh. I see." Sarah Beth put the extra money in one of the mason jars.

"You don't like me, do you?" Anderson asked.

"I never said–."

"Some things don't have to be spoken," Anderson replied. "Your attitude says it all."

"I find it hard to hide my distaste for adding *commissions* on the material and supplies we buy to rid the city of the plague," Sarah Beth snapped. "I also find it hard to be gracious when you insist on hiring men for political reasons."

"What *else* have you to report?" came Anderson's curt demand.

Sarah Beth straightened her skirt, hat and gloves as a means of controlling her temper. She wanted to be composed when she discussed the Griswold incident. Before she could continue, someone knocked on Anderson's office door and opened it.

"Boss, I need you out here," Billy Struve, Anderson's assistant, said.

"Not now, Billy," Anderson snapped. "Can't you see I'm busy?"

"I think you'll want to come out here anyway."

Anderson stormed from his office. Billy closed the door, but not before he gave Sarah Beth an ominous look.

At first, Sarah Beth assumed Anderson would be gone only a moment. She sat in her chair fussing with her clothes and trying to prepare herself for the ordeal of telling Anderson about Griswold and Chicken Dick. When the minutes dragged by and Anderson did not return, she walked to the window.

Fate had made her an aficionado of window screening and she examined Anderson's, made from fine bronze wire and very expensive. The usual wire gauze rotted very quickly, which is why Sarah Beth believed cheesecloth, or a good ducking material, made better cistern covers. *Only the best for Tom Anderson,* she thought as she fingered the window screening. *I wonder if momma ever bought the window screening like I suggested? Who'd put it up? Not paw. Well, maybe on sorry-day. More than likely, Jeremy did it.*

When Anderson still did not return, she strolled around his office, dawdling with the scarlet-gold curls that framed her face. Testimonials, plaques and proclamations filled the walls saying Tom Anderson was a wonderful this or an honorary that. Interspaced among the awards she found pictures of famous people, autographed with personal messages to The Tzar of Storyville. The photographs and their inscriptions proved Tom Anderson knew such august personages as John L. Sullivan and Gentleman Jim Corbett, whose famous fight took place in New Orleans in 1892; George M. Cohan; the famous minstrel, Honey Boy Evans; jockey Tod Sloan; and one of the "Immortal Trio"–Chicago Cub's first baseman Frank Chance.

Sarah Beth walked to the middle of the room and surveyed Anderson's trophies. Here was a man to be wary of, a man whose ego required four huge walls to display it.

Loud voices in the outer office caught Sarah Beth's attention. Through the thick walls she could not understand the words, but recognized Tom Anderson's booming bellow. When things quieted down again, she noticed a photograph of the Razzy Dazzy Spasm Band. She knew all the members, the only white musicians in the District, and had pointed them out to Frances the day they first met.

As Sarah Beth thought of Frances and her plans for the girl, Anderson burst into the office. "That's the last straw, woman!"

Sarah Beth had no doubt who had been in Anderson's outer office. "That's one of the reasons I came to see you. To explain–."

"You've got a *lot* of goddamn explaining to do! Hiring clerks and nigger oiling gangs. Firing men I've hand picked. What makes you think you have the right to hire or fire anyone! What makes you think you have the right to make *any* decisions whatsoever! And without even a goddamn by-your-leave!"

Sarah Beth forced herself to remain calm, glancing at the plaques and pictures on the walls and reminding herself she must play to Anderson's ego rather than fight it. "In any war, things happen in the field that must be dealt with immediately. If I run and ask your permission before I do each little thing–."

"Little thing? *Little thing!*" Anderson bellowed. "These are not little things! Hiring people. Firing them. No, these are not little things at all! They have repercussions far beyond what your poor, female brain can imagine!"

"*MY POOR FEMALE BRAIN!* I've had just about enough of you, you pompous, sanctimonious bastard!" In spite of her anger, Sarah Beth smiled at herself. *Oh, well, so much for playing to his ego.*

"Pompous? Sanctimonious? Listen here, woman!" Anderson rushed toward her.

"No! You listen to me!" Sarah Beth lunged at her nemesis.

They stood toe to toe, nose to nose, hands on hips, glaring at each other.

"I don't mind doing all the work and you getting all the credit," Sarah Beth yelled. "But if I'm to do the work, let me get it done. Otherwise, there'll be no credit to be had!"

"Oh, and I can't get rid of a few, lousy mosquitos?"

"You'd do a fantastic job if you weren't so busy lining your pockets!"

Anderson's face turned scarlet, and blue veins on his nose stood out. "Be careful, chippie! Your doctor-friend might find out a thing or two about you!"

"If he does, you'll lose the next election, Mr. Tzar of Storyville!"

"You dare threaten me, woman! I'll–."

"It's not a threat, it's a fact." Sarah Beth forced herself to quiet down. She had to extricate herself from the latest hole her temper had dug for her. "If you tell Frank, I'll quit and you'll hire Griswold back. Then you'll get the blame."

"Blame? Blame! What blame?" The distended veins in Anderson's neck shrank a bit.

"The blame for turning a noble cause into the means for blackmail."

"What are you talking about?"

"You just spoke to Griswold, didn't you?"

"Yes."

"And he told you I fired him."

Anderson nodded.

"Did he tell you why?"

"He said there was no reason." Anderson spoke in a much more civil fashion. "You had a gang of thugs beat him up and take several hundred dollars from him. And, from the look of him, I'd say your men did a good job. He offered me a finder's fee if I got his money back."

"No reason!" Sarah Beth paused to regain control of her temper again. "No reason? He was only extorting money from the girls to cover the cisterns, or taking payment in trade. He and Chicken Dick."

Anderson looked surprised. "I told Chicken Dick–."

"That's right. But he was working with Griswold just the same. Griswold's worse at following your orders than I am."

"That son of a–." Anderson flopped into the chair in front of his desk. "I had no idea."

"Because you didn't give me a chance to explain." Sarah Beth sat on a sofa across from him. "I came just as soon as I could to tell you what happened."

"The clerks, the nigger gang, you've had plenty of time to tell me about them, but you didn't. Why should I have expected you to tell me about this?" Anderson asked quietly.

"Mr. Anderson, I've kept nothing from you. I might not have had the time to personally speak to you about the people I've hired, but I've sent you the payroll vouchers," she said. "If I were trying to hide these people from you, surely I would have found another way to pay them."

"That's true." Anderson was thoughtful for a minute. "Did you pull a gun on Griswold and have him beat up? Did you take money from him?"

"The facts are accurate, but not the slant I'm sure Griswold put on them," Sarah Beth said. "I used a gun to defend myself. Griswold is a big man and Chicken Dick had a straight razor. As for the so-called thugs, Liam Ryan and his men came to my rescue when Griswold and Charlie decided to rape me before slitting my throat. I took the money Griswold stole from the girls and gave it to Liam to return."

"That's very trusting of you. Do you think he will?"

"Yes, don't you?"

Anderson nodded. "Get word to Liam that one of his men should act as foreman for the oiling gang till I send a replacement. Now about this clerk."

"I needed help. There's a great deal of administration that goes with this job."

"I don't doubt that." Anderson found his cigar stub and lit it. "But I must be judicious in who I place in these positions."

"For political reasons, I suppose."

Anderson sat up, preparing for another argument. "Yes."

Sarah Beth decided on a different tack. "Can't some of *my* political interests be included, too?"

"What?" Anderson laughed. "You have no political interests, my dear. You don't run for office. I do. But if you did, you'd realize the folly of hiring a female clerk. Women don't vote. It's just that simple. If you were a man running for political office, you'd have realized that straight away."

"I see." Sarah Beth conjured up as much remorse as she could muster despite Anderson's patronizing attitude. *Play to his ego.* She found the voice to say, with convincing sincerity, "I *am* sorry for not seeing that beforehand. But in the press of getting the job done, I hired the best people I could find. I can't promise that it won't happen again, either. What I can promise is to be more aware of your political situation. And to seek your counsel as much as the situation allows. For that promise I would like your agreement to keep my clerk."

Tom Anderson studied Sarah Beth and spun the end of his waxed, handlebar moustache between thumb and index finger. "Agreed," he said eventually. "But you'll have to get rid of the nigger gang."

"I can't do that."

Anderson adopted a more fatherly attitude. "Miss LaBranche, though niggers can't vote, I have the entire Fourth Ward, mostly niggers, to contend with. And to do so, I have to deal with their leaders. The men you hired do not–."

"I understand, Mr. Anderson," Sarah Beth said with as much contrition as possible. "Really I do. But these men have been hired already. We need many more workers in Smokey Row. Surely your cronies–. I'm sorry, your associates will be happy with all the other jobs you can provide."

"Damn it, woman!" Anderson slapped the top of his desk. "You don't know the meaning of the word 'compromise', do you? Griswold's gone and you've got your clerk. That's it, damn it! Your niggers go!"

"Then I go, too."

Anderson walked to the window and looked out on to Basin Street, clasping and unclasping his hands behind his back. When he turned he said, "Your niggers go and you stay. Or your precious doctor finds out everything you don't want him to know."

There was no rancor in Anderson's voice, no malice, but the brutality of his words shocked Sarah Beth into silence.

"You've played your trump, Miss LaBranche," Anderson continued. "I know not to hire Griswold back, thanks to you. So you see, my dear, you *will* do what I say."

Sarah Beth stared vacantly around the room. Then, she shook her head and gathered up her purse. "I'll not fire them and I'll not work on the fever project if you do. Good day."

"Good Lord, woman! That's ridiculous! Surely your doctor means more to you than a bunch of no account–."

"That's not the point." Sarah Beth stood next to the sofa with her back to Anderson, forbidding herself to turn and face him. She spoke slowly, with great effort–the sorrow her words would bring shredding her soul. "Don't get me wrong. Titan is very special to me. A good friend. But that's not why I won't fire him. You won't understand this, but I *can't* fire him. I may be only a whore to you, but I gave my word."

"You don't think very much of me at all, do you, Miss LaBranche? Besides pompous and sanctimonious, what other words would you use to describe me? Scoundrel? Profiteer?"

Sarah Beth did not answer.

"But you and I are very much alike, you know. We both whore for a living. And, despite our whoring, we're both true to our word. I've lost considerable sums of money because I gave my word to someone. And you, you're willing to lose your precious doctor because you gave your word to a nigger. That makes us very much alike, doesn't it?"

"I suppose." Sarah Beth choked out the words.

"So, quite by accident I'm sure, you've hit on the only argument that could make me change my mind." Anderson spoke softly. "Keep your niggers, my dear. I'll get some of my own."

Sarah Beth held on to the back of the sofa for support and nodded her thanks, not turning to face him, refusing to let him see her cry, not even tears of joy.

WHEN THE WORK GANGS REPORTED back to the fire house at six o'clock the following Saturday evening, Frances and Sarah Beth checked in their tools and equipment. With almost everyone gone, Liam, the unofficial lead foreman, took Sarah Beth to the side.

"Beggin' your pardon, mum, but there's somethin' I think ya ought to be seein'."

"My God, what now?" Sarah Beth demanded.

"Oh, no, mum. T'ain't like that a'tall. Ike found somethin' I think ya should know."

"I'm sorry, Mr. Ryan," Sarah Beth said. "It's been a long week and I'm exhausted."

"Aye. No need to go apologizin', mum. We all need a hot bath, a bottle of good Irisher whiskey and a night's sleep."

Ike joined them. "Hello, Miss Nice Lady. Liam tell you?"

"Tell me what?"

"Cleaning gutters this week, I make a find-out."

"And?" Sarah Beth asked.

"Come, we show you." Ike picked up two five-gallon oil cans and told Liam, "Take that small-little can and the broom."

With Ike leading her and Liam out of the fire house, Sarah Beth called Frances to join them.

The Greek guided the little band across Conti Street and put his cans down next to the whitewashed stucco wall of St. Louis Cemetery No. 1. "Here. Look." Ike pointed to the gutter, littered with trash and several puddles created by garbage dams. Mosquito larvae covered the surface of each small reservoir. "Now I show you. We all the time take away the trash like you say, but, for you to see, I leave it this time. Okay?"

Sarah Beth nodded.

"First, we make water go way." Ike swept a small pool into the dusty street. "See, no more water." He bent down and scraped the gutter with his hands until he found dry mud. Looking at Sarah Beth, he raised a dirty hand and wormed his fingers. "No more wiggly tail, neither. But tomorrow she rains." He stood and dusted himself off. "Always tomorrow she rains," Ike said, giving the standard weather forecast for New Orleans in summer. From May through September, the days were mostly the same: extremely hot with afternoon thundershowers. "And the garbage, she always comes back, too. So the puddle, she's there when momma mosquito comes buzz, buzz, buzz and make more wiggle tails. And the coal oil, she don't do no good 'cause the sun, she burn it away. So, what ya gonna do?"

Sarah Beth shrugged. "Oil the gutters again."

"Aye, mum. But maybe not. Ya best be listenin' to him."

"I worry this in my head all week till I make me an idea." Ike picked up the small can Liam had carried. "So, then, I axed a friend if he's got some little creosote and he said, 'Yes,' so I borrow me some. Now look. I mix me half creosote with another half coal oil. Now I pour it in the gutter, like this. Now it rains." Ike looked from Sarah Beth to Liam to Frances. "Wait. I need rain. And some them wiggly tails." He went through the side entrance of the cemetery, returned with two glass flower vases from one of the crypts and poured the contents of the vases into the gutter. "See, Miss Nice Lady. Ike got him rain and wiggle tails all together. But wait." A sheen of oil covered the water and the larvae fell from the surface, unable to breathe. "But, wait some more." Ike swept away the water and went back into the cemetery for more vases. He poured more larvae infested water into the gutter and the process repeated itself. "So, now you see what happen. I make a think that the creosote, she hold the coal oil and piss it out a little at a time. When the sun, she burn off the coal oil, the creosote, she piss out some more. So, I make another think and say if Miss Nice Lady get Ike some creosote then Ike can make the gutters much more better for everybody. Maybe we don't worry with them so much all the time."

"Ike," Sarah Beth exclaimed, "that's wonderful! It's so wonderful, in fact, I'm going to ask Mr. Anderson to give you a dollar bonus!"

Sarah Beth turned to Liam. "I'm glad you showed this to me. How much creosote do we need?"

"Start with two barrels and then we see," Ike suggested.

Sarah Beth and Frances started back to the Hook and Ladder Company with Ike and Liam following behind.

In the middle of Conti Street, Frances stopped and turned to Ike. "How did you know there'd be wiggle tails in the cemetery vases?"

"Them little scoundrels always be there in the summer when I visit my dead brother."

"Tomorrow, first thing," Sarah Beth said, "I want your gang to empty all the vases in that cemetery. And the cemetery at the back of the District, too, all three blocks of it. Tell the people you see in the cemetery what you're doing and why. Tell them to tell their friends. We've got to spread the word to clean up the cemeteries. Oh, and while you're emptying the vases, check for standing water in other places."

"But, mum, he ain't got the men t' do that and clean the gutters and screen the sick houses, too," Liam said.

"You're right, of course. Ike, Monday have your gang start on this cemetery in the morning. I'll talk to Mr. Anderson tomorrow about getting you some more men." Renewed by these two small discoveries, Sarah Beth imagined sharing them with Frank. No, she had a better idea.

At the fire house Liam and Ike bid Sarah Beth and Frances good evening.

When they were alone, Sarah Beth told her young friend, "I want you to tell Frank about using creosote and the larvae in the cemeteries."

"Me? Shouldn't you tell him?" Frances asked.

"Why?"

"Well, because you…He…." Frances picked up a clipboard and turned to hang it on the wall.

"Do you think there's something between the doctor and me?"

"You're in love, aren't you?"

"No, my dear, we're not." Sarah Beth did not know how badly the lie would affect her until she told it. The words caught in her throat, drove the breath from her and she held on to their work table for a moment. She had known pairing Frances and Frank would be difficult, but, until she said the words, had no idea precisely how devastating it would be.

Frances turned and said, ecstatically, "Oh, but that's wonderful!" Then, dispirited, she added, "Are you sure? I've seen the way he looks at you. He adores you."

"No, he doesn't." Sarah Beth worked strenuously to appear nonchalant. "We're just good friends. Nothing more."

"If a beau of mine looked at a *friend* the way he looks at you, I'd give them both what for."

"You're mistaken, Frances. Frank and I are…colleagues. I've helped with his accounts and research. Now we're fighting this epidemic as, ah, collaborators. There's absolutely nothing romantic between us. Besides, even if he did love me, what would he think when he found out what I was?"

"You think that would make a difference?" Frances put her hat on and adjusted the pins.

"Of course. It makes a difference to any decent man." *Except Liam.* Sarah Beth wondered why she had that thought, then dismissed it. "But what's clear, at least to me, is that *you* are in love with the good doctor."

"Me!" Frances fumbled her purse open, took out her handkerchief and blotted her cheeks. "Ah, I, ah, I don't know what you're talking about."

"Don't you, now." Sarah Beth's right eyebrow arched. "You're not fond of him?"

"Fond? Well, yes, I suppose you could say I'm fond of him." Frances lifted her chin and patted her neck.

"Fond and, perhaps, attracted to him."

"Well, perhaps a little," Frances admitted. "After all, he *is* a very handsome man. Oh, and those eyes! Sometimes, when he looks at me, I feel like I'm being pulled into–." Frances composed herself. "Yes, I suppose you might say I'm somewhat attracted to him. Who wouldn't be?"

"Fond and attracted," Sarah Beth said, "but not in love with him."

"Ohhhh! Even if I am, what good does it do me?" Frances sat heavily in a chair next to their worktable and pouted forlornly at the fire wagon. "He doesn't even know I'm alive. And what chance would I have with a man like that, anyway? He's a brilliant doctor and I'm just…just…just an ignorant nobody."

"No you're not." Sarah Beth put her hand gently on her friend's shoulder. "You've come a long way these past few months. But you're right. Frank hasn't quite noticed yet the woman you've become. That's why I want you to tell him about the creosote and the larvae in the cemetery vases."

"Will that help?" Frances appeared a little less downcast.

"Of course it will. Those are very important discoveries. Frank will tell others, which can't help but increase his reputation, and he'll have you to thank. And in the process, he'll have to notice the woman you've become."

"Humph! Woman!" Frances said, sulking again. "He thinks of me as a child. If I tell him about using creosote, I'll just be a bright child."

"Come here." Sarah Beth took her young friend's hand and led her to the fire wagon. Pointing to Frances' reflection in the bright red paint, she said, "Look at yourself. You've learned to dress and hold yourself like a refined lady. You're learning to speak like one, too. If we can just get Frank to notice how smart you are, he'll *have* to notice the rest."

"Do you really think so?" Frances gushed. "I mean, I *am* almost eighteen. Do you really think he'll notice I've become a woman? He won't think I'm too young, will he?"

"Men generally like younger women."

"Why?" Francis asked.

"Because, if they know what they're doing, young women are very active in bed."

Obviously flustered at the turn the conversation had taken, Frances stammered, "Frank's not like that. He couldn't be."

"Why not?"

"Because…Well, because he's not. He just couldn't be. And he certainly wouldn't want his wife to be so…so dirty."

"Sex is dirty?"

"Everybody knows that! Mother says holding hands with a boy makes you a whore."

"Is that why she wanted to get rid of you?"

Frances' lips formed a hard line and she turned away.

Perhaps some other time, Sarah Beth thought. *What's important now is for her to understand what the relationship between men and women should be.* "Why do you think there are whores?"

"Because most men are animals."

"No."

"Then why?" Frances snapped.

"Because men have physical needs that both sexes have been taught are bad," Sarah Beth explained patiently. "Women are not supposed to enjoy sex and, if they do, they're evil. Men are taught to take only *good* women for their wives, women who don't enjoy sex. Husbands and wives are only supposed to have sex to procreate. What happens to the men whose wives are pregnant or too old to have children? What do they do about their needs?"

"Control them," Frances said firmly.

"Try to understand, my dear, they can't. The need grows so strong sometimes it's like telling a man not to eat or breathe. And the needs of a woman can be just as strong, though both men and women have been taught those needs are a sin. So men visit the District. And the wives know their husbands go to the District. Of course, they won't admit it. And poor, confused women that they are, many are even thankful their husbands don't debase them by asking them to satisfy the need, while, at the same time, the wives suffer physical deprivation of those same needs and the guilt of having them."

"The animal lust, you mean," Frances said.

"Call it what you will. But the entire thing has been made up to keep women in their place."

Her curiosity piqued, Frances asked, "What do you mean?"

"As long as men maintain that we are the weaker sex–."

"The gentler, nobler sex, don't you mean?"

"However you say it, it comes out the same. We can't do for ourselves so we must be protected. And who's there to protect us? Men, of course. They control everything–money, property, the government. If we're so gentle and noble, why can't we vote? Why can't we run for office?"

"Because we'd become just like men," Francis suggested.

"Or is it because we'd take over? Change the world and make it a better place? Eliminate their greed and corruption?" Sarah Beth put her hands gently on her young friend's shoulders again. "It will take a very long time, Frances, but women will be freed just as the slaves were. We will take our rightful place in the world and the first battle in this revolution will be the bedroom. There's no reason we can't enjoy sex. There's nothing dirty about sharing such ecstasy with the man you love. I suspect many husbands and wives already know that, though they'd deny it if you asked them. You'd do well to learn it, too, Frances, and keep Frank in his own bed with you."

Conspiratorially, Frances hunkered close to Sarah Beth and whispered, "Is it really grand? Do you–? I shouldn't ask, should I?"

"Sometimes, with a man I'm fond of, it's wonderful. I can only imagine what it would be like with one I truly loved," Sarah Beth said wistfully.

"Tell me what I should do. To make Frank happy in bed, I mean"

"Not now."

"Oh, but why? You've taught me so much already. The most important thing in my life will be keeping Frank away from the District. Won't you help me?"

Sarah Beth linked arms with Frances and they walked toward the firehouse door. "After you and Frank are married, I'll tell you everything you need to know. Right now, we have to keep you innocent. No man wants an experienced bride on his wedding night. All you need to know now is that there is nothing to fear, nothing to be ashamed of when Frank lays next to you for the first time."

Frances hugged her friend tightly.

At the door to the Hook and Ladder Company, Sarah Beth said, "You go on ahead. I just remembered something else I need to do. I shan't be long."

"Can I help?"

"No, thank you, dear."

"Then I'll wait."

"No," Sarah Beth said too abruptly. Her voice softened. "Run along. I'll see you a bit later."

With a questioning look, Frances waved and walked down Basin Street.

After watching her young friend cross Bienville Street, Sarah Beth trudged through the thickening gloom of the empty firehouse, ignoring the laughter and piano music from Willie Barrera's parlor house next door. As the District came to life on a Saturday night, she sat alone at the cluttered work table. Giving up Frank would be the hardest thing she had ever done in her life, even more difficult than leaving her beloved mother. But she adored him too much to do otherwise.

Outside a man and woman serenaded each other with a bawdy drinking song as Sarah Beth began to sob softly.

CHAPTER 20

SARAH BETH HAD JUST RETURNED from an inspection of the District when one of the young boys the gangs used as messengers came running into the fire house.

"Miss, oh Miss, Liam needs ya real quick!"

The boy led Sarah Beth to Villere Street where she found Liam and Tim's gangs milling around smoking. Several rough looking men stood guard in front of a house with a closed landau parked in front of it.

"What's wrong, Mr. Ryan?"

Liam jerked his head toward the rogues blocking the *banquette*. "Sure and they won't be lettin' us screen the cisterns of the next few houses."

"And why not?"

The Irishman jabbed his thumb over his shoulder at the carriage. "The owner don't want none of it."

"Why?"

"Aye, and I'm sure I don't know, mum. Ya'll have t' be askin' him ya own self."

Sarah Beth stalked toward the carriage as a man in his late twenties got out.

"Are you the owner of these houses?" Sarah Beth demanded.

"No. I work for him."

"Is he in the carriage?"

The man nodded.

"I'll speak directly to him." Sarah Beth moved to step around the man, but he blocked her way.

"The owner wishes to remain anonymous. I'm empowered to speak for him."

"And your name, sir?"

"That is of no consequence," the man snapped.

"Oh, I see. Do you and your employer know what we are trying to do here?"

"Yes. Trying to enter private property without the owner's consent."

"But do you know why?" Sarah Beth asked reasonably.

"On some pretext about fighting the plague."

"Pretext? Pretext!" Sarah Beth shouted, her patience gone. "Why else would anybody want to go in there?"

"I'm sure I wouldn't know. But you don't have the owner's permission and those fellows," the young man said, pointing to the thugs lining the *banquette*, "will see his wishes are carried out."

Her adversary's arrogance made Sarah Beth even angrier. "I want to speak directly to the owner, not some third-rate messenger boy." She tried to step around the man and he roughly grabbed her arm.

"Hold on now," Liam called. "That ain't no way to be treatin' a lady."

As the Irishman came to Sarah Beth's rescue, the landlord's thugs and the oiling gangs began circling.

Sarah Beth yanked her arm away from her captor. "I'm fine, Mr. Ryan. You and your men stand down." To the young man, Sarah Beth said, deliberately striving to be civil, "Sir, all we wish to do is help the city in it's efforts to fight the fever. Surely, your employer understands our intentions are–."

"My employer understands all this mosquito business is balderdash. He owns these houses and no one, I repeat, no one, will do any reconditioning or repairs without his express permission, which he has no intention of giving."

"Why?"

"Are you too stupid to understand? These are his houses and he says no. He doesn't have to justify himself to you."

Liam now stood beside Sarah Beth clenching and unclenching his fists. She put an arresting hand on the Irishman's forearm and asked the young man, "Are you familiar with the ordinance the City Council passed a few weeks ago because of the likes of him? The law requires him to screen his cisterns."

The young man cleared his throat several times. "Ah, t-that ordinance clearly violates, ah, a man's right to control his own property. It should have never been passed and–."

"We can debate the merits of the law another day." Sarah Beth smirked as she moved in for the kill. "It passed. And several prominent men have been fined and jailed for refusing to obey it. Does your employer wish his name added to the list?"

The young man stood mutely.

"So that's it. He hides and sends some toady out to do his dirty work. Because I don't know his name or yours, you both think you can get away with this. Will I recognize him if I see him?" Sarah Beth tried to move around the young man and he blocked her path again.

Liam grabbed the man's shirtfront. "Sure and I've had me just about enough o' ya gettin' in the way, lad."

The oiling gangs and the landlord's thugs converged on each other again.

Sarah Beth quickly caught hold of the Irishman's cocked fist and glared at the landlord's hireling. She had backed down the most powerful man in Storyville and had no intention of letting some minor despot stop her. "Stand down, men," she ordered. "There's more than one way to skin this cat." To the young man she said, "Tell your employer he has a choice. Either he lets my men screen his cisterns or he does it himself. If he chooses to do it himself, my foreman will inspect the property to insure the job has been done correctly. Tell him if his cisterns are not screened by this evening, I will go to the Hall of Records tomorrow and find out who he is. Then I will file a complaint with the Board of Aldermen. He will be fined and jailed, and I will personally see to it his name appears in the newspaper." Sarah Beth used the threat most persuasive on a New Orleans blue-blood, the same tactic Josie Arlington proposed to rid the French Balls of unwanted uptown visitors. "And when the newspapers report this prominent, upright gentleman's lack of civic responsibility, they'll also be informing the entire city he owns property in the District. That should make interesting after-dinner conversation among his friends and family, don't you think?" Sarah Beth aimed her index finger at the carriage. "Now go! Tell him what I said!"

The young man hesitated.

"Go, I said." She stomped her foot for emphasis.

After conferring with the owner through the carriage window, the young man returned. "My employer wishes to know if you will assume liability for damages done to the–."

"No."

"That's unacceptable. If rain spouts are damaged, if the cistern itself is–."

"Then he can do it himself. He has until this evening." Sarah Beth walked away.

"Wait!" the young man commanded.

Sarah Beth continued walking.

"Wait...Please."

She turned.

The young man went back to the gig and conferred again with the owner. When he returned, the carriage drove away. "My employer asks that your men be careful."

"Call off your dogs." Sarah Beth waved at the thugs still standing on the sidewalk glaring at her gangs.

The young man nodded and his henchmen ambled off in twos and threes.

Feeling smug, Sarah Beth turned to her crew and smiled. With a brogue as thick and fine as Liam's, she said, "T' work with ya, lads. Time's a-wastin'."

Liam grinned at Sarah Beth and took the handkerchief she had given him from the breast pocket of his shirt. "From the look of it, mum, I'd say ya'd be needin' a knight in shinin' armor more often than not."

"Not this time," she replied.

"Maybe not, but t'was touch and go there for a while, that's for sure."

Liam returned the keepsake to his pocket and called to his men, "Ya heard the lady, lads, it's back t' work with ya." Tipping his cap to Sarah Beth, he asked, "Have ya given any more thought t' what I said about keepin' company?"

"No, Mr. Ryan, I'm afraid I haven't," Sarah Beth said softly, trying to make her rejection as gentle as possible. "And I'm afraid I never will."

Liam's smile did not waver, nor did the tender look leave his eyes. "I hope ya don't find it off-puttin' if I ask after it from time t' time. Just t' make sure ya ain't had a change o' heart."

Sarah Beth said nothing and, as the tallow-haired giant returned to work, thought, *What a temptation he is.* But over the years, cynicism had armored her against all tender feelings and only one man had vanquished her defenses. She remained convinced no one else ever could.

SARAH BETH'S SATISFACTION WITH HER victory over the landlord lasted for all of two blocks as she walked back to the Hook and Ladder Company. Passing a crib-house, she heard a feeble cry for help and followed the sound into a seemingly deserted building. The bleating came again as she entered what once was a front parlor. A web-work of ropes, overhung with old blankets gone to rag, had been used to subdivide the room into stalls. Mattress ticking, broken crockery and furniture fit only for kindling littered the floor. The thick, musty air smelled of sweat, spent passion and pestilence.

At the back of the house, in the last of four rooms, Sarah Beth found the remains of a bed occupied by a limp female form clad only in an open chippie–the loose-fitting, short kimono favored by the crib girls.

"Ya'll jus' gotta help me," the woman said, her face contorted in pain. Thick, damp hair lay matted on her face and her skin had a decidedly yellow cast. Black slime ran in rivulets on the floor, puddled on the bare mattress and spattered the woman herself.

"How long have you been here?" Sarah Beth asked, stepping gingerly around the muck on the floor to reach the bed.

"A day, a month, a year. Shit, who the hell knows?"

Sarah Beth brushed the woman's hair from her face. "You!"

"I know ya'll?"

"No. No, I'm sure you don't." Sarah Beth's tone was more virulent than the contagion overwhelming Inez Breaux. "But you should. You ruined me, you bitch. You ruined me and don't even remember who I am."

"W-Whoever ya'll are, ya'll gotta help me. I'm dying. Can't ya'll see that. I'm sorry for whatever I done. I'll make it up to ya'll when I get back on my feet. Anything ya'll want. I promise. Just help me. Please." Inez's infirmed hand reached out.

Sarah Beth stepped backwards before Inez could touch her. "Help *you. NEVER!*"

Awash in a malevolent rage, Sarah Beth stumbled from the room, down the dank hall and into the bright sunshine. Finding Inez Breaux dying from yellow fever almost made her believe in God, in a universal justice that exacted an eye for an eye. She walked back to the firehouse fantasizing how she would personally supervise the screening and fumigation of Inez's crib, delight in telling the dying whore how the work would protect the world from the scourge slowly chewing away her life.

At the Hook and Ladder Company, Sarah Beth astonished Frances with her cheerful report of finding a near-dead fever victim. Beside using unoccupied *demimonde,* the Storyville Fever Committee had hired four young boys to help make pasteboard tack covers at twenty-five cents a day. Sarah Beth sent one of them to tell Ike to meet her at Inez's crib.

Sarah Beth paced the *banquette* in front of the dilapidated house waiting for her crew, savoring the picture in her mind of Inez's suffering, Yellow Jack's tightening embrace slowly smothering the life from the woman who had brought Sarah Beth to damnation.

"Hello, Miss Nice Lady." Ike's greeting was always the same. "You got some job for me?"

"There's someone in there with the fever. In the last room." Sarah Beth pointed at the house.

"Why you here?" Ike asked as he supervised the unloading of equipment from his wagon. "Miss Nice Lady think Ike do sloppy work maybe?" From his voice and expression he plainly teased her.

Sarah Beth did not recognize the joke. "Oh, no, Ike. You and your men do very good work. It's just that this…this *person* is very important…very, very important to me." She smiled like a snake with a rat in its coils.

"Oh. Then Ike do extra 'specially good job."

The screening gang moved their equipment into the house. Sarah Beth watched as they fumigated the room next to Inez's, then scrubbed it with disinfectant. Before the gang began to screen the window, Sarah Beth ordered Inez moved in.

"But that ain't how you say do it. You told Ike before, you say, 'Ike put it up, the screen, first.' Now you don't want it, the screen up before the people. How come?"

"Just this one time, Ike," Sarah Beth said. "I think it's better if we do it this way. But just this once."

Ike shrugged. "Okay."

Two men carried Inez into the fumigated room. As she passed Sarah Beth, she reached out her hand. "I won't forget this, ya'll hear. I'll never forget what ya'll done for me. I'll pay ya back, I swear."

"You've already paid me," Sarah Beth said.

"How?" Inez asked as the men laid her down on a bed nearly as tattered as her own, then began screening the window and door.

Sarah Beth imagined the crew used bricks and mortar instead of wire gauze. "By letting me show you my Cask of Amontillado."

BACK AT THE FIREHOUSE, SARAH Beth reveled in her revenge. Images swirled through her mind: Inez writhing on her bed, Inez puking up the blackness of her soul, Inez gasping her last. Immersed in her daydream, Sarah Beth forgot about the mosquito war until Liam approached her that evening after his gang turned in their equipment.

"Aye, mum, what we gonna do 'bout that woman ya found t'day?"

"Make sure she doesn't infect anyone else." Sarah Beth could not keep the satisfaction out of her voice, nor did she try, as she looked up at Liam from her seat behind the work table she and Frances used as a desk. Idly she twirled one of the golden-red curls that habitually framed her face.

"Done that already, mum, but she needs more. She ain't got no one t' look after her. She'll die f' sure if someone don't tend her."

"Then she'll die," Sarah Beth said.

Liam stared in disbelief. "Ya ain't gonna help her?"

"Help her? *Me* help *her*! I should say not!"

Liam began twisting his cap in his hands and looked as if he might say something but didn't.

The silence became so taut it pulled a terse, "You don't approve?" from Sarah Beth.

"Ain't my place t' approve or no, mum."

"Then why are you looking at me like that?" Sarah Beth demanded.

"Ain't looking at ya no kinda way, mum."

"You most certainly are."

Liam looked from his mangled cap to Sarah Beth and back, but did not speak.

Sarah Beth straightened some papers she had ignored all afternoon and told Frances, who had been watching the scene, to inventory their supplies. With her assistant gone, Sarah Beth said, harshly, "You might not be so quick to judge if you knew what that woman has done."

"Aye, mum. Sure and I don't know none of it...."

"But?" Sarah Beth insisted.

"But whatever it is," Liam said letting his own anger show, "I know one thing f' sure."

"And just what do you *think* you know, Mr. Ryan?"

Liam stood to his full height, intense blue eyes studying Sarah Beth from under his mop of tallow hair. "I know the devil himself don't deserve to kick off like that. And I know ya ain't the kind not t' help a body dyin' like she is, least I didn't think so till this very second." Roughly pulling on his cap, Liam spun and stormed out of the firehouse.

Who the hell does he think he is? Sarah Beth thought, glowering at the Celtic giant's back. *What goddamn right does he have to judge me?* The more she thought about what Liam had said, the madder she became. *What goddamn right does he have to shame me into helping that bitch?* And why, damn him, was it working?

Sarah Beth sat in the gloomy firehouse, her anger festering. As the darkness thickened, she remembered the night she and Frank had first discussed meeting with the delegation from the District. He had told her that all God's creatures deserved her kindness. *Surely, that doesn't apply to Inez Breaux.* Yet, he had been so proud of her "charity" work in the Tenderloin. What would he think of her if he knew how she treated Inez?

What would her momma say? Sarah Beth recalled the exact details of the night she had tried to shoot her paw and heard her momma's words again as the battered woman defended her husband, "*He's a good man down deep...He had dreams just like you once.*"

What were Inez Breaux's dreams? How had she lost them? Angered by her weakening resolve, Sarah Beth shouted emphatically to the fire wagon, "Damn it, I don't care!"

Liam's words came back to her. *"I know the devil himself don't deserve to kick off like that. And I know ya ain't the kind not t' help a body dyin' like she is, least I didn't think so till this very second."*

Sarah Beth stood so roughly she knocked over her chair. "Goddamn it, I hope you all are happy," she raged at the ghosts of her past and present as she blustered out of the fire station.

SARAH BETH HALF WALKED, HALF RAN to The Mansion. Remembering the texts and articles she had read in Frank's library, she commandeered linen, buckets and rags. Titan drove her to the Cheramie's. She hoped to see Frank, but he was out on rounds. In his clinic she found *sodium sulphate, calomel, ingluvin, potassi nitratis, ammoneæ acetatis* and *aurant flor.* Though there was no known cure for Yellow Fever, Sarah Beth knew the treatment for the disease required these medicines. Then she had Titan drive her to Inez's crib.

Even though the sun had set, the temperature hovered in the high eighties, and the humidity near one-hundred percent. Walking through the bleak, abandoned rooms toward what she had hoped would be Inez's tomb, Sarah Beth felt as if she had been wrapped in a blanket soaked in hot water. There was no breeze. Sweat ran through her cleavage and down her spine to soak the waist-band of her skirt.

Her footfalls made the wooden floorboards creak and rasp the dirge of the deathwatch as she moved through the deserted house. Eerie shapes wafted around her, the moth-holed rags separating the old cribs stirring as she passed. She lost her bearings and walked into a tattered blanket, screaming as the musty wool covered her nose and mouth. Fighting her way out of the dank cloth, she used the smell of the sulphur fumigation to lead her to her destination.

With the shutters closed, the feeble light from the street lamps could not penetrate the gloom of Inez's cell. In the blackness, Sarah Beth could just make out a form sprawled on the bed. "Are you awake?"

No answer.

She's dead. "Inez, it's me, Sarah Beth LaBranche."

No response. The shape on the bed did not seem to breathe.

I've killed her. Sarah Beth went closer. *What have I done? What a horrible way to die. What an awful, terrible thing I've done!* Tears welled in Sarah Beth's eyes as she opened the shutters. The meager light from outside seemed to bounce off the inky fabric of darkness enshrouding Sarah Beth and her victim. She lit a match and, as the light flared, Inez moaned. Sarah Beth found herself both thankful and angry the woman had not died.

Sarah Beth stared down at Inez until the flame burned her thumb and she dropped the lifeless match, engulfing the room in darkness again. She lit another and looked for a lamp. Finding none, she walked to the front of the house, guiding herself by the rectangle of lighter blackness that was the doorway to the street. "Ty, go to The Mansion and get me a lamp, please."

"Yaz, 'um." Titan applied the reins to the horse's rump.

Sarah Beth's third trip through the unearthly gauntlet was just as frightening as her first two. The brimstone stench of Inez's sulphur-fumigated dungeon convinced Sarah Beth she had truly descended into hell. To fight the suffocating darkness, she rummaged through the dilapidated chest-of-drawers by match light. Finding the butt of an old candle, Sarah Beth lit it and carried it to the bed, careful not to drop hot wax on the dying woman. Dabbing at the vile black ooze covering Inez's chest, Sarah Beth's thoughts tried to hasten her driver along, *Hurry up with that lantern, Ty.*

The seconds dragged by, the gloom swallowing both women as the candle nub sputtered and gutted. Behind her, Sarah Beth heard the floorboards creak. "Put the lamp on the chest, please, Ty," she said and wondered why he had not lit it. When no one answered, she spun around and the candle went out. Sensing rather than seeing a large shape looming in the doorway, her hand searched the folds of her skirt for her derringer as she demanded, "Who's there?" Whoever it was, he would not take her without a fight.

A match flared and its scant glow flickered shadows in a shock of tallow hair. "Didn't mean t' give ya a fright, mum."

Sarah Beth slipped the derringer back into the secret pocket of her dress. "What are *you* doing here? Haven't you caused me enough trouble for one day, Mr. Ryan?"

The match Liam held burned out, but, even in the dark, his broad smile was evident in his voice. "Sure and I waited 'round the engine company t' see what ya was up t' after our little talk. I knew, after ya thought on it a while, a woman such as yaself couldn't let a body die like this, no matter what she done. So I come by t' see if I could help."

"Hrump! I'd say you've done enough for one day, but, being as you're here, do you have another match? There's not much of this candle left, but maybe–."

"Where y'at, Miz Sarah Bet'?" Titan's voice and the tromp of his boots on the wooden floor carried to the darkened room.

"In here, Ty," Sarah Beth called.

The hall brightened as Titan strode to the back of the house. "'Scuse me, Marse Ryan."

In the glow of Titan's lantern, Sarah Beth saw again how terrible Inez looked. Damp hair matted on her face, black gore covered her body and bedding.

"There's not much I can do for her except clean her up a bit," Sarah Beth said, almost to herself.

"Why?" Liam asked.

"She has to drink the medicines I've brought and she can't keep anything down."

As if on cue, Inez gagged and a slurry of black coffee-grinds dribbled from her mouth.

Sarah Beth turned the woman on her side so she would not drown in her own vomit. "See?"

"Ain't nothing we can do for her?" Liam asked.

"No," Sarah Beth said. "She needs an injection of ergot directly into her stomach. Only a doctor can do that. Ty, see if you find Doc Jessup."

"That old drunk! Faith, mum, the man learned doctorin' in the stock yards."

"*WHO THEN*!" Sarah Beth yelled. "First you want me to save her, now you won't let me! What do you want from me, Liam!"

"Sure and I want ya t' send for that doctor friend o' yours. They say–."

"Who says?" Sarah Beth demanded. "And what do they say? Tell me, damn it!"

Liam stepped backwards. "Aye, mum. All they say is he's a good doctor and a friend of yours. Had Tom Anderson and a bunch o' ladies from the District up t' his house when the fever started."

Sarah Beth needed to sit down. The room's only lopsided chair looked too weak to hold the weight of the heavy, humid air much less her own so she slumped against the wall.

"How 'bout gettin' one of them doctors Miz Myda sees?" Titan asked.

"They're all uptown. She'd be dead by the time they got here, Ty. Besides, I doubt if any of them would come to the District."

"Miz Myda sees 'um."

"They don't know about her!" Sarah Beth snapped.

Titan hung his head.

"I'm sorry Ty," Sarah Beth said softly. "I know you're trying to help. But it's Dr. Frank or nobody."

She looked at Liam, his eyes pleading with her to be the woman he thought her to be.

Why did he demand such nobility from her? Why did she care? Men had ruined themselves for her in the past–fights and horse races, wagers and bankruptcy. Some may have even died for her. She didn't know what became of the men she had manipulated, too unconcerned, indifferent and apathetic to even ask. Now, with just a look, this Irish bumpkin raised emotions she did not know she had. Why him? Why now? And why, oh why, with *this* worthless whore?

Sarah Beth pressed her forehead against the peeling plaster of the small cell, dimly aware the turmoil within her had nothing to do with Liam, or even Inez. She confronted her personal demon, and the fiend wore her own face.

Pushing away from the wall with great effort, Sarah Beth said, "Ty, please see if you can find Dr. Cheramie."

She looked at Inez, wet hair stuck to her face and neck, skin burnished with jaundice, breathing shallow, body and bedding awash in billows of congealed blood. *Goddamn your heart to hell if Frank finds out about me because I've helped you!*

CHAPTER 21

SARAH BETH USED HUMOR TO belie the dread that solidified her stomach into a hard, pig-iron ball. "All this time I thought you were practicing medicine, Frank," she said lightheartedly as her insides mutinied at the thought of him being in the same room with her and Inez. "Now I find you've been keeping bees." Her fingers unconsciously groped for the curls at the side of her face.

Frank wore a Panama hat, and from its wide brim a billowing cloud of mosquito netting settled on his shoulders and trailed down his chest and back. Bicycle clips held his pant cuffs and coat sleeves tightly closed, and the gloves he wore were outrageously inappropriate for the hot, humid summer night. Not an inch of his skin could be seen.

"Laugh all you want, but what am I to do? I am not fortunate enough to be immune to the fever like *some people* I know."

"Do you tend all your patients in that get-up?" Sarah Beth stole a glance at Liam, who watched them intently. *Does he suspect we're anything but friends?* she wondered.

"Of course," Frank said.

"A new treatment plan, Doctor? Scare the fever away." Suddenly Sarah Beth's nervousness made her feel as if she had lost control of the muscles in her face. It felt as if her cheeks slid slowly onto her chest and there was nothing she could do to stop them. Could it actually be happening? Could Frank see huge dollops of skin hanging from her jaw? Could Liam?

"It *is* rather ridiculous." Frank adjusted his hat, gloves and the clips on his trousers and coat sleeves. "But not as bad as some things I have read that doctors have done. During the Black Plague in Europe, we looked even worse. Back then, doctors wore leather suits with a helmet that had an exceedingly long proboscis. Inside the nose-piece they put herbs to cleanse the air. They must have looked like something invented by Jules Verne." Frank struck a pose. "Would you not say my outfit is much more fetching? It certainly is much more practical."

Sarah Beth tried to smile but the imagined weight of her cheeks hanging down on her chest only allowed the corners of her mouth to turn up the slightest bit.

"How long has she had the fever?" Frank asked, opening his bag on Inez's bed.

Sarah Beth wanted to answer, but her tongue and brain refused to cooperate.

"Sure and I'd say more than a couple days. Like as not, near on t' a week." Liam spoke to Frank but studied Sarah Beth.

Frank noticed the medicines Sarah Beth had lined up on the dilapidated chest. "What have you administered?"

"N-Nothing. She can't keep anything down. So I cleaned her up, wrapped her in wet sheets to keep the fever down, and sent for you. She needs an injection of ergot."

"Do you have creosote and magnesia in your little pharmacy here? If that does not help, then we will give her ergot." Frank picked up several small vials from the dresser-top and read the labels. "By Jove! These are all from my clinic. Look here, they must be mine, I can hardly make out the writing." Though his face was hidden by the mosquito netting, the smile in his voice was unmistakable. "You little sneak-thief. But you do know your medicine. Where did you study?"

"Ah, nowhere. W-Well, in your library, I guess. Browsing." Sarah Beth wanted to see Frank's eyes, those mysterious windows to his soul whose secret fascination she had not yet fathomed, but they remained hidden by the mosquito netting. Did he know? Did he suspect?

"You certainly browse well."

"B-But I didn't think to bring creosote or magnesia. I can send Ty to–."

"No matter. I have some in my bag."

As Frank compounded the prescription, Sarah Beth glanced at Liam. The Irishman remained suspiciously quiet. *What's he thinking?* she wondered.

Lifting Inez's head as little as possible, Frank put a spoonful of medicine to her lips. Her mouth remained closed and a small trickle of liquid ran down her chin. "Squeeze her cheeks a little for me, please," he instructed Sarah Beth. With Inez's lips puckered, he poured the medicine into her mouth. Laying the patient's head on the mattress, he held her nose to make her swallow.

After a moment, Inez drew a deep breath through her mouth, gagged, coughed and spit the creosote and magnesia mixture all over Frank. She choked again and retched a thin stream of black vomit on to the sheet Sarah Beth had wrapped around her.

"Perhaps you are correct," Frank said to Sarah Beth. He rummaged in his bag, took out the hypodermic and prepared the ergot injection.

The tension and hot night drove Sarah Beth to the window. She filled her lungs with the humid air to no avail. What *was* Liam thinking? Would he tell Frank about her, destroy her relationship with her beloved doctor in a bitter attempt to win her for himself? How fitting for Frank to learn about her here, in front of Inez, the cause of her damnation, the very person who had insured that Sarah Beth would never be worthy of him.

Frank carefully unwrapped the sheet until he exposed his patient's stomach. When he pushed the needle into her skin, Inez winced, but remained unconscious. "There, I can do no more for her now. It is in God's hands, if He still cares for a woman like her."

"Aye, sir, ya can bet on it. Sure and He ain't never givin' up on none of His children."

"Of course," Frank answered. "Please forgive me. I must be overtired."

"Long days'll do it."

Sarah Beth watched, panic-stricken, as Frank closed his bag and stood, extending his hand to Liam.

"In the press of attending to this poor woman, I am afraid I forgot my manners. I am Doctor Frank Cheramie."

"Ryan, Liam Ryan."

"Are you, ah…associated with, ah…" Frank waved a hand in the direction of Inez's bed.

"Faith, sir, not on ya life. Me and the lads work for the Miss, there. Sure and I knew she'd be needin' a hand lookin' after this sick lass, so I come t' see what I could do."

"I see." Frank's hat turned toward Sarah Beth, his face hidden under the mosquito netting. "There is really nothing more I can do for her, you know."

Sarah Beth nodded as a fleeting thought told her something else could be done, but, in her state of mind, she could not think what it was.

"I *do* have other patients to attend. Surely you know that if it were otherwise, I would stay here with you. But all that can be done for her now is to keep the sheets damp and fan her to bring down the fever. She will live or die as God decides and there are others I may be able to help." Frank's hat turned away from Sarah Beth as he looked around the room. "Will you be safe here by yourself?"

"Sure and there's no need t' go worryin' after the Miss, doctor. I'll be stayin' here with her me own self."

"Excellent. Well then, all that remains is to say good-night. Mr. Ryan." Frank nodded to Liam, then his hat swivelled in Sarah Beth's direction. "Good-night, Nurse," he said, a smile in his voice.

"G-Good-night," Sarah Beth managed to say in a hoarse whisper.

Sarah Beth stood by the open window, Inez sprawled haphazardly on her thin mattress and Liam leaned against the wall as Frank's footsteps reverberated on the wooden floor and out the house. No one moved until Liam straightened himself and walked to the foot of Inez's bed. "Sure and I know now why ya said I can't keep company with ya."

"W-Whatever do you mean, Mr. Ryan?" Sarah Beth held on to the window sill to steady herself.

"Takes a blind man not t' see how ya feel about the doctor, mum."

"I, ah, I–."

"Aye. But ya know what really cuts? That ya'd think I'd let on t' him about ya."

"I didn't say–."

"Ya didn't have t'. T'was writ all over ya face."

"I'm sorry. It's just that some men might use it to come between Frank and–."

"Aye, mum, but I ain't some men. If he's the one ya want, then…." Liam looked at her and the love in his eyes was unmistakable.

"Then what, Mr. Ryan?" Sarah Beth asked gently.

"Then I'll do me best t' see ya get exactly what ya after, no matter who it may be."

"Thank you, Mr. Ryan. You're a true friend."

"Aye, mum, that I am. That and more."

Sarah Beth picked up a pasteboard fan and began cooling Inez.

"Sure and ya got a busy day ahead of ya tomorrow," Liam said, taking the fan. "Get yaself home and t' bed. I'll be lookin' after the lass."

"Your work's harder than mine. Shouldn't you be the one sleeping?"

"'T'is the good Irisher stock, ya see, mum. I don't hardly notice missin' a night's sleep now and again. But you–."

"Being a woman," Sarah Beth said.

"Sure and that's got nothin' t' do with it, mum. Many's the Irisher lass I seen skip the mattress ball a night or two and be none the worse for it.

Aye. And with that fine, full head o' scarlet hair ya have, ya just might think ya can be passin' yaself off as one."

"So I'm just poor stock, am I?"

Finally realizing that Sarah Beth teased him, Liam smiled. "You're a fine one for trippin' me up, now ain't ya, mum? But that ain't it, neither. If ya can't see ya've worn yaself to a fare-thee-well, there's others who can."

"Thank you, Liam, for being so concerned about me. It's very sweet and I'm grateful for it." Sarah Beth rested her hand on the Celtic giant's arm. "And I think I will take your advice. I could use the rest," she said, knowing, as she spoke, she had lied. There would be no sleep for her until she saw Frank. *I must know if he suspects.* "Do you need anything before I go?"

"No, mum."

Sarah Beth had reached the door when Liam said, "Aye, mum. And ya know what ya just done?"

"No," she said from the hall.

"Called me by me given name f' the first time."

"That's because we're friends, Liam. Good friends."

"Sure and then I'm wonderin', Sarah Beth," Liam said expectantly, "if one good friend can come a-callin' on another?"

"You still want to see me knowing how I feel about Dr. Cheramie?"

"Aye."

It wouldn't be fair to you, Sarah Beth thought as she sadly shook her head.

"Sure and ya won't be gettin' no argument from me then. But ya oughtta know I'll be askin' from time t' time."

Sarah Beth smiled. "I'd be disappointed if you didn't."

"Before ya go, as one good friend t' another, let me ask ya somethin'."

Sarah Beth raised her eyebrows.

"Well, if it ain't too personal now, could ya be tellin' me why you was gonna let this here lass pop off without even liftin' a finger."

Sarah Beth hesitated. *He wants my heart, but he'll settle for my friendship. Surely, I can give him that.* She took a deep breath. "Inez put me on the turf when I was thirteen and had no idea what she was doing."

"Aye. But ya done ya Christian duty by her."

"Christian duty be damned! I left home to make money so I could get my momma and brother away from my paw. That bitch took me in with a story about a wonderful orphanage in New Orleans where I could go to school. She brought me to the District, sold me to cure Big Casino, then ran me off when I was no longer any use to her. She deserved to die. She still does."

"Sure and ya've every reason t' want the woman in hell, lass. Aye, and that's where she'll end up, too, I'm thinkin'. But there's one thing ya should be knowin', Sarah Beth LaBranche, and I'm the man t' tell ya."

"What's that?"

"'T'is a fine good thing ya done for the lass here, seein' what she's done t' ya and all. And even if ya doctor friend won't never know, sure and he'd be proud of ya if he did."

"Thank you."

"And another thing, though it won't be meanin' too much to ya, I'm sure. I'm thinkin' t'is a grand thing ya done, too."

"That's where you're wrong, Liam. What you think means a great deal to me. A very great deal."

WHEN SARAH BETH ARRIVED AT the Cheramie's, Frank had not yet returned to his clinic. She did not expect him to be in, though she desperately wanted to see him, talk to him, be reassured by the tone of his voice and the look in his eyes that he had not discovered her secrets.

From the clinic Sarah Beth went to her room and collapsed into one of the chairs, her eyes fixed on the backyard garden and her ears tuned to the sound of Frank's carriage on the cobblestone drive. Through the open door to the hall, she heard Annadette grumble her way up the stairs.

"Would you like coffee, my Dear?" the old woman asked from the landing. When Sarah Beth nodded, Annadette called down the stairwell in a voice several sizes too large for her frail body, "Mary, bring coffee for two to Miss LaBranche's room." Annadette ambled over and sat in the chair next to Sarah Beth's. "You don't mind if I join you?"

Sarah Beth agreed without speaking and they sat in silence until Mary brought the coffee.

"Would you like to talk, my Dear?" Annadette asked after the maid had left.

Sarah Beth shook her head.

"It might make you feel better."

Only seeing Frank would make her feel better, and then only if she had kept her secret safe. Sarah Beth smiled her thanks weakly and shook her head again. They sat quietly letting the evening drift by. Annadette dozed. Sarah Beth, mind-numbed, stared at the firmament of fireflies twinkling in the backyard and ignored her now-cold coffee. The crickets' chirping rose and fell, reaching a crescendo whenever a bullfrog's croak announced the basso section of the chorus had joined the nightly serenade.

"Perhaps you should retire," Annadette said when the sound of Mary clearing the coffee service jarred her awake.

"I doubt I could sleep," Sarah Beth said. "I think I'll work on Frank's research for a while. I've been neglecting it lately. Too much else to do."

Annadette shuffled to the breakfront and poured a glass of sherry. "Take this with you. I know Frank's handwriting. Between it and the wine, your eyes'll droop soon enough."

In the crowded library, cramped among the medical journals and supplies, Sarah Beth found a tiny bit of solace. She worked at Frank's desk, occasionally rubbing the worn wood to find the feel of him.

Annadette had been right. The lantern warmed the already hot and humid air and conspired with the wine and Frank's scrawl to leaden her eyes. But she did not want to sleep. Not before she had seen him, inhaled the air he breathed to take some small part of him away with her, if only for the last time.

She wandered to the yellow fever collection at the back of the library and paged through it, her amazing memory capturing and cataloging the information. Remembering the French pamphlet and the Yellow Fever vaccine promised by its title, the thought that had escaped her while she and Frank tended Inez, she began to reach for it when she heard the tromp of footsteps on the back porch. Her skirt bunched in her hand, she ran into the small waiting area just as Frank entered.

"How is our patient?" He took off his hat with its veil of mosquito netting.

"Resting, as far as I know. Liam stayed with her."

"Quite an interesting fellow, that Irishman of yours."

Had Liam lied to her? Had he betrayed her to Frank after all? "What did he say? You *must* tell me!"

"Why are you so on edge?" Frank asked as he unhooked the bicycle clips from his pants and sleeves.

"I am not on edge. Now what did Liam tell you?"

"Did I say he told me anything? No, I said he was an interesting fellow."

"Well, what makes him so damn interesting?" Sarah Beth demanded.

Frank took Sarah Beth by the elbow and steered her toward the door. "You are obviously tired and very overwrought. We can discuss your Irish friend in the morning."

Sarah Beth wrenched her arm from him and stomped her foot. "I don't want to wait till morning! I want to know now! What did he say?"

"Nothing." Frank held up his hands as if to protect himself from physical attack. "I just thought it was interesting–humorous, if you will–the way he follows you around like a little puppy dog. I almost expected him to wag his tail when you spoke to him."

"Oh."

"It seems I have a rival for your affection."

Sarah Beth clenched her jaw to keep from blurting out how much she loved him, that he could never have a rival, that no one could ever take his place. Instead of rushing into his arms as every fiber of her being wanted, she stood mutely and watched his heart break.

"Oh, I see," he said slowly, with immense sorrow, misreading the look on Sarah Beth's face. "He is not the rival. I am."

CHAPTER 22

THE EPIDEMIC PEAKED IN AUGUST with one hundred new fever cases reported each day. New Orleans' mayor, Martin Behrman, proclaimed Wednesday, August 9, a holiday, recommending all businesses close so employees could take part in a city-wide clean-up. Public Health officers declared certain weekends as General Cleaning and Fumigation Days, urging every household in the city, working under the supervision of federal health authorities, to cut weeds, clean yards and gutters, and remove trash that might, with a small amount of water, act as an incubator for the *stegomyia*.

To kill mosquitos that might have bitten a victim, buildings that housed yellow fever patients were fumigated with sulphur donated by the ward committees. Doors and windows were screened to keep mosquitos out. Cleaning Days became huge, city-wide parties celebrating New Orleans' deliverance from the Saffron Scourge that had haunted the city since its founding and the resultant crippling quarantines that periodically brought the city to its economic knees.

In her rush to fight the plague, Sarah Beth had forgotten Inez Breaux's death two nights after Frank and Liam met. She became a one-woman flying squad around the Tenderloin, rushing to settle a squabble in Smokey Row, then making an unannounced check of the work gangs. At the firehouse, she extolled her clerks—Frances and two men sent by Tom Anderson—to keep accurate records, then reviewed files to insure they were in order. She would lecture the *demimonde* on how to fight the epidemic and, as often as she could, reported to the Tzar of Storyville. Days blurred together. At night she fell exhausted into a dreamless sleep. Frank Cheramie became more a cherished memory than a reality as she saw less and less of him.

Despite her frenetic pace, Sarah Beth found time, along with Myda and many of the other *demimonde*, to attend the funeral of one of the most beloved men in the city. Archbishop Placide Chapelle's piety and goodness could not overcome the sting of an insect almost too insignificant to notice. Ignoring the advice of the health authorities, the *demimonde* joined the thousands of New Orleanians jammed into St. Louis Cathedral and Jackson Square, the heart of the French Quarter's Italian slums and epicenter of the epidemic, the worst infected part of the city, to attend the Archbishop's funeral.

In the press of the standing-room-only throng, in the midst of loud lamentations protesting the loss of the city's cherished prelate, Sarah Beth found a soul-soothing serenity in the back corner of the historic old church. Perhaps God called her from the huge, gilded carving of the Holy Spirit descending from heaven as a dove behind the main altar. Not that she believed in any deity after the despicable life fate had bequeathed her. Yet, some innate sense bade her return to the Cathedral, and several days later she did, making August the month she attended church twice more than the rest of her life.

In the flickering light of votive candles, Sarah Beth knelt near a side altar dedicated to Our Lady of Prompt Succor. New Orleans—a city of frequent hurricanes, major fires and all manner of pestilence—needed a patroness who acted quickly.

Two pews in front of Sarah Beth, a short, gnarled, black-shawled woman prayed loudly, as if the Virgin Mother might be as hard of hearing as the old woman herself. "*Ave Maria, piena di grazia….*"

Sarah Beth had no worship in her own heart, but found a strange tranquility in the faith of the fragile woman praying so loudly. Why had she been called here, Sarah Beth wondered. Was it because of Myda? That precious woman's health had taken a bitter, downward plunge recently and Sarah Beth worried about her. Several doctors had examined Myda and prescribed various potions, none of which had the desired effect. Sarah Beth begged Myda to let Frank help her, but Myda steadfastly refused.

"It could ruin everything between the two of you," Myda insisted.

"There's nothing to ruin," Sarah Beth had replied time and time again. "It's all a dream. He'll find out about me some day and, if it could make you well, it should be today."

But Myda remained adamant. She forbade Frank to be called. Unable to change her mentor's mind, Sarah Beth resorted to deceit. The following day she tried to enlist Lou Belle and Titan in her scheme to have Frank tend Myda. They refused.

"She done made us promise hard not t' do nothin' t' put frights on you and Marse Frank gettin' together," Lou Belle had explained.

Titan was more explicit. "Marse Frank come in the front door, I's carry Miz Myda out the back. He come through the back, we go out the front. Iffen he climb in by the window, I slam it shut 'fore he can...I's sorry, Miz Sarah Bet', I truly is. That's what Miz Myda say and that's just what I's gonna do."

Myda's refusal only applied to Frank, so Sarah Beth decided to ask her beloved doctor for a referral, someone who might help Myda. She would need a good reason for Frank himself not to attend her friend and a convincing lie had not yet occurred to her. She knew, in time, it would.

The quiet church comforted Sarah Beth, allowed the knots in her muscles and mind to loosen. Sitting in the stillness of the half-dark nave she found unexpected release from the pressures she faced daily–Myda's illness, the epidemic, the constant fear that Frank would find out the truth about her. In her mind's eye, she saw her mother's face. How Sarah Beth wanted to pray for her! But words of supplication to a God in which she did not believe would not come. Instead, Sarah Beth hoped the mighty force of the love she had for her mother would somehow finds its way across the miles separating them. *Momma, how I miss you! I love you so much.*

The voice of the old woman in front of Sarah Beth pulled her back to the present. The Hail Mary, lyrically recited in Italian, washed over her like a cool, soothing balm as the ancient dame prayed her beads. "*Ave Maria, piena di grazia. Il Signore sia con te. Sei benedetta fra tutte le donne e benedetto è il frutto del tuo ventre, Gesù....*"

Finally the old woman finished. Bowing deeply, she made the sign of the cross, rose painfully and struggled to the end of the long, wooden pew. In the aisle, she held on to the end of the pew and fought age-stiffened joints to graze her knee on the black and white marble floor-tiles, which had endured the fire that turned four-fifths of the city into ashes in 1788. The present cathedral had been rebuilt on the site of the original one. The old woman struggled up again, turned slowly and shuffled toward the back of the church. She stopped before a gray marble cherub which towered over her, dipped her fingers in the clamshell holy water font the angel held and blessed herself. The two cherubs, which flanked the end of the aisle, were the only other survivors of 1788 fire.

Watching, then mimicking the old woman's rituals, Sarah Beth learned why fate had returned her to the cathedral. Her fingers in the same clamshell holy water font the old woman used, Sarah Beth saw wiggle tails, mosquito larvae, in the marble bowl. She showed her discovery to one of the priests and, finally, the rector, who agreed to empty all the holy water containers until the plague had passed. Another small victory over Yellow Jack.

By September the city had gotten the upper hand on the epidemic. Reported cases of fever began to fall. A public celebration, sponsored by the Elks Club, was held on a Saturday in mid-month to bolster the city's morale and raise funds to continue the fight. The day of the parade provided Sarah Beth with her first respite after two grueling months in the trenches of the mosquito war. She spent the morning with Myda.

Sarah Beth found her mentor in her bedroom-office and, despite her illness, seated at the huge Wooton desk.

Sarah Beth had been fascinated by the desk since she first took up residence at Myda's. When closed it looked like a *chiffonnier* with large doors that curved outward. Opened, the left door was a warren of cubbyholes and the center section a slide-out desk top and more compartments. The right door held row after row of green, felt-covered drawers with brass label holders and handles. Each of Myda's girls kept her valuables in the one or two drawers with her name on them–safer than in any bank.

Sarah Beth sank into a chair next to Myda. "It's so good to see you feeling better. I'm sorry I haven't had much time for my duties here."

"Nonsense," Myda said. "You've been busy and your work is far more important. The girls understand. We're all very proud of you."

Sarah Beth smiled her thanks.

"Why aren't you at the celebration?"

"The obvious reason."

"Dr. Cheramie went."

"He wanted me to go with him, but too many of my callers might…I suggested he take Frances instead."

"And where does he think you are?"

"Visiting the lady I work for, which wasn't a lie." Sarah Beth looked forlorn.

"Sometimes I wish I had never suggested you take a room outside the District. It's only caused you pain, not the happiness I had intended." Myda closed the ledger she had been working on and slipped it into one of the slots in the desk.

"I've never felt that way." Sarah Beth walked to the window and looked across Iberville Street at Groshell's Dance Hall. "I've always thought of it as a blessing. I met Frank because of it. How can I think otherwise?"

"Should you be thanking anyone for meeting Frank Cheramie?"

"Oh, yes, Aunt Myda." Sarah Beth whirled from the window. "Frank is the most wonderful man in the world. I'll always be happy I met him, even though nothing will ever come of it." She sank into the chair again, tears brimming in her eyes. "This is the life I made for myself, Aunt Myda. God knows it's not the life I should have chosen. I should have listened to you when you suggested I live at the House of the Good Shepherd. But I didn't and now I'll live the life I chose, and I'll live it damn well. If it means Frank and I can never be together, so be it. I'm thankful I've known him and helped him, in some small way, with his work. I'm happy for that and would never change it, even if I could." Sarah Beth sighed and looked across the room at Myda. "But at this moment I'm concerned about you? Are you feeling any better?"

Myda shrugged and rang for Lou Belle. "Good days and bad, my Dear. Good days and bad."

"What do the doctors say?"

"That I'm a decrepit old woman not long for this world. At least the fever can't get me. I had it when I was young."

Sarah Beth knelt by Myda's side. "Please stop talking like that. You're the only family I have and I don't want to lose you."

"It's inevitable, my child. You know that. And probably for the best. Then you won't have an excuse." Myda and Sarah Beth had this discussion many times in the past. Myda had often offered to give Sarah Beth money to live somewhere else and start a new life. "After I die you can move away, if you want. The business will be yours. My will is all drawn up. Sell The Mansion. Go to California or New York. Anywhere. All I ask is that you take Lou Belle and Titan with you."

As if on cue, Lou Belle brought coffee. She and Sarah Beth hugged, and the three women spent the rest of the morning in Myda's bedroom, talking and sipping steaming cups of *cafe au lait*. Of course, Lou Belle did her talking and sipping standing up, convinced that it would be a terrible affront to sit in the presence of her mistresses.

SARAH BETH PASSED THE EARLY afternoon of that same day with Annadette Cheramie. About three o'clock the old woman retired for her afternoon nap and Sarah Beth, full of restless energy, found herself bored. After an hour of paging through books she had no interest in, she decided to work on Frank's eye research. She sat in the small library next to the clinic pouring over his journal and did not hear him come in.

"The whole city is celebrating and here *you* are still hard at work. I thought you stayed home to rest." He sat next to the roll-top desk scratching his neck.

"I rested. I slept late, had a delightful carriage ride and spent some time with *Gamé*."

"What, you did not see that Irishman of yours?"

Sarah Beth ignored the barb. "Did you and Frances have fun?"

"Yes, and well deserved, I might add. You really should have joined us."

Sarah Beth shrugged. "Tell me about it."

"It all started with a parade. The mayor and seven hundred Elks. I am not exaggerating, seven hundred of them tromped through the streets downtown, swathed in cheesecloth and wearing silly hats made to look like cisterns. I was so proud of you. I told everyone within ear-shot that I knew the lady who first discovered cheesecloth screening." Frank looked tenderly at her.

Sarah Beth did not want the conversation to turn to their relationship. "Then what?"

"Lots of marching bands. Every now and then someone chanted the slogan of the day, 'And the female of the species is more deadly than the male.' There is no doubt what is behind the whole thing, at least not to an intelligent observer. It is all to get people not to slough their responsibilities to fight the fever, to redouble their–."

"That's wonderful, isn't it?"

"Of course it is, but a bit obvious. The costumes, the slogan reminding people the fever can only be communicated by the female mosquito."

"Frank, we have to get the message to the lower classes, don't we? You yourself have lectured on the mosquito theory anywhere someone throws down a soap box. People get tired of harangues. This was a wonderful way of getting the message out and not bore people."

"You are right, of course, but it is just so obvious that I wonder–."

"Obvious to you, Frank, but I doubt it was obvious to many others. So what happened then?"

"We all marched out to Athletic Park." Frank turned the paper on which Sarah Beth had been summarizing his *phlyctenular ophthalmia* treatment so he could read it. "Baseball…ugliest man contest…speeches extolling everyone to redouble their efforts," he said absently. "And, naturally, the politicians told us how wonderful they were and how lucky we are to have them…Damn it all, Sarah Beth, there is still not one treatment clearly better than the others."

"Be patient, Frank. I still have several more years to review. Something might turn up." She took the paper from him. "At least you and Frances enjoyed the day."

"Well, I have to admit there was some business. The quarantine has not let up yet and we tried to decided what to do about that. Someone suggested inviting the President to the city to show the rest of the country that it is safe to do business with New Orleans again. I doubt if that will happen, though. I cannot see Mr. Roosevelt taking the time out of his busy schedule. And we met a number of officials from the Public Health Department. Lunched with them and some of the mosquito committeemen from other wards. That was a very interesting conversation." Frank rubbed his forehead quite hard and scratched his neck again.

"Headache?" Sarah Beth asked.

"Yes. Been getting worse all day." Frank rolled his shoulders. "And I ache. My back, my arms, my legs."

Alarmed, Sarah Beth felt his forehead. "You're a bit warm, too. Shouldn't you lie down. Chew some willow bark, perhaps."

"Willow bark? Are you a voodoo priestess or just a regular witch doctor?"

"It just so happens, *Monsieur le Docteur* Know-It-All, that willow bark works. I've used it myself."

"If I don't feel better in the morning I might try some of your potions. Right now–."

"Please don't joke about it Frank. I'm concerned." Sarah Beth felt his forehead and cheeks again. "You're very warm. Perhaps–."

"I am warm because I have been in the heat all day. And because I am tired. And because I am here with you. Nothing warms me as that does." He took her hand in his. "I assure you, there is nothing wrong with me that a good night's sleep will not cure."

Sarah Beth withdrew her hand and walked along the rows of Frank's medical books. Hadn't she done everything she could to discourage his infatuation? Nothing worked. Her references to the affection Frank imagined she had for Liam only made Frank escalate his efforts to woo her. As for Frances, Sarah Beth had done everything but drop her on Frank's head and he still ignored her. Perhaps she had been too subtle in advancing Frances' cause. Perhaps she needed to be more direct.

Frances was a wonderful girl, rough-cut but basically intelligent and very pretty. Sarah Beth directed Frances' education and was molding her into the perfect mate. Why couldn't Frank see it?

Lou Belle and Tilda taught Frances to cook, a talent Sarah Beth had never acquired. Sarah Beth herself tutored the girl in literature, mathematics, science, grace, charm and, after Frank and Frances were married, would add a few lessons the nuns at the House of the Good Shepherd never thought of: the wiles to keep Frank in his own bed and out of the District. On this last point, Sarah Beth knew she had to fight the ridiculous mores of society, the notion that a good wife did not enjoy sex, only endured it. No doubt she could persuade Frances, having already begun that part of her education. Frank might be a bit harder to convince.

Deciding her indirect attempts to garner Frank's interest in Frances had not worked and immediately was always the best time to start a new project, Sarah Beth asked, "Did Frances have a good time?"

"I suppose."

"Did you talk to the poor girl at all?"

"Of course. We talked quite a bit today, actually."

"What about?"

"This and that."

"Could you be a bit more specific, Frank?"

"Mostly about what needs to be done once we rid the city of the fever."

"And?" Sarah Beth prompted.

"Actually, she sounded quite a bit like you, explaining how sanitary conditions in the city should be improved to prevent future outbreaks of fever. A sewer system to replace the cisterns and privies, closing the gutters, paving the streets. Things I have spoken to the other committeeman about. But I found it remarkable for someone so young to be so sensible. She's a bright girl."

"More like an intelligent and very pretty young woman, Frank."

"I suppose."

Sarah Beth had been browsing the titles of Frank's books as he spoke and now she turned to see him rubbing his forehead and eyes. "Frank," she said, a note of alarm in her voice.

He quickly took his hand from his face. "Yes?"

"Frank, are you sure you're–."

"I am fine," he insisted

She cupped his chin in her hand and lifted his head to see better. "Your eyes are glassy."

"Very tired, nothing more," he replied.

"Then get yourself to bed." Sarah Beth caught him under the arms and hauled him out of the chair.

"Yes, Dr. LaBranche." He walked toward the small waiting area. "And if I am not better in the morning, which I will be, but if I am not, you can set up your cauldron in the kitchen and brew up your potions. Hrump, works for a doctor, no less, and suggests willow bark. Indeed!" At the door he stopped and turned. "Are you going upstairs just now?"

"No, I have to straighten up in here."

"Good night, then."

"Good night."

When he had gone, Sarah Beth slumped into the chair next to his roll-top desk and rubbed the silky smoothness of the curl that framed her face against her cheek. She thought she had found the lowest place in hell when she had considered, if only for the briefest moment, Emma Johnson's offer to bed the pony. Now she knew how high up that was in the order of damnation. The terror of thinking Frank Cheramie might have contracted yellow fever pushed her into the gutters of hell.

CHAPTER 23

SARAH BETH SLEPT THAT NIGHT in fits and starts. Whenever she finally settle into disturbed slumber, horrible images churned relentlessly behind her eyelids. Mosquitoes as large as harpies swooped down at Frank, tied helplessly to something she could not quite make out. She tried to run to him, shoo the insects, but could not move, her feet captured and held fast in some inescapable quagmire. She bent to unfasten her shoes. First the morass caught one hand, then the other. She sank deeper into the black muck, to her waist, her shoulders, her neck. And all the while the mosquitoes grew larger, Roc-size, and spewed on her beloved Frank a slimy, virulent pestilence. Sarah Beth swam in the sludge, desperate to help him. "Frank! Frank! *FRANK!*"

The sound of her own screaming woke her. Now wide awake, she tossed in the gigantic, teaster bed for an hour, finally realizing the ability to sleep had fled. Several times she started for Frank's room, reaching the bottom of the stairs to the second floor on one attempt. Each time she turned back. *Frank's a doctor,* she told herself. *Surely he knows if he has the fever. But what if...* No, Frank knew what he was doing. Besides, what would he think of her barging into his bedroom in the middle of the night? Especially if she were wrong. *I can wake up Gamé.* No, Frank knew what he was doing. Then she asked herself, *If Frank knows what he's doing, why am I so worried?* She had no answer.

Sarah Beth tried to read but could not concentrate. First light found her dressed and pacing the back gallery waiting for the maid. *Damn him!* she thought. *He knows the symptoms as well as I do, if not better. This is all so his patients…* Her anger left as quickly as it came. Wasn't his self-sacrificing nature one of the reasons she loved him so much? *Maybe he's right. He's been working hard enough to completely exhaust a team of horses.* Another part of her mind quickly deflated her self-assurance, *Maybe he's fooling himself.* Sarah Beth knew how quickly the fever gripped its victims and consoled herself by thinking, *We'll know when he wakes up.* Then the dreadful reality crashed down on her. *Whether we knew last night or find out this morning makes little difference. There's no cure. The fever has to run its course.*

Six o'clock came, then five more minutes passed. Mary was late. Sarah Beth stood at the rail listening for the squeak of the side gate. Nothing. She paced to a white wicker chair, sat, then jumped up to listen at the banister again. When the hinges announced Mary's arrival, Sarah Beth ran down the porch steps and met her in the narrow service alley. "Quick, Mary, see to Dr. Cheramie."

"Why the fuss?"

"When he came home last night he was tired and flushed. He said he was all right, but–."

"Ya let him all night with no tendin'? Lawdy be, Miz Sarah Beth, what you thinkin' 'bout, not lookin' in on him like that."

The two women rushed into the house and up the stairs, Mary still wearing her hat.

The maid knocked on the bedroom door. "Dr. Frank?" No answer. She knocked again and called louder, "Dr. Frank." Still no response.

"Open the door, Mary," Sarah Beth insisted.

"Why you ain't done this youself last night?"

"He said he'd be better…If he wasn't sick and I went to his bedroom…He could have gotten the wrong impression…He said he was–."

Mary opened the door. "All this here worryin' 'bout right and wrong and 'pressions and all like that and a man might be dead to sick. Some white folk don't make *no* sense."

Sarah Beth did not have time to be guilty about her poor judgment. As they entered the room, Frank, lying in a tangle of sheets and pillows, moaned. Both women dashed to his bedside. Sarah Beth laid her hand on his forehead and sucked in her breath.

"He hot?" the maid asked.

"Burning up."

"Lawd, oh, Lawd. Why You done this to a fine man like Dr. Frank? What we's gonna do, Miz Sarah Beth?"

"Get *Gamé* Annadette."

"Yes, 'um. But what we gonna do 'bout–."

"Later, Mary! Get *Gamé*!"

The maid scurried from the room and Sarah Beth began straightening Frank's bed. He groaned again, and tossed roughly. Sarah Beth took his hand in hers. His skin had a distinct yellow cast.

Annadette hobbled into the room on her cane, still in her night gown, not having taken the time to fumble into her robe. "How is he?"

"Not good, I'm afraid."

Annadette looked down at her grandson. "Frank." Then she said louder, shaking him, "Frank."

"Hmmm. Oh, my head!" Frank tried to brace himself on his elbows, grabbed his forehead and fell back. "Someone is shooting off a cannon in my head."

"Don't get up, Frank. Please," Sarah Beth said.

"My patients–."

"Most of your patients are a damn sight better off than you are right now." Annadette put her hand on her grandson's cheek and shook her head. "Mary, get the doctor's bag from the clinic." Looking at Sarah Beth, she asked, "Who's the best fever doctor in the city? Besides him." She nodded toward her grandson. "Frank must have mentioned someone."

"He always talks about Dr. Kohnke," Sarah Beth said.

"Don't bother the Director of the Board of Health," Frank managed to say.

"Then who?" Sarah Beth asked.

"Dr. Rice, Edgar Rice," Frank whispered.

"Where–."

"The address book in my bag. Look him up."

Sarah Beth hurried from the room to return a few minutes later. "I've sent Mary in a cab to find Dr. Rice. Frank, when's the last time you ate? Do you feel nauseous?"

Frank answered the second question by retching over the side of the bed. When he recovered, he said, "About four this morning, I guess. A chicken sandwich. Oh, my head is really going to explode. I will try some of that willow bark now, Sarah Beth. Anything to get rid of this headache."

"What were you thinking of, Frank?" she demanded. "You're a doctor, for God's sake. You should know better than to eat when–."

"I thought–."

"What's done is done. What can we do about it?" Annadette looked to Frank for the answer and scowled when Sarah Beth replied.

"A purgative. Sodium sulphate."

"And where did you study medicine, Miss LaBranche?" the old woman snapped.

"In Frank's library. I've read–."

"Read indeed. I suggest we let a doctor decide the treatment." Annadette turned to the only doctor available. "Frank, what do you–."

"Sarah Beth is correct." Frank could not speak much above a whisper. "But first *calomel* to settle my stomach so the purgative will stay down."

For an instant Sarah Beth's eyes went blank as she searched her prodigious memory for everything she had read about yellow fever. "A quarter grain of *calomel* mixed with a grain of *ingluvin*."

"Yes," Frank struggled to say, "administered–."

Sarah Beth interrupted. "Four times, twenty minutes apart. Then, a half hour after the last of the *calomel*, a half ounce to an ounce of sodium sulphate dissolved in a glass of water."

Frank gave her a weak smile. "Yes, nurse…or should I say, Dr. LaBranche. I would recommend an ounce, though. My stomach is in such a pitiful state."

Sarah Beth left to compound Frank's prescriptions with Annadette staring after her in amazement.

DR. RICE ARRIVED JUST AFTER Sarah Beth gave Frank the final dose of calomel. "There's really nothing for me to do here. The *calomel* and sodium sulphate are clearly indicated. Within an hour of giving him the purgative, I suggest a preparation of–."

"*Potassi nitratis*, one dram; *Ammoneæ acetatis*, three and one half ounces; *aurant flor*, one half ounce." Sarah Beth rattled off the prescription from memory. "It's already prepared. He'll have one-half ounce of the mixture every two hours until the fever's gone."

"Why did you send for me when you're such a competent physician?" Dr. Rice demanded, clearly annoyed a mere woman knew so much about his profession. "You're not one of those women doctors working with Sara Mayo in the Irish Channel, are you?"

"No, *sir*, I'm not!"

Dr. Rice snorted his displeasure. "Then how–. Never mind. However, in your medical training you may not have learned that hot foot baths can relieve the headache. It's old-fashioned, but I've had quite a bit of success with it."

"Thank you, Doctor Rice. Of course, you're correct. How could someone like me know about foot baths?" Sarah Beth tried to use the same charm on the physician as she did on her callers. She only succeeded in sounding sarcastic. "We'll certainly remember that wonderful piece of advice."

"Edgar," Frank strained to say.

"Yes, Frank."

"I-I know you must be terribly busy, but, if you could, please look in on my patients. I hate the idea–."

"Certainly, Frank. And knowing you, there's quite a few, I imagine, who can't pay. But if you'll give me a list, perhaps I can divide it with some of–."

"Sarah Beth has it all written down."

"Naturally," Dr. Rice snorted. He took the paper Sarah Beth handed him and said to her, "You had better make arrangements to fumigate this room."

"Yes, Doctor." Sarah Beth did not bother to tell Dr. Rice those preparations were underway. Titan would fumigate a room down the hall where Frank would be transferred so his room could be treated, after which Frank would return to his own mosquito-free bedroom.

AFTER DR. RICE LEFT, SARAH Beth stayed with Frank almost constantly and applied the three cardinal rules for managing a case of yellow fever. Dr. Rice had instructed her on what to do, confirming what she already knew from her readings in Frank's library. She kept her patient quiet and absolutely prone, lying flat in bed without a pillow. He fasted and drank as much water as he could hold. At first Sarah Beth gave him carbonated water, as most of the medical literature suggested. When it became clear seltzer only increased his nausea and vomiting, she switched to plain water and ice. Frank's stomach settled a bit, but the heaving did not stop completely. Finally, following the instructions of several prominent New Orleans physicians whose articles she had read, Sarah Beth began giving Frank an enema twice a day, with three quarts of saline solution to insure the thorough emptying and cleansing of his lower bowels.

When Dr. Rice left, Frank's fever was 101. Despite Sarah Beth's constant ministrations, at the end of the day it had risen to 102. By sundown of the second day, it climbed to 103, and Sarah Beth decided on a new treatment plan.

"Mary," Sarah Beth instructed, "get all the clean towels and sheets in the house. Bring them here, along with as many buckets of water as you can carry."

"What are you doing?" Annadette demanded.

"We'll wrap him in wet towels and fan him to bring his fever down."

"Dr. Rice didn't say to do that." Annadette had aged centuries in the last two days. "You shouldn't do anything Dr. Rice hasn't said to do."

"*Gamé*, I've read many of Frank's papers on yellow fever. Dr. Salomon–."

"Never heard of him."

"Dr. Lucien Salomon was Secretary of the Louisiana State Board of Health from 1889 to 1893. He's written on the external application of water as a means of reducing the temperature of yellow fever victims."

"And you remember all this? Dr. Rice didn't say anything about wet towels. I think we should send for him."

Sarah Beth slumped on the foot of Frank's bed and rubbed her eyes with the heels of her hands. "We can send for Dr. Rice, if you'd like. He may not be able to come right away. Wouldn't it be better if we started with the towels while we waited?"

"Are you sure about this?"

Using the bedpost, Sarah Beth pulled herself up and trudged downstairs. It took her fifteen minutes to locate Dr. Salomon's article. She sagged into the chair next to Frank's roll-top desk and reread it, weaving the curls that framed her face around her fingers as she did. The words in her mind were exactly the same as those on the page.

Back in Frank's bedroom, Sarah Beth, "I remembered it correctly. Wet towels and fanning. Dr. Salomon has gotten a fever down in a half hour sometimes."

"Then we should use ice water," Annadette urged.

"Dr. Salomon says never to use ice water."

"Why not? Why wouldn't ice water be much better than–."

"I don't know why not. All I know is–."

"Are you sure you've read it correctly? We should send for Dr. Rice and—."

Sarah Beth, shoulders drooping, stared fiercely at the old woman. She wanted to scream. Frank was not getting better and Annadette was only making the situation worse. Pushing back several strands of hair that had escaped her bobby pins, Sarah Beth left the room, passing Mary coming in with another load of towels.

Returning with Dr. Salomon's article, Sarah Beth found Annadette seated in a chair looking out on the oak trees lining Esplanade Avenue. "Dr. Salomon writes, 'Water externally, either by sponging or the application of the wet towel, will almost invariably reduce the temperature. Never use ice water.' There, are you satisfied now?"

Annadette looked forlornly at the younger woman. "I'm sorry. I'm not helping, am I? We should be working together, not fighting. Trouble is, we both love him so much."

Sarah Beth turned to hide the tears welling in her eyes.

"No use denying it, you know. It's as plain as day," Annadette added absently.

Sarah Beth sank on to the ottoman next to Frank's chest of drawers, desolation compounding her utter exhaustion. "I'm not worthy of a man like him."

"That's absolutely ridiculous. You're not, but I suppose your little friend, Frances What's-her-name, is? Don't think I don't know what you've been up to, though for the life of me, I don't know why."

And you never will, if I can help it.

Mary came in with another bucket of water. Sarah Beth began dunking the towels. "Take off his pajamas, please, Mary."

"I'll do it," Annadette said. "I diapered him when he was a baby, I can do it again."

When Frank had been covered with wet towels, Sarah Beth began fanning him. Moving the pasteboard fans in long, sweeping motions, one woman cooled his upper torso, the other his legs and one took a turn resting.

Two days with almost no sleep quickly took its toll on all three women.

"We can't do this by ourselves," Sarah Beth said. "Keep him covered with wet towels. When they start to dry, change them. Mary, if you can, sponge him off whenever you change the towels. I'm going to get help."

Sarah Beth returned almost two hours later with Frances, Lou Belle and Titan, leaving Liam to supervise the mosquito war in the District.

After another night of catnaps, Sarah Beth took Frank's temperature, 104, and sent for Dr. Rice again. He arrived shortly before noon.

Dr. Rice completed the examination of his patient. "Has there been any change in his urine?"

"In what way?" Sarah Beth asked.

"Quantity, for one thing. Any tapering off or cessation. Any debris in it. Bile."

"I don't know." Turning to the maid, Sarah Beth asked, "Mary, have you noticed anything unusual in the chamber pot when you emptied it?"

"What you mean?"

"Is there grit in the bottom of the pot?" the doctor asked.

"Ain't seen no grits, but they be some sand."

The doctor nodded and ushered Annadette, Frances and Sarah Beth into the hall. "He's getting worse."

The three women exchanged frightened glances and Sarah Beth said, "I don't know of anything else we can do."

"We must have had the same training, madame, because I'm at a loss, also." Dr. Rice glared at Sarah Beth for a long moment, then said, "Continue the *potassium-ammoneæ-aurant* compound every two hours. The wet towels are good. Whose idea were they?"

"Mine," Sarah Beth acknowledged. "I had the fever when I was much younger and that's what momma did. Dr. Salomon confirms–."

"Then you *have* had medical training," Dr. Rice said.

"No, I read his article."

"I see," the doctor huffed. "Well, remember, use tepid water. In a situation like this there is a temptation to use ice water on the theory that if cool water is good, cold water is better."

"Miss LaBranche has already told us about the danger of using ice water," Annadette said, smiling at Sarah Beth.

"Watch him carefully, then." The doctor picked up his bag and put on his hat. "Send for me if there is any change."

Over the next two days Frank's temperature increased. No amount of sponging, wet towels or medicine brought it down. His skin became more jaundiced, with a mottled, purplish tint. His urine decreased despite the copious amounts of water he drank.

Sarah Beth's cosmos shrunk. The stars, the planets, the space between, their matter and purpose, all became focused on a three-by-six-foot mattress covered with rumpled, damp sheets and the reduced form of the man she loved wallowing among them. She thought of nothing else but how to save Frank. Sleeping, eating, bathing, the normal activities of a normal life vanished. And as the man she loved so desperately withered, so did she.

For five days, Frank ransacked the bed, tossing in fever-induced fits, groaning, moaning, varnished eyes wide and unseeing. Most of that time Sarah Beth spent ministering to him, fanning him, giving him enemas, wiping his forehead with a cool, damp cloth. On the afternoon of the fifth day, as she sat on the side of his bed staring at him, willing him to recover, she unraveled the mystery of his eyes. His pupils were misshapen; instead of circular, they were oblong, like a cat's. She began to cry. How cruel fate was! She solved the puzzle of his enigmatic eyes when he was almost dead!

On the morning of the sixth day, after a short nap in the chair by the window overlooking Esplanade Avenue, Sarah Beth awoke to find Frank in quiet sleep. She sighed. Relieved, she thought the crisis had passed. Turning his head from the side to make him more comfortable, she gave a short, soundless shriek when she saw a dark red stain on the bed linen. Bending closer, she found the thin trickle of blood running out of his ear. Waking Annadette and Frances, she called downstairs from the banister for Lou Belle and Titan.

Rushing back into Frank's room from the stairwell, Sarah Beth found him sitting up in bed. For an instant she thought he had passed the crisis. Then she noticed his glassy eyes–unfocused, delirious. Without warning, he clutched his stomach and gagged, spewing a thick column of black vomit; as if the miasma consuming him took corporeal form and he could only survive if he cast it out. Then, eyes closed, he slumped back in bed.

"Oh, my God!" Sarah Beth screamed.

Springing from the chair in which she had slept, Frances ran to the bed, averted her eyes and began to gag herself. "Lord Almighty," she said when she recovered. "What *is* that? He hasn't eaten a thing in days."

"Congealed blood," Sarah Beth answered. "Lou Belle, you and Mary get clean sheets and towels. Frances, water. Several buckets to wet the towels and clean him up. Titan, find Dr. Rice and bring him here."

With her soldiers assigned their duties, Sarah Beth turned her attention to Frank, sprawled in a puddle of black gore. She threw the soiled towels on the floor. Ignoring his nakedness, she turned him over and sucked in her breath when she saw the red stain under his buttocks.

"What can I do?" Annadette asked, hobbling over to the bed with the help of her cane.

Sarah Beth, fear chiseled in her face, looked at the old woman. "Pray."

DR. RICE ARRIVED TO FIND Frances holding an ice pack on Frank's throat, Sarah Beth fanning him, Annadette sitting by the window mumbling her rosary beads and the servants bustling in and out with supplies.

"What happened?" he asked.

Sarah Beth told him.

Dr. Rice ordered Frances away, looking annoyed at the sight of the ice bag. He lifted Frank's closed eyelids, checked his temperature, then asked Sarah Beth, "What else have you done, besides the ice."

"I've given him two minims of creosote mixed with milk of magnesia."

"Damn you, madame! Why do you insist on bothering me when you've treated him already! Ice. Creosote. What do you expect me to do for him? You've done it all!"

"Damn *you*, sir! If you'd stop being so resentful that a woman–."

"I will not have this!" Annadette shouted, shaking her cane at Dr. Rice and Sarah Beth. "My grandson is dying and the two of you stand here and argue! No more! Why did you summon the doctor, Sarah Beth?"

"Frank's urine production has stopped. From that and the black vomit, an injection of *ergot* is clearly indicated."

"Haven't you done that *already*?" Dr. Rice sneered.

"Stop it, I say!" Annadette yelled.

"I-I don't know how," Sarah Beth said.

"I *am* surprised. So there is something you can't do after all."

Annadette tottered over to the doctor. "They'll be no more of this, Edgar Rice," she said, her eyes slits. "See that big nigger over there." She pointed to Titan and, shaking her cane in the doctor's face, shouted, "If this bickering doesn't stop I'll have him hold you down while I personally ram this stick down your throat. And don't get ideas about not coming back here, either. When we need you, you'll come or I'll have Titan drag you here by the hair on your head! Now help my grandson!"

Dr. Rice pinched the bridge of his nose. "Madame Cheramie, I'm truly sorry, but there's not much I can do for Frank. Please believe me, I wish I could. Frank is a dear friend. Despite my frightful behavior, for which I apologize and plead forgiveness on account of fatigue, Miss LaBranche has done as much as I or any other physician could do." He turned to Sarah Beth. "My dear, you now face the most difficult part of being a doctor. You've done everything there is to do and your patient is dying." The doctor held up his hand. "No, Miss LaBranche, let me finish. Any doctor will tell you that at a certain point in a patient's treatment, the outcome is beyond the control of the physician. Frank is in a coma. His fever is nearly one hundred seven. There is nothing anyone can do for him. It's in the hands of God now."

"B-But what about the injection?" Annadette looked from Dr. Rice to Sarah Beth and back. "Won't the medicine you just spoke of help him?"

"Of course I'll administer *ergot*. And I'll show Miss LaBranche how to do it so she can continue the treatment." The doctor lifted the rosary Annadette still held. "But I'm afraid, dear ladies, this may be the only medication that will help poor Frank now."

Sarah Beth buried her face in her hands, quickly wiped her eyes and said with fierce determination, squeezing Annadette's arm, "There must be something else. I don't know what it is yet, but I'll find it!"

SARAH BETH HAD ALWAYS FEARED her phenomenal memory would desert her one day. Not knowing how she acquired it, she feared it would abandon her when she needed it most, and that she would not know it had gone. To allay this anxiety, she spent the rest of the day reading the yellow fever section of Frank's library.

Sarah Beth read like other people shuffled cards, flipping pages, scarcely looking at them. She went through the yellow fever reports twice and not one detail had escaped her. Yet something was missing, some errant scrap of information. Perhaps something she had read in one of the general medical journals, something that, when combined with everything else she knew about yellow fever, would give her the cure she so desperately sought.

Nightfall found Sarah Beth at Frank's roll-top desk in the glow of a kerosene lamp, skimming the tables of contents of years of New Orleans Medical Society publications. Suddenly, from some recess of her mind the words came to her, *Statistique des Vaccinations patiquees avec la culture attenuee du microbe de la Fievre Jaune.* The French pamphlet she had noticed in the library months ago, the one she had tried to read on several occasions, but something had always stopped her. Oh, the promise of that title! A yellow fever vaccine!

Sarah Beth ran to the back wall of the library and found the slim text still half hidden behind a thick tome. She grabbed it and rushed back to Frank's desk, rifling through the pages of the booklet, absorbing the information in the original French.

Dr. Domingos Freire had studied the mortality of yellow fever patients in Rio de Janeiro, Jurujuba and Nietheroy. First protesting the lack of accurate data on fever victims, Dr. Freire gave statistics on the age of those vaccinated and their length of residence in Rio, the epicenter of yellow fever in Brazil. When Sarah Beth came to the General Résumé she stopped and reread the details very carefully. In 1886, thirteen hundred eighty-nine people died from yellow fever, which included only seven of the almost thirty-five hundred people inoculated!

Why didn't Edgar Rice tell her of the vaccine? How could he let Frank die without offering him this salvation?

Sarah Beth sent Titan to fetch Dr. Rice again. Then she waited, pacing Frank's bedroom as Frances held the ice bag on his throat to reduce his vomiting and Annadette prayed.

Dr. Rice arrived and Sarah Beth hurled herself at him while he still stood in the doorway. Grabbing his lapels, she demanded, "Why didn't you give Frank the vaccine! Tell me! Tell me! Why? Why?"

"You're hysterical, madame. What vaccine are you talking about?"

"Dr. Freire's. Why didn't you give it to Frank!" She pulled harder on his coat.

"I don't know any Dr. Freire, nor anything about his vaccine."

Sarah Beth grabbed the pamphlet from Frank's dressing table and slammed it against Dr. Rice's chest. "Here!"

"This is in French. I can't read it."

Sarah Beth summarized Dr. Freire's study.

Dr. Rice looked genuinely astonished. "My God! There's a *vaccine*?" He leaned his hand against the door jam. "There have been vaccine studies in the United States, but none proved successful. My God. Now this. I am truly sorry, Miss LaBranche, but if there is a vaccine, we don't know about it in this country."

Sarah Beth stared at him. "It's an attenuated culture of the yellow fever microbe, that's what the title says."

"How is it made?"

"It doesn't say."

"Then how do you expect me–."

"Don't you know about it?"

"Of course not! I just told you that! If I knew of a vaccine, don't you think I would have given it to Frank by now? To all of my patients? Wouldn't every doctor in the city be using it, including Frank? In the United States there is no known, effective vaccine. I'm very sorry. I truly am."

Sarah Beth sat on Frank's bed across from Frances and stroked her beloved's scorching forehead and cheeks. There was something else, something that tickled the bottom of her mind.

"Ladies, I really must go," Dr. Rice said, "I have other–."

"Wait, please." Sarah Beth's eyes closed and her brows furrowed. With one hand resting on Frank's arm, the other gently pressed her forehead, then tapped it. "Blood!"

"Blood? What has blood to do with it?" Dr. Rice asked.

"Dr. Freire used an attenuated culture of yellow fever," Sarah Beth explained. "Attenuated means weakened. Someone who has had yellow fever should have weakened yellow fever microbes in their blood. Shouldn't such blood act as a vaccine?"

Dr. Rice stroked his chin. "Theoretically, I suppose it could."

"Oh, no, doctor, it's much more than theory." Sarah Beth flew from the room. She rushed back in a few minutes later with an 1859 volume of the *New Orleans Medical News and Hospital Gazette* from Frank's library. "Look, in 1858 Dr. N.B. Benedict transfused blood from a healthy yellow fever survivor to his sister, who was dying from the disease. She had no more than four hours to live when they performed the operation, and afterwards she began to recover almost immediately...Dr. Rice, how much longer do you think Frank has?"

Edgar Rice walked to the patient's bed and the dying man's attendants gathered around him. The doctor examined his stricken comrade; inspecting Frank's yellow and purple mottled skin, taking his temperature, listening to his heart and lungs through a stethoscope, feeling for a weak, fluttering pulse and measuring his blood pressure, which registered very low–68 millimeters of mercury on the sphgmanometer Dr. Rice took from his bag.

"Well?" Sarah Beth asked as the doctor put away his equipment. "How long?"

Edgar Rice would not look at the people gathered around him. "Four to six hours."

"Then we must give him a blood transfusion," Sarah Beth said. "I had the disease when I was younger and I'm very healthy now. We'll use my blood."

"No, Miss LaBranche, it's much too dangerous. The effectiveness of transfusions can never be predicted. Sometimes the patient improves, sometimes he dies. It's only recently that Dr. Landsteiner has identified certain antigens in blood that may allow us someday to match one person's blood with another's. Until then, I can't allow it. It may kill him."

"But, Dr. Rice," Frances pleaded, retrieving the ice pack and placing it lovingly on Frank's throat, "he's dying now. You just said so. If he's dead one way and got a chance to live the other, don't we have to give him that chance?" The desperation in Frances' voice told of the deep feeling she had for Frank Cheramie.

"My argument exactly," Sarah Beth said.

"Yes, Doctor. That seems to make the most sense," Annadette added.

Edgar Rice slowly looked at each woman in turn. "When I'm at death's door, I certainly want you three by my bedside. Show me the kitchen. I'll sterilize the hypodermic."

Dr. Rice returned holding the syringe in a small towel. "Please expose your arm, Miss LaBranche."

Sarah Beth rolled up her sleeve. The doctor examined the vein in the crease of her elbow, a faint blue trace against pure white skin, and tapped it several times to make it rise. "We need a tourniquet"

Tearing a strip from the hem of her petticoat, Frances tied it around Sarah Beth's upper arm. When the vein bulged sufficiently, Dr. Rice slowly slid the tip of the needle into her soft flesh.

With three ounces of Sarah Beth's blood in the hypodermic, Dr. Rice took Frank's arm from under the damp towels, easily found his vein and inserted the needle. Three desperate women watched as the plunger slowly pushed the maroon liquid into the dying man.

"When will we know if Frank, ah, Dr. Cheramie's going to get better?" Frances asked.

"I don't know. This is all experimental," Dr. Rice said. "I'll be back in a few hours to check on him."

"You're not leaving, are you?" Annadette demanded.

"Madame Cheramie, please understand. I must. I have other patients to attend."

"But Cyprian is–."

"Madame Cheramie, my dear friend, Frank, will live or die as God decides. My being here will make no difference." Dr. Rice looked sadly at the old woman, then at Sarah Beth and Frances. "We all know he would want me to look after the others. He was that kind of man."

"Please don't speak as if he were already dead," Sarah Beth begged.

"I'm very sorry, Miss LaBranche. Now you must excuse me, I have to go. Let me know if there's any change."

Dr. Rice had reached the door when Sarah Beth called after him, "What was Frank's temperature when you took it just now?"

"A hundred seven. His pulse was weak and fluttering. Good evening, ladies."

At fifteen-minute intervals, Sarah Beth took Frank's temperature and checked his pulse. There was no change in the first half hour. Forty-five minutes after the transfusion his temperature dropped half a degree and Sarah Beth thought she felt a stronger pulse. He continued to improve. His fever fell half a degree every thirty minutes, his pulse strengthened, the mottled look of his complexion improved. When Frank's temperature dropped to one hundred five, all five women, Sarah Beth, Frances, Annadette, Mary and Lou Belle, hugged each other in a circle and cried.

Titan excused himself. "Gots t' find me a mirror. Somethin' stuck up in this here eye," he claimed, wiping his cheek.

Frank's temperature remained stable for another hour, then began decreasing rapidly. One hundred four, one hundred three, one hundred two. A soft pink glow began to replace his jaundiced coloring. His sleep went from labored to restful. Ninety-nine, ninety-eight, ninety-seven.

"Don't worry, *Gamé*, a below-normal temperature is typical in someone recovering from yellow fever," Sarah Beth said, still fanning the wet towels they kept wrapped around their patient.

Ninety-six.

Frank stirred and pulled the towels around him as if they were blankets. His eyes opened. "Damn, I am cold." He looked around bleary-eyed. "How did I get so damn wet?"

The six of them gathered around the bed, weeping at the sweetest curses they had ever heard.

Frank looked from face to face. Finding Sarah Beth's his search stopped. "Have I been sleeping long?"

Everyone but Frank laughed.

MARY AND LOU BELLE HAD to help Sarah Beth to her apartment, fatigue making her legs rubbery and the stairs to the third floor insurmountable without assistance. Once in her room, she fell on the bed without undressing. She had never been more exhausted, nor more euphoric. Frank would live! At the frontier of sleep, she realized she had another reason to be happy. She saw in her mind's eye the hypodermic in Frank's arm, Dr. Rice pushing her warm, dark-red essence into her beloved. She might never have him, never wake to his touch, never give him children, nor share his life as she so desperately wanted, but she would always be a part of him. Her blood would course through his veins, giving him life and strength forever. Not much comfort, not near as much as her aching heart wanted, yet something. A remembrance to warm her soul far beyond her last breath.

CHAPTER 24

SARAH BETH HELD THE SPOON to Frank's lips and he made a wry face. "Is this all I can eat? How long did you say since my last meal?"

"Children make better patients than you do, Frank. Open your mouth."

He did as instructed, slurping the chicken broth and curling his lips. "A man needs meat, dearest Sarah Beth. Red meat." He pulled his head back and looked hungrily at her finger, then felt it, causing her to spill the broth.

"Now look what you've done," she said, scolding him while she smiled.

He squinted and spoke like an old hag. "Hansel, Hansel, where are you? This finger is too thin. Needs fattening up."

Sarah Beth laughed and spooned more chicken stock into him.

"Perhaps a nice sandwich of hand," Frank teased. "Aha, I have it. A succulent, supple arm. Roast of forearm, a bit of that will do me a world of good." He took her arm and gnawed it. Suddenly he became serious. "Is this the arm? The one Edgar took blood from? The arm that saved my life?"

Sarah Beth nodded.

Frank gently kissed the crease of her elbow.

She let his lips burn into her skin, felt the fire, wanted the heat to devour her. *No. Never encourage him.* Gently she took her arm away.

"Thank you so very much for not giving up on me." Frank's captivating cat-eyes gave Sarah Beth a look of undeniable love. "If not for you…Well, without you, there would be no me. But then, I have known that since I first met you. How can I ever repay you?"

"You don't owe me anything, Frank." Sarah Beth turned away from the tender gaze melting her resolve. "That's what friends are for."

"Friends?"

"Yes, friends. That's what we are, Frank. Friends."

"I see. Well, one of my other friends was by a little while ago. Dr. Rice said to give you his best."

Sarah Beth smiled.

"You made quite an impression on him, you know."

"How's that?" She held up another spoonful of broth.

"Your medical knowledge, and acting like a mother lion protecting her cub. Believe me, Edgar does not take easily to women doctors."

"How well I know!" Sarah Beth's pique rattled the spoon against Frank's teeth.

"Please! I am delighted to have been your patient. Hit Edgar in the mouth, not me."

"What else did the dear, condescending doctor have to say?"

"Have you heard about that business of getting the President to visit the city?"

Sarah Beth nodded. "You mentioned it before you became ill."

"Well, Edgar says everyone involved is quite excited. They think it is exactly the right thing to do to show the world the city has the fever under control and the quarantine can be lifted."

"But surely Mr. Roosevelt is much too busy."

"That is the amazing part," Frank said, "Edgar says the President has agreed."

Sarah Beth looked a bit dumbfounded. "That *is* amazing."

Frank rearranged his pillows and settled himself. "Of course, there will be any number of official functions. I have been included in several. Edgar said…." Frank cleared his throat, obviously embarrassed.

"Dr. Rice said what?"

"Well, it seems my name has come to the attention of both the federal and state health authorities." A slight flush built from Frank's neck onto his cheeks. "That business about larvae in the cemetery vases, mixing creosote with coal oil and the wiggle tails in the holy water. Please do not be mad. I have told everyone they were Frances' ideas, but, somehow, I have been given the credit." His eyes grew round with wonder. "Now, it seems, Mr. Roosevelt wants to meet me."

"Oh, that's wonderful." Sarah Beth offered Frank a sip of buttermilk.

"I would like you to accompany me when the President comes to town. Together, we can set the record straight on who thought of what. Perhaps when the truth is known, Mr. Roosevelt will agree to meet Frances and congratulate her in person. Oh, *do* say you will come this time, Sarah Beth. It will be grand. Bands. Parades. Lots of fun. Will you?"

Sarah Beth wanted to go with him as much as she had wanted anything in her life, as much as she wanted to see her momma and Jeremy again. "No, thank you."

"No. No? Why no? Why not yes?"

"Frank, this is something very special, isn't it?"

"Of course. We will meet the President, perhaps have our photograph taken with him. That would be grand! We could hang it here in our house and everyone…Did I say something wrong?"

Sarah Beth walked to the window looking out on Esplanade Avenue. For a moment she watched carriages pass on the oak-lined street and listened to the clop-clop-clop of the horses pulling them along. *No, Frank, you didn't say anything wrong,* she thought. *"Our house" is everything my heart every wanted to hear.* She turned from the window. "For such a special occasion, I think you should take a special person."

"I agree. I just asked her."

"Let me finish, please, Frank. The most special person I know of in your life is Frances. I think you should ask her."

"I've already asked the most special person in my life. She said no, and I want to know why. Is it because of that Irishman?"

"Liam has nothing to do with this," she said, but her tone implied he did.

Frank threw back the bed linen and swung his feet over the side.

"Don't you dare get out of that bed, Frank Cheramie!" Sarah Beth aimed her index finger as if it were a dueling pistol.

"Then come sit by me."

"I'll stand right here, thank you."

Frank sagged back against the pillows. "Have I done something to offend you?"

"Yes. You won't take Frances to meet the President. That's very mean, Frank. And after all, if it weren't for her, *you* might not have been invited. You just said so yourself. Besides, she thinks a great deal of you. And if you intend to set the record straight with Mr. Roosevelt about who's ideas were whose, Frances *should* be with you. They were all Frances' ideas and the President can thank her straight-away."

"She's just a child."

"She's much more than a child, Frank." Sarah Beth folded her arms. "She's a young lady. I admit she's not as refined as she might be, but I'm working on that. She's bright and she learns quickly. And she cares for you very much."

"Don't think I don't know what you've been up to, Miss *Devious* LaBranche. You're trying to foist–."

"Foist? Foist! I'll have you know Frances will make you a fine wife. You could do much worse than to have her *foisted* on you." Sarah Beth grabbed the bowl of chicken broth, the glass of buttermilk and headed for the door.

"If you leave, I will follow you," Frank threatened.

"Dr. Rice said you shouldn't get up."

"Dr. Rice also said I shouldn't be upset. You only seem to follow his advice when it suits you."

Sarah Beth put the bowl and glass on Frank's dressing table and stood at the foot of his bed. "I'm sorry. I just get so mad when you talk about Frances like that. She cares very much for you."

"And I care for her, too, in an uncle-ish, sort of cousin-ish way."

"Frank!" Sarah Beth stamped her foot.

"What do you want me to say? That I adore the girl. Well, I do not. She is nice enough and I like her, but I do not adore her. I adore you."

"Frank, please."

"Please what? Please lie?" He spoke in a sing-song voice, "Please, Frank, please pretend to be in love with someone you could not possibly be interested in." He stopped mocking her. "Is that what you want from me, Sarah Beth?"

"I want you to be reasonable. We, you and I, we're…we're friends, Frank. That's all. Friends." Sarah Beth clenched her jaw. *Why does he have to make this so damn hard? If he only knew, if only I could tell him! But it can never be! This is the life I've made, damn it! I'll live it and live it well, no matter how much it hurts.*

"What is love if it is not a deep, abiding friendship?" Frank asked. "Two people so committed to each other that they want to spend the rest of their lives together. To share everything. Like we have done. To share their souls and minds. To share–."

"Their bodies," she said.

"Is that what has you distressed, my precious Sarah Beth? Come, sit by me." He held out his hand to her. When she remained at the foot of the bed, he said, "I would never force myself on you. Of course, to have children…But only to have children. And only when–."

"And the rest of the time you'd visit the District."

"Of course not! How can you even think that?"

"You've been there before, haven't you?" she asked.

Frank said, his tone as contrite as if he were in a confessional, "The man is often not proud of what the boy has done."

"Why did the boy go?"

Frank found lint on the sheet and picked it off. "This is not a proper topic of conversation for a man and woman. I am sorry if that offends you, but it is the way I feel."

Sarah Beth sat on the foot of the bed. "Isn't this sharing, Frank? Our minds, our intellects. Isn't this what love is about? Why did the boy go?"

"There are some things that are not shared between a man and a woman." He looked at her pointedly. "A man and a *good* woman."

"Don't be so old fashioned, Frank! We're friends having a conversation. Why did the boy go? Adventure? Did he enjoy himself?"

"I am ashamed of it."

"Why?"

"It is not what a proper person should do–evil, vile."

"To enjoy what God has given?" she asked.

"God has nothing to do with it!" More in control of his temper, Frank continued. "The devil, more likely. And those women, they sell themselves, debase themselves. And for what? Thirty pieces of silver."

The words lashed Sarah Beth like a metal tipped cat o' nine tails. She flinched, physically bludgeoned by each syllable. Yet she pressed on, determined that Frances would not one day find herself the victim of some terrible disease brought home by a husband whose lust had conquered reason. "Did it ever occur to you that physical love *should* be pleasurable? That husbands should have wives that are just as exciting as hired women?"

"How can you even think such a thing?" he snapped. "A woman, a *good* woman, only subjects herself to her husband in order to bring children into the world. You make it sound as if lust in a woman is good!"

"Why not, Frank?" Sarah Beth demanded. "Why can't a woman enjoy physical love as much as a man. I've seen it in the District. With those women…Not *seen* it, you understand, but heard of it, talking to them. The women, that is."

"If I had known working in the District during the epidemic would affect you this way, I would have never permitted–."

"*Permitted!*" Sarah Beth's became indignant. "You didn't *permit* me to work there and don't ever think you did. It's something I wanted to do. *You* had no control over it."

Frank waved his hand. "Whatever. The point is, my dear, that dealing with those people has warped your perspective. Besides, we should not even be having this conversation."

"Well, we are. Friends sharing intellects, remember?" Sarah Beth snapped. "Frank, isn't it better for a wife to satisfy her husband rather than him pen up his needs until he is literally forced to rent a woman? As a doctor, Frank, you have to agree. If only as a means of controlling the spread of disease."

Frank hesitated. "Well, ah, from that point of view, you may have the color of an argument." He punctuated his reluctance to grant Sarah Beth's point by pulling the blanket up high on his chest, as if to fortify himself against the onslaught of her radical ideas.

"Now if a wife should serve her husband's needs, strictly for public health reasons, of course, shouldn't there be some reward for her?" Sarah Beth asked.

"You are turning this all around. Besides, it is not something we should be talking about."

"And you're being prudish…Shouldn't there be some reward for the wife?"

"For the sake of argument, let us say I agree." Frank looked a bit uneasy.

"Then isn't it reasonable to assume God gave pleasure to women as their reward for acquiescing to their husbands. Perhaps God is the great Secretary of Public Health in the sky."

"Can you be a little less sacrilegious?"

"God can take a joke. He's certainly played enough of them. But you've changed the subject again, Dr. Cheramie. Given our discussion, is it reasonable to think women should enjoy physical love with their husbands?"

"I-I suppose," Frank said.

"Then remember that with Frances. Things may be as they are, but they don't have to stay that way. Your view of how men and women should act when they're alone is just that, an *opinion*. In the past, people may have believed differently, and they may do so again in the future. Be a little more open-minded, Frank, a little more tolerant. And think about treating Frances better than most men treat their wives." Sarah Beth picked up the bowl and glass from Frank's dressing table and swooped from the room.

"Wait. Wait!" Frank called. "She is not my wife."

From down the hall Sarah Beth's voice came back to him. "Yet."

FRANK'S CONVALESCENCE CONTINUED FOR TWO weeks. Sarah Beth sped his recovery along with chicken soup and buttermilk, and, when he had gathered enough strength, the red meat he craved, all spiced with her radical philosophy.

"Of course, women should vote," she told him. "If men insist that women are the noble gender, then logic demands it."

"I am afraid to ask how."

"Not only vote, Frank, but hold political office, run businesses, do all the things we're not allowed to do now."

"Quite candidly," Frank said, "that is a bit ridiculous. No amount of logic can conclude–."

"Oh, but it can." Sarah Beth sat on the side of his bed while he ate. "If women are as pure and noble as men are base, then shouldn't the pure and noble rule the base?"

"But women do not have the strength to–."

"That again, Frank? I thought we settled this argument the night I helped you with Professor Anderson's wife. Tender sensibilities you called them, remember? Frank, women have the babies. As a doctor, you know what that's like. Admit it. If men had to bear children, mankind would be extinct. No man should talk about the strength women don't have until after his third child."

WHEN DR. RICE DECIDED FRANK had recovered sufficiently, Dr. Cheramie began attending his patients. At first Sarah Beth accompanied him to make sure he did not overwork himself. By mid-October, Dr. Rice and Sarah Beth determined Frank could return to his normal practice and Sarah Beth took up the supervision of the mosquito war in the District again.

Not much needed to be done. The oiling and screening gangs had continued their work and done an admirable job. At Sarah Beth's urging, Tom Anderson had put Liam in charge in her absence. Liam had stopped by the Cheramie's every evening to discuss with Sarah Beth the day's work and seek her advice on what needed to be done next. Frank had misinterpreted these visits as courting and Sarah Beth had done nothing to correct his misunderstanding.

Returning to the Hook and Ladder Company, Sarah Beth found Liam behind the bank of tables they used for desks giving orders to Frances and the two male clerks Tom Anderson had hired, arranging for more supplies and assigning the work crews to their tasks. She decided she was no longer needed and said so.

"Oh, no, lass," Liam said. "That t'ain't the right of it a-tall. Aye. I been runnin' the whole she-bang while ya was gone, but only 'cause ya had it set up good and proper beforehand and gived me the help I needed in the evenin'. Sure and if I had t' do it me own self from the beginnin', we'da been swattin' bugs with rolled-up newspaper all this time. Aye, lass, you can be havin' this job back and we'll all be the happier for it, 'specially me."

Sarah Beth knew anyone could do the job now. The mosquito war had clearly been won and, with the first cool weather, would be over. They only needed to reinspect the cisterns, privies and wells, reoiling them and the gutters as needed until the first chilly night in November destroyed the enemy.

IN LATE OCTOBER THE CITY celebrated. President Roosevelt had agreed to visit New Orleans, and the days leading up to his arrival were as uproarious as the weeks before Mardi Gras. His actual stay was acclaimed more joyously than the Fat Tuesday when the twenty-two year old Russian Grand Duke Alexis Romanoff followed the actress Lydia Thompson to the city and began the modern tradition of Mardi Gras.

Sarah Beth got her way. Frank invited Frances to accompany him on the President's tour of the port aboard the Southern Pacific's vessel, *Comus,* and Sarah Beth spent the week before coaching her young friend on how to behave and what to say.

Late in the afternoon of the big day, Frances swirled into Sarah Beth's room overlooking the Cheramie's garden. Sarah Beth had been reading and set the book down on the small table next to her chair when Frances came in. "What happened? Did you have fun? Tell me everything."

"Oh, it was wonderful! Absolutely, perfectly, deliciously wonderful."

"Well, what happened? Quick. Tell me."

Frances sat on the floor in front of Sarah Beth. "It was the grandest day of my life. It was ex–, ex–." Frances stopped to think of the word. "Extraordinary!"

"I'm on pins and needles." Expectant, Sarah Beth leaned forward.

Giddy, Frances said, "I actually met the President!"

"That's wonderful. What's he like? What did he say?"

"Well, the President got on the boat earlier in the morning, straight from a special train that stopped right there at the wharf. And later the guests came on the boat, and there's this line everybody stands in and all the guests go up and say hello to the President and his party. Oh, and I think I met the mayor, too."

"You think? Surely you'd remember meeting the mayor." Sarah Beth smiled.

"Yes, I'm sure of it. Only I can't remember what he looks like."

"Go on."

Frances hugged her knees to her chest. "Frank was so wonderful."

Good, they're on a first name basis, Sarah Beth thought.

"He introduced me to all the people there. And he's so famous. Everyone knew him and asked how he was feeling, and he introduced me to the President, and the President shook my hand and said, 'How do you do, Miss Kay. So nice to meet you,' and I was so surprised the President actually knew my name." Frances took a deep breath. "And I was so nervous I said, 'It's a horror to meet you, Mr. President,' and I was so embarrassed, because, of course, I meant to say honor but I was so flustered that I said "horror.' But he smiled and patted my hand and said I looked lovely, and I smiled and said, 'Thank you for coming to our city, Mr. President, it means so much to us,' and then Frank said hello to the President, and the President said he had heard about Frank and all the wonderful things Frank did during the epidemic." Another deep breath. "And Frank said I had helped, but that you had helped a lot, too, and the President wanted to know why you hadn't come, and Frank said you were ill and that it was nothing serious, but that you sent your regards, and you were right, Sarah Beth, when you said not to say 'delighted' to the President because everyone said 'delighted' and he didn't say it once that I heard, but I did hear him say 'Bully' and that was so exciting to actually hear the President himself say it." A lack of air in her lungs forced Frances to breathe again. "But, you know something curious? Mr. Roosevelt's teeth aren't nearly as big as they draw them in the newspaper, and I wondered about that all day. It's very curious, don't you think? Why would they draw somebody's teeth so big when they're not?"

"Did you say anything about the President's teeth to Frank?" Sarah Beth asked.

"No, I was going to, but I didn't. I wanted to ask you first. I remembered what you said about foolish questions making me look like a foolish young girl and how Frank shouldn't think that."

"You were right to wait and ask me first. Frank would have thought the question very foolish. You see, when someone draws a picture of someone else, sometimes, to be humorous, they exaggerate a prominent feature, like a nose or ears. In the President's case, they overstate his teeth. It's called a caricature." Sarah Beth leaned back in the chair and stared at the air above Frances' head. "Frank actually mentioned my name to the President."

"Yes, and you could see how proud he was of you when he said it." Suddenly, all the excitement left Frances. "He wanted you with him, not me. I could tell."

"Nonsense. You two make a wonderful couple."

"Not as wonderful as he thinks *you* and he make," Frances said.

"That's not true. I…He…The two of you were made for each other."

"Oh, do you really think so, Sarah Beth? I-I feel very deeply for him, but he doesn't feel the same about me."

"Of course he does," Sarah Beth said.

"He doesn't act like it," Frances said sadly. "All he talks about is you."

"Me?" Sarah Beth glowed. Frank had talked about her. She would savor the memory forever. "What did he say?"

"He wanted to know about you and Liam?"

"And what did you tell him?"

"What we agreed, that you and Liam are very fond of each other. But if Frank cares for me, why doesn't he act like it? Why is he always talking about *you*?

"He doesn't quite know he loves you yet. Men are like that sometimes. He'll come around, you'll see." Sarah Beth realized she had better change the subject before Frances guessed her true feelings for Frank. "Did you really tell the President it was a 'horror' to meet him?"

"Oh, yes. It was so funny."

Both women laughed.

"What else happened?" Sarah Beth asked.

"We had lunch and listened to a lot of speeches."

"Where did you sit? How was the room arranged? You must tell me everything," Sarah Beth urged.

"There were two long tables at the front." Frances pointed behind Sarah Beth as if they sat in the salon where the luncheon was held. "One higher than the other. That's where the President sat. And all the guests were at small, round tables, eight or ten people in a group. I met all the people at our table, but, for the life of me, I can't remember their names."

"You were too nervous, my dear. But that's all right. This was the first important function you've attended in your whole life. You'll get better with experience," Sarah Beth said. "What did you talk about?"

"What you said we would, how to make sure we don't have another epidemic."

"Yes." Sarah Beth sat on the edge of her chair again.

"Well, almost everybody agreed the city needs a better water works to do away with cisterns so the mosquitoes wouldn't have any place to breed. Oh, and that we need to change the sewerage system so there are no more open gutters and privies. But this one old man said no. He said it was too expensive and he didn't want to pay more taxes. But I convinced him," Frances said proudly.

"You did? That's wonderful. How?"

Frances arranged her skirt on the floor around her, savoring the moment. "Well, I was very polite, didn't want to seem pushy, and asked him if he had given money to fight the mosquitoes, and he said yes. Then I said, 'I don't know a lot about business, but giving money to fight the fever seems a lot like a tax. Isn't it almost the same?' He gave me a sour look and nodded. Then I asked him, 'Did you lose much business during the quarantine?' The mere mention of the word sent him on a rampage about how unfair the quarantine was and how much money he lost. He became ever so mad. I don't think I've seen a man that angry before. His face was red and his whiskers almost stood out straight from his face. And I sat politely listening until he finished, then I said, 'Isn't all the money you lost during the quarantine a lot like a tax, too?' And you should have seen his face!" Frances clapped her hands. "He looked like he had sucked dill pickles all morning. Then I said, 'Between the money you gave to fight the fever and what you lost with the quarantine, wouldn't you be better off paying a tax to clean up the city and make sure we never had another epidemic?" Frances smiled triumphantly. "Then *he* said I was right and how smart I was."

"That's wonderful. You stood up to him," Sarah Beth said.

The younger woman smiled.

"What did Frank say? I imagine he was very proud of you."

Frances sounded unsure. "I-I don't know."

"Give him time, dear," Sarah Beth said. "He'll come to see just what a wonderful girl…No, what a wonderful *woman* you are."

"Do you think so? I mean, really? You're not just saying what I want to hear, are you?"

Sarah Beth smiled. "I'm sure of it."

"If he does, it will be all because of you." Frances laid her head in Sarah Beth's lap. "Oh, I love him so much. I'll just die if he doesn't love me back. I almost swoon whenever he looks at me with those enchanting eyes of his."

Sarah Beth kept the ache in her heart out of her voice as she stroked Frances' dark hair with one hand and wound one of her cheek curls around the fingers of the other. "He'll love you, never fear. He'll love you forever," and added to herself, *Just as I will love him.*

CHAPTER 25

WITH THE COOL WEATHER CAME the end of the mosquito war and a return to normal life. Sarah Beth apportioned her time between Myda's establishment and the Cheramie's, working on Frank's research, sending out his bills and acting as his nurse when the opportunity arose.

The end of November brought Thanksgiving and sadness. During the month, most of Myda's strength had forsaken her. Sarah Beth had been surrogate head of The Mansion for some time, but now became the acknowledged madam as her beloved friend's health failed, leaving Sarah Beth no time to spend with callers and little opportunity to seek sanctuary at the Cheramie's. She explained her absence to Frank as the demands of her employer with the holiday's approach. He made sure she plainly understood he was none too happy about seeing her so infrequently.

By the second week in December, all Myda's strength left her, and she spent most of her time bedridden. Sarah Beth's apprehension increased to anxiety. As she worked on the brothel's accounts and listened to the older woman's arduous breathing from where she sat at her mentor's huge Wooton desk, Sarah Beth could almost see Myda laboriously exhaling her life.

Sarah Beth put down her pencil, closed the ledger and slumped back in her chair. Surveying the nooks and pigeon-holes in the desk, she thought how much like the old desk her life was; segmented, compartmentalized. She dipped into and out of this or that niche in her life, just as her hand reached in and out of the desk's cubbyholes. She ran her fingers along the smooth, hand-rubbed maple and suddenly brought them to her lips, as if the touch of the wood sparked an understanding she did not have before. *It's not my life that has these little crannies, it's me. Look at all the things I am. Bookkeeper, mosquito fighter, nurse, researcher, courtesan, and, now, madam.* She smiled. *Not much of a corny-zone any more,* she thought, mispronouncing the word as she had done the day she first met her mentor. *No time with the epidemic and, now, Myda so sick.*

She watched the older woman as she slept, a small corner of the bed linen near her mouth fluttering with each breath. *Corny-zone.* The word brought back memories of the day Myda had saved Sarah Beth's life. How fortunate she had been that Myda took her in. And how sad. Sarah Beth remembered the head-strong young girl she had been, insisting that working for Myda was preferable to living at the House of the Good Shepherd. Now she wished she had listened, had done for herself what she had done for Frances, kept herself off the turf and worthy of Frank. But this was the life she had made for herself and an important part of it, perhaps *the* most important, lay dying in the bed across the room.

Sarah Beth knew something must be done. Maybe now was the time to bring the compartments of her life together. As she watched, Myda's eyes opened and Sarah Beth's dear friend spoke, her voice very weak, "Daydreaming?"

"Deciding." Sarah Beth sat on the bed.

"And what have you decided this time, my dear?" Myda's futile attempt to be light-hearted only underscored the seriousness of her condition.

"That you need to see another doctor."

"Not again. Haven't I been poked and prodded and made to swallow God-knows-what enough?"

"No, nothing's enough until you're well," Sarah Beth said.

"Who this time?"

"Now you have to hear me out before–."

Myda picked at the coverlet. "Why am I thinking we've had this argument before?"

"Because you're a suspicious old woman." Sarah Beth took Myda's hand. "I thought I'd ask Frank–."

"No."

"You didn't let me finish. Frank is a very good–."

"No. We've talked about this a thousand times and a thousand times I've told you the same thing. *NO!*"

Where Myda got the strength to raise her voice Sarah Beth could only guess, but the younger woman refused to be out-argued this time. "Aunt Myda, Frank is the best doctor in the city. And whether or not you agree, I'm bringing him here."

"Unless I have your solemn promise before you leave this room that you won't, I won't be here when you return."

"Please be reasonable."

"It's you who are not being reasonable." Myda took back her hand. "I will not risk Frank finding out about you in a pointless attempt–."

"It's not pointless. Before, when Frank was so sick, Dr. Rice said I was being ridiculous, and look how that turned out. Please let me do the same for you."

"I know, the magic blood transfusion. But don't you see that can't help me. Haven't you stayed up nights reading Frank's medical texts, looking through his journals for something that would help, something all the doctors you've brought here might have missed? Have you found it?"

"I'm not a trained doctor. There could be things I missed, things they teach in medical school," Sarah Beth insisted.

"And how many trained doctors have you had up here to see me? Four? Five?"

"But Frank–."

"Frank Cheramie is a wonderful doctor, the most wonderful doctor in the world. I know that, Dear. But no more wonderful than the other ones I've seen already."

Sarah Beth stood and walked toward the door.

"Do I have your solemn word?"

Sarah Beth shook her head.

"Then kiss me good-bye, for I shan't see you again. By the time you get back, Titan and Lou Belle will have–."

Sarah Beth turned, twisting her hands together. "Why won't you let me help you?" Dropping to her knees at the side of the bed, she laid her head on Myda's breast. "Oh, please say yes. I can't just let you…I must do *something*."

"My dear, dear Sarah Beth, you've done all there is to do. Ruining your life won't keep me on this earth one minute longer. It's my time, dear." Myda gently stroked Sarah Beth's hair.

"My life is ruined already. It was ruined years ago. I saw to that myself. Whether Frank finds out about me now or six months from now makes no difference. He and I can never be together. Sooner or later he'll discover the truth about me and, when he does, he'll never want to see me again. I'd rather he find out sooner if it means making you better."

"You're wrong, you know." Myda picked up the strand of Sarah Beth's scarlet-gold hair that hung by her face and inspected it casually. "I think you and Frank may have a chance. That is, if you haven't botched it up already with this business about Frances. Grooming her to be the wife of the man you love. The very idea is preposterous."

"Haven't you heard of a dying woman choosing a new wife for her husband? What's so different about what I've done?"

"For one thing," Myda said, "you're not dying. For another, he's very much in love with you."

"How would you know? You only met him that one time at the mosquito lecture."

"Lou Belle and his maid, Mary, became friends while you were nursing him," Myda said. "They talk and Lou Belle tells me. Mary says it's plain as day how Frank feels about you."

"That's because he doesn't know. Once he finds out–."

"That's the point. He doesn't have to." Struggling, Myda lifted herself up on her elbows. "Fluff these pillows for me, please, so I can sit up. Thank you." After she settled herself she said, "For want of a better term, let's say Frank fell in love with the good side of you. You're very much the good person he fell in love with, you know. Why else would he love you to begin with? Don't let him find out the rest."

"What if he does?" Sarah Beth asked. "Then he'll hate me for it?"

"That's why you can never let him know."

Sarah Beth walked to the desk, rubbed her fingers lightly on the green felt covering the drawers where the girls kept their valuables. "And what if some day he finds out? What happens then? And how can I keep such a secret when I've had so many callers? Some are very important men in the city. Frank is a prominent doctor. He's bound to meet some of the men I've…some of my callers. How can he avoid it?" She leaned her head gently on the desk's huge, curved door.

"If he finds out, you're no worse off than you are now, are you? But the way you're going about it, there's no chance of you and he ever being happy. Remember, 'T'is better to have loved and lost then never to have loved at all.' Make the most of whatever time you two can have together. Take whatever happiness you can get. If some day he finds out and leaves, aren't you still better off than you are now?" Myda patted the mattress. "Sit by me, dear."

Sarah Beth sat on the bed and took her mentor's hand again.

"I'm going to say something you don't want to hear, but listen to me, please," Myda said. "I've made a will, but you know that. I want you to know it's in my drawer in the desk."

Sarah Beth stood up. "I won't listen."

"Please."

Myda looked so frail, so infirm, her eyes pleading, Sarah Beth could not refuse her. She sank slowly on to the bed.

"I've left everything to you, my dear. This house and everything in it is paid for. Sell it or keep it, as you wish. But I think you should sell it. All I ask is that you take care of Lou Belle and Titan. They've been with me all my life. Besides you, they're my only family. Oh, and see to Tilda. She's been with me a good number of years, too." Myda pointed to her desk. "In the door with all the drawers, there's a secret compartment. I want you to know how to find it. Go take the bottom two rows of drawers out."

Sarah Beth did as instructed. After kneeling and arranging her skirt, she placed the drawers in two lines to her right so she could return them to their proper places when she finished.

"Now look inside." Myda said. "That large piece of trim at the bottom lifts up and out. Remove it and you'll see a keyhole. The key that locks the desk fits it. Open it, please, dear."

Sarah Beth laid the strip of molding in front of the first row of drawers and unlocked the hidden recess.

"Take out the strongbox and bring it here."

Sarah Beth sat on the bed with the small, metal box on her lap.

"Open it," Myda said. "I don't keep it locked. It's too flimsy to worry with that. But I've hidden it well, don't you think?"

Sarah Beth nodded and unhooked the latch. "My Lord! How much money is in here?"

"Two hundred thousand dollars or so. I'm not sure exactly, I haven't counted it lately. But it's more than enough for you and Frank to make a new life. You can put it back now." As Sarah Beth returned the cash box to the desk, Myda said, "It's all yours. With the proceeds from the house and the cash, you two can live anywhere–."

"Frank will never leave New Orleans." Sarah Beth locked the hidden compartment, replaced the drawers and returned to sit on the bed. "He loves this city and its people too much. And his patients, he'd feel he was abandoning them. I know him. He won't do it."

"Then you'll have to convince him otherwise. I've seen you charm some very head-strong men into doing things your way."

"I had to take my clothes off to do it." Sarah Beth smiled slyly. "I can't do that with Frank."

"But the promise is there, my–." Myda coughed weakly. "Excuse me. If he marries you, he'll get to take your clothes off soon enough."

"Frank's too straight-laced. I've tried to talk to him about that, in regards to Frances."

"That is the silliest–." Myda patted her chest to help catch her breath. "I can't understa–." She began a strangling cough.

Sarah Beth hurriedly took a glass of water from the night stand. Sitting Myda up, she made her take small sips till the spasm passed. Then, rushing to the head of the stairs, she called, "Lou Belle! Titan! Tilda! Somebody! Come quick! It's Aunt Myda!"

Titan arrived first with Lou Belle close behind.

"I'm going to get Dr. Cheramie," Sarah Beth said. "Stay with her until I get back."

Myda raised her head. "No," she whispered.

"She don't want ya to," Lou Belle said. "She's 'fraid Dr. Frank will find–."

"She doesn't have anything to say about it. Stay with her. Both of you." Then Sarah Beth rushed from the room.

Out the front door. Down the steps. Into the street. Sarah Beth frantically looked for a cab. Without hat, gloves, purse or coat, hair streaming, skirt and petticoats bunched in her hands so she could run like the tomboy she once was, she rushed down Iberville toward Basin Street. At the corner of Iberville and Liberty, she looked right and left. No cabs by Groshell's Dance Hall or the Casino. She dashed past the cribs lining Iberville Street between Liberty and Franklin. The din from the Pig's Ankle, the Shoto Cabaret and the Big 25 assaulted her, but all the customers must have arrived on foot.

The train station! She could find a cab at the train station on Basin Street!

Sarah Beth arrived at the corner of Iberville and Basin Street out of breath. At last a cab. In front of Fewclothes' Cabaret. Sarah Beth launched herself inside and gave the driver the address. "Hurry! Oh, please, hurry!"

The gig rushed past the most notorious establishments in the Tenderloin, Tom Anderson's Saloon, the Arlington, Mahogany Hall, the firehouse from which Sarah Beth had waged her mosquito war and St. Louis Cemetery.

"Faster!" she called to the driver, pounding on the roof of the Hansom with her fist. "Can't you go any faster? This is a matter of life and death!"

The driver flicked his whip and his horse broke into a trot.

Sarah Beth pulled at the armrest of the rocking cab, not for support but to speed it on through force of will. *Why, oh, why had she listened to Myda? Can't this thing go any faster?* She reached out the front window and smacked the horse's rump with her hand. "Giddy-up! Haw! Haw! Giddy-up!"

The animal broke into a gallop and the driver shouted, "Hey, lady, leave m' horse alone!"

Why hadn't she insisted Frank see Myda a month ago; two months ago? She had, but Myda had become very upset. Sarah Beth chastised herself for not insisting, demanding that Frank treat Myda anyway. Stupid, stupid, stupid! Now her only family lay dying as a result.

A block from Esplanade Avenue, Sarah Beth heard a commotion behind her.

"Out de way! Out de way!" a booming voice called.

She stuck her head around the side of the cab and saw Myda's stately landau careening down the street. Titan stood in the driver's box, lashing the matched chestnut pair, urging them on and yelling for everyone to clear his path.

Sarah Beth beat on the roof of the cab. "Don't let him catch us! Faster! Faster!"

The driver opened the small trap door in the roof. "Lady, you tellin' me that crazy nigger's after ya?"

"My aunt sent him to stop me."

"Now that's different...Whoa." The driver jerked on the reins.

"No," Sarah Beth yelled. "You don't understand."

"I understand I ain't gonna help no young gal run away from home," the driver said. "Say, what ya was doin' in the District anyway?"

Sarah Beth ignored him and jumped from the still moving cab. She ran down the street, no match for Titan's team. He drove the carriage past her in a swirl of dust and a clatter of traces. In front of her, he swerved the rig to block her path. The two chestnut geldings reared and the landau tilted to the side on two wheels. Titan used his massive three hundred pounds to right the carriage and jumped to the ground. As he did, a crowd began to gather; men with angry eyes, incensed by a black man chasing a white woman.

"Miz Myda say t' bring ya back. Now I's carried ya off from one ruination, Miz Sarah Bet', and I'll do it again, iffen I gotta."

"No, Titan, no!" Sarah Beth screamed, holding her skirt and crouching like a panther ready to spring. "She needs Doctor Frank, Titan! You've got to help me get him!"

"Doctor Frank ain't gonna help her none. Ain't nobody gonna help her none now." The giant spoke with a catch in his voice as tears rolled down his cheeks, liquid crystals set against the ebony of his skin. "Miz Myda done passed, Miz Sarah Bet'. And the last thing she say t' me was to stop ya'll from ruination."

Sarah Beth fell to her knees in the middle of the street, buried her face in her hands and bent her head to the ground, her soft sobs muffled by her palms. Titan slowly knelt in front of her, then sat back on his haunches. A number of women in the crowd dabbed their eyes with lace or linen handkerchiefs and one or two of the men quickly brushed something from their cheeks.

"Ya'll gotta come home now, Miz Sarah Bet', and tend t' Miz Myda. Ain't nobody left t' do it."

Her face still in her hands, crying softly, Sarah Beth nodded. Titan took her elbow and led her to the carriage.

METAIRIE CEMETERY, ONCE NEW ORLEANS' premier horse track, had long since been transformed into a domain of granite sepulchers, recumbent lambs and marble angels. Because of the high water table and frequent floods, the city buried its dead in above-ground vaults, which often kept the deceased citizens drier than the living ones. Several times in the past, the corpses of hastily buried yellow fever victims had floated down the streets after a heavy rain. To prevent this, the city's dead occupied long rows of mausoleums and walls of vaults the locals called ovens or fours.

Sarah Beth had selected a small tomb for Myda, its architecture reminiscent of a Greek temple. Large enough for two occupants to await Judgement Day, it had a small chamber in the bottom—a *caveau*, as the city's early Spanish settlers called it—for the remains of earlier occupants when the upper compartments needed to accommodate new arrivals. Sarah Beth knew the *caveau* would never be used. The crypt's only tenants would be her beloved Aunt Myda and, when the time came, Sarah Beth herself.

The *demimonde* of the District, the great—Tom Anderson, Jose Arlington, Lulu White, the Countess Willie Piazza—the near-great—Hilma Burt, Lizette Smith, George Fewclothes—and the ordinary, gathered on a dreary, cold December day to pay their last respects to the most revered madame in the District. Behind the crowd, the Razzy Dazzy Spasm Band, joined by a young black trumpet player called Satchmo–a shortened version of his original nickname, Satchel Mouth–grieved Myda's passing in dirges slow and languished.

Myda DuBoisblanc, proprietress of the most fashionable and expensive brothel in the Tenderloin, was also a kind and gentle lady. Given to philanthropy, she donated generously to the House of the Good Shepherd and many other charities. At The Mansion, the lowest harlot, down on her luck or abused by her fancy man, always found a sanctuary–warm food, a safe bed and the support to keep on living–with no payment ever asked or expected. Today, they all came to say good-bye and, if they believed, to thank whatever God they adored for allowing them to know this wonderful woman.

Sarah Beth, flanked by Frances, Lou Belle, Titan and Tilda stood close to the crypt and watched through tear-filled eyes as the pallbearers slid the polished walnut casket into the tomb. Their dearest friend was gone.

From the crowd several people stepped forth and eulogized Myda briefly. Not even Sarah Beth's prodigious memory would recall who they were or what they said, so all-consuming was her grief. All she would remember later was that Liam appeared by her side and held her arm, giving her a much-needed brace for legs that had gone useless with grief.

A slow, chill drizzle began. Black umbrellas blossomed like inverted tulips. Titan held one over Sarah Beth to protect her from the rain.

Happy the bride the sun shines on, happy the corpse the rain falls on, Sarah Beth thought, remembering the proverb she had heard all her life. She had never considered its meaning until now. "What makes rain at a funeral such a good omen?" she asked aloud to no one in particular.

"Sure and it's because the angels are cryin', lass," Liam explained gently. "Tears o' joy they are for a new soul with 'em in heaven."

Sarah Beth found Liam's words curiously consoling and drew strength from the immense, work-worn hand that cupped her elbow. Though she herself had no faith, if there was a God, Sarah Beth knew he would take Myda straight to Him, no matter what others might say.

The rain came down harder and the crowd, in ones and twos, fled until only Sarah Beth, Lou Belle, Titan, Tilda, Frances, Liam and the Razzy Dazzy Spasm Band remained. Lightening crackled, the sky roared and the last few notes from the band sounded like cats in heat before they, too, ran for cover.

Liam nudged Sarah Beth toward the carriage and she shook her head, rain mingling with the tears streaming down her cheeks.

"Gots t' go now, Miz Sarah Beth." Lou Belle took the new mistress of The Mansion gently by the other arm.

Sarah Beth refused to move.

"Can't have none o' this, now. Gonna catched ya death o' cold out in this here rain. And you know Miz Myda, Gawd rest her soul, wouldn't want none o' that."

Myda's name acted as the incantation that broke Sarah Beth's spell. "Oh, Lou Belle, I miss her so much already. What am I to do without her?"

"What we alls gonna do? Me, I don't know. Alls I know is what she want for the folks she left behind. T' laugh wit' the chil'ens, and smile when the birds sing, and 'joy the grass just bein' green. She want us t' go on and live our lifes like we oughtta and 'member her tender from time t' time. Now ya'll come on along, Miz Sarah Beth. Miz Myda, she in the joy o' the Lawd now, and it don't rain up there like it do down here. We gots t' get us on home."

As Liam looked on, slowly Sarah Beth's head found Lou Belle's shoulder. Frances, Titan and Tilda huddled around the two women and all five embraced, each moaning and whimpering the misery infecting them all. Without lifting her head, Sarah Beth reached out and took Liam's hand.

THREE DAYS LATER, SARAH BETH joined the girls of The Mansion for four o'clock lunch for the first time since laying Myda to rest. The *demimonde* expected her to take her place at the head of the table. Instead, she sat in her usual chair, immediately to the right of the one holding the black wreath.

Sarah Beth remained quiet until after dessert, when she tapped her spoon on her water goblet. The *demimonde*, somber and reflective during the meal, hushed.

"Over the past few days I've thought a lot about the future, both mine and yours. There's no tactful way to say this, so I think it's best to be direct. You are all my friends and I'm sure you'll all understand." Folding her napkin, Sarah Beth placed it next to her coffee cup as eleven pairs of eyes stared expectantly at her. "I've decided to sell The Mansion."

At first Sarah Beth confronted silent faces of varying expression, from acceptance to long-suffering resignation to open hostility. Then bedlam erupted.

"…doesn't care about us. If she did…."

"…got the right to do what she wants…."

"…not fair. None of us are rich like she is…."

"…told you. Didn't I tell you…."

"…can't work with bawds in a five-dollar house…."

"…our friend and we should be happy…."

Consuella, a ravishing dark haired girl who claimed descent from Hernando DeSoto, raised her voice above the rest. "How long, *señorita*, before you evict us?"

"Evict?" Sarah Beth slumped in her chair. "I said nothing about evicting you. You haven't even given me a chance to explain, and already you think the worst."

Consuella stood up. "Ladies. Ladies! Sarah Beth is correct. We are all jumping onto her conclusions. Let us hear her, *por favor*."

Sarah Beth, looking at each woman in turn, said, "First, let me assure you that no one is being evicted. I have no deadline, but I wanted you to know my decision as soon as possible so you could look for other positions, if you choose."

"How long do we have?" Grace, a petite blonde asked.

"I'm not sure you have to move at all," Sarah Beth said. "You may want to wait until you see who the new owners are and work for them. Whatever you decide, I'd like the business sold in three to six months. But I want you to be honest with me and tell me if that gives you enough time to make arrangements."

"That might be a tad short," Lydia, a tall, statuesque brunette said. "Some of us may want to snag a husband and six months may not be enough time."

"Not if you know how to do it, Honey," someone said and the *demimonde* laughed.

"Have you decided how much you want for the place?" Juliette asked. "Some of us may be interested in buying the business ourselves."

"Why, ah, no. I-I haven't given it any thought," Sarah Beth said. "Just this morning I decided what I wanted to do. How much do you think The Mansion is worth? Five thousand dollars?"

"Oh, no, that's much too low," Juliette said. "The furniture, drapes and rugs alone are–."

Hilda, blonde and buxom like her sister, Juliette, said, in a candied, sarcastic tone, "If she wants to sell it to us for five thousand dollars, *why don't you let her*?"

Juliette took Hilda's hand and kissed it. "Because, my love, we should be fair. Miss Myda and Sarah Beth have always treated us well. Who else would any of us trust enough to hold our money? Has it ever come up short? Wasn't it always there when we needed it? And how many broken hearts have they helped mend? The two of us, darling, should be the most grateful. How many times have they helped patch things up between us?"

"If you weren't so jealous, there'd be nothing to patch up," Hilda snapped.

"Whatever the reason, they've been good to us." Juliette turned to Sarah Beth.

Being snubbed only made Hilda madder. "I'm not the only one with a wandering eye. Don't think I don't know about that little high yellow at Lulu White's."

Juliette shifted in her chair. "That was a long time ago."

"I don't know how you tell time. You were over there last week."

Juliette turned to her sister and smiled stiffly. "Let's talk about this later on, in our room."

"That's right. Everything looks better to you in bed. Does your little Chocolate Split agree?" Hilda's tone was peevish. "Didn't think I knew what you called her, did you?"

Juliette released Hilda's hand. "Can we please keep our personal business private?"

"Juliette," Sarah Beth said, trying to defuse the argument, "how much do you think I should ask?"

When Juliette turned to answer, Hilda stuck her tongue out.

"The furnishings are worth at least three thousand," Juliette estimated, "and the house itself seven or eight, so let's say eleven thousand for the whole kit and caboodle. Then there's the business itself. When you're working, Sarah Beth, there's twelve of us receiving about three visitors a night. The house get's a twenty-five percent commission on each caller, so that's fifteen dollars a night per girl. For twelve girls–. No, that's wrong. Usually three, or so, can't have callers because it's their time of the month. So let's figure it on an average of nine girls a night. Let's see, that's ought, carry the four." Juliette wrote imaginary numbers in the air with her finger. "One hundred thirty dollars a night. Plus each of us pays five dollars a day room and board, that comes to one ninety, plus what you make on the food and drinks. So I'd guess The Mansion takes in about two hundred twenty-five dollars a day. Am I close?"

Sarah Beth nodded, amazed at a side of Juliette she had never seen before and the accuracy of her estimate. "Of course, we didn't do near that well during the epidemic."

"I realize that. But normally, without a quarantine or embargo or anything like that, two hundred twenty-five dollars a day is about right, isn't it?"

"Yes. Oh, and by the way, Lou Belle, Titan and Tilda are coming with me," Sarah Beth said.

"Damn. I'd sure like Tilda to stay on as cook. I'll talk to her, if you don't mind?"

Sarah Beth nodded.

"Anyway, I know you have expenses, but the gross is," Juliette did more arithmetic in the air above the table, "carry the three makes eighteen, eight plus three, seven plus one carry the one, $91,250 a year."

One of the *demimonde* whistled.

"Sarah Beth, for the furniture, house and this little gold mine, I wouldn't accept a penny less than $30,000, maybe more," Juliette concluded.

"Fine, just fine!" Hilda complained. "How do you expect us to raise that much money?"

"Don't worry." Juliette patted Hilda on the arm. "A banker's in love with me."

"That's supposed to make *me* feel better?" Hilda groused.

"Will you take a mortgage?" Juliette asked.

Sarah Beth smiled and shook her head. "No, I'm sorry."

"Sarah Beth, why sell The Mansion if it's such a money maker?" Lydia asked. "Hire someone to manage it instead."

Juliette and Hilda both frowned at the intrusion.

Sarah Beth wondered if any of them could understand. Yes, she decided. Each of them, even Juliette and Hilda, must harbor the same secret wish she had discovered in herself since laying Myda to rest. A dream that had been buried deep within her since the day Inez Breaux discarded her. A hope Sarah Beth had denied for such a very long time. "Because, Lydia, I want to leave the District without any ties. This part of my life is over."

CHAPTER 26

IN NEW ORLEANS, WINTER HARDLY deserves the name. From December to March, cold-weather fronts pass through, making some days as balmy as summer and others chill and damp. On a day in January that required all the coal grates in The Mansion to be lit and stoked frequently, Juliette, Hilda and Sarah Beth settled on $40,000 as their sale price. With great ceremony the purchasers and seller met at the Wooton desk that had been transferred to Sarah Beth's room. The *demimonde* took money from the drawers assigned to them and gave Sarah Beth a $4,000 down payment in exchange for a receipt.

That evening, Juliette met her paramour from the bank and, between the sheets of her four-poster bed, opened negotiations for the loan. Just after midnight, she introduced him to her co-signer and he examined both applicants' qualifications and collateral until well after sunrise. When he left, weary but smiling, one of the girls overheard him saying he looked forward to a month or two of hard dickering, considering the terms of the arrangement from all angles and examining all possibilities before approving the loan.

Sarah Beth spent December, January and February furthering her plans for Frances and Frank. She quizzed Frances on current events so the younger woman could discuss them intelligently.

"Why did the members of Congress rush back to Washington on New Year's Eve?" Sarah Beth asked, seeming more like head mistress than friend.

"To get one last free ride before the railroads revoked their passes."

"What happened in Nicaragua?"

"The San Diego volcano erupted causing an earthquake."

"What special machine is being built and why?"

"An airship to explore the North Pole."

Sarah Beth also read Frank's medical texts, distilled the information and presented it in ways Frances could understand. If Frances asked a question Sarah Beth could not answer herself, she, in turn, asked Frank.

Sarah Beth and Frank had finished a discussion about a particularly complicated anatomy question, when he asked, "What were you like as a child?"

Painful memories of her mother's terrible suffering inundated her mind and Sarah Beth barely held them in check. "W-Why do you ask?"

"Because, my dear, you are the only real genius I know. I was wondering if, as a child, you were a prodigy and, if so, in what field?"

Sarah Beth relaxed, thinking her only talent as a child was staying out of her father's way and comforting her mother what little she could. "Quite an ordinary little girl."

They sat at the table in Frank's library with thick medical tomes opened and spread all around. Frank reached for her hand and she suddenly decided to re-shelve the books.

"I doubt that," he said. Angry at the space between them, he moved to help her.

"It's true. My family had little, and I didn't begin school until my teens."

"That's sad. A mind like yours, almost wasted. What schools did you attend?"

This is dangerous, Sarah Beth thought. "None, really. I'm self-taught. Hand me that book, please."

"That is even more amazing. Surely, you had to have some idea of how smart you were though…Here, let me." He helped her put a very heavy book on the shelf.

"As I look back on it now," she said, "I suppose I should have. But when I was young, I only had hints of my unusual memory. After I realized what it was, I never understood it. In fact, it's always frightened me."

"Why?" Again he tried to take her hand, but she slipped away.

"I was always afraid that I'd lose it just when I needed it most. When you were so sick, I re-read your entire yellow fever collection to make sure I hadn't forgotten something that might have helped you."

"And did you?"

"No, it was all there," she said tapping her temple.

"At least you can stop worrying about losing it. From what I have read, it seems never to be lost, save for some trauma to the head. But that is only part of your genius, you know. Remembering is one thing. Assimilating what you remember into a coherent whole is something else again." He followed her around the table, almost as if they played tag. "Edgar told me how you discovered the pamphlet on the Brazilian vaccine and, from it, concluded a cured fever victim's blood might have the same effect. Have you any idea how the process works? In your mind, I mean."

"No." She reached up high to put a book away. "It's a complete mystery. And it wasn't genius, Frank, just remembering."

"But that in itself is genius."

Sarah Beth seemed on the verge of losing her balance, and Frank's hands circled her tiny waist.

"Dissimilar ideas," he said, his face close to Sarah Beth's, "juxtaposed in a way that results in startling new conclusions." His eyes and their feline allure searched hers. "And, the fact is, your conclusion is worth a considerable amount of research."

Sarah Beth let him hold her for the briefest instant, wanting his embrace to go on forever. Then she peeled his fingers away and scooted down the aisle between the bookshelves and the table. "How exciting," she said, her breathing somewhat ragged. "Frances should be able to help you with that now."

"Frances, indeed! That is all I ever hear about from you, Sarah Beth. Frances this and Frances that, Frances the next thing. I very much wish that you would stop–."

Go ahead, Frank, Sarah Beth thought, *tell me I'm foisting her on you again.*

He changed the subject instead."While your yellow fever vaccine conclusion is worthy of research, I think the time can be better spent elsewhere."

"Oh?"

"Not making light of your discovery, I do not think a yellow fever vaccine will be important in the future. We can control the fever through sanitary measures, which the civil authorities can address. The medical profession needs to concentrate on fighting other epidemic diseases."

"Such as?"

"Bubonic plague, for one. Five years ago there was an outbreak here and in Seattle. Since the ancient Greeks and Romans, bubonic plague has been the scourge of civilization. Ten million people in India alone have died from it."

Sarah Beth thought for a moment. "Could it, too, be transmitted by mosquitoes?"

Frank sat down, tired of chasing after Sarah Beth. "I doubt it, *Doctor* LaBranche. Yellow fever–."

Sarah Beth laughed. "I swear, sometimes you're as pompous as Edgar Rice. I suppose you don't approve of women doctors, either. And that's really not fair, you know. You, yourself, said I was a genius, but, genius or not, I can't study medicine, can I? Because I'm a woman."

"Please, Sarah Beth, I was just joking. You suffragettes are such a touchy lot. Anyway, as I was saying, yellow fever occurs within a definite band around the earth's equator. The band, we now know, in which the *stegomyia* mosquito lives. The black death, bubonic plague, knows no such bounds. If there is a carrier, it must be something other than the *stegomyia*."

Sarah Beth returned two more books to the shelves, then sat at Frank's desk. "Is anyone looking for the carrier, like Dr. Reed and Dr. Carrol did for yellow fever?"

"I am sure someone is. By the way," he added as he stood, "unlike my dear friend, Edgar, I have absolutely nothing against women doctors. And if you choose to be, I am quite certain you would be an excellent one. In fact, with that mind of yours, I think you *should* study medicine." He looked at his watch. "I would like very much to stay and talk, but I have patients to see. There are some, ah, personal matters I would like to discuss. Could we, ah, perhaps, ah, have dinner one evening, not too late, of course, and–."

"Friends don't need to have dinner, Frank. Take Frances to dinner, with *Gamé* as chaperon. Friends can talk here in the library, or on the front porch."

"Friends indeed!" he grumbled as he left, slamming the door.

SARAH BETH HAD NO TROUBLE teaching Frances the management skills necessary to oversee a household, both the handling of accounts and day-to-day administration. Lou Belle taught the young woman the crafts of homemaking–sewing, knitting and the like–and, as a result, Frances soon became a refined, polished and competent homemaker.

Sarah Beth wanted her student-bride-to-be familiar with the details of her future husband's work, so Frances began helping Sarah Beth with Frank's *phlyctenular ophthalmia* research.

One afternoon, Frances flitted into Frank's library as Sarah Beth worked. The younger woman skipped around the center table trailing one hand along the rows of books beside her. "Oh, Sarah Beth, you'll never guess what's happened."

Sarah Beth tried not to look smug and knowing. "Frank's asked you to marry him."

"Oh, no." Frances stopped her gambol and looked a bit woebegone. "Not yet." Then she smiled again. "But it's almost as good." She hugged herself and spun around. "Guess again."

"Hmmmm. Let's see. Could it have anything to do with…No, your birthday's some months away. Does it have something to do with Mardi Gras?" Sarah Beth smiled inwardly, knowing all her conniving and goading of Frank had produced it's intended result.

"Yes. Oh, yes. Oh, yes." Frances knelt next to Sarah Beth's chair and said, "Frank's asked me to the Momus Ball." Then she popped up and skipped around the table again. "Not only are we going to the ball, we're going to the King's supper afterwards! And Frank's arranged for me to have a call-out! Imagine that! A call-out! I'll dance before the king and queen and see the court. And the great, wonderful, exciting, thrilling, never-before-seen-by-my-eyes tableaux of a real, actual Mardi Gras ball. And I'll dance–. But I said that…Of course, I don't know how to dance, but you can teach me." She suddenly looked terrified and ran to Sarah Beth's chair, hanging on to the arm. "You *will* teach me to dance, won't you? Oh! Do you think I can learn? Is it hard? I mean, what if I can't dance? I've never tried. Where do my feet go when I waltz?" She arranged her arms as if she were holding an imaginary dance partner. "Is this right?" She looked down. "Do I start with my feet together, like this?…Or apart, like this?"

Worn out just watching Frances' boundless energy and enthusiasm, Sarah Beth pushed herself from the chair with a sigh. "You'll have absolutely no trouble learning to dance. Here, I'll show you. First, your arms go like this." After a bit of a skirmish, they arranged themselves properly. "Now, when you dance, you must listen to the rhythm of the music." Sarah Beth began to sing in waltz tempo. "1-2-3…1-2-3. Don't-look-down, 1-2-3,…At-your-feet, 1-2-3…And-we-must, 1-2-3…Find you a dress-2-3–."

"Oh, goodness!" Frances stopped in mid-step and her hands flew to her face. "I hadn't thought of that. Can we find one?...Or should we have one made? There's so little time. I can pay for it. I saved up all my money from when I worked as your clerk and–."

"Frances, this will be the most important dress you will ever wear in your entire life. We want Frank to fall madly, desperately, head-over-heels in love with you the second he sees you in it. You're the only family I have now, so please let me buy it for you."

"But you've done so much–."

"And there's so much more I want to do," Sarah Beth said and beamed her happiest smile despite the terrible rending deep in her chest. "Your wedding gown, your trousseau. Oh, my dear, darling Frances. Your wedding will be so wonderful."

MOMUS PARADED THE THURSDAY BEFORE Mardi Gras. Sarah Beth fretted away the afternoon and evening getting Frances ready, fussing more over her young friend than a queen before her coronation. The gown needed minor alterations, Frances took three baths before she smelled right and mind-numbing hours were spent rejecting various hair styles.

When Frances descended the stairs, Sarah Beth thought Frank could do nothing but fall in love with the magnificent raven-haired beauty she had created.

Standing in the foyer in white tie, tails and top hat in hand, Frank barely glanced at Frances, saying as he did, "How very pretty you look." Then he turned his mysteriously fascinating feline gaze on Sarah Beth. "Are you sure you will not change your mind? I am certain I can find an extra invitation. We could wait for you to dress."

Frances did not miss Frank's point, nor how he looked at Sarah Beth when she refused. And the younger woman certainly did not miss the tender pantomime of him blowing Sarah Beth a parting kiss.

Distraught, Sarah Beth paced the evening away waiting for Frances and Frank to return. *The man's impossible!* she thought. *What else do I have to do to discourage him?* Most men Sarah Beth knew would have risked their fortunes to have such a enchanting young woman as Frances on their arm. Frank Cheramie wasted the opportunity!

Evening became night, and night early morning before the clatter of hooves in the drive announced the couple's return. After writing her weekly letter to her mother, Sarah Beth had settled in the front parlor half-heartedly reading a book and waiting for them. Now she rushed upstairs, fearing another *faux pas* if Frank saw her again. Perhaps the enchantment and romance of the ball had magically focused his eyes where they should be.

Sarah Beth measured her bedroom in long strides, twisting the curls at the side of her face around her fingers and hoping Frank and Frances would tarry downstairs. A glass of sherry, some quiet conversation alone. It would be a good sign.

Too soon she heard their footsteps on the stairs.

"Good night, Frances. I hope you enjoyed yourself." Frank's voice sounded as if he had stayed on the second floor.

Damn nincompoop doesn't even have the sense to see her to the door, Sarah Beth thought.

"Oh, I did, Frank," Frances bubbled, her tone sweet enough to attract bees. "The most wonderful, the most thrilling night of my life. All the more wonderful, the more thrilling because you were there."

Then Frances stormed into Sarah Beth's room.

"Well," Sarah Beth said, brightly, "it sounds as if the outing was a success."

Frances threw her clutch on the bed. "A damn disaster."

"W-What happened?"

"That little scene as we left set the tone for the whole damned evening."

"I'm sorry, Frances, I had no idea Frank would–."

"Oh, that was just the beginning!" Frances marched back and forth in front of the Mallard armoire. She saw her reflection in the mirror and stopped, hands on hips, to look at herself. "What a waste of time and energy. Frank hardly noticed me." She spun to face Sarah Beth. "*You* knew an escort couldn't sit with his lady if she has a call-out, didn't you? Why didn't you tell me?"

"I didn't know. I've never been–."

"Dinner was an absolute disaster." Frances began pacing again. "We didn't sit together there, either. I bet if you would have gone with him, he'd've sat next to you!"

"You can't dictate seating arran–."

"He'd've found a way for you! And don't pretend you don't know it."

"Surely in the carriage," Sarah Beth suggested, fidgeting with the scarlet wisps framing her face. "Moonlight, a soft breeze, and–."

"Sarah Beth LaBranche is all he talked about!" Frances hissed. "You're this, you're that. You're the most wonderful thing since God created the sun! Well, I'm sick of it! No matter what I do, I can't please that man because of you!"

"I'm truly sorry you had such an awful evening," Sarah Beth said. "Let me help you out of your things. A good night's sleep will–."

"I'm not staying here."

"It's late, Frances, where will you go?"

"A hotel somewhere, thank you very much."

"And how will you get there?"

"A cab."

"There are no cabs out at this hour."

"Then I'll walk."

"You'll do no such thing. I forbid it."

"You *forbid* it!" Frances spat. "*You* forbid it! *You* can't forbid me–."

"Fine. We'll see what Frank has to say."

Frances glared at Sarah Beth, arms folded tightly across her chest, chin quivering. "All right then, have it your own way. You usually do." Frances yanked open the door. "But I'm leaving in the morning!"

"Promise you won't–."

"I said I'd stay the night and I will!" Frances slammed the door behind her.

Sarah Beth rubbed her eyes, then twisted the curl at her temple. Now what would she do? *Hold his thick head behind a mule and let it kick some sense into him!* she thought. *Why can't the man be more understanding? Like Liam.*

Hoping a good night's sleep would give Frances a better perspective and her a new strategy, Sarah Beth dressed for bed.

AT BREAKFAST, FRANK EXUBERANTLY REPORTED on the ball and the supper-dance while *Gamé* Annadette reminisced about the soireés and cotillions of her youth. Only Sarah Beth seemed to notice that Frances remained petulant and aloof. With Frank and his grandmother lingering over coffee, Frances excused herself. Sarah Beth followed her a few minutes later.

Standing in the doorway of Frances' room, Sarah Beth watched her friend pack a small valise, throwing clothes in haphazardly.

"I'm very sorry," Sarah Beth said softly.

Frances stopped venting her ire on the suitcase. Hands on her hips, her shoulders heaved as she breathed deeply, then she turned. Sarah Beth saw a complex of emotions on the girl's face, in her ceramic smile and hardened eyes.

"I suppose you think I should be the one to apologize," Frances snapped.

"I didn't say that. But I'm truly sorry the evening didn't go as we planned."

"With Frank, nothing will go as planed as long as you…Perhaps its unfair to blame you." A small note of contrition slipped into Frances' voice. "You were the one who said what a great man he was and how lucky I would be if he fell in love with me. So I fell in love with him and…And now look what's happened."

"You know if I could, Frances, I'd dig into his heart and tear out his love for me like a weed. I'd plant you there in my place."

"That's right. There's a weed in the garden of love." A small, ironic smile twitched at the corners of Frances' mouth.

Sarah Beth misread her friend's expression as forgiveness rather than deception. "May I help you unpack?"

"Please," Frances said. "But first forgive me for the terrible way I acted last night and this morning."

Sarah Beth's eyes filled with tears. "There's nothing to forgive…But tell me, dear, how can I make this up to you?"

The two embraced. Frances shrugged, then asked, with a malevolent gleam in her eye, "Take me to the Ball of the Two Well-Known Gentleman Saturday night?"

Sarah Beth held her friend at arms length and gave her a loving, reproving look. "I'll do no such thing."

"Because of what's going to happen?"

"Partly, and partly because–."

Frances picked up a night dress from her suitcase and began folding it. "Then Jose Arlington and the girls still expect to play their little prank."

Sarah Beth started re-folding clothes, too. "They've talked of little else since the epidemic broke."

Frances unpacked a chemise. "The plan's the same, isn't it?"

Sarah Beth nodded.

"You're going, aren't you?" Frances asked.

"Yes." Sarah Beth sighed. "I don't really want to, but I promised several of the girls from The Mansion I would."

"Promise me, too. I'd love to see what happens, but the next best thing is for you to tell me. Please go. Promise? Please."

Sarah Beth pouted a bit. *What could it hurt?* "I promise."

CHAPTER 27

JUST AS IN POLITE NEW Orleans society, several organizations sponsored the District's Mardi Gras celebration, the infamous French Balls. Historically, the three most prominent groups were the Red Light Social Club, the C.C.C. Club and the Two Well-Known Gentlemen. By 1906 the Red Lights, once politically well connected, had disappeared, and the C.C.C. Club and the Two Well-Known Gentlemen arrived at a truce. The surviving syndicates jointly sponsored one Carnival Ball the Saturday before Mardi Gras and one Fat Tuesday night. Unlike the city's traditional Mardi Gras clubs, C.C.C. and the Two Well-Known Gentlemen charged three dollars per person admission to their masquerades and split the profits. As Sarah Beth had explained to Frances the day they met, greed energized the District.

The French Balls had become popular with the young women of the upper strata of New Orleans society; *tres chic* to attend and, masked of course, look down their noses at the tawdry women they only heard of in whispers. This haughty attitude had spurred Jose Arlington to devise the surprise for these patrician damsels when the Society of Venus and Bacchus met in The Mansion the preceding spring.

The Saturday of the first French Ball arrived. Without Jose's prank, the gala would have been only a prelude to the excitement of crowning the *demimonde*-queen of Mardi Gras on Fat Tuesday. With the promise of revenge whetting their interest and full pockets from an exceptionally profitable week before Mardi Gras, the bawds and their fancy men showed up at Odd Fellows Hall on Camp Street ready for fun.

Juliette, Hilda and Sarah Beth all had something else to celebrate. After strenuous negotiations in Juliette's boudoir, she and Hilda, working as a team, had secured the loan they needed from Juliette's happily-exhausted banker friend. The act of sale transferring The Mansion took place the morning of the ball in front of the buyers and seller's lawyers and the assembled girls of the house; a joyous time for all concerned, amid champagne, happy tears for bright futures and sad thoughts for dear friends soon lost.

Saturday evening, Sarah Beth and several of the girls climbed into the carriage Titan drove to Odd Fellow's Hall, where the ball was to be given. When they arrived, Sarah Beth saw many of the inhabitants of her soon-to-be past in the large crowd waiting for the doors to open: the four queens of the *demimonde*, Jose Arlington, Countess Willie Piazza, Lulu White and Emma Johnson; the lesser *demimonde* like Josephine Icebox and Deanie Jean the Suicide Queen; Tom Anderson, who everyone knew to be one of the Two Well-Known Gentlemen; the men who had worked with her in the fever fight, Ike, Tim Ryan and his brother, Liam–with corn-silk hair sticking out from under his ever-present newsboy cap. Sarah Beth saw John Griswold's head towering over the crowd and knew, though she could not see him, his runt friend, Chicken Dick Charlie, would be close by.

Ten minutes past the appointed time, the assembly became rowdy, but not more noticeably so than any other gathering in the District. Five minutes later, when the doors remained closed, the mob began to chant, "O-pen, o-pen, o-pen." Caught up in the excitement of their adventure, fashionable young ladies and their gentlemen escorts shouted as loud as the whores and pimps next to them.

Suddenly the New Orleans aristocracy decided they deserved better positions in line than the bawds and their beaus and began jostling toward the doors. The *demimonde* shoved back. Sarah Beth, sensing the impending riot, worked her way behind the crowd just as shutter-girl, Dixie Smith, climbed onto a lamppost. Someone handed Dixie a trumpet and she produced, long and loud, the most horrible sound ever to come from a musical instrument.

When she had the crowd's attention, red-faced Dixie yelled, "By all rights, we oughtta let the uptown ladies in first, dearies." She laid a finger on the side of her nose, winked and snorted a belly-laugh. "Then they'll have the best seats in the house. The ones far away from the doors. Ha-ha."

Everyone laughed, including those who would soon be the brunt of what some already called the world's greatest practical joke. Sarah Beth laughed, too; delighted the condescending hypocrites who made sport of other people's misery faced their comeuppance.

Dixie played an awful encore and kept the mob otherwise amused until the doors finally opened twenty minutes later. The mob surged forward. Sarah Beth, at the fringe of the crowd, managed a proper, decorous entrance into the jammed auditorium.

Inside, the audience was a study in contrast and contradiction. Rich young women, in taffeta and silk, jewels set against the black serge of their escorts' tuxedos, searched the room with opera glasses, whispering among themselves and pointing. The *demimonde*, bedecked in their gaudiest petals and plumes, shimmering in the saccharin sparkle of too many rhinestones, huddled in their own conversations, selecting victims to watch when the prank began.

Sarah Beth noticed one particularly poignant encounter between a District girl and a socialite. Except for different masks, they wore the same ensemble, including hat, gloves and purse. Yet, anyone noticing them could differentiate the polluted from the pristine. The difference lay in the details: harsh lip paint, feather boa, rough cuticles, red hands. Sarah Beth saw the eloquent anguish in the prostitute's eyes as she looked at her twin for the evening and realized, all too painfully, what might have been.

Sneering, the gentlewoman inched her way around the sporting girl, exaggerating her obvious struggle to avoid touching such a social leper. Decimated, the prostitute stood rigid as a stone gargoyle, tears gathering in her eyes, her tormented expression saying, "There, but for the curse of God, go I."

Is the whole world totally without compassion? Sarah Beth wondered, her earlier light-heartedness destroyed as she fully comprehended the tragedy about to take place. She followed the rich, triumphant twin with her eyes. *Doesn't she know how close she is to being exactly what she despises most, how close we all are to that disaster? Our lives turn on moments too insignificant to measure or record. How different mine would be if Paw had come home five minutes earlier or later that day, if his aim had been a tad better or worse when he went hunting; if I had stopped to pull a sticker from my foot, crossed the road in the dust of Inez's carriage rather than in front of it. It's not 'the road not taken' that controls our fortune. That would mean a conscious decision. Blind chance, fate, kismet, destiny, a twinkle in the cosmic eye makes one soul king, another clown; determines who is queen or concubine.*

Sarah Beth watched the genteel victor regally seat herself and chatter happily with friends, nodding occasionally at the wretched woman she had so soundly vanquished.

She has no idea, Sarah Beth thought. *She lives her pampered life and dreams her pampered dreams, never knowing only a sheen in the air prevents her from being what she fears or hates or desires most. Comes the day she loses all, she'll root and ferret for the grand conspiracy she knows beyond doubt has done her in, or die sour after a lifetime vainly searching for the nefarious plot. Yet, if there's a God and He's honest, He'll tell her, when she asks, that fate guaranteed the outcome fifty or a thousand-thousand years before when the wind swept some amoeba onto one pile of dung rather than another.*

Sarah Beth held up her hands, palm out, looking for a seam, a small rip in the gossamer, impenetrable cocoon fortune weaves around

everyone. If she could but find some insignificant fracture, some purchase for a fingernail, she could expand it and slip through to become
the other self the cosmos had denied her. Could she? Could anyone?

Sarah Beth slowly surveyed the *demimonde*. Tyrannized by the
pompous uptown invaders, each wanted revenge. She saw no forgiveness, no understanding of how close the twain might be. Tonight's
shenanigans continued an endless line of tits-for-tats stretching from
forever to infinity.

*Perhaps I'm one of the few lucky ones. Perhaps I've found that tiny split
in the airy gauze of my cell. I've sold The Mansion. I'm leaving the District.
Maybe that's how we break free. Our position in the universe may be determined by minutia, whether or not we stay there is up to us. Myda was
right. I was punishing myself. And for something over which I had no control. Rather than live the life I've made, I'll make the life I want. And who
knows, Frank may even–. No, that can never be.* Sarah Beth sat back in
her seat and scanned the scene before her–the jealousy, the arrogant
pretension, the class warfare. *That's the true ullage of a heart. Its capacity
to forgive: the down-trodden for their failure, the rich for their success;
knowing neither are responsible for anything, save their own desperation.
When someone owns their success or failure, when conscious choice has
overcome cosmic coincidence, only then we should esteem or pity, honor or
scorn them.*

All alone despite the crowd filling Odd Fellows Hall on the Saturday
night before Mardi Gras 1906, Sarah Beth LaBranche forgave those who
had destroyed her life–her father, Inez Breaux, the long line of men
whose lust had debased her. First and foremost, she forgave herself–for
all the deliberately destructive choices she had made, for all she had
allowed herself to become and for everything she never permitted herself to be. That would change now. Having decided to leave the District,
the first full moon of her future rose tonight and in its silvered incan-
descence she would seize her tomorrows by the throat and throttle them
until they returned the birthright she had squandered.

The lights dimmed, the crowd hushed, the orchestra began and the master of ceremonies–tuxedoed, plumed, black masked–took center stage. Sarah Beth had arrived at the ball anxious to see the uptown ladies get their due. Now the mere thought of such a massive exchange of hate exhausted her. She stood to leave.

"Where you going?" Juliette asked.

"Back to The Mansion."

"Oh no, not yet," Juliette urged.

"Stay, stay," Grace insisted. "You'll be sorry if you miss it."

Seated in the precise center of the row, to Sarah Beth's left and right stretched an obstacle course of feet, knees, legs and laps. Daunted, she sat down. The evening had been instructive thus far, perhaps there would be something else to learn.

"Ladiessssss and Gentlemennnnn," the impresario began, "a big howdy-doody t' you-dy and welcome t' the first one o' the C.C.C. Club and Two Well-Knowed Gentlemen's world *re*nowned French Balls f' this year."

Applause, whistles, cat-calls.

"All ya'll know the C.C.C. Club, and the Two Well-Knowed Gentlemen is so well knowed, ain't no need t' introduce none o' 'em, now is there?"

Laughter.

"But before this here shindig gets goin', we gotta little surprise."

The *demimonde* and their fancy men snickered.

"Past few years or so, it's been the thing t' do f' all you uptown bitches and ya snot-nose boyfriends to come slummin' in the District at Mardi Gras. But ya don't never invite none o' us up t' ya shindigs, now do ya? So we axed ourselves, 'Why let the likes o' them come t' ours?'"

Opera-glasses fell and cultured heads moved together for whispered conversations. Several skiddish upper-class couples began shuffling nervously toward the aisles.

"Well, this year, we gotta special treat for all you high falutin' folks. This here's a ball for what they call lewd and abandoned women, so every woman here must be a sport. And in this city, can't be no sport without no license. So ya'll get ya licenses out, ladies, 'cause the coppers wanna check 'em. If ya left 'em home, there's a Black Maria outside t' give ya a free ride t' the hoosegow." Pandemonium erupted and the master of ceremonies shouted through hands cupped around his mouth, "Read the newspaper tomorrow f' the names o' the gals in jail f' being lewd and abandoned without no permit!"

Half the audience rushed for the doors, the other half tried to block their way. Whistles blaring, the police swarmed into the auditorium from doors around the sides and back, and from the stage itself.

Fashionable women shrieked, yelled and elbowed their way to the exits. None fainted, too lady-like a display would cause more trouble than it overcame.

"Cough it up, Miss," a policeman said, grabbing the arm of a socialite one row in front of Sarah Beth. "No license and it's into the Black Maria with you."

"No! You can't put me in there!" the elegant young woman screamed. "I know what you do to women when you get them inside. You can't make me go in there! Horace! Horace, where are you? Make this beastly man let me go! Tell him I'm not one of these dreadful women."

One of the *demimonde* yelled in the young woman's face, "Aw, but ya gotta be, dearie. That's who this ball's for. Ya gotta be one of them dreadful women, as ya calls us. If ya here, you're a whore, and a whore needs a license. Go 'head, show 'em yours, dearie. Go on, shows it to 'em. If ya ain't got one, shame on ya f' being lewd and abandoned w'out one."

The young woman twisted her arm away from the policeman, hiked her skirt and began climbing over the chairs. "Horace! Horace, where are you?" She lost her balance and fell on to the back of another policeman.

"Oh, so ya wanna play rough," the second officer said and grabbed her around the chest. With a hand deliberately cupping each breast, he dragged her toward the exit. "Off we go, chippie."

"Stop that!" the woman shouted, trying to pry away the policeman's fingers. "Don't you dare touch my–. Stop it, I say! That's no way to treat a lady!"

Sarah Beth shook her head at the vengeance being exacted. Eye for eye, tooth for tooth, degradation for degradation. When would it stop?

Behind her, Sarah Beth heard a familiar voice. "There she is! There she is! I told you she'd be here! I told you what she was, didn't I? This proves it!" Frances screamed.

"It proves nothing," Frank replied. "You are here and you are not one of these vile women, are you?"

"Of course not!"

"My point exactly," Frank said. "Sarah Beth is here on a lark, just like you and so many of these other young ladies."

"No! No, she's not! I can prove it!" Frances shoved her way through the crowd, pulling Frank by the arm.

Her newly discovered philosophy suddenly forgotten, Sarah Beth pushed against writhing, jostling, shoving, yelling bodies that would not move. While an infinitesimal sliver of her mind reminded her of her amoeba/dung theory, the rest of her adrenalin-charged brain told her to escape the calamity she had fought so hard to avoid these past months.

Frances and Frank, fighting against currents of humanity washing them toward the exits, closed in on her.

"Just a minute." A policeman grabbed Sarah Beth's wrist. "Let's see ya license."

Sarah Beth, eyes white-ringed, could not tear her gaze from Frances, fighting tenaciously through the mob. "I-I d-don't have one," she managed to say.

As the officer began herding Sarah Beth off, Frances yelled, "No! No! She's a whore! You can't arrest her! She's a whore, *SHE'S A WHORE!*"

With Frank close behind, Frances seized the sleeve of the policeman holding Sarah Beth. "You can't arrest her! She's a whore, I tell you!"

"Look," the officer said, "if she's a whore, she'd be showing me her license, now wouldn't she? With as much time in the hoosegow as these whores get, she'd spare herself a trip if she could, don'tcha think?"

"Listen to me. It's because of him." Frances caught Frank's lapel and dragged him forward. "She doesn't want *him* to know!"

The officer held Sarah Beth's wrist tightly with one hand and rubbed his chin with the other. "Mighty peculiar if ya ask me, Miss. Sounds like a real tall tale. A whore goin' t' jail 'cause of some john. Must be a mighty special trick–."

"Sure and it looks like ya got ya hands full, Johnny," Liam said, pushing his way through the crowd and giving the policeman a friendly pat on the back. "What's the trouble here?"

"Damndest thing ya ever seen." The policeman nodded toward Sarah Beth. "This one here says she ain't a whore 'n' wants me t' cart her off. That one there says she is and wants me t' leave her be. All 'cause of this guy." He jerked his thumb in Frank's direction.

Jostled as the members of the audience around him either sought to escape or help in the arrests, Liam looked from bewildered Frank to vengeful Frances to terrified Sarah Beth. "Aye. And I been knowin' this lady a good, long time now, Johnny, and if there's one thing I can be sayin' f' sure, it's that she ain't no more jolly good fellow than you are."

"It's a lie!" Frances screamed. "He's in love with her. He's trying to protect her! Look, I can prove it!" Frances snatched Sarah Beth's purse before Liam could stop her.

"Damn woman, gimme that!" Liam shouted.

Frances dodged into a knot of hysterical women and began rummaging through the handbag. "It's here!" she yelled. "I know it is. She knew what was going to happen tonight. She told me. They planned it in the house where she works, her and that Arlington woman. She told me all about it and laughed. I know she'd bring–. Here it is! Look, Frank, look!" Frances triumphantly shoved a piece of paper at Frank's nose. "See what it says! Read it!"

Frank took Sarah Beth's license. At first the words did not seem to register: Sarah Beth LaBranche...so on and so on...lewd and abandoned woman.

In a moment that lasted a millennium, Sarah Beth saw unequivocal loathing and absolute contempt flood Frank's eyes as the words on the paper penetrated into his brain.

"Damn it! How could you do this to me?" Raging, Frank seized Sarah Beth's shoulders and shook her. "Tell me! Goddamn you, woman, how could you do this to me!"

"Ya can't be believin' the black-haired one, Johnny." Liam, knocked off balance by a surge of the crowd, tried to push his way to Sarah Beth. "Ain'tcha never seen a switch before. I seen her slip it out her sleeve."

"Lemme see that." The policeman took Sarah Beth's license from Frank. "This you?" he demanded holding up the license.

Sarah Beth nodded mechanically.

"Lewd and abandoned, all right. Here, little darlin'," Johnny said, handing the license to Sarah Beth and letting go her wrist, "keep it handy. You'll be needin' it a bunch 'fore this night's over." The policeman pushed past Liam. "Look at her. Who'da thought?"

"Aw, Johnny, ya ain't believin' none of that blarney, are ya now? Didn't ya see the switch. Didn't ya see the little black-haired one sneak it out her–."

"Blarney, huh? If there's blarney around here, it's yours. I seen that paper come out the purse with my own two eyes."

"Sure and what about the other one then? Check her papers, did ya?"

The policeman turned to Frances. "What about it, honey. Got a paper ya want me t' see. Takes one t' know one, I always say."

"Me? *Me*," Frances said. "I'm not a whore."

"Don't go puttin' me on now," Johnny said, "I seen enough chippies steal a fancy man, one from the other, t' know what's going on here. Lemme see that purse."

Frank grabbed the policeman's arm. "I am no such thing and neither is she! I am a doctor, not a whore's fancy man, though I came closer than I would ever like to think. But, surely, you can't think this young lady–."

The policeman raised his billy. "Best let go if ya don't want ya head split."

Indecisive for only a moment, Frank stepped back.

"You crazy, stupid or both?" Johnny spat at Frank as he snatched Frances' arm. "If ya can't see what's goin' on here, find somebody to take you home, you're too blind t' make it by ya'self."

"I will have you know I *am* a doctor. Though I might have been both crazy and stupid for ever thinking–. I certainly am not any more." Though Frank spoke to the policeman, he looked directly at Sarah Beth. All the mystery and magic gone from his feline eyes, his stared at her like an enraged carnivore stalking its prey. "As for this young lady," he said, putting his arm around Frances, "I vouch for her. She definitely is not one of these terrible women. I guarantee it."

"I'm not! Oh, I'm not. Here, look in my purse." Frances dumped its contents on the seat next to her. "See, no license. I live at this man's house and–."

The policeman's eyebrows raised. "Married?"

"No, not like that. I–."

"Aye, a whore one way or another, eh, Johnny?" Liam said. "If she ain't got no license, do ya duty, lad."

"No, no, it is not what you think," Frank insisted. "She boards there. And it's my grandmother's house."

Liam chuckled. "Likely story, eh, Johnny, boy-o."

"Don't make no difference t' me," the policeman said. "She's here and she don't got no license. Let's go, honey." The policeman pulled Frances toward the door.

"No! Wait! You can't," Frank yelled.

"Look, buster," Johnny said, raising his billy again. "Don't go tellin' me what I can and can't do, or I'll haul your ass in with her right after I bust it black and blue."

"Yes, take me with her," Frank argued. "I can make sure nothing happens to her on the way to jail. I know what you people do in the Maria."

"Ain't likely tonight. Not with a bunch of high falutin', uptown gals with daddies t' have a man's job in the blink of an eye f' just thinkin' about liftin' her skirt."

"Wait," Frank pleaded. "How much to take us both out of here safely?"

"Hmmmm." The policeman lowered his billy.

"Five dollars."

"Ten."

"Done." Frank took out his wallet. "Five now and five more outside."

"Got no time for that. Unlicenced, lewd and abandoned women need arrestin'."

"And I do not have enough money to pay every policeman in this God-forsaken place. Fifteen dollars?"

"I donno."

"Twenty. Ten now and ten outside." Frank shoved money into the policeman's hand. "Pretend you have arrested both of us. None of your friends will stop us."

"Twenty-five."

Frank pushed more bills at the policeman, dropping several on the floor. "More when we get outside. Now go!"

Frances, Frank and the policeman pushed through the crowd toward the door.

As Sarah Beth watched them, Frances turned and called, "I'm sorry, Sarah Beth. I had to do it. It was the only way. He couldn't see me because of you. Please forgive me. I'm so sorr–." The crush of people swallowed Frances up, and the noise drowned out her words.

Sarah Beth stood quietly, ignoring the ruckus around her, watching the spot where she had last seen Frank and Frances. After a moment, she started moving slowly toward the exit.

"Aye, lass, and the least I could be doin' is t' help ya make ya way through this."

"Thank you," Sarah Beth said softly to the Irishman's back.

Stopped several times by policemen, Sarah Beth hauled her license out like some gargantuan weight and showed it to amazed officers who, from the looks of her, had no idea she belonged to the *demimonde*.

On the *banquette* outside Odd Fellows Hall, Liam said, "Sure and I could be seein' ya home, if ya want."

"No, thank you."

"Will ya big nigger be comin' to fetch ya?"

"No."

"Sure and I could be hailin' a cab for ya then?"

"No, thank you."

"For God's sake, lass, ain't there somethin' ya need doin'?"

"Whatever needs to be done can only be done by me."

"Aye."

"Good night, Liam, and thank you for everything. I know what you tried to do in there. Considering how you think you feel about me–."

"'Tain't thinkin'."

"You were very kind, very generous."

"I'm only after makin' ya happy. I'd be doin' it me own self if you'd let me. But time's runnin' out."

"We're each responsible for our own happiness. As far as time running out, you should have given up on me long ago."

"Aye. Don't see how I ever could. But that ain't what I mean. I'm after packin' meself back to Belfast. But if I thought ya might–."

Sarah Beth smiled sadly into his expectant blue eyes. "Do what you must."

Liam appeared to hold his breath as long as he could before the words exploded, "I'd be sayin' I take ya along, but all I can offer is a berth in steerage and that ain't no place for a lass like you."

"That's sweet, Liam, but it's not fair to you."

"Sure and I don't want ya to be worryin' 'bout what's good and what ain't as far as I'm concerned. Just say the word, lass, and–."

Sarah Beth shook her head. "I'm sorry."

"Aye. So am I, lass. So am I."

As Liam walked away, Sarah Beth leaned against one of the fluted metal posts holding the second floor balcony over the sidewalk. A small marquis advertised the night's festivities: a beautiful, buxom young woman, masked and seductively posed, enticed passers-by with the promise, 'FUN! FUN! FUN! DON'T MISS THE FRENCH BALL.' Tonight Sarah Beth had planned to celebrate her rebirth. FUN! FUN! FUN!

I made this life and lived it well. But I should have made it different, so different Frank would have–. No regrets. I promised myself no regrets. What's done is history. With a trembling finger twisting the curl at the side of her face, she thought, *One tear.* A single droplet meandered down her cheek. *Just one for all that was, all that might have been.*

As the small bead of sorrow hung from her chin, in her mind Sarah Beth saw Frances dragged from the hall, her plea echoing in Sarah Beth's brain. *Sorry, sorry, sorry, sorry…Had to, had to, had to, had to…Forgive, forgive, forgive, forgive.*

Sarah Beth steadied herself on the post, then began stumbling down the street, trusting her feet to find their way back to The Mansion, not noticing Liam following in the shadows. *Of course, I forgive you, Frances. It's not your fault. This all began eons ago when some little bug landed on one pile of shit rather than another.*

CHAPTER 28

WITH THE GIRLS OF THE Mansion still at the French Ball and not expected back for several hours, Sarah Beth decided a long bath might convalesce the excruciating pain in her heart. Soothed somewhat by the hot, fragrant water, she lingered over her toilette, thinking of her life and what it might have been. As she swept a brush through her fine, scarlet-gold mane, someone pounded on her door.

"Miz Sarah Beth, oh, Miz Sarah Beth. Y'all better get you'self downstairs quick."

"Come in, Lou Belle." When the housekeeper opened the door, Sarah Beth said, "I'm ready for bed. What is it?"

"It's terrible, that's what it is. He done barged his'self in here hollerin' afta ya. Got his'self lit up like one them sparkles on the Fourth of July, all drunk on whiskey. It's jus' horrible. I ain't never seen a man so crazy drunk afore, and I seed plenty in my day. He clothes all out he pants and he rantin' and ravin'. Any other man I would've told Titan t' pitch out, but him bein' Dr. Frank and all, I didn't knowed what all t' do, so I come up here t' fetch–."

"Calm down, Lou Belle," Sarah Beth snapped. "Did he say what he wanted?"

"Yeah zum. He say he got money and wants t' call on ya."

"Oh, he does, does he!" Sarah Beth slammed the brush on her dressing table, tore off her night dress and threw it to Lou Belle. "Do something with that!"

Naked, hair flying like a banshee, Sarah Beth ran to her chest of drawers and rummaged through it until she found her most seductive peignoir, pale green with frosty lace and emerald ribbon trim. She wrapped herself in it and cinched it closed with a sash the same color as the trim. Running to the mirror, she inspected her reflection. The diaphanous peignoir molded itself to her breasts, accentuated her tiny waist, clung to the graceful spread of her hips. The thin fabric hinted and tantalized, promising the most magnificent female form a man could ever hope to possess. She touched her hair in several places, curled the wisps of hair framing her face with her fingers and asked in breathless whisper, "Am I beautiful, Lou Belle?"

"My, my. You 'bout the prettiest woman a man ever did see."

"Good, Goddamn it!" Sarah Beth's hands went to her hips, her eyes blazed and her lips curled. "Now where is the bastard!"

"But, Miz–."

"There's no buts about it, Lou Belle. If he thinks he can call on me, he's got another think coming. All he'll see is what he can't have. Now where is the son of a bitch?"

"Still in the foyer, I 'spect."

Sarah Beth floated down the stairs, a woodland fantasy, a consort for Puck and his sprightly friends. Her gown billowed behind and clung in front; gorgeous calves and thighs peeked from the folds of the gauzy peignoir, dazzling hair framed her beautiful angel-pixie face. Rounding the final bend in the stairs, she glided to a stop above the stand-off in the foyer.

Frank, swaying like a ship's mast in a storm, stood just inside the front door, and the hulking form of Titan guarded The Mansion from further trespass. In whatever direction Frank's eyes focused, Titan shifted his bulk to ward off a drunken lurch.

"Good evening, Dr. Cheramie," Sarah Beth said sweetly from her position above him.

When Frank saw her, he stood straighter, teetered less. "My God! This is what it must be like to meet your guardian angel."

Sarah Beth used her most beguiling smile. "How kind of you to say, especially after your behavior earlier this evening."

Frank bowed low and, with a grand sweep of his arms, said, "You must…What must you do? I forget…Ah, yes. You must forgive me. I had then just recently the misfortune of discovering the woman I loved, the woman I cherished above life itself was a…was a…was a *WHORE!*" He spit the word, baring his teeth. As quickly as his fury came, it passed. "I am sure you can…What?…Oh, you can understand how supset I made it…Rather, it made me."

"Then why did you come here, Doctor?" Sarah Beth asked, still cloyingly sweet.

"To see you."

"Now that you've seen me, good night."

"No. Wait. I'm your greatest…." Frank shook the fog from his head. "Your greatest admirer and I come calling, like all the rest. I want my turn. Where am I in line, Sarah Beth? Hundredth? Thousandth? Ten thousandth? Tell me, dear, sweet, damnable, contemptible *BITCH*, where am I?"

"On your ear in the Goddamn street! Now that you've seen what you'll never have, get out! Titan, show him the door!"

"Wait." Frank rifled his pockets looking for his billfold. "You don't understand. I have money. I know you take money. That's what women like you do. It's here somewhere." He turned his pants pockets inside out and a few bills fluttered to the floor. "Not enough. I know I have my wallet." He found it in his inside coat pocket. "See." He opened it and held it up for her to look inside.

"I don't want your Goddamn money, Frank Cheramie! I want you to go home!"

"I most certainly will not! This is a spotting house, and I'm a spot...ah, sport. And you, I'm told, are a very great spot. A jolly good fellow, as they say," Frank sneered. "And I've seen the papers to prove it. Are you a good spot, dear Sarah Beth?"

"Not any more, Frank. And never with you. Go home. You're too drunk to stand up."

"Say, what kinda place this is, anyway? You must have one of those sayings. "Come to-." Frank looked around–bleary eyed, waving his hands and swaying. "Come to wherever-the-hell-I-am for a swell time, or something like that. What do they say about you in the District newspaper? Bet you thought I didn't know about the *Sunday Sun*. Well, in my day, I got around, and you better never forget it. What does the paper say about you? 'When in town, don't forgot to visit Miss Sarah Beth BraLaunch. She'll show you a swell time. No one leaves Miss BraLaunch's place un-dissatisfied.' Well, I'm visiting you, Sarah Beth, and I'm un-dissatisfied. Whatcha gonna do about it?"

Sarah Beth's eyes narrowed. "*You* don't have enough money, Frank."

"Sure I do." He held out his billfold again. "Look at all that money. How much to spent, for spindling–. How much for you to show me a swell time, my darling, damnable *WHORE*! Name your price. Go on, Goddamn you, name it!"

"One hundred dollars."

"Outrageous! A man could have twenty women in the best house on Basin Street for–."

"I've named my price. Take it or leave."

Frank fumbled through his wallet. "Not enough," he mumbled. Picking up the money that had fallen on the floor, he counted his cash again. "Still not enough. Wait, I'll be back."

"I won't be here."

"But you have to. Just let me go home–."

"And stay there," Sarah Beth yelled. "Titan, take–."

"Wait. Here. I have sissy-two dollars and…." Frank counted coins from his pocket. "And forty-two, no, forty-three cents."

"Not enough."

"Wait. Wait. My watch, take my pocket watch. It was my father's and it's very valuable."

"I don't want your watch, Frank," Sarah Beth said.

"And my stick pin." He pulled the jewel from his cravat. "It was my mother's engagement ring."

"Frank, for the last time, go–."

"What will it take for you to whore with me, you damnable *BITCH*! Let me lay between your legs like everyone else!" Frank lunged for the stairs, but Titan wrapped his huge arms around Frank's chest and held him as he struggled. "Whore with me, Goddamn you!" he screamed as Titan dragged him toward the front door. "I loved you, I trusted you, I wanted to marry you and you ruined it all! Whore with me, Goddamn you! Take my money and my watch and my mother's ring. Take everything I own, you dirty, filthy Jezebel. You've already taken all that has meaning for me. Take the rest! I have no need for it anymore. Only whore with me, bitch, so there will be no doubt in my mind whatsoever of what you are, so my heart can be rid of you forever! Please," he begged, his voice catching, "please help me be free of you."

Sarah Beth prowled down the stairs. "So that's what this is all about. Take me to bed so you can forget me, is that it? I saved your Goddamn life and this is the thanks I get!"

"Why did you do it? I never asked you to! You should have let me die, you *BITCH*! Then I would never have known. Why, oh, why couldn't you let me die!"

Crouched, ready to pounce, Sarah Beth made her decision. "Let him pass, Titan, if that's what he wants." She spun and ran up the stairs to her room.

Frank, plodding on leaden feet, followed after. Standing in her door-way as she paced back and forth on the other side of the room, he asked, "What about payment?"

"Put it on the dresser. Close the door."

He put his money and jewelry on her bureau, then slammed the door. Still swaying from the liquor, he stood waiting. When she contin-ued pacing, Frank demanded, "Undress me. Women like you do that."

"Undress yourself."

Frank tore at his clothes until they lay in a heap around him, all except his shoes, socks and garters.

Sarah Beth continued marching in front of the windows.

"Well…Wash me."

"Wash yourself."

"You're supposed to wash me. Women like you do that. Wash me, *WHORE!*"

Sarah Beth faced him with her hands on her hips and said, coolly, "Contrary to what your male conceit would like to believe, we don't wash you because we like to, or because you like it. We wash you for our own protection, to make sure you don't have a disease. You're a doctor, Frank. Do you have gleet? Maybe you don't know it by that name. Frank, dear," she asked sweetly, "do you have syphilis or gonorrhea?"

"Of course not."

"Then wash yourself or stick the soap up your ass, I don't much care which."

"This isn't the jolly good time a man expects from a woman like you."

"It's your Goddamn jolly good time, not mine. I do this for the money, remember."

Frank looked down at himself. "Surely you can do something to help me, to repair me–prepare me, I mean–get me ready to–."

"Do it yourself. You remember how."

"Listen here! I'm paying for this with my soul, you Goddamn bitch, the least you can do–."

"Here, Frank, maybe this will help." Sarah Beth plopped on the bed. She arranged her peignoir to reveal ivory thighs and adjusted the bodice to bare the downy-white rise of her breasts. "Some of my admirers tell me they can't look at me like this without coming on too fast. Does it help? Take a good look. This is what you paid for." Sarah Beth's eyes fell to his flagging manhood. "Not much of a bull, are you, Frank? No horns. More like a cow's udder, if you ask me."

Frank fell slowly to his knees, then on all fours. Crawling to the foot of the bed, he rested his chin on the edge of the mattress. His bleary, blood-shot eyes had lost their ability to captivate. "Why are you doing this to me? I've been shamed enough by you, why this? I've paid your price. God, I've paid with my soul! Give me what I paid for and let me go."

"What you paid for is right here," Sarah Beth whispered and rubbed her thighs together tantalizingly. "And right here." She opened her bodice, giving him complete view of her voluptuous breasts. "You've paid for a smile." She grimaced. "A kiss." She blew him one. "A soft caress to your fevered brow." She pantomimed the movement with her hand gracefully in the air. "You've paid for it all. Come." She held her arms out to him. "Come and get your just desserts, *you ungrateful bastard!*"

He climbed on the bed, dragged himself to lay next to her. "Why!" he sobbed, punching the pillow. "Why, why, *why!*" he demanded to the rhythm of his fist fighting feathers. "I loved, loved, loved, you, you, you. How could you do this to me?"

Sarah Beth threw open her gown. "Here, Frank. Take what you paid for."

He looked at her, then buried his face in the pillow. "I can't," he said in a muffled sob. "You won't help me get ready, damn it! Why do you do this to me?"

Why, indeed? Sarah Beth wondered. She loved Frank beyond rage, beyond vengeance, beyond all petty, human failings. And tonight would be the last time she saw him, her last opportunity to love him as she had dreamed of so often these past months, her final chance of thrilling to the ecstasy of totally surrendering herself to him. Regardless of his reasons, regardless of everything he had said and done, she realized *she* needed the memory of loving him completely, to sustain her for the rest of her life. Tentatively, she reached her hand out, then took it back. Softly she answered his question, "Because you'll have everything and I'll have nothing."

"What a lie!" he yelled into the pillow. "How will *I* have everything?"

"You'll have the memory of a night of passion and ecstasy with a woman who loves you more than you can ever imagine. A man as straight-laced as you has no idea what that means. All you know of passion is the lust that brought you to the District as a boy. But tonight, you'll know the bliss of unrestrained love between a man and a woman. A love you could have had for the rest of your life." Sarah Beth reached out for him, but denied herself again, and, almost whispering, said, "And so will I…But then you'll leave me. Go back to your neat, compact world where men and women are slotted perfectly in their little nooks. Where everyone, women included, believes the lies you do. That's how you'll have everything. You'll have the safety of your nice, ordered existence and the memory of tonight. You'll feed on that memory, Frank, and it will give you sustenance for the rest of your life…How do I know?…I'm the expert. I've lived on reminiscence and fantasy all my life. And I mean to make tonight a long-sustaining memory…I'm so sorry, Frank, for all the hurt I've caused you. Come to me. Put your hate aside for just one more night. Take it up again in the morning if you must, but tonight can't we give each other the love that's always been between us?" She finally touched him gently on the shoulder. "Forgive me for being so harsh before. I wanted to hurt you as much as you had hurt me. Now I no longer need that revenge. It settles nothing. Let's each absolve the other for all the hurt we've caused each other. Let's have this one night of incomparable love. Then we'll part, each to live without the other…I in a world more shadow than light. But there will be a remembered glow, my darling. The memory of you, of tonight." Her voice had become warm, loving. She slid next to him, pressing herself hard on him, kissing his neck, his shoulder, his ear. "I'll even help you get ready. Would you like that? Turn over…Frank…Frank? …*Frank!*"

His regular breathing said her memory of that night would be confessing her love to a sleeping drunk.

"Shit!" Sarah Beth rolled to her side of the bed and closed her gown. "Shit!" Jumping up, she left Frank passed out on the bed and, at the door to her bedroom, yelled, "Titan!"

"Here I come, Miz Sarah Bet'." The giant's boots thundered up the stairs and he stood before her, hat in hand. "Here I is. What y'all need?"

"Take this drunken lout home," Sarah Beth ordered bitterly. "No need to dress him either. I hope all his friends see him carried to his house naked and drunk."

Lou Belle wagged her finger at her mistress as she entered the room. "Now, Miz Sarah Beth, ain't no need to be mean like that."

"*Me* mean? What about *him*?"

"He just a man. They 'posed t' be stupid. Not you. You is a lady."

Sarah Beth looked down at the open bodice of her gown, at her thigh exposed almost to the hip. "Some lady."

"You got mo' lady in ya than all them uptown womanezes rolled up t'gether. And don't ya never go thinkin' otherwise, neither…Ty, carry him on out o' here."

"Lou Belle's right, Titan. Dress him before bringing him home."

"You done the right thing, Miz Sarah Beth. Findin' that there man drunk and naked on the front stoop would mortify ol' Miz Annadette t' her grave."

The giant Negro slung Frank over one massive shoulder, then bent and scooped up the doctor's clothes.

"Dress him up and pass him by he house," Lou Belle instructed. "But, before all that, he do need some fixin' fo' what he done. Haul ya big, old man self over here, Ty. I got just the thing t' make Miz Sarah Beth feel better." When Titan carried Frank over, Lou Belle said, "Aim he buck-naked ass this-a-way…Go on now, Miz Sarah Beth, give him a good whack. It sure will make ya feel better, honey. Go on now."

Sarah Beth gave a short, mirthless snort. "What good will that do?"

"A world o' good, 'cause ya doin' it ya'self. Go on now," Lou Belle urged. "See if it don't make ya feel better."

Sarah Beth shooed Titan with her hand. "Just take Dr. Cheramie home."

"Well, if you ain't, I is…Act like a chil'en and gets treated like one," Lou Belle told Frank's bare behind. Then she reached far behind herself and brought the flat of her hand, as hard as she could, smartly on Frank's buttock, leaving a bright, red palm print. Shaking the sting out of her hand, she said, "Ooee! That sure do a heart and soul some good…Dress that man and take him on home now, Ty."

Sarah Beth climbed into the massive bed and huddled under the thick, down comforter.

Lou Belle sat next to her. "There, there, honey child, everythin' be alright come tomorrow"

Sarah Beth heard echoes of her momma in the old Negress' patois and began to cry.

"Just bawl till it all out, if that's what ya need, but I knows things'll look bright again when them tears wash out all the sad. That's what tears is for, ya know."

"Lou Belle, why did things have to be like this? Why did I have to be what I am? If I had only listened to Aunt Myda when she wanted me to go to the House of–."

Lou Belle pulled Sarah Beth to her massive breasts. "Miz Myda, God rest her soul, tried with all her might t' do right by ya. But what be, be and what ain't, ain't. Cry all ya want, child, but a body can't never make ain't int' be. Ya just gotta get on livin'. Forget 'bout what ya been and that there man."

"I can't," Sarah Beth sobbed, "I loved him too much. Oh, God, Lou Belle, I still do. I always will."

Lou Belle lifted Sarah Beth's chin. "Love him. Love *him*? After all he done ya."

"It's what I did to him."

"Go on blamin' ya'self 'bout that, too, if ya want. Ya done that all ya life and look what it got ya…Love him if ya want, ain't nothin' I can say t' stop ya. But, by and by, ya gonna find out what ol' Lou Belle say is true. So listen t' me good. This here the worstest hurt ya heart ever gonna know, 'cause it the first. I seed what ya done all the time ya was here. Never let no man get next t' ya till Dr. Frank. Now in a lot o' ways, you the smartest people I ever knowed. But lovin', ya don't know nothin' 'bout 'cause ya ain't never let ya'self fall in love afore. There be lots of men ya gonna love. And they gonna love ya right back. Just wait. They be out there looking for ya right now. And believe you-I-me, they gonna find ya."

"I don't care about other men," Sarah Beth moaned. "I never wanted anybody but Frank."

"In a little while, when some the hurt go 'way, ya head and ya heart'll say different."

"Lou Belle, I have to leave The Mansion," Sarah Beth said suddenly. "My life here is over."

"I knowed that. Ya done sold the place already."

"You don't understand. I have to leave *now!*"

"Can't. Got no place t' go. Gots t' look for one."

"Tomorrow then," Sarah Beth insisted.

"Fine…'Cept we gots t' wait f' after lunch so all the righteous folk can sober up and get theyself to mass. They's lots of late sleepin' goin' on right now, ya know. It bein' Mardi Gras time and all."

Sarah Beth sprang from the bed and rushed to the bedroom door. "It can't end like this, Lou Belle. How else did I expect him to act when he found out? Didn't I know something like this would happen? This is exactly what I feared all these months."

She flew down the stairs with her gown flowing behind her, the picture of every nymph that ever graced a myth. In the foyer, she found Titan still struggling to pull Frank's trousers up.

She knelt on the floor next to the only man she would ever love and took his head in her hands. In the eternity of an instant, she memorized again the angles and planes of his face, the curves of his brow, the arc of his cheeks and chin; and, as Frank's bleary eyes focused on her, said, "Good-bye, my darling. Remember, I will love you forever and always." Pressing her mouth to his with the totality of her being, with measureless adoration and yearning, she engraved her love on his lips hoping it would linger to honey his every breath as this, their once and only kiss, would sweeten hers.

A FEW MEMENTOES CRATED IN BOXES, Sarah Beth stood on the *banquette* looking at The Mansion and examining pictures of her past called up by her prodigious memory. Titan waited, tall and proud in the driver's seat of the carriage behind her.

How monumental this moment is, she thought, *yet how insignificant it feels. I've walked down these same steps and gotten into this same carriage almost every day for a good part of my life. This is the final time, yet it seems so ordinary. What a strange sensation, to know something is so important but not feel it.*

A voice behind her said, "Aye. 'Tis a big day for the both of us, lass. You're off and so am I." Liam put his valise on the sidewalk and removed his newsboy cap.

"Where are you going?" Sarah Beth asked.

"Belfast."

"Visiting your family?"

"Goin' home."

"Oh, I thought you liked America."

"Aye. But there's trouble brewin' and me place is with me kin. Besides, ain't nothin' to keep me here, is there?"

Ignoring his question, Sarah Beth opened the carriage door. "What kind of trouble?"

"With the damn Brits, what else?" Liam offered her his hand and helped her into the gig. "Sure and there won't be a end to it till us Irishers own back what they stole. 'Tis the land, don'tcha see. That's all we've ever wanted, our own land back."

Sarah Beth settled herself. "Can I offer you a ride?"

"Aye. 'Tain't far to the train station, but the company would be grand, seein' how this'll be the last time I see ya." Liam climbed in and sat next to her.

Titan flicked the reins of the matched grays and the carriage started forward just as an automobile sputtered and coughed past. The horses shied, jerking the carriage and throwing Sarah Beth into Liam's arms.

"So now maybe ya won't go on not answerin' me question."

Sarah Beth felt the reassuring strength of the Irishman's embrace, a lifetime of security hers for the taking. "And what question is that?" She sensed his reluctance to let her go as she gently pushed away from him.

"Sure and there's no need t' be coy with me, Sarah Beth LaBranche. I asked plain as day if there be reason I shouldn't go. And now I'll be thankin' ya for a proper answer."

Any temptation he might have offered evaporated in the heat of Frank's remembered kiss still burning her lips. "Liam–."

No need to explain. His eyes said *he* understood but his heart never would. "Aye. Then I'd feel like a thief if I didn't offer this back t' ya." From his breast pocket he took her handkerchief, the one she used to wipe the blood from him the day he came to her rescue, the one he claimed as a knight's favor from his lady. "Before ya go sayin' anythin' a'tall, I want ya to know I never was gonna keep it without offerin' t' buy it off ya."

"Why? I'd never miss it."

"Ya would one day, the way that head of yours works. And when ya remember me, lass, I want it to be as a man that didn't take more from ya than he gived. That's why I done what I done at the French Ball. Sure and it took a blind man not t' see how much you're was wantin' after that doctor of yours. And if he was what ya was wantin', then he's what I wanted for ya. Then I followed ya home t' make sure ya found it safe and sound, pining so hard for him as ya were. But even a poor plough-man can dream." Liam held up the handkerchief. "And this here's the stuff me dreams are made of. But now I'm off t' wakin' up and it's all I'll have t' remember ya by. So I'm offerin' to buy it off ya at a good and fair price."

Sarah Beth took his hand, the one holding the handkerchief, in both of hers. It was so large it overflowed her palms. Folding his calloused finger over the lace, she said, "Please keep this as my gift to you for all you've given me. Besides Titan, you're the only man I've ever considered a true friend."

Liam looked down at the keepsake. "'Tis much more than I deserve and much less than I want."

Titan stopped the carriage at the train station, the horses skittering a bit at the steam huffed by one of the engines. Liam climbed out, turned and covered Sarah Beth's hand with his as she closed the door. "Remember, lass, if there's ever a knight ya needin', ya can order one through the post." He slipped a piece of paper into her hand. "This here's me da's house in Belfast. Likely he'll know what I'm up t' and how t' get me."

"Thank you. Good-bye, Liam, and God's speed."

An enigmatic smile on his face, he took several steps backwards and waved. "Now if ya was a proper Irisher lass," he called, "ya'd be sayin', 'May the wind be always at ya back, may the road be downhill, and may God hold ya in the palm of His hand till we meet again.' And that's what I'm sayin' t' you, Sarah Beth LaBranche."

She watched the hulking Celt turn and disappear into the crowd, wondering if...*No, damn it!* she thought with the sternness of a head-mistress, *he deserves much more than a heart-broken whore. So much more.* Yet, she found her hand on the door handle and her eyes searching the crowd for a glimpse of straw-yellow hair. Dismal, she fell back against the carriage seat and, refusing herself the consolation of even one tear, whispered, "Good-bye, Sir Knight."

PART III

FALL 1906

CHAPTER 29

AS A VERY RICH AND beautiful young woman, Sarah Beth would have been considered quite a matrimonial prize by the uptown bachelors in her new neighborhood, if only they had known about her. Withdrawn, she deliberately kept to herself, save waving to a neighbor as she worked in the garden. She had no social life, hardly speaking to anyone except the occasional tradesman.

At first her longtime friend and housekeeper accepted Sarah Beth's introversion as mending from the grievous losses, in quick secession, of Myda and Frank. But as spring wore on to summer, then to fall, the situation ground away Lou Belle's patience. By the second week in November the housekeeper could restrain herself no longer. Finding her mistress reading in the upstairs parlor of the house Sarah Beth had bought, Lou Belle unsheathed a feather duster from her apron and began fencing with the furniture and bric-a-brac, mumbling loud enough for her mistress to hear, "Nothin' else left but get on with the wake, I 'spect."

Sarah Beth looked up from her book. "Did someone pass away?"

"Yeah zum."

"I'm sorry to hear that. Someone I know?"

Lou Belle parried and thrust at a lamp. "Yeah zum."

Sarah Beth marked her place and closed the book. Lou Belle clearly had something on her mind. "Who?"

"You, that's who."

"That's silly. I'm not dead and don't intend to be for a long time."

"Might as well be." Lou Belle made a flanking attack on the bookcase.

"Why?"

"Ain't my place t' say."

Smiling, Sarah Beth sat on the arm of a love seat close to the bookcase. "Then why bring it up?"

"'Cause I loves ya like my own and can't stands t' see what ya doin' t' you'self."

Sarah Beth smiled at the machinations of her friend, so transparent, so endearing. "And what exactly am I doing?"

"Hidin'. Don't knows what else t' calls it. Hidin' from the whole world, plain and simple."

Sarah Beth strolled to the windows that stretched from floor to ceiling. "I'm not hiding. I'm living a very full life, although, I admit, a very quiet one. But I'm happy. I have my books. I have my collections. You may not know it, but the furniture and tapestries in this house are very valuable. The furniture, alone…Well, it's a very fine group of antiques from the famous old New Orleans cabinetmakers."

"Yeah zum. If ya say so. But I can't see no kind o' life hangin' rugs on the walls. Ain't never heard o' that a'fore, nohow. And buyin' up stuff dead folks built 'fore the war. If ya gonna collect up stuff, then, I declare, ya oughtta collect up new stuff."

With her back to Lou Belle, Sarah Beth tried to keep the smile out of her voice. "Are you saying I'm crazy?"

"Oh, no, ma'am." Lou Belle looked up from her duel with the knickknacks in the bookcase. "Ya just been a little partic'lar f' the past while now."

"But I'm happy."

"No you ain't."

"If I say I'm happy, shouldn't you believe me?"

"No, ma'am. Don't mean no disrespect, but I knows a fib when I sees one and that one there's big enough to ride home on."

Lou Belle crossed the room and put her arm around Sarah Beth. The two women stood looking out at the street, Sarah Beth holding back the lace curtains with one hand.

"It ain't right, Miz Sarah Beth, you stuck in this big, ol' house with nobody but me and Ty. This here a grand house. 'Members me of Whitewood Hall in the old days. Back then, we had shindigs up t' the big house all the time. You could, too, but ya don't never see nobody."

"Of course, I see people. All the time. The people I buy furniture from, the–."

"Them don't count, they ain't real people. Looka there." Lou Belle pointed to the house next door. "What them people's name?"

"Ah. I've seen the wife several times, but her name escapes me."

"I 'spect it do. Miz Adams. What 'bout them there?" Lou Belle pointed to the other next-door neighbors.

"Ah…ah…."

"Miz Huckerman, Hackerman, something like that. But I's a damn sight closer than you. What 'bout them people 'cross the street. Who they is?"

"All right, you've made your point. But I've had a lot to think about," Sarah Beth said.

"Sunshine make a body think mo' better. G'wan outside f' a walk and do ya thinkin'."

"It's a bit cool today, don't you think?"

"Gawd make shawls for that."

Lou Belle bundled Sarah Beth out of the room and downstairs onto the front porch, wrapping her in a short stole Sarah Beth had crocheted–another occupation the recluse had taken up to fill her days.

"G'wan for a walk, now. They some nice think-under trees down the block that-a-way." Lou Belle pointed toward the Mississippi River half a mile away. "And some more back the house on Fourth Street. I seed some more down on Prytania Street, too." The old colored woman pointed away from the river toward St. Charles Avenue and its trolley line. Then her wide, calico back disappeared into the house as Sarah Beth looked after her.

It is a beautiful day, Sarah Beth thought. She patted the slight bulge in her stomach that had not been there six months ago. If she were not careful, she would lose her figure to *crème brûle. Lou Belle cooks as well as Tilda. I could do with the exercise.*

Walking down the front steps, past her well-tended garden and a lawn that looked like the felt on a card table, Sarah Beth hesitated at the black, wrought-iron gate of the fence surrounding her front yard. That boundary had become her horizon, the edge of the earth to her. It took the courage of an old-world explorer for her to push open the gate and step onto the *banquette.*

The hinges glided effortlessly and, as she hooked the latch after her, she remembered that first day at the Cheramie's. How that gate had creaked! It had a certain charm, though. And the brick walk, running this way and that, dappled with moss and trying to trip anyone who—. She shoved such thoughts from her mind. *Oh, Lou Belle, if you only knew. That's why I stay in. Everything I see reminds me of him.*

Sarah Beth's house stood in the center of the Garden District, on Third Street between Coliseum and Chestnut, a few blocks from Emile Commander's restaurant. The Garden District was originally part of the Livaudais plantation. Wealthy Americans built the *faubourg,* as the city's original French called their neighborhoods, during the battle with the haughty Creoles for control of New Orleans.

The natives resented the *Kaintucks* and their invasion of the Isle of Orleans after the Louisiana purchase. The Americans returned the enmity. With Creole honor not allowing them to engage in any occupation other than farming, brokering cotton and gambling, Yankee traders filled the void in the city burgeoning commerce, quickly amassing fortunes. Wanting a place of their own, away from the Creole stronghold of the French Quarter and away from the wharves, tanneries, stockyards and immigrant tenements that produced their wealth, prosperous Americans built their own city of Lafayette on the New Orleans and Carrollton Railroad line. Originally laid out with no more than four houses to a square, the waxing and waning of fortunes led to further development as land was sold and houses built. But the character of the original Garden District remained the same and distinctly different from the French Quarter. In the old Creole city, houses abutted the *banquettes*, with private walled patios in the rear. In the Garden District, the mansions stood back from the sidewalk, separated from the street by iron fences that once kept wandering cattle out of the beautifully landscaped grounds.

Sarah Beth strolled down a street dappled by the shade of oaks and magnolias. Eclectic architectural styles–Greek Revival, Italianate, Swiss and turreted Victorian–contributed to the glorious diversity of the old American suburb, the luxuriant flower beds giving the *faubourg* its name. Dull green azalea leaves and the glossy bushes of gardenias vowed dazzling color and sweet perfume to come. Evergreen camellias anticipated the coming winter and remembered their glory of years past. Crepe myrtles and mimosas pined for their grandeur of the summer just gone and yearned the year along so their splendor could return. Wherever she looked, Sarah Beth found nature, like her, waiting. But, unlike her, the trees, the flowers, the shrubs, even the grass, all knew, deep in their roots, change would come. Sarah Beth felt no such stirring in her soul.

She pulled the shawl around her and wondered when the normal cycles of her life would return. *Never, unless I, myself, do something to make them begin again. Lou Belle knows that and, I'm sure, Titan does, too. I seem to be the only one who has taken such a long time to reach that momentously obvious conclusion.*

Quickening her pace, Sarah Beth hoped making her heart beat faster would pound and pump away the malaise engulfing her and strengthen her resolve. *I must do something now, even the smallest thing, to change what I'm letting myself become.* She remembered the philosophy she had considered the night of the French Ball. *Neither God with His practical jokes, nor the meanderings of some infinitesimal microbe will dictate my life. They can try, but, damn it, I won't let them!*

Coming up to her own front gate again, Sarah Beth noticed a neighbor sitting on the front porch of the house next door. "Good morning, Mrs. Adams. How are you today?" Sarah Beth smiled and waved.

"Fine, thank you. Won't you join me for a cup of coffee?"

"I'd love to." Sarah Beth stepped through the gate of the Adams' front yard and into her future.

LOU BELLE WAS DUSTING IN the dining room when Sarah Beth returned.

"Her name is Louise Adams," Sarah Beth said without preface. "She has three children, all girls, twelve, ten and seven. Her husband is a successful coffee broker and her father owns a cotton gin he inherited from his father. They've lived in that house for–."

"G'wan, I knows that. But I's mighty glad you do, too."

Sarah Beth hugged her dear friend. "Thank you so much. I needed someone to shake me from my lethargy."

Lou Belle laughed. "I the best, when I gets me m' shakin' dandruff up. But it's natural, child, with all ya been through. Miz Myda passin', Gawd rest her soul, and Dr. Frank doin' what he done. But see, all ya needed was one little shake."

"It's not just Myda and Frank, I've been thinking about something else." Sarah Beth led Lou Belle from the dining room, through large French doors, into the front room.

"Sit with me, please. I've something to discuss with you."

"Ain't fittin' me settin' in the parlor. Standin' just fine with me."

"Please sit down, won't you? Lou Belle, you're my best friend. Can't we sit and talk?"

Lou Belle's eyes filled with tears. "Yeah zum." She sat on the edge of a chair next to Sarah Beth's, her dark eyes darting constantly to the front foyer as she twisted her apron into a knot.

Realizing she could never span the social chasm Lou Belle saw separating them, Sarah Beth asked, "Would you be more comfortable in the kitchen?"

"Oh, yeah zum. That'd be fine. Then I can fix ya up some lunch."

"Fix *us* some lunch."

"Now, Miz Sarah Beth, why ya wanna go cause all that ruckus. Ain't fittin', me eatin' in the dinin' room and all. What if a body comes t' call?"

"Is it fitting if I eat with you in the kitchen?"

Lou Belle chuckled. "Lawd, Lawd. Sure is. Long as you don't go 'round doin' it every day. By and by a body gots to have some time to herself."

In the kitchen, Lou Belle fried ham and sliced bread for their sandwiches. "Got no lettuce and tomato, but I can melt some cheese for ya. Heats up some that vegetable soup from last night, if ya want."

"Fine." Sarah Beth boiled water for tea. "As I said, it's not just the loss of Myda and Frank that's been on my mind. I've been thinking, a lot, about my momma. I write her every week, sending money and telling lies, but it's not enough anymore. I live in this huge house with more rooms than I can–."

"No needs t' tells me 'bout that. I cleans 'em all."

"And for what?" Sarah Beth filled the tea ball with tea leaves. "Nobody uses them. And I know how momma must be living. Probably not as bad as when I left. That is, if paw drank himself to death, and I hope to God he did! But even so, she could come here, and Jeremy, too, if he wants. He's much older now. He might even have a family of his own, but I have more than enough room for everybody. They could all come. But you, Titan and I would all have to agree on what to tell her. And we would have to talk about it a lot so we'd have our stories straight and she wouldn't suspect."

Lou Belle put the sandwiches on the table and returned to the stove for the soup. "Ya sayin' we all gots to get the lie straight."

"That's right. But I think we can do it. And I don't think she'd ever meet anyone I knew in the District, so there'd be no danger of her ever finding out what I was."

"'Less ya told her."

"I'd never do that. Why should I?" Sarah Beth poured the tea and sat at the table. "And I think I can make sure she never finds out, if you and Titan help."

"Ain't gonna turn out no good, iffen ya'll go on like ya sayin'. Ya gonna live till ya die worryin' 'bout who say what t' ya momma and what she gonna hear from the neighbor lady. Iffen somebody give ya an eye, ya gonna walk the floor all night t' figure what it mean and if they know and is they gonna say. It ain't no good, I tell ya. Ya fixin' t' worry you'self t' a frazzle."

Sarah Beth sighed. "I'm afraid your right. I thought perhaps we…But there is another way. I could move. To Baton Rouge, or even back to St. Francisville. I'd sell this house and buy another. One big enough for momma and Jeremy, and his family, if he has one."

"Ain't no good, neither." Lou Belle put the soup bowls on the table and sat across from her mistress. "I knows ya, Miz Sarah Beth, and ya ain't never run away from nothin' in ya whole life, not them bullies back in the District, not even that Mr. Anderson when he tried t' do in Titan and them boys ya hired t' swat skeeters for ya in Smokey Row."

"How do you know about that?"

"That Mr. Anderson, he got colored folk workin' for him and sometimes little pitchers got big ears. 'Sides, no matter where ya at, if ya don't tell ya momma, ya gonna jump out ya skin every time the knocker on the front door bangs. Wonderin' who it be and what they know. Ya don't want no life like that."

"Then how–."

"Ya gots t' tell ya momma the truth."

Sarah Beth's soup spoon clattered against the side of the bowl. "Impossible! How could I do that? Write a letter, 'Dear Momma, I couldn't send for you before because I was a whore. Now I'm a rich, retired whore and you can come live with me.' Lou Belle, she'd die. She'd never forgive–."

"Didn't mean ya got t' give her all the truth at one time. A big lump o' truth kills a body sometimes. What ya got t' do is cut the truth up int' little, bitsy pieces, then give 'em t' ya momma a speck at a time."

"That will just make it worse for her."

"Child, don't ya know nothin' 'bout mommas." Lou Belle took a bite of sandwich. "Mamas is the forgivin'est peoples in the whole world. When she knowed what that she-devil, Inez Breaux, done ya when ya was so little, her heart gonna break 'cause she couldn't stop that woman from ruinin' ya. What's more, she gonna say it her fault for tellin' ya t' go on off. Mark my words."

"What about Jeremy?"

"He a man, I 'spect he ain't even gonna notice."

They finished eating in silence, Sarah Beth pondering Lou Belle's advice. After lunch, Sarah Beth prowled the big house. In room after room, she wondered what her momma would say about the furniture, the lamps, the drapes, the accessories. Would momma like the color scheme, the styles? By late afternoon, she made her decision.

In the library on the first floor, she sat at Myda's huge Wooton desk and, in a beautiful, cursive script, wrote the letter she had begun composing in her mind ever since the day she left home.

Dearest Momma,

What a wonderful and joyous day has been sent to us. After nine long years, our plans come to fruition. Today I write to ask you and Jeremy to join me.

Your mind and heart cannot comprehend how happy those words make me, what gladness comes from keeping my promise to you. How I so love the ink that forms each letter, how I do adore the quill and paper that lets me write of my fidelity to you. My soul soars to the highest clouds as my eyes read the phrase again and again. Join me. What ecstasy it brings!

At once you must fly to me so my heart does not burst from waiting. Say good-bye to no one, for fear it will cost you precious minutes. Take nothing with you as that, too, keeps us apart the longer. I have here everything you will ever need. With the money I enclose, pause long enough only to buy the clothes you and my precious brother may need for the journey. And in the blessed circumstance Jeremy has a family, bring them, too, for the bounty life has given me will support us all for as long as we take breath.

What a heartwarming, happy word: family. To be with my family again is all I have ever dreamed.

Then, with winged Mercury as your guide, secure passage to New Orleans by the swiftest means available. Yet, however you come, it will be much too slow. Agonizingly so. Even if the birds of the air could carry you and Jeremy to me, I would stand on the tallest building urging them ever faster.

Tarry not to wonder how this has been accomplished. Know only that it has been my sustaining dream for, lo, these many years, the millennia of seconds since last I saw you. Rejoice that we are in the summer of our life. Harsh winter has passed. Spring's glorious promise is fulfilled. Now we will revel under a warm sky with the triple suns of our hearts loving each other in a magic land where wishes appear instantly at the tips of our fingers. How these wonders obtain will be made fully known to you as we lounge on the hillsides and in the valleys of our delight.

Now fly to me, lest my heart languish at the thought that precious moments we might spend together are spent apart. The years of loneliness and separation are over. Come swiftly into the sunshine of my love, so I may bask in yours.

Your loving and adoring,
Honey Girl

Sarah Beth addressed the envelope and, for the first time, wrote her return address. For nine long years, she had penned weekly lies to her momma and sent them, along with money for her family's support, with no hint of where she could be found. Today, released at last from any need for deceit, she affixed her whereabouts with flourish.

Before sealing the envelope she considered how much money to include. One hundred dollars did not sound enough. Two hundred had a better ring, yet doubt lingered. What if Jeremy had a family? She settled on three hundred dollars, placed the bills in the envelop and read her letter one last time. Then crumpled it into a rough-edged ball. That lyrical, poetic missive was a song to her own vanity, not a letter for the poor, plain woman that was her momma.

Sarah Beth began with a clean sheet of paper and her beautiful script formed the simple words she would have said if her momma sat next to her.

Dear Momma,
The is the happiest day of my life. At last I can keep my promise to you. I own a big house now and I want you and Jeremy to join me. Please do. It's all I've thought of since the day I left home. I remember exactly how you looked that day. It was the fall of 1897, after the cotton harvest was in. I remember working so hard to get the money to leave. Lottie Mae and I worked out how much I needed sitting on that old log on the road to the Talbot cabin. By the way, if you see Lottie Mae, tell her I…

Finishing the letter and darting from the house, Sarah Beth vacillated as she stood on the front gallery. Perhaps she should go to St. Francisville herself, then she would see her mother sooner. She turned and started back into the house. Titan could come with her to face the wrath of her paw, if whiskey had not killed him yet.

No. Momma said to send for them. She had her reasons. Sarah Beth retraced her steps and posted the letter.

CHAPTER 30

WRITING HER MOMMA RELEASED Sarah Beth back into the world. The days after she mailed the letter saw her energetic, no longer cloistered in her mansion. Gardening meant waving to passing neighbors, chatting with them, learning their names and family circumstance. On daily walks, she became familiar with the cadence of her Garden District neighborhood, the comings and goings of new acquaintances, the noise of children playing, and vendors hawking their wares from early morning to late afternoon.

For Sarah Beth the vendors gave continuity to her life. She remembered them as the street-music of the city for as long as she had been in New Orleans. Over the years, each class of itinerant merchant reached tacit agreement on how best to advertise themselves. Some did it through what they wore, others by the ditties they sang to hawk their merchandise, or a combination of the two. Wherever she found herself in New Orleans, Sarah Beth could guess what she would see outside by what she heard.

The knife and tin man—the frame of his grindstone high on his shoulder and his tall, tin Hessian hat gleaming in the sun—announced himself with a piercing four-note whistle and the bell that jingled from the leg that powered his grindstone while he worked. The produce peddlers sang out a litany of the fruits and vegetables available, with the summer favorite of all children being, "Watermelon. Get ya watermelon, red to da rind." The clothes-pole man, a bundle of long, V-notched sticks strapped to his back, could not be missed.

In the few weeks of beautiful weather that comes to New Orleans in late fall, the whole Garden District braced for the coming of the cool, sometimes cold, damp winter. Preparing her garden for the seasonal change, the bustle of the neighborhood formed a lively background as Sarah Beth and Titan worked the warm, moist soil. The charcoal-man made his rounds calling, "M' horse is white, m' face is black. I sell m' charcoal, two bits a sack." The chimney sweeps, in silk top hat and dove-tail coats, sang through the streets, "Lady, I know why ya chimney won't draw, oven won't bake and ya can't make no cake." Their refrain continued as they worked, both advertisement and warning to the household to stay away from the grates.

Directing Titan in his pruning, Sarah Beth, gloved hands muddy and canvas apron smudged, heard the horn of the rag and bottle man and turned to watch the children flock to his call. Unique among the vendors, the rag man, dressed in his own merchandise, paid his customers rather than being paid by them.

With hampers of bottles and bags of rags, the neighbor children raced to be first to barter for the trinkets and candies in the drawer at the back of the push-cart. The older boys and girls wrangled for coins the skinflint reluctantly gave as a last resort only to the most skilled negotiators.

A boy about seven, in knickers, shirt-sleeves and a newsboy cap, arrived first and swapped a large sack of rags for a few small toys and a licorice whip. Sarah Beth saw the dismay on his face grow as his friends exchanged much smaller hordes for greater booty. As each companion ran off with their loot, his disappointment multiplied. The boy hung back and, as the rag man reached for the shafts at the back of his cart, said, in typical New Orleans patois, "Mister, that ain't no fair. You gave Tommy 'n'nem a lot more for their stuff than ya gave me."

With a smirk, the rag man lifted the handles of his cart. "Dat's life, boy," he said as he pushed off down the street. "Learn from it."

The boy's lower lip grew large as he looked at his few trinkets. Wiping his eyes with the back of his hand, he turned and ran after his friends. On the *banquette* in front of Sarah Beth's gate, he tripped and fell. The pain of skinned hands, elbows and knees adding to his frustration, he began to cry.

Sarah Beth threw down her soiled gloves and ran to help him. "There, there, don't cry," she said, standing him up and trying to hug him.

"Lemme alone!" He pulled away.

"I just want to help. Come let me clean those cuts. If they're not taken care of, they might get infected."

"Don't wanna go in *there*!" The boy pointed at Sarah Beth's house. "Don't want *you* fixin' nothin', neither."

Sarah Beth could not understand the child's fear of her. "Why?"

"'Cause you're…Dr. Cohen'll fix 'em."

"Where does Dr. Cohen live?"

The boy pointed toward the river. "Round the corner."

"Can I take you?" Sarah Beth thought the child's fear unreasonable. Perhaps he was just shy with strangers. "What's your name?"

The boy looked down the street, back at Sarah Beth, then at her house. "Cleo," he whispered.

"Cleo, I'm Miss LaBranche and I haven't lived here very long. I'd like to know where Dr. Cohen lives in case I ever skin my knee and need somebody to look after it. Can I walk with you so I can find out?"

Cleo glanced at Sarah Beth between sniffles. "I don't…ah, well…."

"It won't be like I'm taking you. Anybody can see you're too big to need my help. It's you taking me. How's that?"

"Okay, I guess."

Sarah Beth gave her apron to Titan, then she and her young companion walked around the corner to a three-story Victorian house in the middle of the block. Once inside the gate, Cleo charged onto the gallery and, on tip toes, pounded the door-knocker. A white-uniformed maid answered and Cleo showed her his skinned hands.

"Dr. Cohen in the back. Ya'll come on in. You, too, Miz." As Sarah Beth climbed the stairs, the maid, her eyes white rimmed with fear, looked directly at Sarah Beth for the first time.

Why does everyone seem so afraid of me?

The maid led them down semi-dark halls toward the back of the house, their footsteps amplified to a loud, hollow knocking by the varnished, red-pine floor. Several times the maid glanced over her shoulder at Sarah Beth, and on each occasion Sarah Beth felt the other woman's fright.

First the boy, now her.

Sarah Beth found herself in an airy room of straight-back chairs and glass-paned cabinets full of medical equipment. The place reminded her so much of Frank Cheramie's clinic that an overwhelming grief clutched her heart as the maid called, "Doc Cohen, where you is at? Little Cleo Fields out here wit' man-size brush burns."

A woman's voice answered through an open door to Sarah Beth's left. "In the storeroom, Margaret. I'll be right out."

"Ya'll have a sit, Miz," the maid said. "Doc be 'long directly."

As the housekeeper left, an elderly woman, stalwart and thick as an oak, came into the room. Her gray hair fashionably piled on her head, a white blouse contrasting with a navy-blue skirt that swept the floor, she smiled and nodded at Sarah Beth and said to Cleo, "Let's take a look."

The little boy let the woman examine his abrasions and, as she did, she spoke to Sarah Beth. "I'm Elizabeth Cohen, but I'm afraid I don't know who you are, dear...These don't look too bad, Cleo. I have just the thing."

"Sarah Beth LaBranche. I'm very pleased to meet you, Mrs. Cohen. I moved into the neighborhood several months ago and I'm afraid I haven't been very social. I'm just now getting to know my neighbors."

Elizabeth Cohen gave Sarah Beth a quick smile as she said to Cleo, "First, I have to wash these cuts and that might sting a bit. But you don't mind, do you, Cleo? Such a big boy and all."

Cleo minded, trembling at the sight of the bowel of water and cloth the older woman brought from one of the counters.

Elizabeth Cohen wrung water from a white cloth. "I'm sorry, Miss LaBranche. Go on."

"That's all. I've started meeting the neighbors just this week, in fact. I'm sorry our acquaintance couldn't begin under less trying circumstances." Sarah Beth rubbed Cleo's head and he jerked away.

"That's not the way to act when someone's being nice to you, Cleo." The older woman took a small, black medical bag from one of the cabinets. "I have to put medicine on all of those and I'm afraid it will sting more." She lifted her small patient on to an examining table with almost no effort. "Now I think we're going to need Miss LaBranche's help. Look, Cleo, you have one, two, three, four, five, six bo-bos and between you and me, we only have one, two mouths. If Miss LaBranche helps us, how many mouths will we have?"

Cleo pointed at each available mouth in turn. "One, two, three."

"That's right! Shouldn't you say you're sorry to Miss LaBranche for being so rude if you want her to help us?"

"I don't want her to blow on my bo-bos. I'll die. She's a voodoo witch!"

Elizabeth Cohen laughed, deep and hearty. "Of course. I should have known by the red hair."

"Known what?" Sarah Beth asked, taken back by being called a witch by a little boy she hardly knew.

"You bought the Deppie house some time back, didn't you?"

"How does that make me a witch?"

"Help me with him and I'll tell you. We'll do his hands first."

Cleo winced as the medicine was applied. Elizabeth Cohen explained as she and Sarah Beth tried to soothe its bite. "You know…how children…make something…out of…anything unusual. Is that better Cleo?" The boy nodded. "Now the elbows."

"Ow!"

"And...the coloreds...are very superstitious...too, my dear...By staying to yourself so much...you've become the witch of the neighborhood."

Baffled and a bit confounded, Sarah Beth said, "I-I had no idea...I meant...There's nothing sinister...."

"I know. Now his knees," Elizabeth Cohen said. "And so should everyone else...But staying to yourself...that huge houseman...the servants living with you...You know how people talk...especially children...They feed each other's delusions...Cleo, you've been such a brave boy and we have just a little more to do. If you don't cry, I have a surprise for you." The older woman called down the hall, "Margaret, bring some cala, please." Turning back to Cleo, she asked, "Would you like some?"

Cleo's face brightened and he nodded.

"Where should...my servants...live?" Sarah Beth asked as she soothed the stinging of Cleo's knee.

"That's no one's...business...but yours. There, all done."

"Is it Miss or Mrs. Cohen?" Sarah Beth asked.

"Actually, it's Doctor Cohen." At the door to the clinic, the older woman called, "Margaret, the cala." To Sarah Beth she asked, "Would you care for tea?"

Sarah Beth nodded.

"And, Margaret, serve tea in the front parlor," Dr. Cohen called. She lifted Cleo from the examination table as the maid came in with a platter of pastries whose wonderful aroma filled the room. "Be careful, now," the doctor admonished Cleo, "they're still very hot."

The maid bent down and offered the small, warm fritters to the little boy. He took two, juggling and blowing on them. "Gee, thanks, Dr. Cohen."

"Don't burn your mouth," the doctor said too late.

The little boy sucked in a huge breath to slake the fire on his tongue. "That's okay," Cleo mumbled as crumbs fell on the floor.

"Makin' a mess again," Margaret said. "Now I gots–."

"We can clean it up."

"Bet he momma don't let him go 'round messin' up her house."

"I'm sure she doesn't," Dr. Cohen said. "But we'll let him be a little boy around here. Miss LaBranche, will you join me in the parlor?"

"Dr. Cohen," Cleo said, "can Regis have some, too?"

The old woman stooped to be eye-to-eye with the youngster, her long skirt billowing out around her as she bent. "Dogs don't eat cala."

"Regis does. He *loves* cala. If he smells it on me, he'll want some and if I don't have none, well, I bet he just might bark all night and keep everybody up."

Dr. Cohen smiled and pinched the boy's cheek. "Then I guess we better let you take some for Regis so people can get some sleep around here."

Cleo snatched two handfuls from the tray and aimed them for his pants pockets.

"I wouldn't do that," Sarah Beth warned. "They'll be crumbs by the time Regis gets them."

Cleo looked perplexed. Sarah Beth took off his cap, noticing its similarity to the one Liam wore, and offered it to Cleo upside down. He smiled, dropped the pastries in, grabbed another handful and ran for the back door.

"Cleo," Dr. Cohen called, "don't you have something to say to Miss LaBranche?"

The little boy turned, glancing back and forth between the two women and his freedom just outside. "Ah…thanks."

"For what?" the doctor asked.

Cleo used the back of the hands holding the cap full of pastries to scratch his nose. "For blowing on my cuts."

"Anything else?" Doctor Cohen asked.

"Ah…for helping me not smush the cala." He held up the pastries.

"What else might you say to Miss LaBranche?" Dr. Cohen asked.

"Ah…I, ah, I don't think you're no voodoo witch. Can I go now?"

Both women laughed and waved as the little boy dashed out the back door.

Dr. Cohen led Sarah Beth to the front parlor where they settled comfortably around a low, mahogany butler's tray-table holding a silver tea service and companion tray of still-warm cala. The room, darkened by heavy drapes almost closed, had a cozy feel, as if the doctor had spent a lifetime collecting knickknacks and crocheting rather than ministering to the sick. Through spaces in the drapes Sarah Beth saw beyond the lace curtains on the floor-to-ceiling windows to the landscaped front yard and the bustle of vendors on the sidewalk and street. Dr. Cohen offered Sarah Beth cala, then poured tea.

"These *are* wonderful." Sarah Beth sniffed the wonderful aroma of the pastry she had just bitten.

"An old, traditional New Orleans breakfast, rice and potato fritters. Try them with powdered sugar and syrup." Dr. Cohen pointed to a small, cut-crystal bowel and matching pitcher. "The children like them, so I have Margaret fix a batch every afternoon. Someone always shows up with a bump or bruise and a little medicine for the soul never hurts. If you don't know about cala, I take it you're not from here."

"St. Francisville."

"Been in the city long?" the doctor asked.

"Ah, actually...No."

"That explains a lot, the servants living with you and all."

"They're the only family I have," Sarah Beth explained. "I didn't know there were rules about where my servants could live."

"Not rules," the doctor said. "Traditions. Folks around here usually have their servants live close by. It's very handy. That's why there are so many colored enclaves around the Garden District and University Section."

"I hope I haven't scandalized too many people," Sarah Beth said. "But if I have, they'll just have to get used to it. Lou Belle and Titan are very important to me. My only family."

"Recent losses, I take it. That's why you stayed to yourself." Dr. Cohen looked deep into Sarah Beth's eyes. "You have my sincerest condolences, my dear."

"Yes, recent losses." Sarah Beth sipped her tea. "And recent joy. After years of separation, I've located my mother and brother. They'll be coming to stay with me."

"But that's wonderful! Though I thought you said the servants were your only family."

In the embarrassed hush that followed, Sarah Beth took a sip of tea, selected another pastry, glanced at the flowered wallpaper and Dr. Cohen's query went unanswered. Finally, Sarah Beth sought safer ground. "I didn't know there were any lady doctors in the city."

"I was the first." Dr. Cohen could not keep the pride from her voice.

"When did you begin practicing?"

"In '58. No, '57."

"My goodness! You don't look, ah…Quite a long time ago."

"You must be thinking I'm a well-preserved old bat, and you've every right." Dr. Cohen smiled. "Thankfully, I am."

Embarrassed, Sarah Beth said, "I didn't mean–."

"Nonsense. Eighty-six and, thank God, still going strong. I *am* a well-preserved old bat."

"It must have been very hard for you," Sarah Beth said. "I've experienced the resentment of male doctors myself."

"How wonderful. You're a doctor?"

"Hardly. Last year I worked on one of the ward committees and did some reading. When…When a friend came down with the fever I…There were some discussions with the attending physician and he certainly resented what he considered to be my interference."

"Did your friend recover?" Dr. Cohen poured more tea.

"In a way."

"Complications? What were the symptoms?"

Sarah Beth's throat closed and her voice sounded tense. "I really can't talk about it."

"I'm sorry. I didn't mean to...Which ward committee?"

"I know it's somewhat unusual, but a committee was formed for, ah, Storyville. Knowing...With so many people...." Sarah Beth realized she had steered the conversation on to unsafe ground again.

"No need to apologize, or be ashamed for that matter," Dr. Cohen said. "Those people needed help as much as anyone...In fact, I believe I heard about you. You're the lady who mixed coal oil with creosote for the gutters."

Sarah Beth nodded. "Actually, one of my workmen."

"Aha. Broke new ground like I did when I came here from Philadelphia. *Men* working for *you* How did the men take to a female supervisor?"

"A few problems," Sarah Beth admitted.

"An understatement, I'm sure, my dear."

"Not nearly as bad as you've experienced." Sarah Beth returned her cup and saucer to the tray-table. "And it's so unfair. A competent doctor should be allowed to do her work regardless of gender. Women should be doctors, lawyers and anything else they've a mind to."

"Perhaps one day." Dr. Cohen smiled and poured more tea. "Right now it would be nice to vote. But the system isn't all bad. It has advantages."

Adding cream and sugar, Sarah Beth rested her cup and saucer on her knee and asked politely, "How can you say that? Women are virtual slaves. How many lives have you saved? Yet, you're not assumed to have enough intelligence to vote. I certainly can't see any advantage in that."

"I didn't say it was perfect. I've experienced my share of enmity for being a doctor. My card reads 'Doctor for Ladies Only,' though there were men glad enough to see me during the epidemics. But the advantage I spoke of is real. There's more than enough important work for women to do."

Sarah Beth remained respectfully adamant. "Then you must see something I cannot. Men control everything. And to keep us under their thumb they've developed this myth. We're either goddesses or devils. We have such tender sensibilities. And most people, including many women, want us to be goddesses. By perpetuating this myth, we're kept in chains. It has to stop!"

"No doubt. Still we mustn't lose sight of the important work we *can* do." Dr. Cohen's voice remained calm.

Sarah Beth's became somewhat strident. "What *little* we can do."

"By concentrating on what women can't do, you fail to see what we can and have accomplished." Doctor Cohen poured herself another cup of tea. "Women like you, of independent means I assume, and those whose husbands can support them well, have much to do. Men tend to ignore the issues we feel strongly about. They let us alone as long as the household accounts balance and the children are well raised. This gives us an enormous amount of time, and, in the better families, the means to concentrate our efforts on the issues most men ignore. In fact, men, in relentless pursuit of the almighty dollar, create most of the ills we try to cure."

"Hmm." Sarah Beth sipped her tea. "An interesting thought."

"Don't misunderstand me. It's ludicrous that women can't vote or run for office, or do anything men do for that matter. And we should fight for our rights. But we should do it like Emma Kendell and her Equal Rights Association Club. They're active in many social welfare issues besides suffrage. Child labor, for example. And securing a water and drainage system last year's epidemic proved we so desperately need, fighting animal cruelty, opening the sides of the Black Maria so women prisoners are not raped by the guards, providing better health facilities for the poor, improving the education of orphans, to name just a few. Pick an issue that makes this world a better place and women are in the forefront."

"I became quite interested in medicine working on the mosquito committee. I-I'm blessed with a very good memory." Sarah Beth felt the heat in her neck as the embarrassment of self praise turned it red. She looked down at the cup and saucer balanced on her knee. "I remember everything I read, word for word. I sometimes think that might be a great advantage if I studied medicine. Then I could help the poor receive the medical care they deserve."

"Are you one of those rare souls who glance at something and remember it exactly? Forever?"

Sarah Beth's cheeks flushed and she nodded.

"How I wish I had a mind like that! Oh, but you're right. Such a memory would be a tremendous advantage in medical school. But have you thought of the disadvantages of studying medicine?"

Sarah Beth sighed. "I've already seen the resentment. I can tolerate it if I must."

"There's much more than just that," Dr. Cohen said. "First...Now mind you, I'm not trying to discourage you. I think it's wonderful. But you do need to understand the obstacles. First, you'll have to give up your beautiful new home, at least for a while, and move away."

"Why? I love this city. I'd want to practice here."

"But you can't study medicine here. Tulane doesn't accept women, none of the southern medical schools do. I trained in Philadelphia. And if you practice in New Orleans, you'll be very limited. Women are not allowed in the Orleans Parish Medical Society and, thus, can't practice at any of the city's hospitals ex–."

"What's the use?" Sarah Beth's teacup rattled as she set it on the tray-table. "They have me blocked no matter which way I turn."

"That's not as much of a problem as you might think. You can always open your own hospital or–."

Sarah Beth snickered. "How likely is that? If I can't practice at–."

"Oh, my dear, it's already been done. Last year, eight women doctors formed a staff and opened the New Orleans Hospital and Dispensary for Women and Children near Kingsley House." Dr. Cohen referred to a well-known settlement house in the Irish Channel. "You could do the same. Or join Sara Mayo's staff." Dr. Cohen gave Sarah Beth a conspira-torial smile and wink. "Your namesake is the leader of the rebels."

Sarah Beth leaned back in her chair, her fingers gently flicking her cheek curls, and focused her eyes on the myriad possibilities floating in the air just above Elizabeth Cohen's head.

"If you want my advice, and you're about to get it whether you want it or not, my dear," Dr. Cohen said.

Sarah Beth smiled. "Dr. Cohen, I'll always welcome your advice and be grateful for it."

"Then visit Dr. Mayo. The rigors of a medical education may entail more sacrifices than you're prepared to make. And it may not be the best way for you to make your contribution. From what I hear, Dr. Mayo desperately needs help. A woman that has supervised work gangs may be more important to her just now than another doctor."

The conversation turned to various topics and the two women chat-ted for another twenty minutes before Sarah Beth noticed Dr. Cohen appeared a bit weary. Not wanting to impose, she excused herself.

On the walk home Sarah Beth felt exhilarated. She had given voice to her wish to be a doctor, an aspiration she had begun to nurture even before that last devastating night with Frank. No longer a dream, not yet a goal, Dr. Cohen's pragmatic encouragement gave Sarah Beth the impetus to explore the possibility.

Moving away to study medicine might prove impossible with momma and Jeremy soon to arrive, but Sarah Beth decided, at the very least, to visit Dr. Mayo. Perhaps she could serve in some non-medical capacity. *After all, Momma and Jeremy won't take up all my time. Besides, it may make things easier for Momma to accept if she sees me helping the poor.*

Jubilant, Sarah Beth rushed up the steps to her house, new dreams replacing old nightmares. In the foyer, she took the mail from a mirrored rosewood hall tree and shuffled through it. Nothing. She sorted through it again, slowly. None of the envelopes had a St. Francisville return address. Perhaps a week was not enough time.

New dreams had replaced old nightmares; now, small, worrisome doubts crept in.

CHAPTER 31

FOR THE NEXT WEEK, SARAH Beth found reasons to hover around the front of her house each morning until the postman arrived. Then, for several mornings, she and Titan mulched the flower beds, preparing them for the coming winter. When that excuse no longer served, she decided on a new tradition, fall house cleaning.

Lou Belle protested. "Ain't never heard nobody doin' no fall house cleanin'. Everybody know it spring the time t' clean." Nonetheless, Lou Belle complied with her mistress' eccentricities.

The end of the second week after Sarah Beth wrote to her mother found her and her servants hard at work cleaning the front parlor. Everything in the room had been dusted the day before–furniture, lamps, picture molding and the long, satin, tasseled cords holding the paintings in place. The rugs covering the varnished pine floor would be beaten that afternoon. The morning's assignment was to clean the large tapestry covering one entire wall of the room. To accomplish the task, Sarah Beth had bought a vacuum cleaner, reasoning that beating the dust from a work of art would damage it. Besides, all science and its application fascinated her. In the years before she had met Frank Cheramie, she had flown in hot air balloons and read voraciously about the doings of the Wright brothers and other aviation pioneers. In addition to the vacuum cleaner, Sarah Beth's latest folly, according to Lou Belle, was a burning desire for a horseless carriage.

The housekeeper grumbled and complained about the new contraption but Titan, in his typical stoic fashion, accepted his mistress' decision, knowing it would be foolish to oppose the inevitable. Sarah Beth almost always had her way.

Lou Belle considered the machine a tortuous appliance, requiring great stamina to operate. The maid had tried but failed. Walking with two long levers attached to the bottom of her feet had proven too much for her. So that morning, as Sarah Beth's eyes incessantly darted to and from the front gate watching for the postman, Lou Belle wrestled the cleaning nozzle back and forth over the tapestry, and Titan operated the foot bellows.

After cleaning the back, they had turned the tapestry over and Titan had mounted the machine again when Sarah Beth saw the postman. She ran on to the front gallery to meet him and returned sorting through several envelopes.

"Anythin' from ya momma yet?" Lou Belle asked.

Sarah Beth sighed. "No, but...." She tore open an envelope and scanned the letter inside. "Dr. Mayo has agreed to meet with me. I have an appointment Thursday afternoon at two."

"Ain't that just fine." Lou Belle grinned. "Now ya'll got somethin' t' do 'stead of bein' cooped up alls the time in this here big, old house."

"I don't have the job yet, Lou Belle."

"Likely so, Miz Sarah Bet." Titan stopped working the foot bellows and caught his breath. "Ain't nobody in they right mind gonna turn down a body what says she'll work free f' nothin'."

"You'd think so," Sarah Beth said, her face and tone somewhat dubious. She opened the other envelopes quickly, hoping one might contain information about her momma, something she had at first overlooked. Nothing.

THE IRISH CHANNEL, WHICH HOUSED Sara Mayo's clinic, separates the Garden District from the Mississippi River. Sarah Beth had heard two conflicting explanations of how this immigrant enclave got its name. The first said that when it rained, drainage from the affluent Garden District inundated the ghetto as the water ran to the river. The second claimed the red light in front of the tenement's most noted landmark, the Bucket of Blood Saloon, appeared to be a channel marker to river mariners. In Sarah Beth's mind, one explanation seemed just as likely as the other.

The day of her appointment with Dr. Mayo, Sarah Beth arrived half an hour early. The clinic was lodged in a brown, three-story clapboard house on Annunciation Street, in the heart of the Irish Channel. The yard and front gallery were overflowing with women standing under palm trees or sitting on benches, all surrounded by children romping about. So many children that, had Sarah Beth not known differently, she might have mistook the building for a school or orphanage.

Worming her way through the crowd toward the front door, Sarah Beth noticed most of the women and children were dressed in the rag man's discards and had not bathed in some time. At the door of the clinic she hailed a passing nurse. "Pardon me. I have a two o'clock appointment with Dr. Mayo."

The nurse smiled. "Has the doctor seen you before?"

"No."

"I'll have to start a chart. Please wait while–."

"Excuse me." Sarah Beth felt a bit uncomfortable. "I'm not a patient. I wrote Dr. Mayo about working here, and she's agreed to see me."

"I'm so sorry." The nurse looked embarrassed. "Dr. Daisy's expecting you, Miss LaBranche. Please come in. I'm Anna Werling."

As Nurse Werling and Sarah Beth entered the infirmary, another nurse passed and called into the yard, "Miss Mary O'Brien and her daughter Ester."

In the foyer of the converted residence, Nurse Werling pointed to a room at Sarah Beth's left. "If you'll wait in there, I'll let Dr. Daisy know you're here."

Sarah Beth entered a room that had obviously been the front parlor of a once fashionable home. Now it served as an office. She sat in a straight-back chair and waited, trying to ignore the hordes of children thundering up and down the metal fire escape just outside the window. Nurses, doctors and administrators bustled about in the yard beyond, ushering patients inside, taking temperatures and recording symptoms. Some children played, others cried as their mothers consoled them. The more desperately ill held their heads and moaned. A young, expectant mother sitting in the shade grabbed her stomach and screamed. A nurse ran to help her.

The strong, antiseptic smell of the place reminded Sarah Beth of Frank's infirmary, and melancholia began to inch its way into her soul. To escape the advancing depression, she unobtrusively studied the women in the room across the foyer, well-to-do matrons seated in chairs obviously more comfortable than the hard benches outside.

Hearing the clop of shoes on wooden stairs, Sarah Beth went to the door and saw a group of women coming from the second floor. Their leader, dark haired, somewhat short, somewhat plump, smiled and laughed while issuing instructions over her shoulder. "Ah, Miss LaBranche," the woman said, her eyes twinkling, "so good of you to come." She ushered Sarah Beth back into the office as she waved good-bye to her companions. "Tea? Coffee perhaps?"

"No, thank you."

"But you must have something. Once we get a volunteer in our clutches, we try to make them happy enough to return."

Sarah Beth felt an immediate rapport with her vibrant hostess.

"Please sit down." Dr. Sara Mayo introduced herself, then asked, "How did you hear about our little enterprise?"

"From Dr. Cohen. She and I are neighbors."

"Elizabeth Cohen?"

Sarah Beth nodded.

"I have heard of her, though I have never had the pleasure of meeting her. I understand she is retired now."

"Semi-retired. When the neighborhood children scrape knees, out comes the medical bag and a plate of cookies." Sarah Beth studied the other woman. Sara Mayo appeared to be in her late thirties and wore her dark hair pulled into a bun on top of her head and had dark, laughing eyes. Even seated, the doctor radiated energy.

"I suppose you would like to know our history before you decide if you want to volunteer."

"And I suppose you'd like to know my experience before you let me," Sarah Beth said.

"Heavens, no." Dr. Mayo slapped her hands to her cheeks in mock dismay. "Whenever someone says they want to help us, we ask no questions. Whatever your talents, we can surely use them. Our only requirement is for volunteers to have a body temperature of ninety-eight point six degrees, or there abouts." Daisy Mayo smiled disarmingly. "Shall I show you our facilities? We can talk while you look around."

Sarah Beth nodded.

In the foyer outside of her office, Dr. Mayo pointed to the room and its occupants that Sarah Beth had been studying when the doctor arrived. "We are very crowded, as you have no doubt noticed. We recently moved here. Rent free, I might add, because of the generosity of Dr. Otis' family. Dr. Otis is one of our staff physicians. We see forty to sixty patients a day, so it is quite hectic most of the time."

Walking down the hall and past the stairs, Dr. Mayo showed Sarah Beth several examining rooms. "We have seven clinics. Medical, surgery, pediatrics, dermatology, gynecology, neurology and dentistry. Plus a pharmacy. Our patients are women and children of little or no means. They pay what they can, but no one is turned away because they have no money."

"Earlier, in the room across from your office, I noticed several ladies who apparently can afford medical care," Sarah Beth said.

"Each of our eight staff doctors have their own practice. I, myself, have an office on Canal Street. But some procedures must be done in a hospital. As none of us are allowed to practice in the local hospitals, our private patients come here. When they do, they receive a bill."

"Dr. Cohen mentioned the problem with the hospitals," Sarah Beth said. "Something to do with the Medical Society."

"Yes. To have hospital privileges, one must be a member of the Orleans Parish Medical Society. The Society will not admit female doctors. So here we are."

"It's so unfair." Sarah Beth knitted her brows. "I'm sure you and your staff are just as competent as–."

"Don't judge too hastily. There are many members of the Society who feel the injustice as keenly as you and I. Were it up to them, women would be admitted."

"Then why–."

"The quaint and curious custom of the blackball. A handful of members, a minority to be sure, have consistently voted against female members. Their excuse is to protect us, to guard against women being exposed to discussions unusual in mixed assemblies. What rot!"

"Yes, I know. We have such tender sensibilities." The bitter-sweet memory of Frank clouded Sarah Beth's forehead momentarily as she remembered the night they tended Maggie Anderson.

"But we have our supporters in the Society, too," Daisy Mayo explained. "A dozen members are consulting physicians here at our dispensary. Our time will come, one day soon. It has to. Women doctors are in demand. Did you know there are women in this city who have never seen a doctor because they refuse to be attended by a male physician? Women of substantial means, mind you. They want female doctors, and their influence will be felt in the end…And a poor woman deserves just as much dignity as a rich one. Not only should a poor woman have the right to see a female physician, she should have the right to do it in private. Without our clinics, indigent patients must submit to examination by the entire medical class at Charity Hospital."

The tour had taken them to the back stairs and they went up to the second floor. "This and the room across the hall are our surgical recovery facilities. We have six patient beds, five for whites and one for coloreds."

Sarah Beth seemed surprised.

"You don't mind working with coloreds, do you?"

"Oh, no. They deserve medical care, too. In fact, I helped compile research on the treatment of *phlyctenular ophthalmia*. As I'm sure you know, the disease is more prevalent in coloreds."

"That *is* wonderful. With whom did you work?"

"I've even done medical billing and worked with one of the ward committees last year." Sarah Beth hoped Dr. Mayo did not notice her evasive answer.

"Then we are indeed fortunate you have chosen to work with us. Which ward committee?" Dr. Mayo asked.

Damn! Every time she spoke of her past, Sarah Beth set another trap for herself. She drew a deep breath. "In…In Storyville."

"Good for you! It takes a brave woman to do what you did." Dr. Mayo clapped her hands together. "While we must abhor those people for their sins, and purge society of their depravity, they are still human beings and should be treated as such. Miss LaBranche, I like the cut of your jib, as they say. May I call you Sarah?"

She answered with a relieved sigh. "Sarah Beth. Please do."

"And you must call me Daisy, everyone else does. And it will make things so much simpler, too, don't you think? Imagine the confusion two Saras would cause."

They continued their tour and ended at Dr. Mayo's office where she said, "Take a few days and think matters over. Then, if you still wish to honor us with your services–."

"There's nothing to think about," Sarah Beth said. "It would be a privilege to work here."

"Wonderful." Daisy Mayo smiled broadly. "When can you begin?"

"Where can I put my hat?"

BECAUSE OF HER EXPERIENCE DURING the epidemic, Sarah Beth became the new quartermaster of the New Orleans Dispensary and Hospital for Women and Children. She began her work late that first afternoon in the general storeroom. Supplies were scant. For the six beds in the two recovery wards, she found five blankets and two extra sets of linen. When she asked, Sarah Beth discovered the beds were changed every third day. The hospital had no pillow cases because it had no pillows. Sarah Beth made a list of the minimum stock needed. She would send Lou Belle and Titan to purchase the items tomorrow.

Dusk came early in late November and Sarah Beth wanted to inspect the physical condition of the building itself before it became too dark. She looked for a kerosene lamp. When she found none, that, too, along with a can of kerosene, was added to the list of supplies.

Outside, Sarah Beth ignored the clinic's cosmetic needs, paint and flower beds long neglected, and concentrated on structural necessities—rotten clapboards that needed replacing, a fence in total disrepair, an empty coal bin and no firewood in the rack. Darkness overtook her project, as did despair over the Dispensary's indigence. She sat heavily on one of the patient benches in the front yard, and its joints gave way, dumping her unceremoniously on the ground.

As she stood and dusted herself off, a vaguely familiar female voice Sarah Beth knew she should recognize said from behind her, "T-The clinic is closed, isn't it?"

Sarah Beth turned.

A fit of coughing caught the woman, and she staggered a few steps. Sarah Beth reached for her but the woman stumbled away, holding a rag to her mouth. "Stay away. I'm contagious."

Sarah Beth, squinting against the night to see the woman's face, said, "If you need help, I'm sure we can arrange it. There's a nurse assigned to the ward who might be able to assist you. I imagine we can send for one of the doctors, if necessary…Don't I know you? Your voice is very familiar."

"No," the woman said too quickly. "I-I don't want to see the nurse. That's not…I have to go." The woman held the rag to her face even though the coughing fit had passed. "I-I don't need any help. Leave me alone." She staggered down the alley toward the Dispensary's back yard looking over her shoulder and calling, "Go away. I don't need any help."

Perhaps the broken fence is a neighborhood short-cut, Sarah Beth thought. She walked back to the Dispensary, but, at the front door, changed her mind and crept silently to the end of the porch. Peeking around the edge of the house, she saw the woman furtively dart around the far corner of the Dispensary and into the back yard. *She's not taking a short cut, she's meeting someone.* Suddenly Sarah Beth realized who the woman was, heightening the mystery. She crept down the shadowy alley until she heard voices.

"Do you have it?" the woman asked.

"'Deed I do," a man's voice replied. "Gots t' pay up first, like always."

"You know I'm sick. You might–."

The man sounded angry. "Ya ain't got clap, does ya, woman? Better not, 'cause if ya do, I takes my stuff and get on outta here."

"N-No. I have a cough, the same as always."

"Ha-ha. Gal, it ain't the coughin' end I wants."

"But–."

"That's it, that's the end I wants. Get by them steps and bends over. Get that skirt on up. Sooner ya gets to payin' me, sooner ya gets what ya want."

In the dark ally, Sarah Beth almost wept, feeling the woman's shame grate upon the remembered desperation woven into her own soul. The man's brutish grunts, the woman's whimpers mingled with echoes of her past and whisked Sarah Beth back to Storyville, back to the degradation she had suffered before Myda found her. No woman should be made to endure such shame; no sin required such atrocious restitution. Sarah Beth's head swirled with only one thought, *SAVE THE WOMAN!*

Automatically Sarah Beth reached into the folds of her dress for her guns. Damn! She had stopped carrying the derringers when she left the District. What now?

Sarah Beth pushed her back hard against the Dispensary wall as second by excruciatingly slow second sired a rash and reckless plan. Stooping down, she searched the ground until she found two sticks the size she needed–one the right length, one to make the right sound–she hoped.

Sarah Beth jumped around the corner of the building and yelled, "Stop right now!"

"Who that?" The man no longer moved and grunted but remained glued to the bent-over woman.

"Let her go!" Sarah Beth commanded.

"Who gonna make me?"

Even in the dark, Sarah Beth could tell the man was of above average height. "I'll shoot if you don't." She raised her hand with the longer piece of wood held like a gun barrel.

"A little ol' white gal perntin' her finger and makin' like she gots a gun ain't scarin' me none." He backed from the woman and took a threatening step toward Sarah Beth, making no attempt to hide his aroused manhood. "Maybe I'll let this here one go iffen ya'll come takes her place."

Sarah Beth brought her other hand up as if to steady her aim. With her hands together, she broke the second stick, hoping the noise would sound like a gun's hammer cocking. "Fingers don't make a noise like that. Now move away from her, I say!" Sarah Beth hoped the man was none too bright. The stick broke with a sickeningly wooden sound.

The woman moaned, "Stop. You don't know what you're doing."

The moon came from behind the clouds and threw a feeble, silver glow on the scene. Sarah Beth saw the confusion on the man's face and hoped he did not see the deception in her hand. She had no choice but to press her bluff. "I said step back! Do it and do it now, you black son of a bitch!"

The man raised his hands, white palms out. "Listen, lady. I ain't done nothin'. Look-a-here, she wanted t'. She done it befo'. Lots o' times. She want the stuff I got, see, and I told her that be the price and she paid it. Ax her." He turned to the woman, now huddled next the Dispensary's back steps. "G'wan, tells her that ain't no lie. G'wan, tells her 'fore that crazy woman shoots me daid!"

"He's right," the woman sobbed. "Let us alone."

Sarah Beth shook the lie in her hands. "Get out!"

The man buttoned his pants and inched toward her.

"Not the alley. Through the back yard. There's a hole in the fence."

"How I know ya ain't gonna shoot me? I ain't givin' ya my back whilst ya points that there gun at me."

"Don't and you're guaranteed I'll shoot you." Sarah Beth aimed the stick at his crotch. "Exactly where it will do the most good, too."

"I's goin'." The man backed up toward the fence. "Don't go crazy on me now, lady. I's goin'." When he reached the hole in the fence, he darted through.

Watching the space through which the assailant had disappeared, Sarah Beth bent down and put her arm around the woman huddled next to the stairs.

"Why couldn't you leave well enough alone?" the woman demanded. "Why couldn't you leave me be? I need his morphine, and that's the only way I can pay for it. I know you think I'm terrible. But you don't understand. I need it and now he's gone. Oh, what will I do?"

"I'll help you."

"You have morphine! Give it to me quickly." The woman struggled to roll up the sleeve on her left arm.

Sarah Beth saw the hope in the woman's eyes, heard the desperation in her voice. "No. I have no morphine."

"T-Then how can you help? Why didn't you leave us alone? Oh God, why didn't you just mind your own business!"

"Where's your husband?" Sarah Beth asked.

"Do I know you?"

"Yes. Where's your husband?"

"Who are you?"

"Sarah Beth LaBranche. Now tell me, Mrs. Anderson, where is Philip?"

"Dead," Maggie Anderson replied.

"Oh my God! How?" *Did he make good on his threat to kill himself?* Sarah Beth wondered.

"The fever."

"And the children?"

"Dead. All dead. The fever took them all." Maggie Anderson's soft sobs were halted by a horrendous coughing fit that racked her thin frame.

"What about your family, your parents? Why haven't you gone to them for help?"

Maggie Anderson's eyes were wide, with very little sanity in them. "Morphine! I need morphine! Please, you've got to help me." She clawed Sarah Beth's arm. "Can you get any? Inside?"

"Is that how he—."

"That man's sister works here. She steals it and gives it to him. He sells it. Please. Let's go inside and look."

"Perhaps." Sarah Beth helped Maggie Anderson sit on the steps. "First tell me what happened."

"Philip changed so much. So suddenly. Began drinking. That's all he did, drink and drink. I'd get up in the morning, and he'd be drunk already. Or maybe it was from the night before. I never knew which. He didn't care about me, the children, his position. He taught at Tulane, did you know that?"

Sarah Beth nodded in the dim moon light.

"He lost his teaching post. He lost everything. No money, no food, behind in the rent. All because of a *woman!*"

Hearing the venom in Maggie Anderson's voice, trembling, Sarah Beth asked, "H-How do you know? D-Did he say that. Did he say who she was?"

"Never a name. But the fever made him delirious and he'd call for her. 'Oh, my scarlet beauty. Why, oh, why did you leave me?' he'd moan over and over. That's how I knew he had a *whore*!"

Sarah Beth held Maggie's shoulders to support her. "Then what happened?"

"He and the children got sick within a few days of each other. Oh, my poor babies! My poor, poor precious little babies! We had no money. Philip drank it all up. The doctor was wonderful. He tended all of them even though he knew we couldn't pay. He came–."

"What doctor? What was his name?" Sarah Beth insisted.

"Dr. Grander. But still there was no money for food. The rent was past due. Our savings were gone. My babies cried from the fever. The landlord came to evict us." Maggie's voice became more and more hopeless. "There was nothing else for me to do. I couldn't have my sick babies thrown into the street. I begged with him, I pleaded. But he had no heart, no soul. He wanted an...an accommodation. He wanted me to...I had no choice. Both Philip's family and mine live up north. No time to ask them for help. And with the quarantine, no way to get to them. There was no other way, I tell you!" With unequivocal despair in her voice, Maggie's eyes begged Sarah Beth to understand the hopelessness of her situation. "And my children were sick. I had no choice, you must believe me. Please, you must believe I would never...The landlord brought scraps of food and made me debase myself for each morsel. As God is my witness, there was no other way! You must believe me! I'm a good, decent woman. At least, I was. And I caught his cough. When the pains in my chest got worse, I began using morphine. It makes the hurt go away for a while. At first, the landlord gave it to me, but I'm sure it was for his own purposes, not to relieve my pain. To increase...to increase my abandon...Oh, God, it hurts so much to cough! I had to do something. Please, Miss, you've got to believe me. And you must help me, help me get my morphine!"

The utter desperation in Maggie Anderson's voice overwhelmed Sarah Beth. She blinked back tears. How many people had she ruined? How many lives had she decimated? She was no better than Inez Breaux. Perhaps the loss of her momma was part of her punishment. She still had no word from the woman she longed with all her heart to see. If the penance for what she had done was never to see her momma and Jeremy again, it still was not enough. In the shadows of the silver-sprinkled Dispensary yard, holding half-dead Maggie Anderson close to her breast, Sarah Beth vowed to make amends for her wickedness, to atone a thousand-fold for each vile deed. And she would start with this woman, whose life she had destroyed.

CHAPTER 32

"SHE COULD NOT HAVE STAYED here," Daisy Mayo said as she sat next to the roll-top desk that occupied one wall of her office. "There was no other way. Please believe me, Sarah Beth. Tuberculosis is very contagious. Your actions, though understandable, were very rash. You put everyone in the Dispensary, the patients, the staff, yourself, at great risk."

"What's to become of her?" Sarah Beth paced back and forth in front of the windows overlooking the Dispensary's front yard.

"She will stay at the sanatorium in Mandeville."

"For how long?"

"We have no cure," Daisy said in a low, hushed voice.

"She'll die there, won't she?" Sarah Beth stopped pacing and looked out the window at the patients.

"We all will die someday."

Sarah Beth touched the curtains lightly with her hand. "But she'll die sooner than most."

"I am afraid so."

Sarah Beth stomped her foot. "Damn! It's so unfair."

Daisy came from her desk and stood next to Sarah Beth. "Life itself is unfair. But we have a duty to all mankind, not just individuals. We must always be conscious of the greater good. Quarantines are always hard, always seem unfair."

"And, many times, unnecessary," Sarah Beth insisted. "Like the yellow fever quarantines. How many people suffered needlessly because of our ignorance? Flags hanging from houses, trains from New Orleans stopped at gunpoint. All so fruitless."

"But you are comparing apples to oranges. Based on current knowledge, the yellow fever quarantines do seem outrageous. And they were definitely based on ignorance. We, as doctors, had no knowledge of how the disease was transmitted and, so, quarantines seemed warranted. That's not the case here. We can say with almost complete certainty that the tuberculosis germ is air-borne, sent from one person to the next by a sneeze, a cough, perhaps just the simple act of breathing." Daisy rested her hand on Sarah Beth's arm. "Knowing the kind of woman she is makes your charity toward her especially admirable. But, while her due as a human being is the best medical care possible, we must insure that she does not contaminate the rest of society through her disease or because of what she is."

"Just what do you mean by that?" Sarah Beth walked away from Daisy in an indignant huff.

"She *is* a fallen woman, and we must purge ourselves of people like her."

Sarah Beth began pacing again. "Are you saying a fallen woman can never redeem herself? What about Mary Magdalene?"

"Certainly she can change her ways through self-discipline and devotion to God. But the inclination toward sin is rooted in the nature of certain social classes. Just because a person of that class controls herself, laudable as that may be, does not mean we can drop our guard."

Sarah Beth held her mouth in a harsh line, speaking through lips that barely moved. "You assume that there are no circumstances where a *good* person could be forced to behave in ways you disapprove."

"Someone with your great charity may not see the issue clearly." Dr. Mayo kept her voice low, her tone soothing as she returned to her desk. "There is a delicate balance to achieve. Alleviate the current suffering and insure the root cause is eliminated. It may be hard for someone of great compassion to accept, but that is what science teaches us. One reads Darwin to understand what one must do to improve our species. I ask only two things of you, study Darwin and keep an open mind."

Sarah Beth let her anger go and sat across from her friend. She knew Sara Mayo echoed the beliefs prevalent in the upper class; an opinion born not of malice, but a sincere desire to better humanity and secure the Utopia of their design. "I will, Daisy, if you promise to keep an open mind, too. When I worked in Storyville during the fever, I learned there are many reasons why people live that life. Not excuses, but explanations. No one deliberately chooses evil, at least *I* don't think so. But sometimes things happen beyond anyone's control. Or the wrong choice is made. Then, making the best of a bad situation can become a way of life and even the best bred person, after a while, loses sight of what they've done wrong. I'll study Darwin, Daisy, if you'll allow a person can be redeemed."

"Ah, but of course they can," Dr. Mayo said. "Individuals can and do redeem themselves. But the lower class as a whole, my dear, cannot."

"We'll discuss that issue later," Sarah Beth said, "right now I must ask a favor."

"What might that be?"

"A leave of absence. There are family matters–."

"Dear Sarah Beth, you do not need my permission to go. It is you who favor us by working here. If you must leave to attend your family, do so, by all means."

"And when I return, may I come back?" Sarah Beth asked.

"We will welcome you with open arms."

FROM THE FRONT GALLERY OF her house on Third Street, Sarah Beth watched Titan load the last of her luggage into the carriage.

The clothes pole man crossed the street and called from the gate, "Need poles, lady? Gots 'em straight and tall."

"Not today, thank you." Sarah Beth turned to Lou Belle. "I shan't be gone long, at least I don't plan to be. Two weeks, three at most. If that changes, I'll write."

"How I gonna know they's a letter f' me?"

"On the back of the envelope, I'll put a cross on each corner. Check the mail each day and if you find an envelope like that, take it to Dr. Mayo. She'll read it to you."

"Yeah zum. Gots everythin' ya'll need? Enough drawers and all?"

Sarah Beth smiled. *Only Lou Belle would say such a thing.* "I'm sure I do. But, if I've forgotten anything, I'll buy it. Oh, speaking of money, I've left three hundred dollars in Aunt Myda's desk for you. It should be more than enough to take care of you and Titan until I return. Here's the key. Do you remember the small green-covered drawers in the desk where Aunt Myda kept the girls' money?"

Lou Belle nodded.

"The money is in a drawer on the top row, all the way to the right."

"I knows where you talkin' 'bout." Lou Bell looked past her mistress, put her hands on her hips and frowned. "Who that gal on the *banquette* messin' with my Ty."

Sarah Beth turned to see Titan come through the gate and up the front walk. On the *banquette*, with her hand on the shoulder of a young boy, stood a colored woman about Sarah Beth's age.

At the porch Titan doffed his hat. "That there gal say she looking for you, Miz Sarah Bet'."

"Did she say why?"

"No, ma'am."

"Did she say who she is?"

"No, ma'am, and me, I ain't axed."

Sarah Beth studied the newcomer. There was something very familiar about her. With a head full of pigtails and a red and black polka dot dress, she could have been a grown up version of–. Sarah Beth flew down the steps and out the gate. "Lottie Mae! Oh, Lottie Mae! It's so good to see you!"

Lottie Mae's head turned toward the sound of Sarah Beth's voice and she lost her balance when Sarah Beth rushed up and embraced her.

"Let me look at you." Sarah Beth held her friend at arms length. "Oh, it's so good to see you again."

Lottie Mae flashed the brilliant white teeth Sarah Beth remembered so well. "Real fine seein' you, too, Miss Sarah Beth."

Sarah Beth slipped her arm around the waist of her childhood friend. "What's all this 'Miss' nonsense?"

"You all growed up now. Ma, she say 'fore I lef' it ain't fittin' not t' call ya Miss."

"That's silly." Sarah Beth pulled her friend close. "I'm the same person that picked blackberries with you for your mother's pies. Oh how is she, Lottie Mae, how is Elona?"

"Fine as can be. Say to tell ya she still think about ya."

"I can't wait to see her. This is such a coincidence. I was just leaving for St. Francisville and here you are in New Orleans." A cloud that Sarah Beth did not notice passed over Lottie Mae's smile. "What brings you here?"

"Come t' see ya."

"I'm so glad we didn't miss each other." Sarah Beth hugged her friend's waist as she lead her toward the porch. "What could possibly bring you all this way to see me after all these years?"

"T' talk 'bout somethin' needs talkin…And ax ya'll t' help me." Lottie Mae had one arm around Sarah Beth as they walked and the other hand on the shoulder of the young boy with her. "Miss–. Sorry. Sarah Beth, you the most smartest gal I ever knowed. I still 'member that time ya did all that with them rocks when you was figurin' money t' run off. Now me, I gots the most terrible, worrisome thing that can happen to a body. Ma, she said the onlyest thing t' do was come see ya. So that's just what I done."

They had reached the porch, and Lottie Mae stumbled against the bottom step.

"Sorry, Lottie," the young boy said as he helped Sarah Beth steady her friend. "Thought the lady'd say."

"Say what?" Sarah Beth asked.

"Where stuff is." Lottie Mae looked for the bottom step with the toe of her shoe. "Like as not, ya ain't took no notice 'cause ya sound so excited and all, but me, I can't hardly see no more. That's what I needs ya help on. I can't see nothin'. I's goin' blind as a bat."

For the first time, Sarah Beth looked closely at her friend's eyes. Covering each was a sheet of tiny white pimples ranging from the size of a grain of sand to the head of a pin. "Oh, God, Lottie Mae! Have you seen a doctor?"

"No, ma'am. Old Doc Boudreaux passed, Gawd rest his soul, and the new doctor come t' town say he got no time for a nigger gal till he catch heself up with all the white folk. But it look like he ain't never gonna have time t' look after me. And this here just gettin' worse. Used t' be I could see some out the right eye. Now that's goin', too. When that last letter come for ya ma, we finally knowed where ya was at. Ma, she say I needed t' get on down here t' see ya. So Ant'ny here—he my littlest brother. Ant'ny lead me on down. Paw, he don't need the boy in the fields just now. Can ya help me, Miss—. Can ya help me, Sarah Beth?"

"Of course, Lottie Mae, of course." Sarah Beth helped her friend up the front steps. "Lou Belle, this is Lottie Mae Talbot from St. Francisville. I've told you about her. We grew up together."

"Yeah zum." Lou Belle took the hand Lottie Mae had on her brother's shoulder and helped Sarah Beth lead her blind friend into the house. Anthony and Titan followed.

Taking off her hat and handing it to Lou Belle, Sarah Beth guided Lottie Mae into the front parlor.

Lottie Mae's congested eyes strained to see her surroundings. "This the big house ya'll talked 'bout in ya letter, ain't it? Downstairs sittin' room, I bet."

"Yes, it's a long story. Please sit down." Sarah Beth helped her friend into an overstuffed chair. "We've so much to catch up on. Would you like tea? Coffee perhaps? Have you had breakfast?"

A patina of fear covered the infection in Lottie Mae's eyes. Her face looked like a run-away slave's hearing blood hounds. "N-No, thank you kindly, ma'am. My belly got all it can hold."

Sarah Beth saw the same class consciousness in Lottie Mae that she had seen when she invited Lou Belle to sit in the parlor with her. "Would you prefer sitting in the kitchen?"

"Oh, yes, 'um."

"Fine. But only if you promise to stop all this 'ma'am' and 'Miss' business." Sarah Beth linked arms with her old friend as they walked to the back of the house.

Seated at the kitchen table, Lottie Mae would only accept a glass of water.

"I'm so excited!" Sarah Beth said with her friend settled at the table. "Tell me about momma and Jeremy. How are they, when did you see them last?"

Lottie Mae's face took on a look of great sadness. "That's the other part o' why I come."

Sarah Beth reached across the table and grabbed her friend's hands. "What's wrong? Oh, God, what's wrong?"

Lottie Mae shook her head. "Ain't no easy way t' say."

Sarah Beth shook her friend's arm. "Just tell me, for God's sake."

Lottie Mae took a deep breath and held it for a heart beat, then blurted out, "Ya ma and brother, they dead. Ya paw, too."

Lou Belle caught Sarah Beth just as she fainted and fell out of her chair.

SARAH BETH REGAINED CONSCIOUSNESS IN her own bed. Lou Belle sat in a rocking chair close by, singing a mournful hymn to herself. The heavy, familiar tramp of Titan's boots could be heard pacing the hall outside. Sarah Beth began to cry softly.

Lou Belle sat on the bed and hugged Sarah Beth to her. "There, there, chil'. I knows how much this hurt. Ya just cry it all outta ya."

For a long while the two women held each other with only Sarah Beth's muted weeping, punctuated by Titan's boots, to break the stillness.

"Where's Lottie Mae?" Sarah Beth finally asked between sniffles.

"In the kitchen. This been hard on her, too."

"Ask her to come up, please?"

"Ty," Lou Belle called, "get ya'self downstairs and fetch that gal up here."

Sarah Beth and Lou Belle sat quietly until Lottie Mae knocked on the door.

Sarah Beth dried her eyes. "Come and sit by me Lottie Mae." With Lottie Mae settled on the bed with Lou Belle's help, Sarah Beth held her pillow tightly to her chest and, with a great effort to be calm, said, "Please tell me what happened."

"This be powerful bad, Sarah Beth, but ma, she say the truth set ya free, so I gonna tell ya all the truth like I know it."

Sarah Beth squeezed the pillow tighter and blinked back tears. "That's all I ask."

"After ya run off, they be a big commotion with ya ma and paw. Ya ma, she come t' town after that mo' black and blue than reg'lar and limpin' a might. Then things settle down and when I seed her later on, she didn't look no more bunged-up then before ya gone. Ya know ya ma, she was always bunged-up somewheres from that man."

Sarah Beth nodded and a tear slipped silently down her cheek.

"Nothin' much happened till plantin' when I heared ya ma gots a letter down t' the General Mercantile. Then ya ma got comin' t' town reg'lar on a Monday while ya paw was sleepin' off the 'shine. And just like sunrise, every Monday they'd be a letter. By and by, folks started sayin' them letters come from ya'll and ya'll was sendin' money. That was real nice, Sarah Beth. I seed ya ma round 'bout sometimes and she say t' me how happy it make her that ya done kept ya promise."

Sheets of tears washed Sarah Beth's face, yet she did not make a sound.

"She tell me how she can buy stuff now. How her life be better 'n' all. Jeremy, too. But she say Addie Thompson say them letters, they gots a strangeness 'bout them. Miss Thompson, she say them letters don't say where y'at. But ya ma, she don't care. All she know is ya kept ya first promise and likely ya'd keep the rest. Ya ma, she was real proud of you, girl."

Her head buried in the pillow, Sarah Beth's body shook as she cried. Lou Belle put a comforting hand on her shoulder.

Lottie Mae waited in respectful silence, listening for her friend to recover her composure, then said, "Things went on reg'lar till just past the second Christmas after ya run off. I heared tell ya paw, he found out 'bout the letters and the money. Ya ma, she stopped comin' t' town, and ya paw, he come by the General Mercantile after them letters now. Miss Thompson, she wouldn't give 'em t' him on account they had ya ma's name on 'em. Ya paw, he made an awful fuss, sayin' how ya ma was his wife and them letters and what's in 'em is his on account of it. And Miss Thompson, she went t' see ya ma and ya ma, she say t' give ya paw the letters, so that's what Miss Thompson done. But then she went back with the sheriff 'cause ya ma, she was in bed the first time and bunged-up so bad Miss Thompson hardly don't knowed her. But the sheriff, he say he can't do nothin' 'cause ya paw say ya ma fell down off the porch and got walked on by a mule. And ya ma, she say that's right. The sheriff, he say ya paw's lyin' and ya ma's swearin' to it, but they ain't nothin' he can do iffen ya ma won't say what happened f' true."

"She was always like that." Sarah Beth looked from Lottie Mae to Lou Belle. "Even after everything he had done to her, she loved him. I remember just before I ran away she told me not to hate him."

Lou Belle stroked Sarah Beth's hair. "Sounds like ya maw's the one ya got all ya goodness from, honey child."

"She was a wonderful woman." Sarah Beth took Lottie Mae's hand. "Then what happened?"

"Ya paw, he drunk all the time now, takin' the money ya send and buyin' more 'shine than a human man can drink. By and by, when he come one day for the letter, he tell Miss Thompson that ya ma dead. From that fall and the mule. Ain't nobody believe that lyin', drunked up ol' bum 'bout ya ma bein' mule-kicked. Miss Thompson, she pass herself by ya cabin and, sure enough, she find a grave. And Jeremy, he say ya ma dead, too. Miss Thompson, she wanna take Jeremy out o' there and put him in a home, but ya paw, he say he need the boy for chores and such. The sheriff, he say he can't help Miss Thompson get Jeremy out from there, so the boy, he stays."

"Poor little Jeremy." Sarah Beth began crying again.

"I sure sorry t' be the one t' tell ya all this, Sarah Beth. Ya sure ya wants t' hear, 'cause it don't get no better. Fact is, it get a lot worser."

Sarah Beth wiped her face with the end of the pillowcase. "Please go on, Lottie Mae. I have to know everything."

"For a while ya paw, he be in town reg'lar on a Monday all drunked up. Then come a Monday and nobody seed him. Come Tuesday, they ain't hide nor hair o' the man. By Wednesday, Miss Thompson, she gets the sheriff and they pass by ya cabin. The way I heared it, it terrible out there. They found little Jeremy hangin' dead by the neck from a tree."

"Oh, my God!" Sarah Beth swooned.

"Ty, get the salts!" Lou Belle yelled as she held Sarah Beth's limp body.

Titan's boots thundered down the stairs and up again. "Where they at?"

Lou Belle raced from the bedroom mumbling about good-for-nothing men. When she returned, she found Sarah Beth conscious but disoriented. "Ty, gets me a wet rag and be quick 'bout it." She sat on the bed. Shaking her mistress, she called, "Miz Sarah Beth…Miz Sarah Beth, honey…Say somethin' t' me, chil'."

Sarah Beth moaned as Titan returned with the compress. Lou Belle applied it to her mistress' forehead. Regaining her faculties, Sarah Beth took the cloth and wiped her face.

"Ya want somethin' t' drink, honey?" Lou Belle asked.

"Yes, please. Water."

Titan rushed from the room.

Lou Belle laid her mistress back against her pillows. "Honey, ya had enough o' all this for one day, ain't ya? Why ya don't try t' get some sleep now?"

"No." Sarah Beth sat up. "Sleep won't change anything. Momma's dead. Little Jeremy's dead. I have to know what happened. It will be worse if I wait. If I don't know, my mind will make up things more terrible…Can you understand, Lou Belle?"

"Yeah zum, I surely can."

Sarah Beth turned to Lottie Mae. "I'm sorry. You've been so kind to come so far to tell me this and I keep interrupting. It's just that–."

"Don't say nothin' 'bout sorry, Sarah Beth." Lottie Mae reached out to find her friend's hand "This be the kind o' thing a natural body can't hardly stand. But maybe Miss Lou Belle, here, be right. Maybe it better to wait and–."

"No, Lottie Mae. I don't want to wait. Please tell me now."

Lottie Mae turned her white-sheeted eyes in the direction of Sarah Beth's voice. "Ain't much left t' tell. Miss Thompson and the sheriff, they look f' ya paw and find him in the cabin. He dead, too. On the bed. Wacked up good with a ax."

"D-Did they catch the people who killed Jeremy?" Sarah Beth begged to know.

"The sheriff and ol' Doc Harrison…I sure is sorry t' be the one t' tell ya all this, Sarah Beth. The sheriff and the doc, they say Jeremy hunged hisself."

An almost soundless keening began deep in Sarah Beth's throat. Becoming louder, it formed a single word. "Nooooooo?" She balled her hands into white-knuckled fists and beat the mattress. "He would never do that! Why would he do that?"

Lottie Mae's sightless eyes turned away from Sarah Beth and she sighed. When she turned back towards the sound of Sarah Beth's sobs, she said, "'Cause o' what the doc figured ya paw done him."

"What? What did paw do?"

"Not now." Lou Belle interrupted, her voice sharp and insistent as she dabbed the wet cloth on Sarah Beth's face. "Ya'll had enough f' one day. Ya gots t' rest. Lottie Mae can stay in–."

Sarah Beth grabbed Lou Belle's arm and looked deep into the older woman's eyes. "No! No, I must find out!" Sarah Beth seized her childhood friend's skirt and knotted it into a ball in her hand. Desperation in her voice, she implored, "Don't leave me like this. You have to tell me, Lottie Mae! Not knowing is the worst of all. Oh, please tell me, or the things I make up in my head will be worse than anything that could have happened."

Lottie Mae's blank eyes looked in Lou Belle's direction for guidance.

Lou Belle nodded, then, remembering Lottie Mae could not see, said, "Go on, chil'."

Lottie Mae turned back to Sarah Beth. Mustering her resolve with a deep breath, she said, "The way I heared it, the doc figured ya paw used the boy for a woman."

Sarah Beth, her eyes round, covered her mouth with her hands as she sucked in her breath. Then, pounding the pillow, she screamed, "That son of a bitch! That bastard! That vile, loathsome spawn of hell! How could he do such a thing to his own son! Shit, shit, shit!" She looked toward heaven and pleaded, "Momma, oh, momma, why didn't you let me shoot the bastard when I had the chance!"

"Can't nobody know what happened f' sure," Lou Belle admonished. "It all be just figurin', ain't that right, Lottie Mae." She wasted a wink on the blind woman.

"Seem t' me it pretty good figurin'. All he front teeths be gone." Lottie Mae grimaced and tapped her own. "They found him in that tree nekked and looked him over good. They say he *be*-hind tore up bad."

Sarah Beth covered her face with her hands and slumped against Lou Belle. Silent sobs shuddered her body until the air in the room seemed to resonate with her grief.

Eventually Sarah Beth stopped crying. Lou Belle, not caring whether her mistress had fainted or fallen asleep, laid Sarah Beth down—carefully taking the battered pillow and placing it at the foot of the mattress. As she guided Lottie Mae to the door, Lou Belle made a silent wish, a prayer that Sarah Beth found solace in the sweet oblivion engulfing her.

SARAH BETH REMAINED SEQUESTERED IN her room for the next week. Her prodigious memory allied with her sorrow to conjure up images of the atrocities Lottie Mae had described. Behind her eyelids at night, on the ceiling above her bed during the day, the terrible visions haunted her. She imagined the abominations from every conceivable angle—as if she witnessed them through the chinks in the cabin's clapboards or from the bushes at the edge of the woods or through the open outhouse door.

Horrible as her brother's suffering must have been, she visualized little of it. Her mind focused, instead, on the agony of her beloved momma. She pictured the weeks and months and years of torture the poor woman had endured at the hands of the drunken sot who had sired her. Her fantasies filled the bedroom. Wherever she looked, she saw her paw pounding, kicking, punching her momma. If she squeezed her eyelids closed, she still saw her momma being beaten, heard the poor woman's moans and her paw's inebriated laughter.

After a few days, Lou Belle and Lottie Mae took up station in the bedroom despite Sarah Beth's protests. The old housekeeper forced her to eat, and Lottie Mae spoke of the childhood she and Sarah Beth had shared. Little by little, as grief and anguish entombed her, the voices of her two friends became Sarah Beth's only connection with the corporeal world.

As time slowly passed, the images in her mind took on substance for Sarah Beth. Soon they became so real she thought she could save her momma. One afternoon, as Lou Belle and Lottie Mae napped in rockers next to the bed, Sarah Beth lunged at the specter shape of her paw, her hands curled into claws, her fingernails aimed at his eyes. It did no good. She fell through the man and landed on the floor on the other side of him. When she looked up, she saw him still beating her momma, but from a different angle.

The noise of Sarah Beth crashing to the floor startled Lottie Mae and Lou Belle awake. As the housekeeper helped her charge back to bed, it seemed to Sarah Beth as if they walked around the spectacle of her paw pummeling her momma, Sarah Beth's angle of view changing with each step.

Occasionally Sarah Beth lapsed into sanity. On these sporadic visits to reality, she understood what was happening to her, yet would do nothing to change it. She refused to use the force of her prodigious intellect to save her from the madness she knew she deserved. Each night, as dusk filtered through the lace curtains on the window, she closed her eyes for what she hoped would be the last time.

One night, other ghosts from Sarah Beth's past arrived, one by one, to haunt her. As her paw beat her momma, Inez Breaux stood next to him, laughing, throwing hot water on her momma, screaming, "Ya'll done this, Sarah Beth," as black bile spewed from her mouth. Bald, fat, wicked Judge Watson raped and ravaged the drugged and drunken innocent young girl Sarah Beth had once been as her momma watched, weeping. Maggie Anderson held her three dead children by the neck, spitting the phlegm of tuberculosis on Sarah Beth as Philip Anderson and every man Sarah Beth had let use her plundered and despoiled the whore with the scarlet-gold hair in ways more odious than Sarah Beth had ever imagined. As the crowd of would-be defilers crushed around her, Sarah Beth glimpsed tallow hair fighting toward her only to be beaten back by John Griswold. Frank and Frances, in wedding attire, watched, pointing at the suffering of Sarah Beth and her momma and laughing uproariously.

Her nightmare became so insufferable, Sarah Beth sprang from tormented sleep to sit bolt upright in bed. All was quiet, except for the light murmur of Lottie Mae and Lou Belle's snoring. Somehow, Sarah Beth's sudden waking kept her demons entombed in her subconscious. For the first time in days she saw the details of her bedroom in the soft glow of a trimmed kerosene lamp: the carved bedposts, the pattern of the quilted comforter, her own reflection in the chiffonnier's mirror across the room.

Suddenly, the likeness in the mirror took on a life of its own and beckoned her. Sarah Beth padded to the chiffonnier to see her other self more closely–the streaming, disheveled, red hair; the nightgown she had ripped during her nightmare. As she recognized the feral dementia in the sunken eyes of her reflection, as she felt the demons of her nightmares clawing the inside of her breast for their freedom, in that one instant of lucidity before her mirror, she knew what she must do.

Sarah Beth stole softly to her high-top dresser. From the bottom drawer, she took one of her pearl-handled derringers. The silver barrel glistened in the dimness as she opened the gun and checked the chamber. The dull brass sheen of the bullet's casing caught the feeble light.

Sarah Beth had raised the small gun to her temple when a voice behind her said, "That ain't the way, honey girl. That ain't never the way."

Sarah Beth spun around. "Momma! Momma is that you?" She saw the specter of her mother in the moonlight on the cabin porch the night she had tried to kill her paw.

"That ain't the way, honey girl. That ain't never the way."

"Oh, momma." Sarah Beth fell into the arms of the phantom. "Oh, momma, I missed you so much. Oh, momma, I'm so sorry for what I did to you and–."

"Ya ain't done nothin', honey girl. If there's someone t' blame, it's me. I done m' best t' save both you kids, but you's the only one I could help. Just keep that in mind, ain't none of this ya fault."

"But, momma, I should have come for you and–."

As Sarah Beth spoke, the spirit of her dead momma led her to bed. "Shush. Ya done what ya thought was right. That's all a body can ask. Maybe I should've let Jeremy go with ya when I knowed ya was headin' off. Maybe I should've let ya kill ya paw that night. Maybe I done right no matter what happened. Maybe, maybe, maybe. What's done is done. Ain't nothing gonna change it now. Not even you dyin'." The ghost laid Sarah Beth in bed, tucked the blankets around her and sat down. "What-all I done, honey girl, I done f' you. Jeremy, too, some, but mostly you. Don't make it a waste by killin' ya own self or pinin' away."

"But, momma–."

"Close ya eyes and get some sleep."

"But, momma–."

The apparition passed its hand over Sarah Beth's eyes and darkness came.

Sarah Beth woke near dawn. Through her bedroom window she saw the leading edge of day banish the stars. Lou Belle and Lottie Mae snored in the semi-darkness, which the meager light of dawn and the lamp did little to dispel.

Sarah Beth wondered if it had all been a dream. Had she really seen her momma's ghost, spoken to her? Was it an illusion, the workings of an over-wrought mind? Was it–.

The demons had vanished! Sarah Beth could feel their absence. Her hand came to her breast. Just a short while ago, the fiends mauled the inside of her chest to escape and torment her again. Now, she could only feel the beat of her heart.

Poor Lou Belle looked so uncomfortable sleeping in the chair, her head cocked over on her shoulder. Sarah Beth knew her old friend would have a stiff neck when she woke. "Pssst. Lou Belle. Lou Belle, wake up."

"Whaaa?"

"Go to bed. I'll be alright now."

Lou Belle rubbed her eyes, stretched and yawned. "I ain't g'wan nowheres till you is back in ya own right mind."

"I am now." In a quiet voice, so as not to wake Lottie Mae, Sarah Beth told her old friend of her vision.

When Sarah Beth finished, Lou Belle said, "Ain't I told ya all along ain't none of it ya fault?"

"Yes. Yes, you did. But don't you see, Lou Belle? Momma had to tell me, too."

CHAPTER 33

LOU BELLE KEPT SARAH BETH in bed for three more days to make sure her mistress had fully recovered. During this forced convalescence Sarah Beth and Lottie Mae reminisced, recounting their youths together. Lottie Mae told Sarah Beth the goings-on in St. Francisville over the past nine years, carefully avoiding mention of Sarah Beth's family until lunch on the third day, when Lou Belle forced the issue.

The housekeeper had brought sandwiches up to Sarah Beth's bedroom and stood with her hands on her ample hips listening to Lottie Mae's stories. When Lottie Mae stopped to take a bite, Lou Belle demanded, "What happened t' all them moneys Miz Sarah Beth been sendin' all these years is what I wants t' know."

"Lou Belle!" Sarah Beth scolded with a reproving look.

"That's okay. She done right t' ax. Me, I brung it with me," Lottie Mae answered. "Lemme gets it. It all in the room ya lets me 'n' Ant'ny stay in out back." Lottie Mae raised her voice to call her little brother who spent the last few days dozing on the floor next to Sarah Beth's chest of drawers, except to eat or guide his sister in her comings and goings. "Get ya'self over here, Ant'ny."

When Lottie Mae and Anthony returned, Sarah Beth's childhood friend stood in the doorway holding a hobo's suitcase of old cloth in one hand, her other on Anthony's shoulder. "All here, 'cept what ya paw used up t' buy he 'shine." Anthony led Lottie Mae to Sarah Beth's bed and she held the bundle out.

Sarah Beth unwrapped the cloth and found several stacks of envelops tied together.

"I-I had t' use me some o' that money t' gets here. Ma, she took it from that last letter ya'll sent. Three hundred whole dollars was in there, Sarah Beth. Ma, she never seed that much money in her whole life. She took a hundred o' them dollars and bought me this here dress and me and Ant'ny a ticket on the packet boat down. What's left is back in there. But, I swanie, I's gonna pay it all back."

"Best look like it, too," Lou Belle said.

Absently, Sarah Beth began opening the envelops and reading the letters. Each contained a ten dollar bill, which she piled on the bed next to her. She said absently as she read, "Of course she won't pay me back. How else could she have come here to tell–." She looked up from the letters. "Thank you so much for coming, Lottie Mae. None of this has been easy for me, but seeing you, learning what happened from a dear friend rather than in a letter from someone…Thank you so much for coming."

Sarah Beth began reading again, each letter a separate entry in the journal of her life. Lou Belle took Lottie Mae by the arm and the two women, along with Anthony, left Sarah Beth alone with her memories.

SARAH BETH DRESSED AND CAME down for dinner that evening. Everyone ate in the kitchen because Sarah Beth was the only one who felt comfortable in the dining room.

With coffee finished and Lou Belle clearing the dishes, Sarah Beth led Lottie Mae onto the back gallery and they sat quietly together. After a while, Sarah Beth extracted several rolls of money from the folds of her skirt and placed them in Lottie Mae's hand. "This is the money I sent momma over the years. I'd like you to have it."

"Can't take ya money, Sarah Beth. That ain't why I come."

"I know." Sarah Beth closed Lottie Mae's fingers around the bills. "But I'd like you to have it. Think of it as payment for the great service you've done for me. A reward."

"Don't want no reward. Ain't why I come."

"You came because we're friends and you wanted to tell me in person. That was very kind of you."

Lottie Mae's hands knotted her skirt. "Partly, but it ain't all."

"Your eyes."

Lottie Mae nodded.

"I'm sure I can help with that."

DAISY MAYO FINISHED HER EXAMINATION, then called Sarah Beth into the room. Closing the door, Sarah Beth asked, somewhat anxious, "And?"

"She is a normally developed woman in good health except for an advanced case of *phlyctenular ophthalmia.*"

The words tugged at Sarah Beth's heart, bringing a rush of memories and Frank's face clearly to mind. "I thought so."

"Are you familiar with the disease?" Daisy looked closely at the eczema on Lottie Mae's face. "This is a classic symptom, other than the eye infestation itself, of course."

"What is?" Lottie Mae asked.

"The rash on your upper lip and eyelids. Hold still." Using the edge of a tongue depressor, Daisy scraped flecks of Lottie Mae's dry skin onto a glass slide which she brought to a microscope set up on the counter at the end of the room. After examining the tissue, she said, "Nothing unusual here."

Sarah Beth and Lottie Mae stood arm in arm. "What do you recommend, Daisy?"

"A hydrogen chloride wash."

Sarah Beth's instincts immediately opposed Daisy's suggestion, but she did not know why. She thought back to the work she had done on the disease for Frank, the treatment tables she constructed clearly in her mind's eye. Hydrogen chloride was one of the least effective regimens.

Suddenly, a random thought made her realize why she and Frank had never found an effective treatment. They had grouped the data by remedy instead of severity.

Using her phenomenal mental ability, Sarah Beth closed her eyes and in her mind rearranged Frank's treatment information according to the numerical system of severity they had developed. Lottie Mae's case was clearly Class 5, the most critical. Eyes still closed, fingers twisting the curl at the side of her face, Sarah Beth mentally reorganized the Class 5 cases according to treatment, assessed each regimen according to the number of days it took to cure the disease and announced her conclusion. "Daisy, the best treatment would be to combine a borax-boracic wash with enzymol."

"You've been studying medical journals at night?"

Daisy's sweet tone held an unmistakable hint of sarcasm and reminded Sarah Beth of her quarrels with Dr. Rice during Frank's bout with yellow fever. Sarah Beth walked over to Daisy Mayo, who leaned against the microscope counter with her arms folded. Her voice low, Sarah Beth said, "I'm *not* challenging you. As I told you, I worked with a doctor in the past and, together, we did extensive research on *phlyctenular ophthalmia*. I'm only suggesting–."

Refusing to look at Sarah Beth, Daisy took the slide from the microscope and tossed it in the waste can. "*My* experience is that a hydrogen chloride wash is best at this stage of the disease."

Sarah Beth made her voice conciliatory. "I'm only suggesting another doctor's experience with cases like this may be more applicable."

Daisy's mouth formed a hard line when she finally looked at Sarah Beth. "Then perhaps you should take your friend to that *other* doctor."

Sarah Beth hesitated only a moment. "Perhaps I should."

SARAH BETH HAD NO INTENTION of taking Lottie Mae to see Frank. Though his memory would be held forever in her heart, he could never again be a part of her life. Instead, the day after Daisy Mayo examined Lottie Mae, Sarah Beth helped her childhood friend down the street to Elizabeth Cohen's house. In sharp counterpoint to Sarah Beth's first visit, Margaret, Dr. Cohen's maid, smiled warmly when she saw Sarah Beth and made small talk as she led the guests to Dr. Cohen's infirmary. The aroma of freshly baked cala filled the house, and Sarah Beth smiled, remembering how Elizabeth Cohen prepared for the triage of the small soldiers, sailors, pirates, cowboys and Indians that did battle on the tree-shaded streets and lawns of the neighborhood.

After seating Sarah Beth and Lottie Mae in the light, airy dispensary, Margaret went to the back yard door and called her mistress.

Elizabeth Cohen, stalwart and sturdy, shuffled up the back steps. On the porch, she brushed mud from her gardening apron and gloves, then laid them over the white arm of one of the wicker chairs. The woman always amazed Sarah Beth. At eighty-five, the only concession she made to age was the stiffness of her gait. "Wonderful to see you, my dear." Dr. Cohen allowed the screen door to bump against her backside so it would not slam as she straightened her light gray blouse and contrasting darker skirt. "What brings you–. Ah, I see."

"Can you help her?" Sarah Beth did nothing to hide the hope in her voice.

"Let's have a look."

Dr. Cohen had Lottie Mae sit on a treatment table and examined her as Daisy Mayo had done the day before, reaching the same conclusion.

"What treatment do you propose?" Sarah Beth held her breath waiting for the answer.

Elizabeth folded her arms under her ample bosom and drummed the fingers of her right hand on her left forearm. "A fifty percent solution of enzymol for six weeks, then calomel until the infection is completely gone. Several months of treatment, I'd say."

Sarah Beth twirled her cheek curl around her index finger and finally asked, "Are you open to suggestion?"

Elizabeth Cohen raised her eyebrows. "If there's justification."

Sarah Beth began to explain when Dr. Cohen raised her hand. "Let's find someplace more comfortable, shall we?"

Margaret served tea and cala in the semi-dark front parlor, then retired to the kitchen to occupy Lottie Mae. Elizabeth and Sarah Beth settled comfortably around the mahogany butler's tray-table and served themselves tea and pastry from the silver service and tray Elizabeth obviously used for all her guests. The room had lost none of its cozy feel since Sarah Beth last sat in it, chatting with Elizabeth and admiring the knick-knacks and crochet that filled it.

"Now, you mentioned a suggestion for Lottie's treatment." Elizabeth blew on the scalding tea before sipping it.

Sarah Beth took a deep breath. "Yes," she said and explained how she had worked with a local doctor on his *phlyctenular ophthalmia* research, her conclusion about the best treatment based on that research and Daisy Mayo's reaction when she suggested the alternative therapy. "From what I've told you," Sarah Beth concluded, "would you consider treating Lottie Mae with a borax-boracic wash and enzymol?"

Elizabeth placed her cup and saucer carefully on the butler tray-table. "I'm afraid, my dear, I'm forced to decline, just as Dr. Mayo did."

Sarah Beth slumped back in her overstuffed chair, disappointment in her eyes. "I was so sure you would understand."

"*I* do. I'm afraid it's *you* who doesn't understand, my dear."

"But–."

Elizabeth held up the teapot offering Sarah Beth another cup. Sarah Beth shook her head and Elizabeth filled her own. "You'll find none of the resentment you sensed in Dr. Mayo in me. In fact, I hope you're correct in your conclusions."

Sarah Beth sat quickly on the edge of her chair. "Then why won't you take my suggestion?"

"Because your conclusions are unsubstantiated." When Sarah Beth tried to interrupt, Elizabeth held up her hand. "I'm sure you're telling me exactly what you believe to be the results of the research. But that's not how medical progress is made. The research must be published, other physicians must study and criticize it, or support it based on their own findings. The process of scientific inquiry takes time."

Sarah Beth's expression held a hint of a pout. "Lottie Mae doesn't *have* time. She needs the treatment now or she'll be blind the rest of her life."

"I understand your concerns, but do you understand mine?"

"Frankly, no."

Elizabeth sipped her tea as she organized her thoughts, then said, "Ethically I'm bound to do what, in my judgement, is in the best interest of my patient. Without verifiable evidence to the contrary, I have only my past experience to base my judgement on. You must understand when I say, Sarah Beth, that, based on my fifty years as a doctor, the best treatment for your friend is enzymol and calomel."

Sarah Beth had long since forgotten the cala and its sweet aroma filling the room. "What if you're wrong? How do I convince you?"

"Publish the research. Let me study it."

"But, Elizabeth, there's not enough time."

"Then you have only two choices as I see it." Unlike Sarah Beth, Elizabeth was not too agitated to ignore the pastries and bit into one.

"Yes?"

With her hand in front of her mouth, the doctor chewed quickly and swallowed. "Either treat her yourself, which I don't recommend, or convince the doctor you worked with of the validity of your claim and have him treat her."

"Why not treat her myself?" Sarah Beth asked.

Elizabeth paused as she dipped her pastry in a bowl of powdered sugar and looked solemnly at her guest. "What happens if you're wrong? What happens if you treat Lottie Mae and she ends up blind for the rest of her life? Are you sure enough of your conclusions, without the benefit of any medical training, to take that risk?"

"No."

"Then your only alternative is to convince the doctor you worked with that your judgment is correct. He's the only person in the city trained in medicine and familiar enough with the research you cite to judge your claims. If you truly believe your treatment is best for Lottie Mae, you *must* take your arguments to him. If you're correct, it may be the only way to save your friend's eyesight."

SARAH BETH WRESTLED WITH THE decision to take Lottie Mae to Frank for days. She worried, fretted and schemed, devising and discarding plans that allowed her beloved doctor to treat Lottie Mae while she avoided seeing him. She imagined Lou Belle and Titan taking Lottie Mae to Frank, or making contact through Mary, the Cheramie's maid. She even thought of enlisting the help of Annadette, but, in the end, decided nothing would do except to see him herself. She alone could convince him to reanalyze their data.

Their data. Oh, how much of her life was tied to his! How often had she thought of him these past months! Now the idea of seeing him again terrified her. Their single kiss that last terrible night in the foyer of the Mansion still burned her lips. Her heart had been broken so often only the memory of that long-ago caress held its fractured parts together, kept it beating. If Frank repudiated her again, she knew it would destroy her. Yet, for the sake of her childhood friend, Sarah Beth steeled herself to face him.

WHEN TITAN STOPPED THE CARRIAGE in front of the house on Esplanade Avenue, Sarah Beth leaned forward to study it from the landau's window. How it had changed! The old dowager of a mansion, the Nottoway her life had earned her by the day she first saw it, had been transformed. No longer in disrepair, the paint shined bright and new, the shutters aligned perfectly, the lawn cut and the gardens well tended. Sarah Beth felt a tremendous satisfaction knowing much of this had been accomplished through her efforts in handling Frank's accounts.

Leaning back in the carriage seat, Sarah Beth rolled one of the scarlet wisps at the side of her face around the fingers of one hand and took Lottie Mae's hand in the other. "We're here," she said in a voice just above a whisper.

The melancholy filling the carriage did not go unnoticed by Lottie Mae. "Why ya so sad?" she asked as her milky white eyes stared directly ahead.

"I'm not sad. I'm really quite happy. I'm sure Dr. Cheramie will be able to cure you."

"Ain't all that good seein', but I hears just fine. Just took them two words, 'We're here,' t' know ya heart's 'bout to break." Lottie Mae's other hand covered Sarah Beth's. "Why ya don't tell me 'bout it?"

Sarah Beth took a deep breath. "Dr. Cheramie and I used to be in love."

"Don't sound like no used t' be t' me. Sounds like comin' here's bustin' up ya heart powerful bad, ain't that so?"

Helping her friend from the landau, Sarah Beth guided Lottie Mae around to the patients' entrance at the rear of the house. "I won't lie to you. Seeing Frank again will be one of the hardest things I've ever done. But there's no other way."

The two women entered the screen door of the dispensary and found six other patients, five obviously unable to pay, in line before them.

The infirmary was just as Sarah Beth remembered it–high ceilings, somewhat cluttered, lined with counters and glass-doored cabinets with white curtains. As she and Lottie Mae took seats, Mary came in from the front of the house.

The maid's hands went to her cheeks and her eyes opened wide. "Oh, Lawdy be, Miz Sarah Beth, yo' sho' is a sight. Lemme tell Dr. Frank directly. He just be in here…"

Sarah Beth stood. "Thank you, Mary, but we'll wait our–."

Frank appeared in the doorway of one of the examining rooms. His eyes locked with Sarah Beth's and she saw the infinite sadness deep in his soul.

With his voice emotionless, Frank demanded, "Why are you here?"

Sarah Beth could not find her tongue. She helped Lottie Mae stand so her blind eyes could speak for them.

"There are other doctors," Frank said.

"B-But none that knows as much...." Sarah Beth held tightly to the straight-back chair in front of her. "Our...Your research...I know now why we...Why you couldn't find a definitive cure." Finding her courage, Sarah Beth spoke with more confidence. "We weren't looking at the data correctly. We categorized it by treatment. If we would have looked at the cases by severity, we would have seen the best cure varies by the intensity of the disease."

"And?"

"No one else will believe me. I've tried. Dr. Mayo. Dr. Cohen. I'm sure others would react the same. They either resent my suggestions or won't use them because they haven't read published reports. And their treatments won't work. I know it. Fra–, Dr. Cheramie, you're our only hope." Sarah Beth wanted to beg his forgiveness for profaning his life again. Instead, she stood in silence–her tongue unable to form the words even if her mind could find them.

The tension between them was so palpable everyone in the room stopped talking and gawked. Sarah Beth held tight to the back of the chair in front of her for support as Frank studied the end of his stethoscope. She swallowed her heart back into place several times during the interminable time it took Frank to answer.

His chest heaved as if the weight of some great burden crushed down upon him, their gazes locked again and, finally, he said, the sadness in his eyes unchanged, "Show me. The folder is still in the library, probably right where you left it. I have not looked at it since you…since I…since we…In a long time."

Sarah Beth hesitated. Frank walked to the end of the row of chairs where she stood and held out his hand. After settling Lottie Mae, Sarah Beth allowed him to escort her to the library.

The room was exactly the same as she had left it–walls of shelves bending under the weight of thick medical books, the large blonde oak table crowding the center of the room, Frank's roll-top desk in the corner next to the door through which they entered.

She avoided looking into the mysterious feline eyes that had fascinated her so. "Where?"

"Surely that wonderful mind of yours remembers where you put it," Frank said, his tone etched in frost and sorrow. "I could not bare to touch it…Too painful. Surely, you must understand."

"Yes," she whispered and, averting her eyes, walked to the shelf where she had filed the study.

"Out of my way," Annadette ordered as she shuffled into the room, her silver hair pulled back severely into a bun just above the collar of her black dress, and shoved Frank aside with her cane. "Oh, my dear Sarah Beth, you don't know how good it is to set these old eyes on you again. When Mary said you were here, I came as fast as these decrepit legs would carry me."

"It's wonderful to see you, too." Sarah Beth rushed to the old woman, a broad smile on her face, and they embraced.

Annadette slipped her arm in Sarah Beth's. "What's the cause of our good fortune?"

Sarah Beth told her of Lottie Mae's condition, the reactions of Doctors Mayo and Cohen and concluded by saying, "I want her to have the best care possible. Frank's research shows a borax-boracic wash combined with enzymol to be the most effective treatment for cases this severe. I came here, hoping Frank would–."

"I'm sure he will, dear," Annadette said. "And if he refuses, I'll–."

From behind them, Frank snapped, "That won't be necessary, *Gamé.* I will see the woman," and strode from the room.

FOR SEVEN DAYS, SARAH BETH washed Lottie Mae's eyes with the borax-boracic solution three times a day and applied enzymol as Frank instructed. The next week she took her childhood friend to Dr. Cheramie's clinic again. Not wanting to offend the doctor any more than she already had on the first of what Frank had said may be months of regular visits, Sarah Beth waited in the carriage as Titan brought Lottie Mae in for her examination. Annadette sent Mary to invite Sarah Beth to join her for coffee. Sarah Beth refused, and the old woman stood on the porch waving her cane and threatening, "Don't make me come out there and get you, young lady!"

Sarah Beth responded with an emphatic shake of her head. But when Annadette attempted to scale the steps–holding tight to the banister–Sarah Beth relented and went inside, beginning a weekly ritual of visits while Lottie Mae kept her appointment.

Frank brought Lottie Mae to the front parlor when he finished his examination and gave Sarah Beth instructions for his patient's continued home treatment. That, too, became a ritual; though, in Sarah Beth's mind, a strange one. Frank's directions for Lottie Mae's care never changed, but he always came to the parlor and gave them to her. *Could it be he wants to…? No, I'm being foolish,* she thought. Though she tried to dismiss the idea, she could not help but wonder if Frank was deliberately finding an excuse to see her?

Two weeks became four, then six, then eight. Lottie Mae's sight improved substantially and the conversations between Sarah Beth and Annadette became more personal. Soon Sarah Beth realized she had told the older woman about her life, and the narrative began to assuage much of the guilt she felt for what had happened to her mother and brother.

At the end of Lottie Mae's third month of treatment, Frank came into the front parlor during Sarah Beth's visit with Annadette and sat in a chair across from Sarah Beth. "Her eyesight has almost returned to normal and there is no further reason for her to return. Continue the eye-wash and salve at home until all the nodules of infection have disappeared. Then proceed with the same regimen for another six weeks." He paused for a long moment, then, looking intently at Sarah Beth, added, "Imagine, a blind man curing the blind."

What riddle is this? Sarah Beth wondered.

The look in Frank's eyes softened. "Would it be too much to hope that you have found a cure for terminal stupidity as well as your friend's obstructed vision?"

Sarah Beth's eyes held his. "W-Who might the patient be?"

"This particular form of witlessness strikes men exclusively, and I have suffered a very bad bout of it."

Sarah Beth put her cup on the coffee table. "What are the symptoms?"

Frank bowed his head. "Getting drunk and acting more asinine than any man in all of history. Throwing away the greatest love a man could ever hope to know. Blaming the woman I love desperately for things she could not control. Being so damn blind that months have gone by without me saying, 'I love you, Sarah Beth' or, 'Please forgive me, Sarah Beth' or...."

His confession startled her. Sarah Beth could think of nothing to say, except to continue the silliness Frank had started. "A-And who d-diagnosed this condition?"

"I did," Annadette said. "I knew something was wrong the night this lout," she swung her cane in Frank's direction, "came home so drunk he couldn't spit and hit the floor. But would he tell me why? Of course not. Stayed drunk for a week. Eyes like a spaniel with his paw in a rat trap. That's why I insisted you join me for coffee when you brought Lottie Mae for her appointments. I'm a fine judge of character and, if what my ignoramus grandson finally told me about your past was true, I knew there had to be a reason." The old woman beamed. "You told me, and I told him…Though, for the life of me, I can't see how this simpleton could have had such a good effect on you."

Frank knelt beside Sarah Beth's chair and took her hands in his. "My darling, I *am* such a fool. Please find it in your heart to forgive me." He stood and gently pulled her to her feet.

With one hand Sarah Beth pushed Frank away, with the other she held tightly to his arm. "What of Frances? How is she–."

"Frances is a dear child," Frank said, pulling Sarah Beth closer, "but, like most girls her age, very fickle. She has gone and fallen in love with someone else, I am happy to say. A Scotsman of all things. Imagine that."

Fire raged in Sarah Beth's eyes and she pushed Frank away with both hands. "So, with no one to love, you've come back to your wh–."

Frank covered her mouth with his hand and said fiercely, "No! And if you ever say that again, I will–."

She pulled away. "Exactly what do you think you will do!"

His voice softened. "Whatever it takes to make you forgive me for the terrible wrong I have done you. Can you not understand how sorry I am? Can you not see I am–."

"What are you, Frank?" Sarah Beth demanded.

"Stupid and pig-headed," Annadette suggested. "Even after I told him what had happened to you, would he go beg your forgiveness? No. Look how long he took!"

Frank ignored his grandmother. "I was too caught up in my own vision of the what the world ought to be, rather than what it is. I required quite some time to realize that fact."

"And how did you arrive at that blinding flash of insight?" Sarah Beth asked, more composed.

"I told him he was an ass," Annadette said, "on numerous occasions."

"Seeing you so often these past months brought me to my senses. I know now, deep in my heart and soul, and, yes, finally in my thick head, that *Gamé* was right." Frank did not give Sarah Beth a chance to interrupt. "I fell in love, so deeply in love, with you when you were our boarder. The woman I knew was the woman you are, regardless of what fate had done to you or the armor you wore to protect yourself. It is the woman I know you are that I love and want to marry. It is she I want to give me sons."

Sarah Beth looked at the floor.

Frank put his finger under her chin and raised her face to his. "I do not deserve you, you know. But seeing *your* courage in bringing Lottie Mae here week after week, knowing how much pain that must have caused you, finally gave *me* the courage to say what I should have said long ago. I love you, Sarah Beth. I love you desperately. I want you to marry me. Please say yes."

"Do you know what you're asking?" Sarah Beth looked into his enchanting eyes. "The human race is not much given to kindness. There are many men who know…my past. You'll meet them. They'll snicker, make snide remarks and tell you to your face they have seen the mole on my–. If I still loved you, and I'm not saying I do, but if I still loved you, do you think I could put you through such torture?"

"If you still loved me, and I am not implying that you do, but if you still loved me, would it matter if I had lost a leg before we met?"

"Of course not."

"Yes, it would," Frank said. "You would prefer I had not lost it."

Sarah Beth considered for a moment. "True, but it wouldn't stop me from loving you."

Frank drew her gently to him. "Exactly. Can I not feel the same? Can I not wish the past were different, but love you just the same?"

Sarah Beth rested her head on his chest. "It will be so hard, Frank." She looked up at him. "People will talk openly about the doctor who married the–."

He put a finger to her lips. "Your whole life has been hard and you survived. If a woman can endure what you have undergone, surely a man can."

"*Frank!*" Sarah Beth drew the word out, making it an accusation.

"Quite right. I forgot the suffragette business. Sorry."

"Don't you see, Frank, it's not only my past. There's so much about me that conflicts with what you believe."

"Vote, you have my blessing. I will even march with you, if you want. Only please say–."

"It's not just the vote, Frank. It's everything about women's rights…And I've changed. A great deal, I'm afraid."

Frank held her tighter. "I know. You live uptown and–."

"Not just surface changes. I know now what I want to do with my life." Sarah Beth rushed to tell him, the discovery still new and exciting to her. "These past months I've helped Daisy Mayo at her clinic, even after she refused to treat Lottie Mae as I suggested. I couldn't help myself. She performs operations that change women's lives! Frank, just being there made me feel so…I don't know how to describe it. But to affect a person's life so much for the better has to be the grandest feeling."

"It is, my darling. The greatest reward of being a doctor."

"Then you understand why I want to study medicine," Sarah Beth said. "I wish I had done so already. Then I could have helped Lottie Mae."

"I am glad you did not. Were it not for Lottie Mae's condition, I might never have found you again. And you *did* help her because *we*, you and I working together, found the cure. But I am afraid, my darling, you can not go to medical school."

"And just why the hell not!" Sarah Beth pushed away from him.

"Because you will have to go up north to do so, and I could not endure that. I have just found you again, darling, and cannot bear to give you up," Frank said with tender insistence. "Once we are married, I want you here with me and the children. I cannot have you living–."

"Then I'll go to medical school in New Orleans."

"You must know they do not accept–. But I guess *you* will change all that." His grin widened and he said, lovingly, as he pulled her to him. "What have I gotten myself into?" He laughed. "I seem to have hold of a tiger's tail."

Sarah Beth sank into his arms. "This will be your last chance to let go."

"Never!"

Annadette beamed. "I've always dreamed of seeing my great-grand-children before I die. The wedding must be soon. Come, my dear, we've much to do," she said shuffling out of the parlor.

Frank pressed his lips to Sarah Beth's, and she felt their promise and commitment. Yet, for the briefest moment she hesitated, the sight of a bright, open face under a crop of tallow hair flitting across the land-scape of her memory. Why, at what should have been the happiest moment of her life, did she think of *him*? Did her heart have a message her mind refused to accept?

She pushed Liam from her thoughts and threw her arms around Frank's neck. *This is the life we'll make*, she thought, *we'll live it, live it well, and the devil take the hind most.*

THE END OF BOOK ONE

Author's Note

Separating Fact from Fiction

The Characters—Many of the people you've met in *Magdalenes* are historical figures. Most are among the *demimonde*: Tom Anderson, Josie Arlington, Willie Piazza, Emma Johnson and Lulu White, as well as some of the lesser denizens of Storyville like Deanie Jean the Suicide Queen and Josephine Icebox. Their actions and dialogue in *Magdalenes* are fictitious as there is no record of a fever committee operating in Storyville during the 1905 epidemic. Elizabeth Cohn, the first woman doctor in New Orleans, and Sara Mayo are also historical figures (see *Women and New Orleans, A History*, by Mary Gehman and Nancy Ries, as well as a number of newspaper articles).

Storyville—All of the background and physical description of Storyville and its inhabitants comes from Al Rose's *Storyville*. The fictionalizations are:

> Vestal House: I could find no record of an establishment specializing in young girls, though the practice of selling virgins, especially as a cure for syphilis, was common at this time; and

> The Mansion: There were no twenty-dollar parlor houses in New Orleans after Reconstruction. Of course, there were no courtesans in Storyville either.

The Practice of Medicine—To the best of my ability as a researcher, all of the scientific and medical terms, practices and procedures (except Sarah Beth's cure–there was no known cure for syphilis in 1897-88) are accurate as of the early nineteen hundreds. All of the physicians mentioned, with the exception of Frank Cheramie and Dr. Rice, are historical figures whose accomplishments, as set out in *Magdalenes*, are well documented. My gratitude goes to all those who did the original research:

> George Augustin, *History of Yellow Fever*
>
> The Louisiana Historical Society and its publication, *Louisiana History*
>
> All of the medical pioneers who practiced in New Orleans (a hell-hole of pestilence for much of its history) and published their work in the Orleans Parish Medical Society's *New Orleans Medical and Surgical Journal.*

In one of history's all-too-often ironies, the 1905 yellow fever epidemic in New Orleans should never have occurred. A vaccine had been discovered and documented in 1887 in the French pamphlet Sarah Beth found in Frank's library. I have a copy of the pamphlet, and a translation, in my files. I could not establish why the existence of that vaccine was not known in the United States.

Channing Hayden
New Orleans
September 2000